I'VE GOT YOUR NUMBER

www.transworldbooks.co.uk

I'VE GOT YOUR NUMBER

Sophie Kinsella

BANTAM PRESS

LONDON • TORONTO • SYDNEY • AUCKLAND • JOHANNESBURG

TRANSWORLD PUBLISHERS
61–63 Uxbridge Road, London W5 5SA
A Random House Group Company
www.transworldbooks.co.uk

First published in Great Britain
in 2012 by Bantam Press
an imprint of Transworld Publishers

A CIP catalogue record for this book
is available from the British Library.

ISBNs 9780593059814 (hb)
9780593059821 (tpb)

Addresses for Random House Group Ltd companies outside the UK
can be found at: www.randomhouse.co.uk
The Random House Group Ltd Reg. No. 954009

The Random House Group Limited supports the Forest Stewardship
Council (FSC®), the leading international forest-certification organization.
Our books carrying the FSC label are printed on FSC®-certified paper.
FSC is the only forest-certification scheme endorsed by the leading environmental
organizations, including Greenpeace. Our paper procurement policy can
be found at www.randomhouse.co.uk/environment.

Typeset in 11/14pt Palatino by
Falcon Oast Graphic Art Ltd.
Printed and bound in Great Britain by
Clays Limited, Bungay, Suffolk

12

For Rex

ONE

Perspective. I need to get perspective. It's not an earthquake or a crazed gunman or nuclear meltdown, is it? On the scale of disasters, this is not huge. *Not* huge. One day I expect I'll look back at this moment and laugh and think, 'Ha ha, how silly I was to worry—'

Stop, Poppy. Don't even try. I'm not laughing – in fact I feel sick. I'm walking blindly around the hotel ballroom, my heart thudding, looking fruitlessly on the patterned blue carpet, behind gilt chairs, under discarded paper napkins, in places where it couldn't possibly be.

I've lost it. The only thing in the world I wasn't supposed to lose. My engagement ring.

To say this is a special ring is an understatement. It's been in Magnus's family for three generations. It's this stunning emerald with two diamonds and Magnus had to get it out of a special bank vault before he proposed. I've worn it safely every day for three whole months, putting it religiously on a special china tray at night, feeling for it on my finger every thirty seconds . . . and now, the very day his parents are coming back from the States, I've lost it. The very same *day*.

Professors Antony Tavish and Wanda Brook-Tavish are, at this precise moment, flying back from six months' sabbatical in Chicago. I can picture them now, eating honey-roast peanuts and reading academic papers on their his-'n'-hers Kindles. I honestly don't know which of them is more intimidating.

Him. He's so sarcastic.

No, her. With all that frizzy hair and always asking you questions about your views on feminism all the time.

OK, they're both bloody scary. And they're landing in about an hour and of course they'll want to see the ring . . .

No. Do not hyperventilate, Poppy. Stay positive. I just need to look at this from a different angle. Like . . . what would Poirot do? Poirot wouldn't flap around in panic. He'd stay calm and use his little grey cells and recall some tiny, vital detail which would be the clue to everything.

I squeeze my eyes tight. Little grey cells. Come on. Do your best.

Thing is, I'm not sure Poirot had three glasses of pink champagne and a mojito before he solved the murder on the Orient Express.

'Miss?' A grey-haired cleaning lady is trying to get round me with a hoover and I gasp in horror. They're hoovering the ballroom already? What if they suck it up?

'Excuse me.' I grab her blue nylon shoulder. 'Could you just give me five more minutes to search before you start hoovering?'

'Still looking for your ring?' She shakes her head doubtfully, then brightens. 'I expect you'll find it safe at home. It's probably been there all the time!'

'Maybe.' I force myself to nod politely, although I feel like screaming, 'I'm not *that* stupid!'

On the other side of the ballroom I spot another cleaner clearing cupcake crumbs and crumpled paper napkins into a black plastic bin bag. She isn't concentrating at all. Wasn't she listening to me?

'Excuse me!' My voice shrills out as I sprint across to her. 'You *are* looking out for my ring, aren't you?'

'No sign of it so far, love.' The woman sweeps another load of detritus off the table into the bin bag without giving it a second glance.

'Careful!' I grab for the napkins and pull them out again, feeling each one carefully for a hard lump, not caring that I'm getting buttercream icing all over my hands.

'Dear, I'm trying to clear up.' The cleaner grabs the napkins out of my hands. 'Look at the mess you're making!'

'I know, I know. I'm sorry.' I scrabble for the cupcake cases I dropped on the floor. 'But you don't understand. If I don't find this ring, I'm dead.'

I want to grab the bin bag and do a forensic check of the contents with tweezers. I want to put plastic tape round the whole room and declare it a crime scene. It has to be here, it *has* to be.

Unless someone's still got it. That's the only other possibility that I'm clinging to. One of my friends is still wearing it and somehow hasn't noticed. Perhaps it's slipped into a handbag . . . maybe it's fallen into a pocket . . . it's stuck on the threads of a jumper . . . the possibilities in my head are getting more and more far-fetched, but I can't give up on them.

'Have you tried the cloakroom?' The woman swerves to get past me.

Of course I've tried the cloakroom. I checked every single cubicle on my hands and knees. And then all the basins. Twice. And then I tried to persuade the concierge to close it and have all the sink pipes investigated, but he refused. He said it would be different if I knew it had been lost there for certain, and he was sure the police would agree with him, and could I please step aside from the desk as there were people waiting?

Police. Bah. I thought they'd come roaring round in their squad cars as soon as I called, not just tell me to come down to the police station and file a report. I don't have time to file a report! I've got to find my ring!

I hurry back to the circular table we were sitting at this afternoon and crawl underneath, patting the carpet yet again. How could I have let this happen? How could I have been so *stupid*?

It was my old school friend Natasha's idea to get tickets for the Marie Curie Champagne Tea. She couldn't come to my official hen spa weekend, so this was a kind of substitute. There were eight of us at the table, all merrily swigging champagne and stuffing down cupcakes, and it was just before the raffle started that someone said, 'Come on, Poppy, let's have a go with your ring.'

I can't even remember who that was, now. Annalise, maybe? Annalise was at university with me, and now we work together at First Fit Physio, with Ruby who was also on our physio course. Ruby was at the tea too, but I'm not sure she tried on the ring. Or did she?

I can't believe how rubbish I am at this. How can I do a Poirot if I can't even remember the basics? The truth is, *everyone* seemed to be trying on the ring: Natasha and Clare and Emily (old school friends up from Taunton) and Lucinda (my wedding planner, who's kind of become a friend) and her assistant Clemency, and Ruby and Annalise (not just college friends and colleagues but my two best friends. They're going to be my bridesmaids, too).

I'll admit it: I was basking in all the admiration. I still can't believe something so grand and beautiful belongs to me. The fact is, I still can't believe *any* of it. I'm engaged! Me, Poppy Wyatt. To a tall, handsome university lecturer who's written a book and even been on TV. Only six months ago, my love life was a disaster zone. I'd had no significant action for a year and was reluctantly deciding I should give that match.com guy with the bad breath a second chance . . . and now my wedding's only ten days away! I wake up every morning and look at Magnus's smooth, freckled sleeping back; and think, 'My fiancé, Dr

Magnus Tavish, Fellow of King's College London,'[1] and feel a tiny tweak of disbelief. And then I swivel round and look at the ring, gleaming expensively on my nightstand, and feel another tweak of disbelief.

What will Magnus say?

My stomach clenches and I swallow hard. No. Don't think about that. Come on, little grey cells. Get with it.

I remember that Clare wore the ring for a long time. She really didn't want to take it off. Then Natasha started tugging at it, saying, 'My turn, my turn!' And I remember warning her, 'Gently!'

I mean, it's not like I was *irresponsible*. I was carefully watching the ring as it was passed round the table.

But then my attention was split, because they started on the raffle and the prizes were fantastic. A week in an Italian villa, and a top-salon haircut, and a Harvey Nichols voucher . . . The ballroom was buzzing with people pulling out tickets and numbers being called out from the platform and women jumping up and shouting, 'Me!'

And *this* is the moment where I went wrong. This is the gut-churning, if-only instant. If I could go back in time, that's the moment I would march up to myself and say severely, 'Poppy, *priorities.*'

But you don't realize, do you? The moment happens, and you make your crucial mistake, and then it's gone and the chance to do anything about it is blown away.

---

1. His specialism is Cultural Symbolism. I speed-read his book, *The Philosophy of Symbolism*, after our second date and then tried to pretend I'd read it ages ago, coincidentally, for pleasure. (Which, to be fair, he didn't believe for a minute.) Anyway, the point is, I read it. And what impressed me most was: there were so many footnotes. I've totally got into them. Aren't they handy? You just bung them in whenever you want and instantly look clever.

Magnus says footnotes are for things which aren't your main concern but nevertheless hold some interest for you. So. This is my footnote about footnotes.

So what happened was, Clare won Wimbledon tickets in the raffle. I love Clare to bits, but she's always been a tad feeble. She didn't stand up and yell, 'Me! Woo-hoo!' at top volume, she just raised her hand a few inches. Even those of us on her table didn't realize she'd won.

Just as it dawned on me that Clare was holding a raffle ticket in the air, the presenter on the platform said, 'I think we'll draw again, if there's no winner . . .'

'Shout!' I poked Clare and waved my own hand wildly. 'Here! The winner's over here!'

'And the new number is . . . 4-4-0-3.'

To my disbelief, some dark-haired girl on the other side of the room started whooping and brandishing a ticket.

'She didn't win!' I exclaimed indignantly. '*You* won.'

'It doesn't matter.' Clare was shrinking back.

'Of *course* it matters!' I cried out before I could stop myself, and everyone at the table started laughing.

'Go, Poppy!' called out Natasha. 'Go, White Knightess! Sort it out!'

'Go, Knightie!'

This is an old joke. Just because there was this *one* incident at school, where I started a petition to save the hamsters, everyone started calling me the White Knightess. Or Knightie, for short. My so-called catchphrase is apparently 'Of *course* it matters!'[2]

Anyway. Suffice it to say that within two minutes I was up on the stage with the dark-haired girl, arguing with the presenter about how my friend's ticket was more valid than hers.

I know now that I should never have left the table. I should never have left the ring, even for a second. I can see how stupid that was. But in my defence, I didn't *know* the fire alarm was going to go off, did I?

2. Which, actually, I never say. Just like Humphrey Bogart never said, 'Play it again, Sam.' It's an urban myth.

It was so surreal. One minute, everyone was sitting down at a jolly champagne tea. The next minute, a siren was blaring through the air and there was pandemonium, with everyone on their feet, heading for the exits. I could see Annalise, Ruby and all the others grabbing their bags and making their way to the back. A man in a suit came on to the stage and started ushering me, the dark-haired girl and the presenter towards a side door, and wouldn't let us go the other way. 'Your safety is our priority,' he kept saying.[3]

Even then, it's not as if I was *worried*. I didn't think the ring would have *gone*. I assumed one of my friends had it safe and I'd meet up with everyone outside and get it back.

Outside, of course, it was mayhem. There was some big business conference happening at the hotel as well as our tea, and all the delegates were spilling out of different doors into the road, and hotel staff were trying to make announcements with loudhailers, and cars were beeping, and it took me ages just to find Natasha and Clare in the mêlée.

'Have you got my ring?' I demanded at once, trying not to sound accusatory. 'Who's got it?'

Both of them looked blank.

'Dunno.' Natasha shrugged. 'Didn't Annalise have it?'

So then I plunged back into the throng to find Annalise, but she didn't have it, she thought Clare had it. And Clare thought Clemency had it. And Clemency thought Ruby might have had it, but hadn't she gone already?

The thing about panic is, it creeps up on you. One minute you're still quite calm, still telling yourself, 'Don't be ridiculous. Of course it can't be lost.' The next, the Marie Curie staff are announcing that the event will be curtailed early due to unforeseen circumstances, and handing out goody bags. And all your friends have disappeared to catch the tube. And

---

3. Of course, the hotel wasn't on fire. The system had short-circuited. I found that out afterwards, not that it was any consolation.

your finger is still bare. And a voice inside your head is screeching, 'Oh my God! I knew this would happen! Nobody should ever have entrusted me with an antique ring! Big mistake! Big mistake!'

And that's how you find yourself under a table an hour later, groping around a grotty hotel carpet, praying desperately for a miracle. (Even though your fiancé's father has written a whole bestselling book on how miracles don't exist and it's all superstition and even saying 'OMG' is the sign of a weak mind.)[4]

Suddenly I realize my phone is flashing, and grab it with trembling fingers. Three messages have come through, and I scroll through them in hope.

Found it yet? Annalise xx

Sorry babe, haven't seen it. Don't worry, I won't breathe a word to Magnus. N xxx

Hi Pops! God, how awful, to lose your ring! Actually I thought I saw it . . . (incoming text)

I stare at my phone, galvanized. Clare thought she saw it? Where?

I crawl out from under the table and wave my phone around, but the rest of the text resolutely refuses to come through. The signal in here is rubbish. How can this call itself a five-star hotel? I'll have to go outside.

'Hi!' I approach the grey-haired cleaner, raising my voice above the Hoover's roar. 'I'm popping out to check a text. But

---

4. Did Poirot ever say, 'Oh my God'? I bet he did. Or 'Sacrebleu!' which comes to the same thing. And does this not disprove Antony's theory since Poirot's grey cells are clearly stronger than anyone else's? I might point this out to Antony one day. When I'm feeling brave. (Which, if I've lost the ring, will be never, obviously.)

if you *do* find the ring, just call me, I've given you my mobile number, I'll just be on the street . . .'

'Right you are, dear,' says the cleaner patiently.

I hurry through the lobby, dodging groups of conference delegates, slowing slightly as I pass the concierge's desk.

'Any sign of . . .'

'Nothing handed in yet, madam.'

The air outside is balmy, with just a hint of summer, even though it's only mid April. I hope the weather will still be like this in ten days' time, because my wedding dress is backless and I'm counting on a fine day.

There are wide shallow steps in front of the hotel and I walk up and down them, swishing my phone back and forth, trying to get a signal but with no success. At last I head down on to the actual pavement, waving my phone around more wildly, holding it over my head, then leaning into the quiet Knightsbridge street, my phone in my outstretched fingertips.

Come on, phone, I mentally cajole it. *You can do it. Do it for Poppy. Fetch the message. There must be a signal somewhere . . . you can do it . . .*

'Aaaaaaah!' I hear my own yell of shock before I even clock what's happened. There's a twisting pain in my shoulder. My fingers feel scratched. A figure on a bike is pedalling swiftly towards the end of the road. I only have time to register an old grey hoodie and skinny black jeans before the bike turns the corner.

My hand's empty. What the hell—

I stare at my palm in numb disbelief. It's gone. That guy stole my phone. He bloody stole it.

My phone's my *life*. I can't exist without it. It's a vital organ.

'Madam, are you all right?' The doorman is hurrying down the steps. 'Did something happen? Did he hurt you?'

'I . . . I've been mugged,' I somehow manage to stutter. 'My phone's been nicked.'

The doorman clicks sympathetically. 'Chancers, they are. Have to be so careful in an area like this . . .'

I'm not listening. I'm starting to shake all over. I've never felt so bereft and panicky. What do I do without my phone? How do I function? My hand keeps automatically reaching for my phone in its usual place in my pocket. Every instinct in me wants to text someone, 'OMG, I've lost my phone!' but *how can I do that without a bloody phone*?

My phone is my people. It's my friends. It's my family. It's my work. It's my world. It's everything. I feel like someone's wrenched my life-support system away from me.

'Shall I call the police, madam?' The doorman is peering at me anxiously.

I'm too distracted to reply. I'm consumed with a sudden, even more terrible realization. The ring. I've handed out my mobile number to everyone: the cleaners, the cloakroom attendants, the Marie Curie people, everyone. What if someone finds it? What if someone's got it and they're trying to call me *right this minute* and there's no answer because Hoodie Guy has already chucked my SIM card into the river?

Oh God.[5] I need to talk to the concierge. I'll give him my home number instead—

No. Bad idea. If they leave a message, Magnus might hear it.[6]

OK, so . . . so . . . I'll give him my work number. Yes.

Except no one will be at the physio clinic this evening. I can't go and sit there for hours, just in case.

I'm starting to feel seriously freaked out now. Everything's unravelling.

To make matters even worse, as I run back into the lobby, the concierge is busy. His desk is surrounded by a large group of conference delegates, talking about restaurant reservations.

---

5. Weak mind.
6. I'm allowed to give myself at least a *chance* of getting it back safely and him never having to know, aren't I?

I try to catch his eye, hoping he'll beckon me forward as a priority, but he studiously ignores me, and I feel a twinge of hurt. I know I've taken up quite a lot of his time this afternoon – but doesn't he realize what a hideous crisis I'm in?

'Madam.' The doorman has followed me into the lobby, his brow creased with concern. 'Can we get you something for the shock? Arnold!' He briskly calls over a waiter. 'A brandy for the lady, please, on the house. And if you talk to our concierge, he'll help you with the police. Would you like to sit down?'

'No, thanks.' A thought suddenly occurs to me. 'Maybe I should phone my own number! Call the mugger! I could ask him to come back, offer him a reward . . . What do you think? Could I borrow your phone?'

The doorman almost recoils as I thrust out a hand.

'Madam, I think that would be a very foolhardy action,' he says severely. 'And I'm sure the police would agree you should do no such thing. I think you must be in shock. Kindly have a seat and try to relax.'

Hmm. Maybe he's right. I'm not wild about setting up some assignation with a criminal in a hoodie. But I can't sit down and relax; I'm far too hyper. To calm my nerves I start walking round and round the same route, my heels clicking on the marble floor. Past the massive potted ficus tree . . . past the table with newspapers . . . past a big shiny litter bin . . . back to the ficus. It's a comforting little circuit, and I can keep my eyes fixed on the concierge the whole time, waiting for him to be free.

The lobby is still bustling with executive types from the conference. Through the glass doors I can see the doorman back on the steps, busy hailing taxis and pocketing tips. A squat Japanese man in a blue suit is standing near me with some European-looking businessmen, exclaiming in what sounds like loud, furious Japanese and gesticulating at everybody with the conference pass strung round his neck on a red cord. He's so tiny and the other men look so nervous, I almost want to smile.

The brandy arrives on a salver and I pause briefly to drain it in one, then keep walking, in the same repetitive route.

Potted ficus . . . newspaper table . . . litter bin . . . potted ficus . . . newspaper table . . . litter bin . . .

Now I've calmed down a bit, I'm starting to churn with murderous thoughts. Does that Hoodie Guy realize he's wrecked my life? Does he realize how *crucial* a phone is? It's the worst thing you can steal from a person. The *worst*.

And it wasn't even that great a phone. It was pretty ancient. So good luck to Hoodie Guy if he wants to type 'B' in a text or go on the Internet. I hope he tries and fails. *Then* he'll be sorry.

Ficus . . . newspapers . . . bin . . . ficus . . . newspapers . . . bin . . .

And he hurt my shoulder. Bastard. Maybe I could sue him for millions. If they ever catch him, which they won't.

Ficus . . . newspapers . . . bin . . .

Bin.

Wait.

What's that?

I stop dead in my tracks and stare into the bin, wondering if someone's playing a trick on me, or if I'm hallucinating.

It's a phone.

Right there in the litter bin. A mobile phone.

TWO

I blink a few times and look again – but it's still there, half-hidden amid a couple of discarded conference programmes and a Starbucks cup. What's a phone doing in a *bin*?

I look around to see if anyone's watching me – then reach in gingerly and pull it out. It has a couple of drops of coffee on it, but otherwise it seems perfect. It's a good one, too. Seems new.

Cautiously I turn and survey the thronging lobby. Nobody's paying me the slightest bit of attention. No one's rushing up and exclaiming, *'There's* my phone!' And I've been walking around this area for the last ten minutes. Whoever threw this phone in here did so a while ago.

There's a sticker on the back of the phone, with *White Globe Consulting Group* printed in tiny letters and a number. Did someone just chuck it away? Is it bust? I press the On switch and the screen glows. It seems in perfect working order to me.

A tiny voice in my head is telling me that I should hand it in. Take it up to the front desk and say, 'Excuse me, I think some-one's lost this phone.' That's what I should do. Just march up to the desk, right now, like any responsible, civic-minded member of society . . .

My feet don't move an inch. My hand tightens protectively round the phone. Thing is, I *need* a phone. I bet White Globe Consulting Group, whoever they are, have millions of phones. And it's not like I found it on the floor or in the cloakroom, is it? It was in a bin. Things in bins are *rubbish*. They're fair game. They've been relinquished to the world. That's the rule.

I peer into the bin again, and glimpse a red cord, just like the ones round all the delegates' necks. I check the concierge to make sure he's not watching, then plunge my hand in again and pull out a conference pass. A mugshot of a stunningly pretty girl stares back at me, under which is printed: *Violet Russell, White Globe Consulting Group*.

I'm building up a pretty good theory now. I could be Poirot. This is Violet Russell's phone and she threw it away. For . . . some reason or other.

Well, that's her fault. Not mine.

The phone suddenly buzzes and I start. Shit! It's alive. The ringtone begins at top volume – and it's Beyoncé's 'Single Ladies'. I quickly press Ignore, but a moment later it starts up again, loud and unmistakable.

Isn't there a bloody volume control on this thing? A couple of nearby businesswomen have turned to stare and I'm so flustered that I jab at Talk instead of Ignore. The business-women are still watching me, so I put the phone to my ear and turn away.

'The person you have called is not available,' I say, trying to sound robotic. 'Please leave a message.' That'll get rid of whoever it is.

'Where the fuck *are* you?' A smooth, well-educated male voice starts speaking and I nearly squeak with astonishment. It worked! He thinks I'm a machine! 'I've just been talking to Scottie. He has a contact reckons he can do it. It'll be like key-hole surgery. He's good. There won't be any trace.'

I don't dare breathe. Or scratch my nose, which is suddenly incredibly itchy.

'OK,' the man is saying. 'So, whatever else you do, be fucking careful.'

He rings off and I stare at the phone in astonishment. I never thought anyone would actually leave a *message*.

Now I feel a bit guilty. This is a genuine voice-mail and Violet's missed it. I mean, it's not *my* fault she threw her phone away, but even so . . . On impulse I scrabble in my bag for a pen and the only thing I've got to write on, which is an old theatre programme.[7] I scribble down: 'Scottie has a contact, keyhole surgery, no trace, be fucking careful.'

God alone knows what *that's* all about. Liposuction, maybe? Anyway, it doesn't matter. The point is, if I ever do meet this Violet girl, I'll be able to pass it on.

Before the phone can ring again, I hurry to the concierge's desk, which has miraculously cleared.

'Hi,' I say breathlessly. 'Me again. Has anyone found my ring?'

'May I please assure you, madam,' he says with a frosty smile, 'that we would have let you know if we had found it. We *do* have your phone number—'

'No you don't!' I cut him off, almost triumphantly. 'That's the thing! The number I gave you is now . . . er . . . defunct. Out of use. Very much so.' The last thing I want is him calling Hoodie Guy and mentioning a priceless emerald ring. 'Please don't call it. Can you use this number instead?' I carefully copy the phone number from the back of the White Globe Consulting phone. 'Actually, just to be sure . . . can I test it?' I reach for the hotel phone and dial the printed number. A moment later Beyoncé starts blasting out of the mobile phone. OK. At last I can relax a little. I've got a number.

---

7. *The Lion King.* Natasha got free tickets. I thought it would be some lame kids' thing but it was *brilliant*.

'Madam, was there anything else?'

The concierge is starting to look quite pissed off and there's a queue of people building behind me. So I thank him again, and head to a nearby sofa, full of adrenalin. I have a phone and I have a plan.

It only takes me five minutes to write out my new mobile number on twenty separate pieces of hotel writing paper, with 'POPPY WYATT – EMERALD RING, PLEASE CALL!!!!' in big capitals. To my annoyance, the doors to the ballroom are now locked (although I'm *sure* I can hear the cleaners still inside), so I'm forced to roam around the hotel corridors, the tea room, the ladies' cloakrooms and even the spa, handing my number out to every hotel worker I come across and explaining the story.

I call the police and dictate my new number to them. I text Ruby – whose mobile number I know off by heart – saying:

Hi! Phone stolen. This is my new mobile number. Cn u pass to everyone? Any sign of ring???

Then I flop back on to the sofa in exhaustion. I feel like I've been living in this bloody hotel all day. I should phone Magnus too, and give him this number – but I can't face it yet. I have this irrational conviction that he'll be able to tell just from my tone of voice that my ring is missing. He'll sense my bare finger the minute I say 'Hi'.

Please come back, ring. Please, PLEASE come back . . .

I've leaned back, closed my eyes and am trying to send a telepathic message through the ether. So when Beyoncé starts up again I give a startled jump. Maybe this is it! My ring! Someone has found it! I don't even check the screen before pressing Talk and answering excitedly, 'Hello?'

'Violet?' A man's voice hits my ear. It's not the man who called before, it's a guy with a deeper voice. He sounds a bit bad-tempered, if you can tell that just from three syllables.[8] He's also breathing quite heavily, which means he's either a pervert or doing some exercise. 'Are you in the lobby? Are the Japanese contingent still there?'

In an automatic reflex I look around. There's a whole bunch of Japanese people by the doors.

'Yes, they are,' I say. 'But I'm not Violet. This isn't Violet's phone any more. Sorry. Maybe you could spread the word that her number's changed?'

I need to get Violet's mates off my case. I can't have them ringing me every five seconds.

'Excuse me, who is this?' the man demands. 'Why are you answering this number? Where's Violet?'

'I possess this phone,' I say, more confidently than I feel. Which is true. Possession is nine-tenths of the law.[9]

'You *possess* it? What the hell are you – oh Jesus.' He swears a bit more and I can hear distant footsteps. It sounds like he's running downstairs.[10] 'Just tell me, are they leaving?'

'The Japanese people?' I squint at the group. 'Maybe. Can't tell.'

'Is a short guy with them? Overweight? Thick hair?'

'You mean the man in the blue suit? Yes, he's right in front of me. Looks pissed off. Now he's putting on his mac.'

The squat Japanese man has just been handed a Burberry by a colleague. He's glowering as he puts it on, and a constant stream of angry Japanese is coming out of his mouth, as all his friends nod nervously.

'No!' The man's exclamation down the phone takes me by surprise. 'He can't leave.'

'Well, he is. Sorry.'

'You have to stop him. Go up to him and stop him leaving the hotel. Go up to him now. Do whatever it takes.'

---

8. Which I think you can.
9. I've never been quite sure what that means.
10. Maybe not a pervert, then.

'*What?*' I stare at the phone. 'Look, I'm sorry, but I've never even met you—'

'Nor me you,' he rejoins. 'Who are you, anyway? Are you a friend of Violet's? Can you tell me exactly why she decided to quit her job halfway through the biggest conference of the year? Does she think I suddenly don't *need* a PA any more?'

Aha. So Violet's his PA. This makes sense. And she walked out on him! Well, I'm not surprised, he's so bossy.

'Anyway, doesn't matter.' He interrupts himself. 'Point is, I'm on the stairs, floor nine, the lift jammed, I'll be downstairs in less than three minutes, and you have to keep Yuichi Yamasaki there till I arrive. Whoever the hell you are.'

What a nerve.

'Or what?' I retort.

'Or else a year of careful negotiation goes down the tubes because of one ridiculous misunderstanding. The biggest deal of the year falls apart. A team of twenty people lose their jobs.' His voice is relentless. 'Senior managers, secretaries, the whole gang. Just because I can't get down there fast enough and the one person who could help won't.'

Oh bloody hell.

'All right!' I say furiously. 'I'll do my best. What's his name again?'

'Yamasaki.'

'Wait!' I raise my voice, running across the lobby. 'Please! Mr Yamasaki? Could you wait a minute?'

Mr Yamasaki turns, questioningly, and a couple of flunkeys move forward, flanking him protectively. He has a broad face, still creased in anger, and a wide, bullish neck, around which he's draping a silk scarf. I get the sense he's not into idle chit-chat.

I have no idea what to say next. I don't speak Japanese, I don't know anything about Japanese business or Japanese culture. Apart from sushi. But I can't exactly go up to him and say 'Sushi!' out of the blue. It would be like going up to a top American businessman and saying, 'T-bone steak!'

'I'm . . . a huge fan,' I improvise. 'Of your work. Could I have your autograph?'

He looks puzzled, and one of his colleagues whispers a translation into his ear. Immediately his brow clears and he bows to me.

Cautiously I bow back, and he snaps his fingers, barking an instruction. A moment later, a beautiful leather folder has been opened in front of him, and he's writing something elaborate in Japanese.

'Is he still there?' The stranger's voice suddenly emanates from the phone.

'Yes,' I mutter into it. 'Just about. Where are you?' I shoot a bright smile at Mr Yamasaki.

'Fifth floor. Keep him there. Whatever it takes.'

Mr Yamasaki hands me his piece of paper, caps his pen, bows again and makes to walk off.

'Wait!' I cry desperately. 'Could I . . . show you something?'

'Mr Yamasaki is very busy.' One of his colleagues, wearing steel glasses and the whitest shirt I've ever seen, turns back to me. 'Kindly contact our office.'

They're heading away again. What do I do now? I can't ask for another autograph. I can't rugby-tackle him. I need to attract his attention somehow . . .

'I have a special announcement to make!' I exclaim, hurrying after them. 'I am a singing telegram! I bear a message from all Mr Yamasaki's many fans. It would be a great discourtesy to them if you were to refuse me.'

The word 'discourtesy' seems to have stopped them in their tracks. They're frowning and exchanging confused glances.

'A singing telegram?' asks the man in steel glasses suspiciously.

'Like a Gorillagram?' I offer. 'Only singing.'

I'm not sure that's made things any clearer.

The interpreter is murmuring furiously in Mr Yamasaki's ear, and after a moment instructs me, 'You may present.'

Mr Yamasaki turns round, and all his colleagues follow suit, folding their arms expectantly and lining up in a row. Around the lobby I can see a few interested glances from other groups of business people.

'Where *are* you?' I mutter desperately into the phone.

'Third floor,' comes the man's voice after a moment. 'Half a minute. Don't lose him.'

'Begin,' says the man in steel spectacles pointedly.

Some other hotel guests in the lobby have stopped to watch. Oh God. How did I get myself into this? Number one, I can't sing. Number two, what do I sing to a Japanese businessman I've never met before? Number three, *why* did I say singing telegram?

But if I don't do something soon, twenty people might lose their jobs.

I make a deep bow, just to spin out some more time, and all the Japanese bow back.

'*Begin*,' repeats the man in steel spectacles, his eyes glinting ominously.

I take a deep breath. Come on. It doesn't matter what I do. I only have to last half a minute. Then I can run away and they'll never see me again.

'Mr Yamasaki . . .' I begin cautiously, to the tune of 'Single Ladies'. 'Mr Yamasaki. Mr Yamasaki, Mr Yamasaki.' I shimmy my hips and shoulders at him, just like Beyoncé.[11] 'Mr Yamasaki, Mr Yamasaki.'

Actually, this is quite easy. I don't need any lyrics, I can just keep singing 'Mr Yamasaki' over and over. After a few moments, some of the Japanese even start singing along, and clapping Mr Yamasaki on the back.

'Mr Yamasaki, Mr Yamasaki. Mr Yamasaki, Mr Yamasaki.' I

11. OK, not just like Beyoncé. Like me imitating Beyoncé.

lift my finger and waggle it at him with a wink. 'Ooh-ooh-ooh
. . . ooh-ooh-ooh . . .'

This song is ridiculously catchy. All the Japanese are singing
now, apart from Mr Yamasaki, who's just standing there, looking delighted. Some delegates nearby have joined in with the
singing and I can hear one of them saying, 'Is this a Flash Mob
thing?'

'Mr Yamasaki, Mr Yamasaki, Mr Yamasaki . . . Where *are*
you?' I mutter into the phone, still beaming brightly.

'Watching.'

'*What?*' My head jerks up and my eyes sweep the lobby.

Suddenly my gaze fixes on a man standing alone, about
thirty yards away. He's wearing a dark suit and has thick black
rumpled hair and is holding a phone to his ear. Even from this
distance I can see that he's laughing.

'How long have you been there?' I demand furiously.

'Just arrived. Didn't want to interrupt. Great job, by the way,'
he adds. 'I think you won Yamasaki round to the cause, right
there.'

'Thanks,' I say sarcastically. 'Glad I could help. He's all yours.'
I bow to Mr Yamasaki with a flourish, then turn on my heel and
head swiftly towards the exit, ignoring the disappointed cries of
the Japanese. I've got more important stuff to worry about than
arrogant strangers and their stupid business deals.

'Wait!' The man's voice follows me, through the receiver.
'That phone. It's my PA's.'

'Well, she shouldn't have thrown it away then,' I retort,
pushing the glass doors open. 'Finders keepers.'

There are twelve stops from Knightsbridge to Magnus's
parents' house in North London, and as soon as I resurface
from the underground I check the phone. It's flashing with
new messages – about ten texts and twenty emails – but there
are only five texts for me and none with news about the ring.
One's from the police and my heart leaps with hope – but it's

only to confirm that I've filed a report and asking if I want a visit from a Victim Support Officer.

The rest are all text messages and emails for Violet. As I scroll down them, I notice that 'Sam' features in the subject heading of quite a few of the emails. Feeling like Poirot again, I check back on the 'Numbers Called' function, and sure enough, the last number that called this phone was 'Sam Mobile'. So that's him. Violet's boss. Dark-rumpled-hair Guy. And to prove it, her email address is samroxtonpa@whiteglobeconsulting.com.

Just out of the mildest curiosity, I click on one of the emails. It's from jennasmith@grantlyassetmanagement.com and the subject is 'Re: Dinner?'.

> Thanks, Violet. I'd appreciate you not mentioning any of this to Sam. I feel a little embarrassed now!

Ooh. What's she embarrassed about? Before I can stop myself, I've scrolled down to read the previous email, which was sent yesterday.

> Actually Jenna, you should know something: Sam's engaged. Best, Violet.

He's engaged. Interesting. As I read the words over again I feel a strange little reaction inside which I can't quite place – surprise?

Although why should I be surprised? I don't even know the guy.

OK, now I *have* to know the whole story. Why is Jenna embarrassed? What happened? I scroll down still further and find a long introductory email from Jenna, who has clearly met this Sam Roxton at a business function, got the hots for him and invited him to dinner two weeks ago, but he hasn't returned her calls.

... tried again yesterday ... maybe using the wrong number ... someone told me he is notorious and that his PA is always the best route to contact him ... very sorry to bother you ... possibly just let me know either way ...

Poor woman. I feel quite indignant on her behalf. Why didn't he reply? How hard is it to send a quick email saying 'No thanks'? And then it turns out he's engaged, for God's sake.

Anyway. Whatever. I suddenly realize I'm snooping in someone else's in-box, when I have a lot of other, more important things to be thinking about. *Priorities*, Poppy. I need to buy some wine for Magnus's parents. And a 'Welcome home' card. And, if I don't track down the ring in the next twenty minutes ... some gloves.

Disaster. *Disaster*. It turns out they don't sell gloves in April. The only ones I could find were from the back room in Accessorize. Old Christmas stock, only available in a Small.

I cannot believe I'm seriously planning to greet my prospective in-laws in too-tight red woolly reindeer gloves. With tassels.

But I have no choice. It's that or walk in bare-handed.

As I start the long climb up the hill to their house, I'm starting to feel seriously sick. It's not just the ring. It's the whole scary prospective in-laws thing. I turn the corner – and all the windows of the house are alight. They're home.

I've never known a house which suits a family as much as the Tavishes' does. It's older and grander than any of the others in the street, and looks down on them from its superior position. There are yew trees and a monkey puzzle in the garden. The bricks are covered in ivy and the windows still have their original 1835 wooden frames. Inside, there's William Morris wallpaper dating from the 1960s and the floorboards are covered with Turkish carpets.

Except you can't actually *see* the carpets because they're mostly covered in old documents and manuscripts which no one ever bothers to clear up. No one's big on tidying in the Tavish family. I once found a fossilized boiled egg in a spare-room bed, still in its egg cup, with a desiccated toast soldier. It must have been about a year old.

And everywhere, all over the house, are books. Stacked up three-deep on shelves, piled on the floor and on the side of every lime-stained bath. Antony writes books, Wanda writes books, Magnus writes books and his elder brother Conrad writes books. Even Conrad's wife Margot writes books.[12]

Which is great. I mean, it's a wonderful thing, all these genius intellectuals in one family. But it does make you feel just the teensiest, weensiest bit inadequate.

Don't get me wrong, I think I'm pretty intelligent. You know, for a normal person who went to school and college and got a job and everything. But these aren't normal people, they're in a different league. They have super-brains. They're the academic version of *The Incredibles*.[13] I've only met his parents a few times, when they flew back to London for a week for Antony to give some big important lecture, but it was enough to show me. While Antony was lecturing about political theory, Wanda was presenting a paper on feminist Judaism to a think-tank, and then they both appeared on *The Culture Show*, taking *opposing* views on a documentary about the influence of the Renaissance.[14] So that was the backdrop to our meeting. No pressure, or anything.

I've been introduced to quite a few different boyfriends' parents, over the years, but hands down, this was the worst

12. Not books with plots, by the way. Books with footnotes. Books about *subjects*, like history and anthropology and cultural relativism in Turkmenistan.
13. I wonder if they all take fish oil. I must remember to ask.
14. Don't ask me. I listened really carefully and I still couldn't work out how they disagreed. I don't think the presenter could follow, either.

experience, ever. We'd just shaken hands and made a bit of small-talk and I was telling Wanda quite proudly where I'd been to college, when Antony looked up over his half-moon glasses, with those bright, cold eyes of his, and said, 'A degree in physiotherapy. How amusing.' I felt instantly crushed. I didn't know what to say. In fact, I was so flustered I left the room to go to the loo.[15]

After that, of course, I froze. Those three days were sheer misery. The more intellectual the conversation became, the more tongue-tied and awkward I was. My second-worst moment: pronouncing 'Proust' wrong and everyone exchanging looks.[16] My very worst moment: watching *University Challenge* all together in the drawing room, when a section on bones came up. My subject! I studied this! I know all the Latin names and everything! But as I was drawing breath to answer the first question, Antony had already given the correct answer. I was quicker next time – but he still beat me. The whole thing was like a race, and he won. Then at the end, he looked over at me and enquired, 'Do they not teach anatomy at physiotherapy school, Poppy?' and I was just *mortified*.

Magnus says he loves *me*, not my brain, and that I've just got to ignore his parents. And Natasha said just think of the rock and the Hampstead house and the villa in Tuscany. Which is Natasha for you. Whereas my own approach has been as follows: just don't think about them. It's been fine. They've been safely in Chicago, thousands of miles away.

But now they're back.

Oh God. And I'm still a bit shaky on 'Proust'. (Proost? Prost?) And I didn't revise the Latin names for bones. And I'm wearing red woolly reindeer gloves in April. With tassels.

My legs are shaking as I ring the bell. Actually shaking. I feel like the scarecrow in *The Wizard of Oz*. Any minute I'll collapse

---

15. Magnus said afterwards he was joking. But it didn't *sound* like a joke.
16. I've never even read any Proust. I don't know why I had to bring him up.

on the path and Wanda will torch me for losing the ring.

Stop, Poppy. It's fine. No one will suspect anything. My story is, I burned my hand. That's my story.

'Hi, Poppy!'

'Felix! Hi!'

I'm so relieved it's Felix at the door my greeting comes out in a quivering gasp.

Felix is the baby of the family – only seventeen and still at school. In fact, Magnus has been living in the house with him while his parents have been away, as a kind of babysitter, and I moved in after we got engaged. Not that Felix needs a babysitter. He's completely self-contained, reads all the time and you never even know he's in the house. I once tried to give him a friendly little 'drugs chat'. He politely corrected me on every single fact, then said he'd noticed I drank above the recommended limit of Red Bull and did I think I might have an addiction? That was the last time I tried to act older sister.

Anyway. That's all come to an end now that Antony and Wanda are returning from the States. I've moved back to my flat and we've started looking for places to rent. Magnus was all for staying here. He thought we could carry on using the spare bedroom and bathroom on the top floor and wouldn't it be convenient, as he could continue using his father's library?

Is he nuts? There is *no way* I am living under the same roof as the Tavishes.

I follow Felix into the kitchen, where Magnus is lounging on a kitchen chair, gesturing at a page of typescript and saying, 'I think your argument goes wrong here. Second paragraph.'

However Magnus sits, whatever he does, he somehow manages to look elegant. His suede-brogued feet are up on another chair, he's halfway through a cigarette[17] and his tawny hair is thrown back off his brow like a waterfall.

The Tavishes all have the same colouring, like a family of

17. I know. I've *told* him, a million times.

foxes. Even Wanda hennas her hair. But Magnus is the best-looking of all, and I'm not just saying that because I'm marrying him. His skin is freckled but tans easily too, and his dark red-brown hair is like something out of a hair ad. That's why he keeps it long.[18] He's actually quite vain about it.

Plus, although he's an academic, he's not just some fusty guy who sits inside reading books all day. He skis really well, and he's going to teach me too. That's how we met, in fact. He'd sprained his wrist skiing and he came in for physio, after his doctor recommended us. He was supposed to be seeing Annalise but she switched him for one of her regulars and he ended up coming to me instead. The next week he asked me out on a date, and after a month, he proposed. A month![19]

Now Magnus looks up and his face brightens. 'Sweetheart! How's my beautiful girl? Come here.' He beckons me over for a kiss, then frames my face in his hands, like he always does.

'Hi!' I force a smile. 'So, are your parents here? How was their flight? I can't *wait* to see them.'

I'm trying to sound as keen as I can, even though my legs are wanting to run away, back out of the door and down the hill.

'Didn't you get my text?' Magnus seems puzzled.

'What text? *Oh.*' I suddenly realize. 'Of course. I lost my phone. I've got a new number. I'll give it to you.'

'You lost your phone?' Magnus stares at me. 'What happened?'

'Nothing!' I say brightly. 'Just . . . lost it and had to get a new one. No biggie. No drama.'

I've decided on a general policy that the less I say to Magnus right now, the better. I don't want to get into any discussions as to why I might be clinging desperately on to some random phone I found in a bin.

---

18. Not ponytail long, which would be gross. Just on the long side.
19. I don't think Annalise's ever forgiven me. In her head, if she hadn't switched appointments, *she'd* be marrying him now.

'So, what did your text say?' I quickly add, trying to move the conversation on.

'My parents' plane was diverted. They had to go to Manchester. Won't be back till tomorrow.'

Diverted?

Manchester?

Oh my God. I'm safe! I'm reprieved! My legs can stop wobbling! I want to sing the *Hallelujah* chorus. *Ma-an-chester! Ma-an-chester!*

'God, how *awful.*' I'm trying hard to twist my face into a disappointed expression. 'Poor them. Manchester. That's miles away! I was really looking forward to seeing them, too. What a pain.'

I *think* I sound pretty convincing. Felix shoots me an odd look, but Magnus has already picked up the typescript again. He hasn't commented on my gloves. Nor has Felix.

Maybe I can relax just a notch.

'So ... er ... guys.' I survey the room. 'What about the kitchen?'

Magnus and Felix said they were going to clear up this afternoon, but the place is like a bombsite. There are takeaway boxes on the kitchen table and a stack of books on top of the hob and even one in a saucepan. 'Your parents will be back tomorrow. Shouldn't we do something?'

Magnus looks unmoved. 'They won't care.'

It's all very well for him to say that. But *I'm* the daughter-in-law (nearly) who's been living here and will get the blame.

Magnus and Felix have begun talking about some footnote,[20] so I head over to the hob and start a quick tidy-up. I don't dare remove my gloves, but the guys aren't giving me the slightest glance, thankfully. At least I know the rest of the house is OK. I went over the whole place yesterday, replaced all the old manky bottles of bubble bath and got a new blind for the

20. You see? It's all about the footnotes.

bathroom. Best of all, I tracked down some anemones for Wanda's study. Everyone knows she loves anemones. She's even written an article about 'Anemones in Literature'. (Which is just typical of this family – you can't just enjoy something, you have to become a top academic expert on it.)

Magnus and Felix are still engrossed as I finish. The house is tidy. No one's asked me about the ring. I'll quit while I'm ahead.

'So, I'll be off home,' I say casually and drop a kiss on Magnus's head. 'You stay here, keep Felix company. Say welcome back to your parents from me.'

'Stay the night!' Magnus sweeps an arm round my waist and pulls me back. 'They'll want to see you!'

'No, you welcome them. I'll catch up tomorrow.' I smile brightly, to distract attention from the fact that I'm edging towards the door, my hands behind my back. 'Plenty of time.'

'I don't blame you,' says Felix, looking up from the type-script and blinking at me.

'Sorry?' I say, a bit puzzled. 'Don't blame me for what?'

'Not sticking around.' He shrugs. 'I think you're being remarkably sanguine, given their reaction. I've been meaning to say so for weeks. You must be a very good person, Poppy.'

What's he *talking* about?

'I don't know . . . What do you mean?' I turn to Magnus for help.

'It's nothing,' he says, too quickly. But Felix is staring at his older brother, a light dawning in his eyes.

'Oh my God. Didn't you tell her?'

'Felix, shut up.'

'You didn't, did you? That's not exactly fair, is it, Mag?'

'Tell me what?' I'm turning from one face to the other. 'What?'

'It's nothing.' Magnus sounds rattled. 'Just . . .' He finally meets my eyes. 'OK. My parents weren't exactly wild to hear we're engaged. That's all.'

For a moment I don't know how to react. I stare at him, dumbly, trying to process what I just heard.

'But you said . . .' I don't quite trust my voice. 'You said they were thrilled. You said they were excited!'

'They will be thrilled,' he says crossly. 'When they see sense.'

They *will* be?

My whole world is wobbling. It was bad enough when I thought Magnus's parents were just intimidating geniuses. But all this time they've been *against us getting married*?

'You told me they said they couldn't imagine a sweeter, more charming daughter-in-law.' I'm trembling all over by now. 'You said they sent me special love from Chicago! Was all that *lies*?'

'I didn't want to upset you!' Magnus glares at Felix. 'Look, it's no big deal. They'll come round. They simply think it's all a bit fast . . . they don't know you properly . . . They're idiots,' he ends with a scowl. 'I told them so.'

'You had a row with your parents?' I stare at him, dismayed. 'Why didn't you tell me any of this?'

'It wasn't a row,' he says defensively. 'It was more . . . a falling-out.'

A falling-out? *A falling-out?*

'A falling-out is *worse* than a row!' I wail in horror. 'It's a million times worse! Oh God, I wish you'd told me . . . What am I going to do? How can I face them?'

I knew it. The Professors don't think I'm good enough. I'm like that girl in the opera who relinquishes her lover because she's too unsuitable and then gets TB and dies and good thing too, since she was so inferior and stupid. She probably couldn't pronounce 'Proust' either.

'Poppy, calm down!' Magnus says irritably. He gets to his feet and takes me firmly by the shoulders. 'This is exactly why I didn't tell you. It's family nonsense and it's got nothing to do with us. I love you. We're getting married. I'm going to do this and I'm going to see it through whatever anyone else says, whether it's my parents or my friends or anyone else. This is about us.' His voice is so firm, I start to relax. 'And anyway, as soon as they spend some more time with you, my parents will come round. I know it.'

I can't help giving a reluctant smile.

'That's my beautiful girl.' Magnus gives me a tight hug and I clasp him back, trying as hard as I can to believe him.

As he draws away, his gaze falls on my hands and he frowns, looking puzzled. 'Sweets . . . why are you wearing gloves?'

I'm going to have a nervous breakdown. I really am.

The whole ring debacle nearly came out. It would have done, if it weren't for Felix. I was halfway through my ludicrous, stumbling, hand-burning excuse, expecting Magnus to become suspicious at any moment, when Felix yawned and said, 'Shall we go to the pub?' and Magnus suddenly remembered an email he had to send first and everyone forgot about my gloves.

And I chose that opportunity to leave. Very quickly.

Now I'm sitting on the bus, staring out into the dark night, feeling cold inside. I've lost the ring. The Tavishes don't want me to marry Magnus. My mobile is gone. I feel like all my security blankets have been snatched, all at once.

The phone in my pocket starts to emit Beyoncé again, and I haul it out without any great hope.

Sure enough, it's not any of my friends calling to say, 'Found it!' Nor the police, nor the hotel concierge. It's him. Sam Roxton.

'You ran off,' he says with no preamble. 'I need that phone back. Where are you?'

Charming. Not 'Thank you so much for helping me with my Japanese business deal'.

'You're welcome,' I say. 'Any time.'

'Oh.' He sounds momentarily discomfited. 'Right. Thanks. I owe you one. Now, how are you going to get that phone back to me? You could drop it round at the office or I could send a bike. Where are you?'

I'm silent. I'm not going to get it back to him. I need this number.

'Hello?'

'Hi.' I clutch the phone more tightly and swallow hard. 'The thing is, I need to borrow this phone. Just for a bit.'

'Oh Christ.' I can hear him exhale. 'Look, I'm afraid it's not available for "borrowing". It's company property and I need it back. Or by "borrowing", do you actually mean "stealing"? Because, believe me, I *can* track you down and I'm not paying you a hundred pounds for the pleasure.'

Is that what he thinks? That I'm after money? That I'm some kind of phone-napper?

'I don't want to *steal* it!' I exclaim indignantly. 'I just need it for a few days. I've given the number out to everyone, and it's a real emergency . . .'

'You did *what*?' He sounds baffled. 'Why would you do that?'

'I lost my engagement ring.' I can hardly bear to say it out loud. 'It's really old and valuable. And then my phone was nicked, and I was absolutely desperate and then I passed this litter bin and there it was. In the *bin*,' I add for emphasis. 'Your PA just chucked it away. Once an item lands in a bin it belongs to the public, you know. Anyone can claim it.'

'Bullshit,' he retorts. 'Who told you that?'

'It's . . . it's common knowledge.' I try to sound robust. 'Anyway, why did your PA walk out and chuck her phone away? Not much of a PA, if you ask me.'

'No. Not much of a PA. More of a friend's daughter who should have never been given the job. She's been in the job three weeks. Apparently landed a modelling contract at exactly midday today. By one minute past, she'd left. She didn't even bother telling me she was going, I had to find out from one of the other PAs.' He sounds pretty pissed off. 'Listen, Miss . . . what's your name?'

'Wyatt. Poppy Wyatt.'

'Well, enough kidding around, Poppy. I'm sorry about your ring. I hope it turns up. But this phone isn't some fun accessory you can purloin for your own ends. This is a company phone with business messages coming in all the time. Emails. Important stuff. My PA runs my life. I *need* those messages.'

'I'll forward them,' I hastily offer. 'I'll forward everything. How about that?'

'What the—' He mutters something under his breath. 'OK. You win. I'll buy you a new phone. Give me your address, I'll bike it over—'

'I need *this* one,' I say stubbornly. 'I need this number.'

'For Christ's—'

'My plan can work!' My words tumble out in a rush. 'Everything that comes in, I'll send to you straight away. You won't know the difference! I mean, you'd have to do that anyway, wouldn't you? If you've lost your PA then what good is a PA's phone? This way is *better*. Plus you owe me one for stopping Mr Yamasaki,' I can't help pointing out. 'You just said so yourself.'

'That *isn't* what I meant, and you know it—'

'You won't miss anything, I promise!' I cut off his irritable snarl. 'I'll forward every single message. Look, I'll show you, just give me two secs . . .'

I ring off, scroll down all the messages that have arrived in the phone since this morning and quickly forward them one by one to Sam's mobile number. My fingers are working like lightning.

Text from 'Vicks Myers': forwarded. Text from 'Sir Nicholas Murray': forwarded. It's a matter of seconds to forward them all on. And the emails can all go to samroxton@ whiteglobeconsulting.com.

Email from 'HR Department': forwarded. Email from 'Tania Phelps': forwarded. Email from 'Dad'—

I hesitate a moment. I need to be careful here. Is this Violet's dad or Sam's dad? The address at the top of the email is davidr452@hotmail.com, which doesn't really help.

Telling myself it's all in a good cause, I scroll down to have a quick look.

Dear Sam

It's been a long time. I think of you often, wondering what you're up to, and would love to chat some time. Did you ever get any of my phone messages? Don't worry, I know you're a busy fellow.

If you are ever in the neighbourhood, you know you can always stop by. There is a little matter I'd like to raise with you – quite exciting actually – but as I say, no hurry.

Yours ever

Dad

As I get to the end I feel a bit shocked. I know this guy is a stranger and this is none of my business. But honestly. You'd think he could reply to his own father's phone messages. How hard is it to spare half an hour for a chat? And his dad sounds so sweet and humble. Poor old man, having to email his own son's PA. I feel like replying to him myself. I feel like visiting him, in his little cottage.[21]

Anyway. Whatever. Not my life. I press Forward and the email goes zooming off, with all the others. A moment later Beyoncé starts singing. It's Sam again.

'When exactly did Sir Nicholas Murray text Violet?' he says abruptly.

'Er . . .' I peer at the phone. 'About four hours ago.' The first few words of the text are displayed on the screen, so there's no great harm in clicking on it and reading the rest, is there? Not that it's very interesting.

---

21. Assuming he lives in a little cottage. He sounds like he does. All alone, with maybe just a faithful dog for company.

Violet, please ask Sam to call me. His phone is switched off. Best, Nicholas.

'Shit. *Shit.*' Sam's silent a moment. 'OK, if he texts again you let me know straight away, OK? Ring me.'

I open my mouth automatically to say, 'What about your dad? Why don't you ever ring *him*?' Then I close it again. No, Poppy. *Bad* idea.

'Ooh, there was a phone message earlier,' I say, suddenly remembering. 'About liposuction or something, I think. That wasn't for you?'

'*Liposuction?*' he echoes incredulously. 'Not that I'm aware of.'

He doesn't need to sound so scoffing. I was only asking. It must have been for Violet. Not that she's likely to need liposuction, if she's off modelling.

'So . . . we're on? We have a deal?'

For a while he doesn't reply, and I have an image of him glowering at his cell phone. I don't exactly get the feeling he's relishing this arrangement. But then, what choice does he have?

'I'll get the PA email address transferred back to my in-box,' he says grouchily, almost to himself. 'I'll speak to the tech guys tomorrow. But the texts will keep coming to you. If I miss any of them—'

'You won't! Look, I know this isn't ideal,' I say, trying to mollify him. 'And I'm sorry. But I'm really desperate. All the hotel staff have this number . . . all the cleaners . . . it's my only hope. Just for a couple of days. And I promise I'll send every single message on. Brownie's honour.'

'Brownie's *what*?' He sounds mystified.

'Honour! Brownie Guides? Like Scouts? You hold up one hand and you make the sign and you swear an oath . . . Hang on, I'll show you . . .' I disconnect the phone.

There's a sheet of grimy mirror opposite me on the bus. I

pose in front of it, holding the phone in one hand, making the Brownie sign with the other and wearing my best 'I'm a sane person' smile. I take a picture and text it at once to Sam Mobile.

Five seconds later a text message pings back.

I could send this to the police and have you arrested.

I feel a little whoosh of relief. *Could*. That means he's not going to. I text back:

I really, really appreciate it. Thx ☺ ☺ ☺

But there's no reply.

THREE

The next morning I wake suddenly to see the phone flashing with a new text from the Berrow Hotel, and feel so relieved I almost want to cry. They've found it! They've found it!

My fingers are fumbling as I unlock the phone; my mind galloping ahead. An early-morning cleaner found the ring clogging up a Hoover . . . discovered it in the cloakroom . . . saw a glint on the carpet . . . now securely locked in the hotel safe . . .

Dear Guest, Summer breaks half price. Please visit www.berrowhotellondon.co.uk. for details. Kind regards, The Berrow Team

I sag back on the bed, leaden with disappointment. Not to mention anger at whoever put me on the mailing list. How could they do that? Are they *trying* to play with my neuroses?

At the same time, a nasty realization is turning round and round in my stomach. Another eight hours have passed since I lost the ring. The longer it's not found—

What if—

I can't even finish my thoughts. Abruptly I get out of bed and pad through to the kitchen. I'll make a cup of tea and send on some more messages to Sam Roxton. That'll take my mind off things.

The phone has started buzzing again with texts and emails, so I turn on the kettle, perch on the window seat and start scrolling through, trying desperately not to hope. Sure enough, every message is just some friend asking if I've found the ring yet and making suggestions like, have I checked my handbag pockets?

There's nothing from Magnus, even though I sent him a couple of texts last night, asking what else his parents had said about me and when was he planning to tell me, and how was I going to face them now, and was he ignoring me on purpose?[22]

At last I turn to Sam's messages. He clearly hasn't had the email function transferred yet, because there are about fifty, just from overnight and this morning. Crikey Moses, he was right. His PA evidently *does* handle his whole life.

There's everything and everyone in here. His doctor, colleagues, charity requests, invitations . . . It's like a mainline into the universe of Sam. I can see where he buys his shirts (Turnbull & Asser). I can see where he went to university (Durham). I can see the name of his plumber (Dean).

As I scroll down, I start to feel uncomfortable. I've never had so much access to someone else's phone before. Not my friends'; not even Magnus's. There are some things you just don't share. I mean, Magnus has seen every inch of my body, including the dodgy bits, but I would never, *ever* let him near my phone.

Sam's messages are randomly mixed up with mine, which feels weird, too. I scroll down two messages for me, then about

22. OK, it wasn't a couple of texts. It was about seven. But I only pressed Send on five of them.

six for Sam, then another for me. All side by side; all touching each other. I've never shared an in-box with anyone in my life. I didn't expect it to feel so . . . *intimate*. It's as if we're suddenly sharing an underwear drawer or something.

Anyway. No big deal. It's not for long.

I make my tea and fill a bowl with Shreddies. Then, as I munch, I slowly pick through the messages, working out which ones are for Sam and forwarding them on.

I'm not going to *spy* on him or anything. Obviously not. But I have to click on each message in order to forward it, and sometimes my fingers automatically press Open by mistake and I catch a glimpse of the text. Just sometimes.

Clearly it's not just his father who's having a hard time getting in touch with him. He must be really, *really* bad at answering emails and texts; there are so many plaintive requests to Violet: 'Is this a good way to reach Sam?' 'Hi! Apologies for bothering you but I have left several messages for Sam . . .' 'Hi Violet, could you nudge Sam about an email I sent last week? I'll reprise the main points here . . .'

It's not like I'm reading through every single email *fully* or anything. Or scrolling down to read all the previous correspondence. Or critiquing all his answers and rewriting them in my head. After all, it's none of my business what he writes or doesn't write. He can do what he likes. It's a free country. My opinion is neither here nor there—

God, his replies are abrupt! It's driving me nuts! Does everything *have* to be so short? Does he *have* to be so curt and unfriendly? As I clock yet another brief email I can't help exclaiming out loud, 'Are you allergic to typing, or something?'

It's ridiculous. It's like he's determined to use the fewest possible words:

Yes, fine. Sam

Done. Sam

OK. Sam

Would it kill him to add 'Best wishes'? Or a smiley face? Or say thank you?

And while I'm on the subject, why can't he just *reply* to people? Poor Rachel Elwood is trying to organize an office Fun Run and has asked him twice now if he could lead a team. Why wouldn't he want to do that? It's fun, it's healthy, it raises money for charity, what's not to love?

Nor has he replied about accommodation for the company conference in Hampshire next week. It's at the Chiddingford Hotel, which sounds amazing, and he's booked into a suite, but he has to specify to someone called Lindy whether he's still planning to come down late. And he hasn't.

Worst of all, his dentist's receptionist has emailed him about making an appointment for a check-up four times. *Four times.*

I can't help glancing back at the previous correspondence, and Violet's obviously given up trying. Each time she's made an appointment for him, he's emailed her, 'Cancel it. S', and once even, 'You have to be joking.'

Does he *want* his teeth to rot?

By the time I'm leaving for work at 8.40, a whole new series of emails has arrived. Obviously these people all start work at the crack of dawn. The top one is from Jon Mailer, entitled 'What's the story?' which sounds quite intriguing, so as I'm walking along the street, I open it.

Sam.
Ran into Ed at the Groucho Club last night, looking worse for wear. All I'll say is, don't let him in the same room as Sir Nicholas any time soon, will you?
Regards
Jon

Ooh, now I want to know the story too. Who's Ed, and why was he the worse for wear at the Groucho Club?[23]

The second email is from someone called Willow, and as I click on it, my eyes are assaulted by capitals everywhere.

Violet.
Let's be grown-ups about this. You've HEARD Sam and me fighting. There's no point hiding anything from you.
So, since Sam REFUSES to answer the email I sent half an hour ago, maybe you could be so kind to print this attachment out and PUT IT ON HIS DESK SO HE READS IT?
Thanks so much.
Willow

I stare at the phone in shock, almost wanting to laugh. Willow must be his fiancée. Yowzer.

Her email address is willowharte@whiteglobeconsulting. com. So, she obviously works at White Globe Consulting, but she's still emailing Sam? Isn't that odd? Unless maybe they work on different floors. Fair enough. I once emailed Magnus from upstairs to ask him to make me a cup of tea.

I wonder what's in the attachment.

My fingers hesitate as I pause at a pedestrian crossing. It would be wrong to read it. Very, very wrong. I mean, this isn't some open email cc-ed to loads of people. This is a private document between two people in a relationship. I *shouldn't* look at it. It was bad enough reading that email from his father.

But on the other hand . . . she wants it printed out, doesn't she? And put on Sam's desk, where anyone could read it if they walked by. And it's not like I'm *indiscreet*. I won't mention this to anyone; no one will ever even know I've seen it . . .

My fingers seem to have a life of their own. Already I'm

___

23. Poirot would probably have worked it out already.

clicking on the attachment. It takes me a moment to focus on the text, it's so heavy with capital letters.

> Sam
> You still haven't answered me.
> Are you intending to? Do you think this is NOT IMPORTANT?????
> Jesus.
> It's only the most important thing IN OUR LIFE. And how you can go about your day so calmly . . . I don't know. It makes me want to weep.
> We need to talk, so, so badly. And I know some of this is my fault, but until we start untying the knots TOGETHER, how will we know who's pulling which string? How?
> The thing is, Sam, sometimes I don't even know if you have a string. It's that bad. I DON'T KNOW IF YOU HAVE A STRING.
> I can see you shaking your head, Mr Denial. But it is. It's THAT BAD, OK???
> If you were a human being with a shred of emotion, you'd be crying by now. I know I am. And that's another thing, I have a ten o'clock with Carter which you have now FUCKED UP as I left my FUCKING MASCARA at home.
> So, be proud of yourself.
> Willow

My eyes are like saucers. I've never seen anything like it in my life.

I read it over again – and suddenly find myself giggling. I know I shouldn't. It's not funny. She's obviously really upset. And I know I've said some pretty screwy things to Magnus, when I've been pissed and hormonal. But I would never, *ever* put them in an email and get his assistant to print it out . . .

My head bobs up in sudden realization. Shit! There's no Violet any more. No one's going to print it out and put it on

Sam's desk. He won't know about it and he won't reply and Willow will get even more livid. The awful thing is, this thought makes me want to giggle even more.

I wonder if this is a bad day or if she's always this intense. I can't resist typing 'Willow' in the search engine, and a whole series of emails pop up. There's one from yesterday, with the title 'Are you trying to fuck me or fuck WITH me, Sam? Or CAN'T YOU DECIDE???' and I get another fit of the giggles. Yikes. They must have one of those up-and-down relationships. Maybe they throw things at each other and shriek and bellow, then have mad passionate sex in the kitchen—

Beyoncé suddenly blasts out from the phone and I nearly drop it as I see 'Sam Mobile' appear on the screen. I have a sudden mad thought that he's psychic and knows I've been spying on his love life.

No more snooping, I hastily promise myself. No more Willow searches. I count to three – then press Answer.

'Oh, hi there!' I try to sound relaxed and guiltless, like I was just thinking about something else altogether and not at all imagining him screwing his fiancée among a pile of broken crockery.

'Did I have an email from Ned Murdoch this morning?' He launches in without so much as a 'Hi'.

'No. I've sent all your emails over. Good morning to you too,' I add brightly. 'I'm really well, how about you?'

'I thought you might have missed one.' He completely ignores my little dig. 'It's extremely important.'

'Well, I'm extremely thorough,' I retort pointedly. 'Believe me, everything that's coming into this phone, you're getting. And there wasn't anything from Ned Murdoch. Someone called Willow just emailed, by the way,' I add casually. 'I'll forward it on. There's an attachment, which sounded quite important. But obviously I didn't look at it at all. Or read it, or anything.'

'Hrrmm.' He gives a kind of non-committal growl. 'So, have you found your ring?'

'Not yet,' I admit reluctantly. 'But I'm sure it'll turn up.'

'You should inform your insurers anyway, you know. They sometimes have a time limit for claiming. Colleague of mine got caught out that way.'

Insurers? Time limits?

I suddenly feel clammy with guilt. I've given this no thought at all. I haven't checked up on my insurance or the Tavishes' insurance or anything. Instead I've been standing at a pedestrian crossing, missing my chance to walk, reading other people's emails and laughing at them. *Priorities*, Poppy.

'Right,' I manage at last. 'Yes, I knew that. I'm on to it.'

I ring off and stand motionless for a moment, the traffic whizzing in front of me. It's like he's pricked my bubble. I have to come clean. It's the Tavishes' ring. They should know it's lost. I'll have to tell them.

Hi there! It's me, the girl you don't want to marry your son, and guess what, I've lost your priceless family ring!

I'll give myself twelve more hours, I abruptly decide, and press the crossing button again. Just in case. *Just* in case.

And then I'll tell them.

I always thought I might be a dentist. Several of my family are dentists, and it always seemed like a pretty decent career. But then, when I was fifteen, my school sent me on a week-long work-experience placement at the physio unit at our local hospital. All the therapists were so enthusiastic about what they did, that focusing only on teeth suddenly felt a bit narrow for me. And I've never regretted my decision for a moment. It just suits me, being a physio.

First Fit Physio Studio is exactly eighteen minutes' walk from my flat in Balham, past Costa and next to Greggs the baker. It's not the grandest practice in the world – I'd probably earn more if I went to some smart sports centre or a big hospital. But I've been working there ever since I qualified, and can't imagine working anywhere else. Plus, I work with friends. You wouldn't give that up in a hurry, would you?

I arrive at nine o'clock expecting to have the usual staff meeting. We have one every Thursday morning, where we discuss patients and targets, new therapies, the latest research, stuff like that.[24] There's one particular patient I want to talk about, actually: Mrs Randall, my sweet 65-year-old with the ligament problem. She's pretty much recovered – but last week she came in twice, and this week she's booked three appointments. I've told her she just needs to exercise at home with her Dyna-Bands, but she insists she needs my help. I think she's become totally dependent on us – which might be good for the cash register but is *not* good for her.

So I'm quite looking forward to the meeting. But to my surprise, the meeting room is set up differently from usual. The table has been pulled to one end of the room with two chairs behind it – and there's a sole chair facing it in the middle of the room. It looks like an interview set-up.

The reception door pings to signal that someone's entered, and I turn to see Annalise coming in with a Costa Coffee tray. She's got some complicated braided arrangement in her long blonde hair, and she looks just like a Greek goddess.

'Hi, Annalise! What's up?'

'You'd better talk to Ruby.' She gives me a sidelong look, without smiling.

'What?'

'I don't think I should say.' She takes a sip of cappuccino, eyeing me secretively over the top.

What's up now? Annalise's quite prickly, in fact, she's a bit of a child. She goes all quiet and sulky, and then it comes out

---

24. There are only three of us and we've known each other for yonks. So just *occasionally* we lurch off into other areas like our boyfriends and the Zara sale.

that yesterday you asked her for that patient file too impatiently and hurt her feelings.

Ruby is the opposite. She's got smooth, latte-coloured skin, a huge, motherly bust, and is packed so full of common sense it's practically wafting out of her ears. The minute you're in her company you feel saner, calmer, jollier and stronger. No wonder this physio practice has been a success. I mean, Annalise and I are OK at what we do, but Ruby is the star turn. Everyone loves her. Men, women, grannies, kids. She also put up the money for the business[25] so she's officially my boss.

'Morning, babe.' Ruby comes breezing out from her treatment room, beaming her usual wide smile. Her hair has been back-combed and pinned in a bun, with intricate twisted sections on either side. Both Annalise and Ruby are totally into their hairdos – it's almost a competition between them. 'Now look, it's a real pain, but I have to give you a disciplinary hearing.'

'*What?*' I gape at her.

'Not my fault!' She lifts her hands. 'I want to get accreditation from this new body, the PFFA. I've just been reading the material and they say if your staff chat up the patients you have to discipline them. We should have done it anyway, you know that, but now I need to have the notes ready for the inspector. We'll get it done really quickly.'

'I didn't chat him up,' I say defensively. 'He chatted *me* up!'

'I think the panel will decide that, don't you?' chimes in Annalise forbiddingly. She looks so grave I feel a tickle of worry. 'I *told* you you'd been unethical,' she adds. 'You should be prosecuted.'

'*Prosecuted?*' I appeal to Ruby. I can't believe this is happening. Back when Magnus proposed, Ruby said it was such a romantic story she wanted to cry, and that, OK, strictly it was against the rules but in her opinion love conquered all, and *please* could she be a bridesmaid?

25. Or rather, her dad did. He already owns a string of photocopying shops.

'Annalise, you don't mean "prosecuted".' Ruby rolls her eyes. 'Come on. Let's convene the panel.'

'Who's on the panel?'

'Us,' says Ruby blithely. 'Me and Annalise. I know we should have an external person, but I didn't know who to get. I'll tell the inspector I had someone lined up and they were ill.' She glances at her watch. 'OK, we've got twenty minutes. Morning, Angela!' she adds cheerily as our receptionist pushes the front door open. 'Don't let any calls through, OK?'

Angela just nods and sniffs and dumps her rucksack on the floor. She has a boyfriend in a band, so she's never very communicative in the mornings.

'Oh, Poppy,' Ruby says over her shoulder as she leads the way into the meeting room. 'I was supposed to give you two weeks' notice to prepare. You don't need that, do you? Can we say you had it? Because there's only a week and a bit till the wedding, so it would mean dragging you away from your honeymoon or leaving it till you're back, and I *really* want to get the paperwork done . . .'

She's ushering me to the sole chair, marooned in the middle of the floor, while she and Annalise take their seats behind the table. Any minute I expect a bright light to be shined in my eyes. This is horrible. Everything's suddenly turned. It's them against me.

'Are you going to *fire* me?' I feel ridiculously panicked.

'No! Of course not!' Ruby is unscrewing her pen. 'Don't be silly!'

'We might,' says Annalise, shooting me an ominous look.

She's obviously loving her role as Chief Henchwoman. I know what this is all about. It's because I got Magnus and she didn't.

Here's the thing. Annalise's the beautiful one. Even I want to stare at her all day, and I'm a girl. If you'd said to anyone last year, 'Which of these three will land a guy and be engaged by next spring?' they'd have said immediately, 'Annalise.'

So I can understand her point of view. She must look in the mirror and see herself (Greek goddess) and then see me (lanky legs, dark hair, best feature: long eyelashes) and think ... WTF?

Plus, as I said, Magnus was originally booked with her. And at the last minute we switched appointments. Which is *not my fault*.

'So.' Ruby looks up from her foolscap pad. 'Let's just run over the facts, Miss Wyatt. On December 15th last year, you treated a Dr Magnus Tavish here at the clinic.'

'Yes.'

'For what form of injury?'

'A sprained wrist sustained while skiing.'

'And during this appointment, did he show any ... inappropriate interest in you? Or you in him?'

I cast my mind back to that first instant Magnus walked into my room. He was wearing a long grey tweed coat, and his tawny hair was glistening with rain and his face was flushed from walking. He was ten minutes late, and he immediately rushed over, clasped both my hands and said, 'I'm most *terribly* sorry,' in this lovely, well-educated voice.

'I ... er ... no,' I say defensively. 'It was just a standard appointment.'

Even as I say this, I know it's not true. In standard appointments, your heart doesn't start to pound as you take the patient's arm. The hairs on the back of your neck don't rise up. You don't hold on to his hand just very slightly longer than you need to.

Not that I can say any of this. I really would be fired.

'I treated the patient over the course of a number of appointments.' I try to sound calm and professional. 'By the time we realized our affection for each other, his treatment was over. It was therefore totally ethical.'

'He told me it was love at first sight!' shoots back Annalise.

'How do you explain *that*? He told me you were instantly attracted to each other and he wanted to ravish you right there on the couch. He said he'd never known anything so sexy as you in your uniform.'

I'm going to *shoot* Magnus. What did he have to say that for?

'Objection!' I glower at her. 'That evidence was procured while under the influence of alcohol and in a non-professional capacity. It therefore cannot be allowed in court.'

'Yes, it can! And you are *under oath*!' She jabs a finger at me.

'Objection sustained,' Ruby interrupts, and looks up from writing, a distant, wistful look in her eyes. 'Was it really love at first sight?' She leans forward, her great big uniformed bosom bulging everywhere. 'Did you *know*?'

I close my eyes and try to visualize that day. I'm not sure what I knew, except I wanted to ravish him on the couch, too.

'Yes,' I say at last. 'I think so.'

'It's *so* romantic.' Ruby sighs.

'And wrong!' Annalise chimes in sharply. 'The minute he showed any interest in you, you should have said, "Sir, this is inappropriate behaviour. I would like this session to end and for you to transfer to another therapist."'

'Oh, another therapist!' I can't help a short laugh. 'Like *you*, by any chance?'

'Maybe! Why not?'

'And what if he'd shown interest in you?'

She lifts her chin proudly. 'I would have handled it without compromising my ethical principles.'

'I was ethical!' I say in outrage. 'I was totally ethical!'

'Oh yes?' She narrows her eyes like a prosecuting barrister. 'What led you to suggest exchanging appointments with me in the first place, Miss Wyatt? Had you in fact already Googled him and decided you wanted him for yourself?'

Aren't we over this?

'Annalise, *you* wanted to swap appointments! I never suggested anything! I had no idea who he was! So if you feel like you missed out, tough luck. Don't swap, next time!'

For a moment, Annalise says nothing. She's getting pinker and pinker in the face.

'I know,' she bursts out at last, and bangs a fist to her forehead. 'I know! I was so *stupid*. *Why* did I swap?'

'So what?' cuts in Ruby firmly. 'Annalise, get over it. Magnus obviously wasn't meant for you, he was meant for Poppy. So what does it matter?'

Annalise is silent. I can tell she isn't convinced.

'It's not fair,' she mutters at last. 'Do you *know* how many bankers I've massaged at the London Marathon? Do you *know* how much effort I've made?'

Annalise cottoned on to the London Marathon a few years ago, when she was watching it on telly and realized it was stuffed full of fit, motivated guys in their forties, who were probably single because all they did was go running, and OK, forties was a bit old, but *think* what kind of salary they must be on.

So she's been volunteering as an emergency physiotherapist every year since. She makes a beeline for all the attractive men and works their calf muscles or whatever, while fixing them with her huge blue eyes and telling them *she's* always supported that charity, too.[26]

To be fair, she's got lots of dates out of it – one guy even took her to Paris – but nothing long-term or serious, which is what she wants. What she won't admit, of course, is that she's extremely picky. She pretends that she wants a 'really nice, straightforward guy with good values', but she's had several of those desperately in love with her, and she dumped them, even the really good-looking actor (his stage play ended and he had no other work coming up). What she's *really* after is a guy who looks like he's out of a Gillette commercial, with a

---

26. She also completely ignores all the poor women with twisted ankles. If you're a girl, never do the Marathon with Annalise on duty.

massive salary and/or a title. Preferably both. I think that's why she's so mad about losing Magnus, since he's a 'Dr'. She once asked me if he would become 'Professor' one day and I said probably yes, and she went a kind of green.

Ruby scribbles something else down, then screws her pen-lid on. 'Well, I think we've covered the facts. Well done, everyone.'

'Aren't you going to give her a warning or something?' Annalise is still pouting.

'Oh, fair point.' Ruby nods, then clears her throat. 'Poppy, don't do it again.'

'OK.' I shrug.

'I'll put that in writing, show it to the inspector, that'll shut him up. By the way, did I tell you I've found the *perfect* strapless bra to go under my bridesmaid's dress?' Ruby beams at me, back to her usual cheery self. 'Aquamarine satin. It's lush.'

'Sounds amazing!' I get up and reach for the Costa Coffee tray. 'Is one of these for me?'

'I got you a flat white,' says Annalise grudgingly. 'With nutmeg.'

As I take it, Ruby gives a small gasp. 'Poppy! Haven't you found your ring?'

I look up to see both Annalise and Ruby staring at my left hand.

'No,' I admit reluctantly. 'I mean, I'm sure it'll turn up somewhere . . .'

'Shit.' Annalise has a hand over her mouth.

'I thought you found it.' Ruby is frowning. 'I'm sure somebody said you'd found it.'

'No. Not yet.'

I'm *really* not enjoying their reaction. Neither of them is saying, 'Not to worry', or 'These things happen.' They both look horrified, even Ruby.

'So, what will you do?' Ruby's brows are knitted.

'What did Magnus say?' chips in Annalise.

'I . . .' I take a gulp of flat white, playing for time. 'I haven't told him yet.'

'Sheeesh.' Ruby exhales.

'How much is it worth?' *Trust* Annalise to ask all the questions I don't want to think about.

'Quite a bit, I suppose. I mean, there's always insurance . . .' I trail off lamely.

'So, when are you planning to tell Magnus?' Ruby has her disapproving face on. I hate that face. It makes me feel small and mortified. Like that awful time she caught me giving ultrasound and texting at the same time.[27] Ruby is someone you just instinctively want to impress.

'Tonight. Neither of you guys have seen it, have you?' I can't help asking, even though it's ridiculous, like they'll suddenly say, 'Oh yes, it's in my bag!'

They both shrug 'No' silently. Even Annalise is looking sorry for me.

Oh God. This is really bad.

By six o'clock it's even worse. Annalise has Googled emerald rings.

Did I ask her to do this? No. I did not. Magnus has never told me how much the ring is worth. I asked him, jokingly, when he first put it on my finger, and he joked back that it was priceless, just like me. It was all really romantic and lovely. We were having dinner at Bluebird, and I had no idea he was going to propose. None.[28]

---

27. It was an emergency, in my defence. Natasha had split up with her boyfriend. And it's not like the patient could see what I was doing. But yes, I know it was wrong.
28. I know girls say that and what they really mean is, 'I gave him an ultimatum and then let him think he'd come up with the idea himself and six weeks later, bingo.' But it wasn't like that. I honestly had no idea. Well, you wouldn't, would you, after a *month*?

Anyway, the point is, I never knew what the ring cost and I never wanted to know. At the back of my mind I keep trying out lines to Magnus like, 'Well, I didn't *realize* it was so valuable! You should have *told* me!'

Not that I'd have the nerve to really say that. I mean, how dumb would you have to be not to realize that an emerald out of a bank vault is worth something? Still, it's been quite comforting not to have a precise figure in my head.

But now here's Annalise brandishing a sheet of paper she's printed out from the Internet.[29]

'Art Deco, fine quality emerald, with baguette diamonds,' she's reading out. 'Estimate: £25,000.'

What? My insides turn to jelly. That can't be right.

'He wouldn't have given me anything that expensive.' My voice is a bit shaky. 'Academics are *poor*.'

'He's not poor! Look at his parents' house! His dad's a celebrity! Look, this one's thirty grand.' She holds up another sheet. 'It looks exactly like yours. Don't you think, Ruby?'

I can't look.

'*I* would never have let it off my finger,' Annalise adds, arching her eyebrows, and I almost want to hit her.

'*You're* the one who wanted to try it on!' I say furiously. 'If it hadn't been for you, I'd still have it!'

'No, I wasn't!' she retorts indignantly. 'I just tried it on when everyone else did! It was already going round the table.'

'Well, whose idea was it, then?'

I've been racking my brains about this again – but if my memory was hazy yesterday, it's even worse today.

I'm never going to believe a Poirot mystery again. Never. All those witnesses going, 'Yes, I remember it was 3.06 p.m. exactly because I glanced at the clock as I reached for the sugar tongs,

---

29. Which I bet she did *not* do in her lunch hour. *She* should be the one getting the disciplinary hearing.

and Lady Favisham was quite clearly sitting on the right-hand side of the fireplace.'

Bollocks. They have no idea where Lady Favisham was, they just don't want to admit it in front of Poirot. I'm amazed he gets anywhere.

'I've got to go.' I turn away before Annalise can taunt me with any more expensive rings.

'To tell Magnus?'

'Wedding meeting with Lucinda first. Then Magnus and his family.'

'Let us know what happens. Text us!' Annalise frowns. 'Hey, that reminds me, Poppy, how come you changed your number?'

'Oh, that. Well, I went out of the hotel to get a better signal and I was holding out my phone . . .'

I break off. On second thoughts, I can't be bothered to get into the whole story of the mugging and the phone in the bin and Sam Roxton. It's all too way-out and I haven't got the energy.

Instead I shrug. 'Just . . . you know. Lost my phone. Got another one. See you tomorrow.'

'Good luck, missus.' Ruby pulls me in for a quick hug.

'Text!' I hear Annalise calling after me as I head out of the door. 'We want hourly updates!'

She would have been great at public executions, Annalise. She would have been the one at the front, jostling for a good view of the axe, already sketching the gory bits to put up on the village noticeboard, just in case anyone missed it.

Or, you know, whatever they did before Facebook.

I don't know why I bothered rushing, because Lucinda's late, as always.

In fact, I don't know why I bothered to have a wedding planner. But I only ever think that thought to myself very quietly, because Lucinda is an old family friend of the Tavishes and every time I mention her Magnus says, 'Are you two getting along?' in raised, hopeful tones, like we're two endangered pandas who have to make a baby.

It's not that I don't *like* Lucinda. It's just that she stresses me out. She sends me all these bulletins by text the whole time, of what she's doing and where, and keeps telling me what an effort she's making on my behalf, like the sourcing of the napkins, which was the *hugest* saga and took her for ever and three trips to a fabric warehouse in Walthamstow.

Also, her priorities seem a little screwy. Like, she hired an 'IT Wedding Specialist' at great expense, who set up whizzy things like a text-alert system to give all the guests updates,[30] and a web page where guests can register what outfit they're wearing and avoid 'unfortunate clashes'.[31] But while she was doing all that, she didn't get back to the caterers we wanted, and we nearly lost them.

We're meeting in the lobby of Claridge's – Lucinda loves hotel lobbies, don't ask me why. I sit there patiently for twenty minutes, drinking weak black tea, wishing I'd cancelled and feeling sicker and sicker at the thought of seeing Magnus's parents. I'm just wondering if I might actually have to go to the Ladies and be ill – when she suddenly appears, all flying raven hair and Calvin Klein perfume and six mood boards under her arm. Her suede spiky kitten heels are tapping on the marble floor and her pink cashmere coat is billowing out behind her like a pair of wings.

Trailing in her wake is Clemency, her 'assistant'. (If an unpaid eighteen-year-old can be called an assistant. I'd call her slave labour.) Clemency is very posh and very sweet and terrified of Lucinda. She answered Lucinda's ad for an

30. Which we've never used.
31. Which no one has registered on.

intern in *The Lady* and keeps telling me how great it is to learn the ropes first-hand from an experienced professional.[32]

'So, I've been talking to the vicar. Those arrangements *aren't* going to work. The wretched pulpit has to stay where it is.' Lucinda descends into a chair in a leggy, Joseph-trousered sprawl, and the mood boards slide out of her grasp and all over the floor. 'I just don't know why people can't be more *helpful*. I mean, what are we going to do now? And I haven't heard back from the caterer . . .'

I can barely concentrate on what she's saying. I'm suddenly wishing I'd arranged to meet Magnus first, on my own, to tell him about the ring. Then we could have faced his parents together. Is it too late? Could I quickly text him on the way?

'. . . and I still haven't got a trumpeter.' Lucinda exhales sharply, two lacquered nails to her forehead. 'There's so much to do. It's insane. *Insane*. It would have *helped* if Clemency had typed out the Order of Service properly,' she adds, a little savagely.

Poor Clemency flushes beetroot and I shoot her a sympathetic smile. It's not her fault she's severely dyslexic and put 'hymen' instead of 'hymn' and the whole thing had to be redone.

'We'll get there!' I say encouragingly. 'Don't worry!'

'I'm telling you, after this is over I'm going to need a week in a spa. Have you seen my *hands*?' Lucinda pushes them towards me. 'That's stress!'

I have no idea what she's talking about – her hands look perfectly normal to me. But I stare at them obediently.

'You see? Wrecked. All for your wedding, Poppy! Clemency, order me a G&T.'

---

32. Personally, I'm doubtful about Lucinda's so-called 'experience'. Whenever I ask her about other weddings she's done, she only ever refers to one, which was for another friend, and consisted of thirty people in a restaurant. But obviously I never mention this in front of the Tavishes. Or Clemency. Or anyone.

'Right. Absolutely.' Clemency leaps eagerly to her feet.

I try to ignore a tiny rub of irritation. Lucinda's always throwing little references like that into the conversation: 'All for your wedding.' 'Just to make you happy, Poppy!' 'The bride's always right!'

She can sound quite pointed sometimes, which I find quite disconcerting. I mean, I didn't *ask* her to be a wedding planner, did I? And we are paying her quite a lot, aren't we? But I don't want to say anything, because she's Magnus's old friend and everything.

'Lucinda, I was just wondering, have we sorted out the cars yet?' I say tentatively.

There's an ominous silence. I can tell that a wave of fury is rising inside Lucinda, from the way her nose starts to twitch. At last it erupts, just as poor Clemency arrives back.

'Oh bloody *hell*. Oh fucking ... *Clemency!*' She turns her wrath on the trembling girl. '*Why* didn't you remind me about the cars? They need cars! We need to hire them!'

'I ...' Clemency looks helplessly at me. 'Um ... I didn't know ...'

'There's always something!' Lucinda is almost talking to herself. 'Always something else to think about. It's endless. However much I run myself into the ground, it just goes on and on and on ...'

'Look, shall I do the cars?' I say hastily. 'I'm sure I can sort them.'

'Would you?' Lucinda seems to wake up. 'Could you do that? It's just, there's only one of me, you know, and I have spent the entire *week* working on details, all for *your* wedding, Poppy ...'

She looks so stressed out, I feel a pang of guilt.

'Yes! No problem. I'll just go on Yellow Pages or something.'

'How's your hair coming along, Poppy?' Lucinda suddenly focuses on my head, and I silently will my hair to grow another centimetre, very quickly.

'Not bad! I'm sure it will go into the chignon. Definitely.' I try to sound more positive than I feel.

Lucinda has told me about a hundred times how short-sighted and foolish it was to cut my hair to above the shoulder, when I was just about to become engaged.[33] She also told me at the wedding-dress shop that with my pale skin,[34] a white dress would never work and I should wear lime green. For my *wedding*. Luckily the wedding-dress shop-owner chipped in and said Lucinda was speaking nonsense: my dark hair and eyes would set off the white beautifully. So I chose to believe her, instead.

The G&T arrives and Lucinda takes a deep slug. I take another sip of tepid black tea. Poor old Clemency hasn't got anything, but she looks like she's trying to blend into her chair and not attract any attention at all.

'And . . . you were going to find out about confetti?' I add cautiously. 'But I can do that too,' I backtrack quickly at Lucinda's expression. 'I'll phone the vicar.'

'Great!' Lucinda breathes out sharply. 'I'd appreciate that! Because there *is* only one of me and I *can* only be in one place at once—' She breaks off abruptly as her gaze alights on my hand. 'Where's your ring, Poppy? Oh my God, haven't you *found* it yet?'

As she lifts her eyes she looks so thunderstruck, I start to feel sick again.

'Not yet. But it'll turn up soon. I'm sure it will. The hotel staff are all looking . . .'

'And you haven't told Magnus?'

'I will!' I swallow hard. 'Soon.'

'But, isn't it a really important family piece?' Lucinda's hazel eyes are wide. 'Won't they be livid?'

Is she *trying* to give me a nervous breakdown?

33. Was I supposed to be *psychic*?
34. 'Deathly white', as she called it.

My phone buzzes and I grab it, grateful for the distraction. Magnus has just sent me a text which dashes my secret hope that his parents would suddenly catch gastric flu and have to cancel:

Dinner at 8, whole family here, can't wait to see you!

'Is that your new phone?' Lucinda frowns critically at it. 'Did you get my forwarded texts?'

'Yes, thanks.' I nod. Only about thirty-five of them, all clogging up my in-box.

When she heard I'd lost my phone, Lucinda insisted on forwarding all her recent texts to me, just so I didn't 'drop the ball'. To be fair, it was quite a good idea. I got Magnus to forward all his most recent messages too, and the girls at work.

Ned Murdoch, whoever he is, has also finally contacted Sam. I've been looking out for that email all day. I glance at it distractedly, but it doesn't seem particularly earth-shattering to me: 'Re Ellerton's bid. Sam, hi. A few points. You'll see from the attachment, blah blah blah . . .'

Anyway, I'd better send it on straight away. I press Forward and make sure it's gone through. Then I type a quick reply to Magnus, my fingers fumbling with nerves.

Great! Can't wait to see your parents!!!! So exciting!!!! ☺ ☺ ☺
PS could we meet outside first? Something I want to talk about. Just a really tiny thing. Xxxxxxxxx

FOUR

I now have historical insight. I actually *know* now what it felt like to have to trudge up to the guillotine in the French Revolution. As I walk up the hill from the tube, clutching the wine I bought yesterday, my steps get slower and slower. And slower.

In fact, I realize, I'm not walking any more. I'm standing. I'm staring up at the Tavishes' house and swallowing hard, over and over again, willing myself to move forward.

Perspective, Poppy. It's only a ring.

It's only your prospective in-laws.

It was only a 'falling-out'. According to Magnus,[35] they never actually said straight out they didn't want him to marry me. They only *implied* it. And maybe they've changed their minds!

Plus, I have discovered one tiny positive. My home insurance policy will pay out for losses, apparently. So that's something. I'm even wondering whether to *start* the ring conversation via insurance and how handy it is. 'You know, Wanda, I was reading an HSBC leaflet the other day—'

35. I finally winkled this out of him on the phone at lunchtime.

Oh God, who am I kidding? There's no way to salvage this. It's a nightmare. Let's just get it over with.

My phone bleeps and I take it out of my pocket just for old times' sake. I've given up hoping for a miracle.

'You have one new message,' come the familiar, unhurried tones of the voice-mail woman.

I feel like I *know* this woman, she's talked to me so often. How many people have listened to her, desperate for her to hurry up, their hearts pounding with fear or hope? Yet she always sounds equally unfussed, like she doesn't even *care* what you're about to hear. You should be able to choose different options for different kinds of news, so she could start off: 'Guess what! Ace news! Listen to your voice-mail! Yay!' Or: 'Sit down, love. Get a drink. You've got a message and it's not good.'

I press '1', shift the mobile to the other hand and start trudging again. The message was left while I was on the tube. It's probably just Magnus, asking where I am.

'Hello, this is the Berrow Hotel, with a message for Poppy Wyatt. Miss Wyatt, it appears your ring *was* found yesterday. However, due to the chaos after the fire alarm—'

What? *What?*

Joy is whooshing through me like a sparkler. I can't listen properly. I can't take the words in. They've found it!

I've already abandoned the message. I'm on speed-dial to the concierge. I love him. I *love* him!

'Berrow Hotel—' It's the concierge's voice.

'Hi!' I say breathlessly. 'It's Poppy Wyatt. You've found my ring! You're a star! Shall I come straight round and get it?'

'Miss Wyatt,' he interrupts me. 'Did you listen to the message?'

'I . . . some of it.'

'I'm afraid . . .' He pauses. 'I'm afraid we are not presently sure of the ring's whereabouts.'

I stop dead and peer at the phone. Did he just say what I thought he did?

'You said you'd found it.' I'm trying to stay calm. 'How can you not be sure of its whereabouts?'

'According to one of our staff, a waitress *did* find an emerald ring on the carpet of the ballroom during the fire alarm and handed it to our guest manager, Mrs Fairfax. However, we are uncertain as to what happened after that. We have been unable to find it in the safe, nor in any of our usual secure locations. We are deeply sorry, and will do our very utmost to—'

'Well, talk to Mrs Fairfax!' I try to control my impatience. 'Find out what she did with it!'

'Indeed. Unfortunately she has gone on holiday, and despite our best endeavours, we have been unable to contact her.'

'Has she *pinched* it?' I say in horror.

I'll find her. Whatever it takes. Detectives, police, Interpol . . . I'm already standing in the courtroom, pointing at the ring in a plastic evidence bag, while a middle-aged woman, tanned from her Costa del Sol hideout, glowers at me from the dock.

'Mrs Fairfax has been a faithful employee for thirty years and handled many very valuable items belonging to guests.' He sounds slightly offended. 'I find it very hard to believe that she would have done such a thing.'

'So, it must be somewhere in the hotel?' I feel a glimmer of hope.

'That is what we are endeavouring to find out. Obviously as soon as I know anything more, I will be in touch. I can use this number still, can I?'

'Yes!' Instinctively I grip the phone more tightly. 'Use this number. Please call *as soon* as you hear anything. Thank you.'

As I ring off, I'm breathing hard. I don't know how to feel. I mean, it's good news. Kind of. Isn't it?

Except that I still don't have the ring safely on my finger. Everyone will still be worried. Magnus's parents will think I'm flaky and irresponsible and never forgive me for putting them through such stress. So I still have a total nightmare ahead of me.

Unless— Unless I could—

No. I couldn't possibly. Could I?

I'm standing like a pillar on the pavement, my mind circling furiously. OK. Just let's think this through properly. Logically and ethically. If the ring isn't *actually* lost . . .

I passed a Boots on the high street, about four hundred yards back. Almost without knowing what I'm doing, I retrace my steps. I ignore the shop assistant who tries to tell me they're closing. My head right down, I make my way to the first-aid counter. There's a glove thing you pull on, and some rolls of adhesive bandage. I'll get it all.

A couple of minutes later I'm striding up the hill again. My hand is swathed in bandages, and you can't tell whether I'm wearing a ring or not, and I don't even have to lie, I can say, 'It's difficult to wear a ring with a burned hand.' Which is true.

I'm nearly at the house when my phone bleeps and a text from Sam Roxton pops into my in-box.

Where's the attachment?

Typical. No hello, no explanation. He just expects me to know what he's on about.

What do you mean?

The email from Ned Murdoch. There was no attachment.

That's not my fault! I just sent on the email. They must have forgotten to put it on. Why don't you ask them to send it again, WITH the attachment? Directly to your computer?

I know I sound a bit exasperated, and of course he instantly picks up on it.

This phone sharing was your idea, if you remember. If you're tired of it, just return my phone to my office.

Hurriedly I text back:

No, no! It's OK. If it comes through I'll forward it. Don't worry. I thought you were getting emails transferred to your address???

Techies said they'd sort it asap. But they are liars.

There's a short pause, then he texts:

Got the ring, btw?

Nearly. Hotel found it, but then lost it again.

Typical.

I know.

By now, I've stopped walking and am leaning against a wall. I know I'm spinning out time before I have to go into the house, but I can't help it. It's quite comforting, having this virtual conversation through the ether with someone who doesn't know me or Magnus, or anybody. After a few moments I text in a confessional rush:

Am not telling my in-laws have lost ring. Do you think that's really bad?

There's silence for a bit – then he replies:

Why should you tell them?

What kind of ridiculous question is *that*? I roll my eyes and type:

It's their ring!

Almost at once his reply comes beeping in:

Not their ring. Your ring. None of their business. No big deal.

How can he write 'No big deal'? As I text back, I'm jabbing the keys crossly.

Is family bloody HEIRLOOM. Am about to have dinner with them right now. They will expect to see ring on my finger. Is huge deal, thank you.

For a while there's silence and I think he's given up on our conversation. Then, just as I'm about to move on, another text beeps into the phone.

How will you explain missing ring?

I have a moment's internal debate. Why not get a second opinion? Lining up the screen carefully, I take a photo of my bandaged hand and MMS it to him. Five seconds later he replies:

You cannot be serious.

I feel a twinge of resentment and find myself typing:

What would YOU do then?

I'm half-hoping he might have some brilliant idea I hadn't thought of. But his next text just says:

This is why men don't wear rings.

Great. Well, that's really helpful. I'm about to type some-thing sarcastic back, when a second text arrives:

It looks phoney. Take off one bandage.

I stare at my hand in dismay. Perhaps he's right.

OK. Thx.

I unpeel a bandage and am stuffing it into my bag just as Magnus's voice rings out.

'Poppy! What are you doing?' I look up – and he's striding along the street towards me. Flustered, I drop the phone into my bag and zip it shut. I can hear the bleep of another text arriving, but I'll have to look at it later.

'Hi, Magnus! What are you doing here?'

'Getting some milk. We're out.' He stops in front of me and rests two hands on my shoulders, his brown eyes regarding me in tender amusement. 'What's up? Putting the evil moment off?'

'No!' I laugh defensively. 'Of course not! I'm just coming up to the house.'

'I know what you wanted to talk to me about.'

'You . . . do?' I glance involuntarily at my bandaged hand and then away again.

'Sweetheart, listen. You *have* to stop worrying about my parents. They'll love you when they get to know you properly. I'll make sure they do. We're going to have a fun evening. OK? Just relax and be yourself.'

'OK.' I nod at last, and he squeezes me, then glances at my bandage.

'Hand still bad? Poor you.'

He didn't even mention the ring. I feel a glimmer of hope. Maybe this evening will be OK, after all.

'So, have you told your parents about the rehearsal? Tomorrow evening at the church.'

'I know.' He smiles. 'Don't worry. We're all set.'

As I walk along, I savour the thought of it. The ancient stone church. The organ playing as I walk in. The vows.

I know some brides are all about the music or the flowers, or the dress. But I'm all about the vows. *For better for worse . . . For richer for poorer . . . And thereto I plight thee my troth . . .* All my life, I've heard these magical words. At family weddings, in movie scenes, at royal weddings even. The same words, over and over, like poetry handed down the centuries. And now we're going to say them to each other. It makes my spine tingle.

'I'm so looking forward to saying our vows,' I can't help saying, even though I've said this to him before, approximately a hundred times.

There was a very short time, just after we'd got engaged, when Magnus seemed to think we'd be getting married in a registry office. He's not exactly religious, and nor are his parents. But as soon as I'd explained exactly *how much* I'd been looking forward to saying the church vows all my life, he backtracked and said he couldn't think of anything more wonderful.

'I know.' He squeezes my waist again. 'Me too.'

'You really don't mind doing the old words?'

'Sweets, I think they're beautiful.'

'Me too.' I sigh happily. 'So romantic.'

Every time I imagine myself and Magnus in front of the altar, hands joined, saying those words to each other in clear, resonant voices, it seems like nothing else matters.

But as we approach the house twenty minutes later, my glow of security starts to ebb away. The Tavishes are definitely back. The whole house is lit up and I can hear opera blasting out of the windows. I suddenly remember that time Antony asked me what I thought of *Tannhäuser* and I said I didn't smoke.

Oh God. *Why* didn't I do a crash course on opera?

Magnus swings the front door open, then clicks his tongue.

'Damn. Forgot to call Dr Wheeler. I'll just be a couple of minutes.'

I don't believe this. He's bounding up the stairs, towards the study. He can't *leave* me.

'Magnus.' I try not to sound too panicked.

'Just go through! My parents are in the kitchen. Oh, I got you something for our honeymoon. Open it!' He blows me a kiss and disappears round the corner.

There's a huge, beribboned box on the hall ottoman. Wow. I know this shop and it's expensive. I tug it open, ripping the expensive pale-green tissue paper, to find a grey and white printed Japanese kimono. It's absolutely stunning, and even has a matching camisole.

On impulse I duck into the little front sitting room which no one ever uses. I take off my top and cardigan, slip the camisole on, then replace my clothes. It's slightly too big – but still gorgeous. All silky-smooth and luxurious-feeling.

It *is* a lovely present. It really is. But to be honest, what I would have preferred right now is Magnus by my side, his hand firmly in mine, giving me moral support. I fold the dressing gown up again and stuff it back amid the torn tissue, taking my time.

Still no sign of Magnus. I can't put this off any longer.

'Magnus?' comes Wanda's high-pitched, distinctive voice from the kitchen. 'Is that you?'

'No, it's me! Poppy!' My throat is so clenched with nerves I sound like a stranger.

'Poppy! Come on through!'

Relax. Be myself. Come on.

I grasp the bottle of wine firmly and head into the kitchen, which is warm and smells of Bolognese sauce.

'Hi, how are you?' I say in a nervous rush. 'I brought you some wine. I hope you like it. It's red.'

'*Poppy.*' Wanda swoops towards me. Her wild hair has been freshly hennaed and she's wearing one of her odd, capacious dresses made out of what looks like parachute silk, together with rubber-soled Mary-Janes. Her skin is as pale and unadorned as ever, although she's put on an inaccurate slash of red lipstick.[36] Her cheek brushes against mine and I catch a whiff of stale perfume. 'The "fi-an-cée"!' She enunciates the word with care bordering on ridicule. 'The "betrothed".'

'The "affianced",' chimes in Antony, rising from his seat at the table. He's wearing the tweed jacket he wears in the photo on the back of his book and surveys me with the same off-putting gimlet-eyed smile. ' "The Oriole weds his mottled mate, The Lily's bride o' the bee." Another for your collection, darling?' he adds to Wanda.

'Quite right! I need a pen. Where's a *pen*?' Wanda starts searching among the papers already littering the counter-top. 'The *damage* that has been done to the feminist cause by *ridiculous*, lazy-minded anthropomorphism. "Weds his mottled mate". I ask you, Poppy!' She appeals to me, and I give a rictus smile.

I have no idea what they're talking about. None. Why can't they just say, 'Hello, how are you?' like normal people?

'What's *your* view on the cultural response to anthropomorphism? From a young woman's perspective?'

My stomach jumps as I realize Antony is looking my way again. Oh my holy aunt. Is he talking to me?

Anthro-what?

I feel like if only he would write down his questions and give them to me with five minutes to look over (and maybe a dictionary) I'd have half a chance to come up with something intelligent. I mean, I *did* go to university. I *have* written essays with long words in them and a dissertation.[37] My English teacher even once said I had a 'questing mind'.[38]

36. Magnus says Wanda has never sunbathed in her life, and she thinks people who go on holiday in order to lie on beds must be mentally deficient. That'll be me, then.
37. 'Study of Continuous Passive Motion Following Total Knee Arthroplasty'. I've still got it, in its plastic folder.
38. She didn't say exactly where it was questing *to*.

But I don't have five minutes. He's waiting for me to speak. And there's something about his bright gaze that turns my tongue to dust.

'Well. Um . . . I think it's . . . it's . . . an interesting debate,' I say feebly. 'Very crucial in this day and age. So, how was your flight?' I add quickly. Maybe we can get on to movies or something.

'Unspeakable.' Wanda looks up from where she's scribbling. '*Why* do people fly? *Why?*'

I'm not sure if she's expecting an answer or not.

'Um . . . for holidays and stuff—'

'I've already started making notes for a paper on the subject.' Wanda interrupts me. ' "The Migration Impulse". Why do humans feel compelled to pitch themselves across the globe? Are we following the ancient migratory paths of our ancestors?'

'Have you read Burroughs?' Antony says to her, with interest. '*Not* the book, the PhD thesis.'

No one's even offered me a drink yet. Quietly, trying to blend in with the background, I creep into the kitchen area and pour myself a glass of wine.

'I gather Magnus gave you his grandmother's emerald ring?'

I jump in panic. We're on to the ring already. Is there an edge to Wanda's voice or did I make that up? Does she *know*?

'Yes! It's . . . it's beautiful.' My hands are trembling so much, I nearly spill my wine.

Wanda says nothing, just glances at Antony and raises her eyebrows meaningfully.

What was that for? Why an eyebrow-raise? What are they thinking? Shit, shit, they'll ask to see the ring, it's all going to implode . . .

'It's difficult to wear a ring with a burned hand,' I blurt out desperately.

There. It wasn't a lie. Exactly.

'*Burned?*' Wanda swings round and takes in my bandaged hand. 'My dear girl! You must see Paul.'

'Paul.' Antony nods. 'Certainly. Ring him, Wanda.'

'Our neighbour,' she explains. 'Dermatologist. The best.' She's already on the phone, winding the old-fashioned curly cord around her wrist. 'He's only across the street.'

Across the street?

I'm paralysed with horror. How have things gone so wrong, so quickly? I have a vision of some brisk man with a doctor's bag coming into the kitchen and saying, 'Let's have a look', and everyone crowding round to see as I take off my bandages.

Should I dash upstairs and find a match? Or some boiling water? To be honest, I think I'd take the agonizing pain over having to admit the truth—

'Damn! He's not in.' She replaces the receiver.

'What a shame,' I manage, as Magnus appears through the kitchen door, followed by Felix, who says, 'Hi, Poppy', and then immerses himself back in the textbook he was reading.

'So!' Magnus looks from me to his parents as though trying to assess the mood of the room. 'How are you all doing? Isn't Poppy looking even more beautiful than usual? Isn't she just lovely?' He bunches up my hair in a fist, and then lets it fall down again.

I wish he wouldn't. I know he's trying to be nice, but it makes me cringe. Wanda looks baffled, as though she has no idea how to reply to this.

'Charming.' Antony smiles politely, as though he's admiring someone's garden.

'Did you get through to Dr Wheeler?' Wanda demands.

'Yes.' Magnus nods. 'He says the focus *is* cultural genesis.'

'Well, I must have read that wrong,' she says tetchily. 'We're trying to see if we can't get papers published in the same journal.' Wanda turns to me. 'All six of us, including Conrad and Margot. Family effort, you see. Felix on indexing. Everyone involved!'

Everyone except me flashes through my mind.

Which is ridiculous. Because do I *want* to write an academic paper in some obscure journal which no one ever reads? No. Could I? No. Do I even know what cultural genesis is? No.[39]

'You know, Poppy's published in her field,' Magnus suddenly announces, as though hearing my thoughts and leaping to my defence. 'Haven't you, darling?' He smiles proudly at me. 'Don't be modest.'

'You've published?' Antony wakes up and peers at me with more attention than he ever has before. 'Ah. Now, *that's* interesting. Which journal?'

I stare helplessly at Magnus. What's he *talking* about?

'You remember!' he prompts me. 'Didn't you say you'd had something in that physiotherapy periodical?'

Oh God. No.

I will *kill* Magnus. *How* could he bring that up?

Antony and Wanda are both waiting for me to reply. Even Felix has looked up with interest. They're obviously expecting me to announce a breakthrough in the cultural influence of physiotherapy on Nomadic tribes or something.

'It was *Physiotherapists' Weekly Roundup*,' I mumble at last, staring at my feet. 'It's not really a periodical. More of a . . . a magazine. They published a letter of mine once.'

'Was it a piece of research?' says Wanda.

'No.' I swallow hard. 'It was about when patients have BO. I said maybe we should wear gas masks. It was . . . you know. Supposed to be funny.'

There's silence.

I'm so mortified I can't even raise my head.

'You did write a dissertation for your degree, though,' ventures Felix. 'Didn't you tell me once?' I turn in surprise and he's looking at me with an earnest, encouraging gaze.

---

39. Although I am rather good at footnotes. They could put me in charge of those.

'Yes. I mean . . . it wasn't published or anything.' I shrug awkwardly.

'I'd like to read it one day.'

'OK.' I smile – but honestly, this is pitiful. Of course he doesn't want to read it, he's just trying to be nice. Which is sweet of him, but makes me feel even more tragic, since I'm twenty-nine and he's seventeen. Plus, if he was trying to boost my confidence in front of his parents it hasn't worked, because they're not even listening.

'Of course, humour *is* a form of expression which one should factor into one's cultural narrative,' says Wanda doubtfully. 'I think Jacob C. Goodson has done some interesting work on "Why Humans Joke" . . .'

'I believe it was "*Do* Humans Joke?"' corrects Antony. 'Surely his thesis was that—'

They're off again. I breathe out, my cheeks still burning. I cannot cope. I want someone to ask about holidays, or *EastEnders*, or anything but this.

I mean, I love Magnus and everything. But I've been here five minutes and I'm a nervous wreck. How am I going to survive Christmas every year? What if our children are all super-bright and I can't understand what they're saying and they look down on me because I haven't got a PhD?

There's an acrid smell in the air and suddenly I realize the Bolognese is burning. Wanda is just standing there by the stove, wittering away about Aristotle, not even noticing. Gently I take the spoon out of her grasp and start to stir. Thank God you don't need a Nobel prize to do this.

At least saving the supper made me feel useful. But half an hour later we're all sitting round the table, and I'm back to my speechless panic-mode.

No wonder Antony and Wanda don't want me to marry Magnus. They obviously think I'm a total dimbo. We're halfway through the Bolognese, and I haven't uttered a single word. It's too hard. The conversation is like a juggernaut. Or maybe a symphony. Yes. And I'm the flute. And I *do* have a tune, and I'd quite like to play it, but there's no conductor to bring me in. So I keep drawing breath, then chickening out.

'. . . the commissioning editor unfortunately saw otherwise. So there will be no new edition of my book.' Antony makes a rueful, clicking sound. '*Tant pis.*'

Suddenly I'm alert. For once I actually understand the conversation and have something to say!

'That's terrible!' I chime in supportively. 'Why won't they publish a new edition?'

'They need the readership. They need the demand.' Antony gives a theatrical sigh. 'Ah well. It doesn't matter.'

'Of *course* it matters!' I feel fired up. 'Why don't we all write to the editor and pretend to be readers and say how brilliant the book is and demand a new edition?'

I'm already planning the letters. *Dear Sir, I am shocked that a new edition of this wonderful book has not been published.* We could print them in different fonts, post them in different areas of the country—

'And would you personally buy a thousand copies?' Antony regards me with that hawk-like stare.

'I . . . er . . .' I hesitate, stymied. 'Maybe . . .'

'Because unfortunately, Poppy, if the publisher printed a thousand books which did not sell, then I would be in an even worse boat than before.' He gives me a fierce smile. 'Do you see?'

I feel totally squashed and stupid.

'Right,' I mumble. 'Yes. I . . . I see. Sorry.'

Trying to keep my composure, I start clearing the plates. Magnus is sketching some argument out for Felix on a piece of paper and I'm not sure he even heard. He gives me an absent smile and squeezes my bum as I pass. Which doesn't make me feel that much better, to be honest.

But as we sit back down for pudding, Magnus tinkles his fork and stands up.

'I'd like to announce a toast to Poppy,' he says firmly. 'And welcome her to the family. As well as being beautiful, she's caring, funny and a wonderful person. I'm a very lucky man.'

He looks around the table as though daring anyone to disagree with him, and I shoot him a grateful little smile.

'I'd also like to say a big "welcome back" to Mum and Dad.' Magnus raises a glass and they both nod back. 'We missed you while you were away!'

'I didn't,' chime in Felix, and Wanda gives a bark of laughter.

'Of course you didn't, you terrible boy!'

'And *finally* . . .' Magnus tinkles his glass again to get attention. '. . . of course . . . Happy birthday to Mum! Many happy returns of the day, from all of us.' He blows her a kiss across the table.

What? *What* did he just say?

My smile has frozen on my lips.

'Hear, hear!' Antony raises his glass. 'Happy birthday, Wanda, my love.'

It's his mother's *birthday*? But he didn't tell me. I don't have a card. I don't have a gift. How could he do this to me?

Men are *crap*.

Felix has produced a parcel from under his chair and is handing it to Wanda.

'Magnus,' I whisper desperately as he sits down. 'You didn't tell me it was your mother's birthday. You never said a word! You should have told me!'

I'm almost gibbering with panic. My first meeting with his parents since we got engaged, and they don't like me, and now this.

Magnus looks astonished. 'Sweets, what's wrong?'

How can he be so obtuse?

'I'd have bought her a *present*!' I say under cover of Wanda exclaiming, 'Wonderful, Felix!' over some ancient book which she's unwrapping.

'Oh!' Magnus waves a hand. 'She won't mind. Stop

stressing. You're an angel and everyone loves you. Did you like the mug, by the way?'

'The what?' I can't even follow what he's saying.

'The "Only Just Married" mug. I left it on the hall stand? For our honeymoon?' he prompts at my nonplussed expression. 'I told you about it! Quite fun, I thought.'

'I didn't see any mug.' I stare blankly at him. 'I thought you'd given me that big box with ribbons.'

'What big box?' he says, looking puzzled in turn.

'And now, my dear,' Antony is saying self-importantly to Wanda, 'I don't mind telling you, I've rather *splashed out* on you this year. If you'll give me a minute . . .'

He's getting up and heading out to the hall.

Oh God. My insides suddenly feel watery. No. Please. No . . .

'I think . . .' I begin, but my voice won't work properly. 'I think I might possibly . . . by mistake . . .'

'*What the—*' Antony's exclaiming resounds from the hall. 'What's happened to this?'

A moment later he's in the room, holding the box. It's all messed up. Torn tissue paper is everywhere. The kimono is falling out.

My head is pulsing with blood.

'I'm really sorry . . .' I can barely get the words out. 'I thought . . . I thought it was for me. So I . . . I opened it.'

There's a deathly silence. Every face is stunned, including Magnus's.

'Sweets . . .' he begins feebly, then peters out as though he can't think what to say.

'Not to worry!' says Wanda briskly. 'Give it to me. I don't mind about the wrapping.'

'But there was another thing!' Antony is poking the tissue paper testily. 'Where's the other bit? Was it in there?'

Suddenly I realize what he's talking about, and give a little inward whimper. Every time I think things can't get worse, they plummet. They find new, ghastly depths.

'I think . . . Do you mean . . .' I'm stuttering, my face beet-root. 'This?' I pull a bit of the camisole out from under my top and everyone gazes at it, thunderstruck.

I'm sitting at the dinner table wearing my future mother-in-law's underwear. It's like some twisted dream that you wake up from and think, 'Crikey Moses! Thank God *that* didn't really happen!'

The faces round the table are all motionless and jaw-dropped, like a row of versions of that painting *The Scream*.

'I'll . . . I'll have it dry-cleaned,' I whisper huskily at last. 'Sorry.'

OK. So this evening has gone about as hideously as it possibly could. There's only one solution, which is to keep drinking wine until my nerves have been numbed or I pass out. Whichever comes first.

Supper is over, and everyone's got over the camisole incident. Kind of.

In fact, they've decided to make a family joke out of it. Which is sweet of them, but means that Antony keeps making ponder-ously funny remarks like 'Shall we have some chocolates? Unless Poppy's already *eaten them all*?' And I know I should have a sense of humour, but every time, I flinch.

Now we're sitting on the ancient bumpy sofas in the draw-ing room, playing Scrabble. The Tavishes are complete Scrabble nuts. They have a special board that spins around, and posh wooden tiles and even a leather-bound book where they write down the scores, dating back to 1998. Wanda is the current leader, with Magnus a close second.

Antony went first, and put down OUTSTEP (74 points). Wanda made IRIDIUMS (65 points). Felix made CARYATID (80 points). Magnus made CONTUSED (65 points).[40] And I made STAR (5 points).

40. No idea what most of these words mean.

In my family, 'STAR' would be a *good* word. Five points would be a pretty decent score. You wouldn't get pitying looks and clearing of throats, and feel like a loser.

I don't often think back about past times or reminisce. It's not really my thing. But sitting here, rigid with failure, hunching my knees, inhaling the musty Tavish smells of books and kilims and old wood fire, I can't help it. Just a chink. Just a tiny window of memory. Us in the kitchen. Me and my little brothers, Toby and Tom, eating toast and Marmite round the Scrabble board. I remember it distinctly; I can even taste the Marmite. Toby and Tom had got so frustrated, they made a load of extra tiles out of paper and decided you could have as many as you liked. The whole room was covered in cut-out squares of paper with biro letters scrawled on them. Tom gave himself about six Zs and Toby had ten Es. And they *still* only scored about four points per turn and ended up in a scuffle, yelling, 'It's not fair! It's not fair!'

I feel a rush of tears behind my eyes and blink furiously. I'm being stupid. *Ridiculous*. Number one, this is my new family and I'm trying to integrate with them. Number two, Toby and Tom are both away at college now. They have deep voices and Tom has a beard. We never play Scrabble. I don't even know where the set is. Number three—

'Poppy?'

'Right. Yes! I'm just . . . working it out . . .'

We're into the second round. Antony has extended OUT-STEP into OUTSTEPPED. Wanda has simultaneously made both OD[41] and OVARY. Felix put down ELICIT, and Magnus went for YUK, which Felix challenged, but it was in the dictionary and scored him lots of points on a double-word score. Now Felix has gone to make some coffee and I've been shuffling my tiles hopelessly for about five minutes.

I almost can't bring myself to go, I'm so humiliated. I should

41. Which apparently *is* a word. Silly me.

never have agreed to play. I've stared and stared at the stupid letters, and this is honestly the best possible word I can make.

'P-I-G,' enunciates Antony carefully as I put my tiles down. 'Pig. As in . . . the mammal, I take it?'

'Well done!' says Magnus heartily. 'Six points!'

I can't look at him. I'm fumbling miserably for another two tiles. A and L. Like that's going to help me.

'Hey, Poppy,' says Felix, coming back into the room with a tray. 'Your phone's ringing in the kitchen. What did you put down? Oh, "Pig".' As he looks at the board his mouth twitches and I see Wanda give him a warning frown.

I can't bear this any longer.

'I'll just go and check who called, if that's OK,' I say. 'Might be something important.'

I escape to the kitchen, haul my phone out of my bag, and lean against the comforting warmth of the Aga. There are three texts from Sam, starting with *'Good luck'*, which he sent two hours ago. Then twenty minutes ago he texted, *'Favour to ask'*, followed up by *'Are you there?'*

That call was from him too. I guess I'd better see what's up. I dial his number, picking morosely at the remains of the birthday cake on the counter.

'Great. Poppy. Can you do me a big favour?' he says as soon as we're connected. 'I'm away from my desk and something's up with my phone. Nothing's going out, and I need to get an email to Viv Amberley. Would you mind?'

'Oh yes, Vivien Amberley,' I begin knowledgeably – then draw myself up short.

Perhaps I shouldn't reveal that I've read all the correspondence about Vivien Amberley. She works in Strategy and has applied for a job at another consultancy. Sam is desperately trying to keep her, but nothing's worked and now she's said she's resigning tomorrow.

OK. I *know* I've been nosy. But once you start reading other people's emails, you can't stop. You have to know what's happened. It's been quite addictive, scrolling down the endless strings of back-and-forth emails and working out the stories. Always backwards. Like rewinding little spools of life.

'If you could send her a quick email I'd be hugely grateful,' Sam's saying. 'From one of my email addresses. To vivienamberley@skyhinet.com, have you got that?'

Honestly. What am I, his PA?

'Well . . . all right,' I say grudgingly, clicking on her address. 'What shall I say?'

'"Hi Viv. I would love to talk this through with you again. Please call to arrange a meeting whenever's convenient tomorrow. I'm sure we can work something out. Sam."'

I type it out carefully, using my non-bandaged hand – then hesitate.

'Have you sent it?' Sam says.

My thumb is on the key, poised to press Send. But I can't do it.

'Hello?'

'Don't call her Viv,' I blurt out. 'She hates it. She likes being called Vivien.'

'*What?*' Sam sounds gobsmacked. 'How the hell—'

'It was in an old email that got forwarded. She asked Peter Snell not to call her Viv but he didn't notice. Nor did Jeremy Atheling. And now you're calling her Viv too!'

There's a short silence.

'Poppy,' says Sam at last, and I picture those dark eyebrows of his knitted in a frown. 'Have you been reading my emails?'

'No!' I say defensively. 'I've just *glanced* at a couple . . .'

'You're sure about this Viv thing?'

'Yes! Of course!'

'I'm looking up the email now . . .' I stuff a chunk of icing in my mouth while I'm waiting – then Sam is back on the line. 'You're right.'

'Of course I'm right!'

'OK. Can you change her name to Vivien?'

'Hold on a minute . . .' I amend the email and send it. 'Done.'

'Thanks. Good save. That was sharp of you. Are you always this sharp?'

Yeah right. I'm so sharp, the only Scrabble word I can come up with is 'Pig'.

'Yes, all the time,' I say sarcastically, but I don't think he notices my tone.

'Well, I owe you one. And I'm sorry for disturbing your evening. It's just a fairly urgent situation.'

'Don't worry. I get it,' I say understandingly. 'You know, I'm sure Vivien *wants* to stay at White Globe Consulting really.'

Oops. That just slipped out.

'Oh, really? I thought you hadn't read my emails.'

'I didn't!' I say hastily. 'I mean . . . you know. Maybe one or two. Enough to get an impression.'

'An impression!' He gives a short laugh. 'OK then, Poppy Wyatt, what's your impression? I've asked everyone else's opinion, why not throw your tuppenceworth in? Why is our top strategist taking a sideways step into an inferior company when I've offered her everything she could want, from promotion, to money, to a higher profile—'

'Well, that's the problem,' I cut him off, puzzled. Surely he realizes that? 'She doesn't want any of those things. She gets really stressed out by the pressure, especially by media things. Like that time she had to go on Radio 4 with no notice.'

There's a long silence down the line.

'OK . . . what the hell is going on?' says Sam at last. 'How would *you* know something like that?'

There's no way I can get out of this one.

'It was in her appraisal,' I confess at last. 'I was really bored on the tube earlier, and it was in an attachment—'

'That was *not* in her appraisal.' He sounds quite shirty. 'Believe me, I've read that document back to front, and there's nothing about making media appearances—'

'Not the most recent one.' I screw up my face with embarrassment. 'Her appraisal three years ago.' I can't believe I'm admitting I read that too. 'Plus she said in that original email to you, "I've told you my issues, not that anyone's taken any notice." I think that's what she means.'

The fact is, I feel a total affinity for Vivien. I'd be freaked out by being on Radio 4 too. All the presenters sound just like Antony and Wanda.

There's another silence, so long that I wonder if Sam's still there.

'You might have something,' Sam says at last. 'You might just have something.'

'It's only an idea,' I backtrack instantly. 'I mean, I'm probably wrong.'

'But why wouldn't she *say* this to me?'

'Maybe she's embarrassed.' I shrug. 'Maybe she thinks she's already made the point and you're not going to do anything about it. Maybe she thinks it's just easier to move job.'

'OK.' Sam exhales. 'Thank you. I'm going to pursue this. I'm very glad I rang you, and I'm sorry I disturbed your evening.'

'No problem.' I hunch my shoulders gloomily and scoop up some more cake crumbs. 'To be honest, I'm glad to escape.'

'That good, huh?' He sounds amused. 'How did the bandage go down?'

'Believe me, the bandage is the least of my problems.'

'What's up?'

I lower my voice, glancing at the door. 'We're playing Scrabble. It's a nightmare.'

'Scrabble?' He sounds surprised. 'Scrabble's great.'

'Not when you're playing with a family of geniuses, it's not. They all put words like "iridiums". And I put "pig".'

Sam bursts into laughter.

'Glad it's so funny,' I say morosely.

'OK, come on.' He stops laughing. 'I owe you one. Tell me your letters. I'll give you a good word.'

'I can't remember them!' I roll my eyes. 'I'm in the kitchen.'

'You must remember some. Try.'

'All right. I have a W. And a Z.' This conversation is so bizarre that I can't help giving a little giggle.

'Go and look at the rest. Text them over. I'll give you a word.'

'I thought you were at a seminar!'

'I can be at a seminar and play Scrabble at the same time.'

Is he serious? This is the most ridiculous, far-fetched idea I've ever heard.

Plus, it would be cheating.

Plus, who says he's any good at Scrabble?

'OK,' I say after a few moments. 'You're on.'

I ring off and head back into the drawing room, where the board has spawned another load of impossible words. Someone has put down UG. Is that really English? It sounds like Eskimo.

'All right, Poppy?' says Wanda, in such bright, artificial tones that I instantly know they've been talking about me. They've probably told Magnus that if he marries me they'll cut him off without a penny or something.

'Fine!' I try to sound cheerful. 'That was a patient on the phone,' I add, crossing my fingers behind my back. 'Sometimes I do online consultation, so I might have to send a text, if you don't mind?'

No one even replies. They're all hunched over their tiles again.

I line my phone up so the screen takes in the board and my rack of tiles. Then I press the photo button.

'Just taking a family snap!' I say quickly as the faces are raised in response to the flash. I'm already sending the photo over to Sam.

'It's your turn, Poppy,' says Magnus. 'Would you like some help, darling?' he adds in an undertone.

I know he's trying to be kind. But there's something about the way he says it that stings me.

'It's OK, thanks. I'll be fine.' I start moving the tiles back and forth on my rack, trying to look confident.

After a minute or two I glance down at my phone, just in case a text has somehow arrived silently – but there's nothing.

Everyone else is concentrating on their tiles or on the board. The atmosphere is hushed and intense, like in an exam room. I shift my tiles around more and more briskly, willing some stupendous word to pop out at me. But no matter what I do, it's a fairly crap situation. I could make RAW. Or WAR.

And still my phone is silent. Sam must have been joking about helping me. Of *course* he was joking. I feel a wave of humiliation. What's he going to think, when a picture of a Scrabble board arrives on his phone?

'Any ideas yet, Poppy?' Wanda says, in encouraging tones, as though I'm a subnormal child. I suddenly wonder if Magnus told his parents to be nice to me while I was in the kitchen.

'Just deciding between options.' I attempt a cheerful smile.

OK. I have to do this. I can't put it off any longer. I'll make RAW.

No, WAR.

Oh, what's the difference?

My heart low, I put the A and W down on the board, just as my phone bleeps with a text.

WHAIZLED. Use the D from OUTSTEPPED. Triple word score, plus 50 point bonus.

Oh my God.

I can't help giving a laugh, and Antony shoots me an odd look.

'Sorry,' I say quickly. 'Just . . . my patient making a joke.' My phone bleeps again.

It's Scottish dialect, btw. Used by Robert Burns.

'So, is that your word, Poppy?' Antony is peering at my pathetic offering. ' "Raw"? Jolly good. Well done!'

His heartiness is painful.

'Sorry,' I say quickly. 'My mistake. On second thoughts, I think I'll do *this* word instead.'

Carefully I lay down WHAIZLED on the board and sit back, looking nonchalant.

There's an astounded silence.

'Poppy, sweets,' says Magnus at last. 'It has to be a *genuine* word, you know. You can't just make one up—'

'Oh, don't you know that word?' I adopt a tone of surprise. 'Sorry. I thought it was fairly common knowledge.'

'Whay-zled?' ventures Wanda dubiously. 'Why-zled? How do you pronounce it, exactly?'

Oh God. I have no bloody idea.

'It . . . er . . . depends on the region. It's traditional Scottish dialect, of course,' I add with a knowledgeable air, as though I'm Stephen Fry.[42] 'Used by Robert Burns. I was watching a documentary about him the other night. He's rather a passion of mine, in fact.'

'I didn't know you were interested in Burns.' Magnus looks taken aback.

'Oh yes,' I say as convincingly as possible. 'Always have been.'

'*Which* poem does "whaizled" come from?' Wanda persists.

'It's . . .' I swallow hard. 'It's actually rather a beautiful poem. I can't remember the title now, but it goes something like . . .'

I hesitate, trying to think what Burns' poetry sounds like. I heard some once at a Hogmanay party, not that I could understand a word of it.

---

42. Stephen Fry off *QI*, I mean. Not *Jeeves and Wooster*. Although Jeeves probably knew a fair bit about Burns' poetry, too.

''Twas whaizled . . . when the wully whaizle . . . wailed. And so on!' I break off brightly. 'I won't bore you.'

Antony raises his head from the 'N–Z' volume of the dictionary, which he instantly picked up when I laid my tiles down, and has been flicking through.

'Quite right.' He seems a bit flummoxed. '*Whaizled*. Scottish dialect for "wheezed". Well, well. Very impressive.'

'Bravo, Poppy.' Wanda is totting up. 'So, that's a triple-word score, plus your fifty-point bonus . . . so that's . . . 131 points! The highest score so far!'

'A hundred and thirty-one?' Antony grabs her paper. 'Are you sure?'

'Congratulations, Poppy!' Felix leans over to shake my hand.

'It was nothing really.' I beam modestly around. 'Shall we keep going?'

FIVE

I won! I won the Scrabble game!

Everyone was gobsmacked. They pretended not to be – but they were. The raised eyebrows and astonished glances became more frequent and less guarded as the game went on. When I got that triple-word score with SAXATILE, Felix actually broke out into applause and said, 'Bravo!' And as we were tidying the kitchen afterwards, Wanda asked me if I'd ever thought of studying linguistics.

My name was entered in the family Scrabble book, and Antony offered me the 'winner's glass of port' and everyone clapped. It was such a sweet moment.

OK. I know it was cheating. I know it was a bad thing to do. To be honest, I kept expecting someone to catch me out. But I put the ringtone on silent and no one realized I was texting Sam all the way through.[43]

And yes, of *course* I feel guilty. Halfway through, I felt even worse when I texted Sam in admiration:

43. Haven't both Antony and Wanda ever invigilated exams as part of their jobs? Just saying.

How do you know all these words?

And he replied:

I don't. The Internet does.

The *Internet*?

 For a moment I felt too shocked to reply. I thought he was *thinking* of the words, not just finding them on Scrabblewords.com or whatever. I typed:

That's CHEATING!!!!

He texted back:

You already crossed that line. What's the difference?

And then he added:

Flattered you thought I was a genius.

Then, of course, I felt really stupid.

And he had a point. Once you've started cheating, does it really matter what your methods are?

I know I'm storing up problems for the future. I know Sam Roxton won't always be on the end of my phone to feed me words. I know I couldn't possibly repeat the feat. Which is why I'm planning to retire from family Scrabble, as from tomorrow. It was a short, brilliant career. And now it's over.

The only person who wasn't entirely fulsome in his praise was Magnus, which was a bit surprising. I mean, he said, 'Well done', along with everyone else – but he didn't give me a special hug or even ask me how come I knew all those words. And when Wanda said, 'Magnus, you didn't tell us Poppy was so talented!' he flashed her this quick smile and said, 'I told you, Poppy's brilliant at everything.' Which was nice – but kind of meaningless too.

The thing is . . . he came second.

He can't be *jealous* of me, surely?

It's about eleven now, and we're back in my flat. I'm half-tempted to go and talk to Magnus about it, but he's disappeared off to do some preparation for a lecture on 'Symbols and Symbolic Thought in Dante'[44] which he's giving tomorrow. So instead I curl up on the sofa and forward some emails which came in earlier for Sam.

After a few I can't help clicking my tongue with frustration. Half of these emails are reminders and chasers. He still hasn't replied about the conference accommodation at the Chiddingford Hotel, or the Fun Run, or the dentist. *Or* the new James & James bespoke suit waiting for him to pick up at his convenience. How can you ignore new clothes?

There are only a few people he ever seems to reply to immediately. One is a girl called Vicks, who runs the PR department. She's very businesslike and curt, just like him, and has been consulting him about some press launch they're doing together. She often cc-s Violet's address, but by the time I forward the email, Sam's already replied to her. Another is a guy called Malcolm who asks Sam's opinion about something nearly every hour. And of course, Sir Nicholas Murray, who's clearly very senior and important and is doing some work for the government at the moment.[45] He and Sam seem to get on incredibly well, if their emails are anything to go by. They zing back and forth like conversation between old friends. I can't really understand half of what they're saying – especially all the in-jokes – but the tone is obvious, and so is the fact that Sam

44. The first time Magnus told me his specialism was Symbols, I thought he meant *Cymbals*. The ones you clash. Not that I've ever admitted that to him.
45. Not that I've been prying or anything. But you can't help glancing at things as you forward them, and noticing references to 'the PM' and 'Number Ten'.

has more emails to and from Sir Nicholas than anybody else.

Sam's company is obviously some kind of consultancy. They tell companies how to run their businesses and they do a lot of 'facilitating', whatever that is. I guess they're like negotiators or mediators or something. They must be pretty successful at it because Sam seems very popular. He's been invited to three drinks parties, just this week, and to a shooting event with a private bank next weekend. And a girl called Blue has emailed for the third time, asking if he'd like to attend a special reception to celebrate the merger of Johnson Ellison with Greene Retail. It's at the Savoy, with a jazz band and canapés and goody bags.

And he still hasn't replied. Still.

I just don't understand him. If I'd been invited to something so amazing, I would have replied instantly, 'Yes please! Thank you so much! I can't wait! ☺☺☺.' Whereas he hasn't even *acknowledged* it.

Rolling my eyes, I forward every single email, then type him a text:

Thx again for Scrabble! Have just sent on some new emails.
Poppy

A moment later my phone rings. It's Sam.

'Oh, hi—' I start.

'OK, you're a genius,' he interrupts. 'I had a hunch Vivien would be working late. I called her for a chat and mentioned the issues we discussed. It all came out. You were right. We're going to talk again tomorrow, but I think she's staying.'

'Oh,' I say, pleased. 'Cool.'

'No,' he says firmly. 'Not just cool. Awesome. Incredible. Do you know how much time and money and trouble you have saved me? I owe you, big time.' He pauses. 'Oh, and you're right, she hates being called Viv. So I owe you twice.'

'No problem! Any time.'

'So . . . that's all I had to say. I won't keep you.'

'Goodnight. Glad it all worked out.' As I ring off, I remember something, and quickly type a text:

Have u booked dentist yet? U will get manky teeth!!!

A few seconds later the phone bleeps with a reply:

I'll take my chances.

Take his chances? Is he *nuts*? My aunt is a dental nurse, so I know what I'm talking about.

I search the Web for the most gross, revolting photo of decaying teeth I can find. They're all blackened and some have fallen out. I click on Send/Share and text it to him.

The phone almost immediately bleeps with a reply:

You made me spill my drink.

I giggle, and text back:

Be afraid!!!!

I nearly add, 'Willow won't be impressed when your teeth fall out!!!' But then I stop, feeling awkward. You have to draw a line. Despite all the texting back and forth, I don't really *know* this guy. And I certainly don't know his fiancée.

Although the truth is, I feel as though I do know her. And not in a good way.

I've never come across anyone or anything like Willow before. She's unbelievable. I would say she's sent twenty emails to Sam since I've had this phone. Each screwier than the last. At least she's given up sending messages addressed directly to Violet. But still, she keeps cc-ing her emails to the PA address, as though she wants to have as much chance of reaching Sam as possible and doesn't care who sees what.

Why does she have to email her most private thoughts, anyway? Why can't they just have these conversations in *bed*, like normal people?

This evening she was going on about this dream she'd had about him last night, and how she felt suffocated but ignored all at the same time, and did he realize 'how toxic' he was? Did he realize how he was 'CORRODING HER SPIRIT????'

I always type a reply to her now, I can't help it. This time I put:

Do you realize how toxic YOU are, Willow the Witch?

And then deleted it. Naturally.

The most frustrating thing is that I never get to see Sam's replies. There's no back-and-forth correspondence; she always starts a fresh email. Sometimes they're friendly – like yesterday she sent one that just said, 'You're a really, really special man, you know that, Sam?' Which was quite sweet. But nine out of ten are whingeing. I can't help feeling sorry for him.

Anyway. His life. His fiancée. Whatever.

'Sweetheart!' Magnus comes into the room, interrupting my thoughts.

'Oh, hi!' I quickly turn off. 'Finished your work?'

'Don't let me disturb you.' He nods at the phone. 'Chatting to the girls?'

I give a noncommittal smile and slip the phone into my pocket.

I know, I know, I know. This is bad. Keeping a secret from Magnus. Not telling him about the ring or the phone or any of it. But how can I start now? Where would I begin? And maybe I'd regret it. What if I confess all and cause a huge rift and half an hour later the ring turns up and I needn't have said anything?

'You know me!' I say at last, and give a little laugh. 'What did you talk to your parents about tonight?' I quickly move on to the subject I *really* want to find out about, i.e. what do his parents think of me and have they changed their minds?

'Oh, my parents.' He makes an impatient gesture and sinks

down on the sofa. He's tapping his fingers on the arm, and his eyes are distant.

'You OK?' I say cautiously.

'I'm great.' He turns to me and the clouds fall away from his eyes. Suddenly he's focused. 'Remember when we first met?'

'Yes.' I smile back. 'Of course I do.'

He starts stroking my leg. 'I arrived at that place expecting the battle-axe. But there *you* were.'

I wish he wouldn't always call Ruby a battle-axe. She's not. She's gorgeous and lovely and sexy, her arms are just a *teeny* bit meaty. But I hide my squirm of irritation and keep smiling.

'You were like an angel in that white uniform. I've never seen anything more sexy in my life.' His hand is moving further up my leg with intent. 'I wanted you, right there, right then.'

Magnus loves telling this story, and I love hearing it.

'And I wanted you,' I lean over and gently bite his earlobe. 'The minute I saw you.'

'I know you did. I could tell.' He pulls my top aside and starts to nuzzle my bare shoulder. 'Hey Poppy, let's get back into that room one day,' he whispers. 'That's the best sex I've ever had. You, in that white uniform, up on that couch, with that massage oil ... Jesus ...'[46] He starts tugging at my skirt and we both tumble off the sofa on to the carpet. And as my phone bleeps with another text, I barely notice.

---

46. OK. Busted. I didn't tell the absolute *full* truth in my disciplinary hearing.

Here's the thing: I know I was totally unprofessional. I know I should be struck off. The physiotherapy ethics booklet practically *starts*, 'Don't have sex with your patient on the couch, whatever you do.'

But what I say is: if you do something wrong yet it doesn't actually hurt anybody and nobody knows, should you be punished and lose your whole career? Isn't there a bigger picture?

Plus, we only did it once. And it was really quick. (Not in a bad way. Just in a quick way.)

And Ruby once used the offices for a party, and propped all the fire doors open, which is *totally* against health and safety. So. Nobody's perfect.

*

It's not until later on, when we're getting ready for bed and I'm rubbing in body lotion,[47] that Magnus lands his bombshell.

'Oh, Mum called earlier.' His speech is muffled with toothpaste. 'About the skin guy.'

'What?'

He spits out and wipes his mouth. 'Paul. Our neighbour. He's coming to the wedding rehearsal to look at your hand.'

'*What?*' My hand clenches automatically and I squirt body lotion across the bathroom.

'Mum says you can't be too careful with burns and I think she's right.'

'She didn't have to do that!' I'm trying not to sound panicky.

'Sweets.' He kisses my head. 'It's all fixed up.'

He heads out of the bathroom and I stare at my reflection. My happy post-sex glow has gone. I'm back to the black hole of dread. What do I do? I can't keep dodging for ever.

I don't have a burned hand. I don't have an engagement ring. I don't have an encyclopaedic knowledge of Scrabble words. I'm a total phoney.

'Poppy?' Magnus reappears meaningfully at the bathroom door. I know he wants to get to sleep because he's got to go to Brighton early tomorrow.

'Coming.'

I follow him to bed and curl up in his arms and give a pretty good impersonation of someone falling peacefully off to sleep. But inside I'm churning. Every time I try to switch off, a million thoughts come crowding back in. If I call off Paul the dermatologist, will Wanda be suspicious? Could I mock up a burn on

---

47. This is part of my pre-wedding regime, which consists of daily exfoliation, daily moisturizing, weekly face mask, hair mask and eye mask, a hundred sit-ups every day, and meditation to keep calm. So far I've got as far as the body lotion.

my hand? What if I just told Magnus everything, right now?

I try to picture this last scenario. I know it's the most sensible. It's the one the agony aunts would recommend. Wake him up and tell him.

But I just can't. I *can't*. And not only because Magnus is always totally ratty if he gets woken up in the night. He'd be so shocked. His parents would always think of me as the girl who lost the heirloom ring. It'd define me for ever more. It'd cast a pall over everything.

And the point is, they don't *have* to know. This doesn't *have* to come out. Mrs Fairfax might call any time. If I can just hold out till then . . .

I want to get the ring back and quietly slip it back on my finger and for no one to be any the wiser. That's what I want.

I glance at the clock – 2.45 a.m. – then at Magnus, breathing peacefully, and feel a surge of irrational resentment. It's OK for him.

Abruptly I swing my legs out from under the covers and reach for a dressing gown. I'll go and have a cup of herbal tea like they recommend in magazine articles on insomnia, along with writing down all your problems on a piece of paper.[48]

My phone is charging in the kitchen, and as I'm waiting for the kettle to boil I idly click through all the messages, methodically forwarding on Sam's. There's a text from a new patient of mine who's just had surgery on his anterior cruciate ligament and is finding it hard-going, and I send a quick, re-assuring text back, saying I'll try to fit him in for a session tomorrow.[49] I'm just pouring hot water on a camomile and vanilla tea bag when a text bleeps, making me start.

48. What, for your boyfriend to find?
49. I don't give my number out to all my patients. Just long-term patients, emergencies and the ones who look like they need support. This guy is one of those types who says he's absolutely fine and then you see he's white with pain. I had to *insist* he should call me whenever he wanted, and repeat it to his wife, otherwise he would have just nobly struggled on.

What are you doing up so late?

It's Sam. Who else? I settle down with my tea and take a sip, then text back:

Can't sleep. What are YOU doing up so late?

Waiting to speak to a guy in LA. Why can't you sleep?

My life ends tomorrow.

OK, that might be overstating it a tad, but right now, that's how it feels.

I can see how that might keep you up. Why does it end?

If he really wants to know, I'll tell him. Sipping my tea, I fill five texts with the story of how the ring was found but then lost again. And how Paul the dermatologist wants to look at my hand. And how the Tavishes are being snippy enough about the ring *already*, and they don't even know it's lost. And how it's all closing in on me. And how I feel like a gambler who needs just one more spin on the roulette wheel and everything might come good, but I'm out of chips.

I've been typing so furiously, my shoulders are aching. I rotate them a few times, and take a few gulps of tea and am just wondering about cracking open the digestives, when a new text arrives.

I owe you one.

I read the words and shrug. OK. He owes me. So what? A moment later a second text arrives.

I could get you a chip.

I stare at the screen, baffled. He does know the chip thing is a *metaphor*, doesn't he? He's not talking about a real poker chip?

Or a French fry?

The usual daytime traffic hum is absent, making the room abnormally silent, save for an occasional judder from the fridge. I blink at the screen in the artificial light, then rub my tired eyes, wondering if I should just turn off the phone and go to bed.

What do you mean?

His reply comes back almost immediately, as though he realized his last text sounded odd.

Have jeweller friend. Makes replicas for TV. Very realistic. Would buy you time.

A fake ring?

I think I must be really, really thick. Because that had never even *occurred* to me.

SIX

OK. A fake ring is a *bad* idea. There are a million reasons why. Such as:
1. It's dishonest.
2. It probably won't look convincing.
3. It's unethical.[50]

Nevertheless, here I am in Hatton Garden at ten the following morning, sauntering along, trying to hide the fact that my eyes are on stalks. I've never been to Hatton Garden before, I didn't even know it existed. A whole *street* of jewellers?

There are more diamonds here than I've ever seen in my lifetime. Signs everywhere are boasting best prices, highest carats, superb value and bespoke design. Obviously this is engagement-ring city. Couples are wandering along and girls are pointing in through the windows and the men are smiling but all look slightly sick whenever their girlfriends turn away.

I've never even been into a jewellery shop. Not a grown-up,

---

50. Is unethical the same as dishonest? This is the kind of moral debate I could have asked Antony about. In different circumstances.

proper one like these. The only jewellery I've ever had has come from markets and Topshop, places like that. My parents gave me a pair of pearl studs for my thirteenth birthday, but I didn't go into the shop with them. Jewellery shops have been places I've walked past, thinking they're for other people. But now, since I'm here, I can't help having a good old look.

Who would buy a brooch made out of yellow diamonds in the shape of a spider for £12,500? It's a mystery to me, like who buys those revolting sofas with swirly arms they advertise on the telly.

Sam's friend's shop is called Mark Spencer Designs, and thankfully doesn't have any yellow spiders. Instead, it has lots of diamonds set in platinum bands, and a sign saying 'Free champagne for engaged couples. Make your ring-choosing experience a special one.' There's nothing about replicas or fakes and I start to feel nervous. What if Sam misunderstood? What if I end up buying a real emerald ring out of embarrassment and have to spend the rest of my life paying it off?

And where *is* Sam, anyway? He promised to pop along and introduce me to his friend. Apparently he works just round the corner – though he didn't reveal exactly where. I turn and survey the street. It's kind of weird that we've never met properly, face to face.

There's a man with dark hair walking briskly on the other side of the road, and for a brief moment I think perhaps that's him, but then a deep voice says, 'Poppy?'

I turn – and of course, *that's* him: the guy with the dark, rumpled hair striding towards me. He's taller than I remember from my glimpse of him in the hotel lobby, but has the same distinctive thick eyebrows and deep-set eyes. He's wearing a dark suit and immaculate white shirt and a charcoal tie. He flashes me a brief smile and I notice that his teeth are very white and even.

Well. They won't be for much longer if he doesn't go to the dentist.

'Hi. Poppy.' As he approaches he hesitates, then extends a hand. 'Good to meet you properly.'

'Hi.' I smile back tentatively and we shake hands. He has a nice handshake. Warm and positive.

'So, Vivien's definitely staying with us.' He tilts his head. 'Thanks again for your insight.'

'No problem!' I shrug awkwardly. 'It was nothing.'

'Seriously. I appreciate it.'

This is odd, talking face to face. I'm distracted by seeing the contours of his brow and his hair rippling in the breeze. It was easier by text. I wonder if he feels the same way.

'So.' He gestures at the jewellery shop. 'Shall we?'

This shop is seriously cool and expensive. I wonder if he and Willow came to choose their ring here. They must have done. I'm almost tempted to ask him – but somehow I can't quite bring myself to mention her. It's too embarrassing. I know far too much about them.

Most couples, you meet at the pub or at their house. You talk about anodyne stuff. Holidays, hobbies, Jamie Oliver recipes. Only gradually do you venture on to personal stuff. But with these two, I feel as if I've been pitched straight into some fly-on-the-wall documentary and they don't even know it. I found an old email last night from Willow which just said, 'Do you know how much PAIN you have caused me, Sam? Quite apart from all the fucking BRAZILIANS??'

Which is something I really wish I hadn't read. If I ever meet her, that's the only thing I'm going to be able to think about. Brazilians.

Sam has pressed the buzzer and is ushering me into the smart, dimly lit shop. At once a girl in a dove-grey suit comes up.

'Hello, may I help?' She has a soft, honey-like voice which completely suits the muted décor of the shop.

'We're here to see Mark,' Sam says. 'It's Sam Roxton.'

'That's right.' Another girl in dove grey nods. 'He's waiting for you. Take them through, Martha.'

'May I get you a glass of champagne?' says Martha, giving me a knowing smile as we walk along. 'Sir? Champagne?'

'No thanks,' says Sam.

'Me neither,' I chime in.

'Are you sure?' She twinkles at me. 'It's a big moment for the two of you. Just a little glass to take care of the nerves?'

Oh my God! She thinks we're an engaged couple. I glance at Sam for help – but he's typing something on his phone. And there's no *way* I'm launching into the story of losing my priceless heirloom ring in front of a bunch of strangers, and hearing all the gasps of horror.

'I'm fine, honestly,' I smile awkwardly. 'It's not— I mean, we're not—'

'That's a wonderful watch, sir!' Martha's attention has been distracted. 'Is that vintage Cartier? I've never seen one quite like it.'

'Thanks.' Sam nods. 'Got it at an auction in Paris.'

Now I notice it, Sam's watch *is* quite amazing. It's got an old leather strap and the dull-gold dial has the patina of another age. And he got it in Paris. That's pretty cool.

'Goodness.' As we walk, Martha takes my arm and leans in, lowering her voice, girl to girl. 'He has *exquisite* taste. Lucky you! You can't say the same of all the men who come in here. Some of them go for absolute horrors. But a man who buys himself vintage Cartier has got to be on the right track!'

This is painful. What do I say?

'Err . . . right,' I mumble, staring at the floor.

'Oh, I'm sorry, I don't mean to embarrass you,' says Martha charmingly. 'Please let me know if you change your mind about the champagne. Have a wonderful session with Mark!' She ushers us into a large back room with a concrete floor, lined with metal-fronted cabinets. A guy in jeans and rimless specs gets up from a trestle table and greets Sam warmly.

'Sam! Been too long!'

'Mark! How are you doing?' Sam claps Mark on the back, then steps aside. 'This is Poppy.'

'Good to meet you, Poppy.' Mark shakes my hand. 'So, I understand you need a replica ring.'

I feel an immediate lurch of paranoia and guilt. Did he have to say it out loud like that, for anyone to hear?

'Just very temporarily.' I keep my voice almost to a whisper. 'Just while I find the real thing. Which I will, really, really soon.'

'Understood.' He nods. 'Useful to have a replica anyway. We do a lot of replacements for travel and so forth. Normally we only make replicas of jewellery we've designed ourselves, but we can make the odd exception for friends.' Mark winks at Sam. 'Although we do try to be a *little* discreet about it. Don't want to undermine our core business.'

'Yes!' I say quickly. 'Of course. I want to be discreet too. Very much so.'

'Do you have a picture? A photo?'

'Here.' I haul out a photo which I printed off my computer this morning. It's of me and Magnus at the restaurant where he proposed. We got the couple at the next table to take a picture of us, and I'm holding up my left hand proudly, with the ring clearly visible. I look absolutely giddy – which, to be fair, is how I was feeling.

Both men stare at it in silence.

'So, that's the guy you're marrying,' says Sam at last. 'The Scrabble fiend.'

'Yes.'

There's something in his tone which makes me feel defensive. I have no idea why.

'His name's Magnus,' I add.

'Isn't he the academic?' Sam's frowning at the photo. 'Had the TV series?'

'Yes.' I feel a flash of pride. 'Exactly.'

'That's a four-carat emerald, I'd guess?' Mark Spencer looks up from squinting at the photo.

'Maybe,' I say helplessly. 'I don't know.'

'You don't *know* how many carats your engagement ring is?' Both men shoot me an odd look.

'What?' I feel myself flush. 'I'm sorry. I didn't *know* I'd lose it.'

'That's very sweet,' says Mark with a wry little smile. 'Most girls know it down to the nearest decimal. Then they round up.'

'Oh. Well.' I shrug, to cover my embarrassment. 'It's a family ring. We didn't really talk about it.'

'We have a lot of mounts in stock. Let me look...' Mark pushes his chair away and starts searching through the metal drawers.

'So he still doesn't know you've lost it?' Sam jerks a thumb at the picture of Magnus.

'Not yet.' I bite my lip. 'I'm hoping it'll turn up and...'

'He'll never have to know you ever lost it,' Sam finishes for me. 'You'll keep the secret safe till your deathbed.'

I look away, feeling twingey with guilt. I don't like this. I don't like having secrets from Magnus. I don't like being the kind of person who has assignations behind their fiancé's back. But there's no other way.

'So, I'm still getting Violet's emails on this.' I gesture at him with the phone, to distract myself. 'I thought the tech people were sorting it out?'

'So did I.'

'Well, you've got some new ones. You've been asked about the Fun Run four times, now.'

'Hmm.' He barely nods.

'Aren't you going to answer? And what about your hotel room for this conference in Hampshire? Do you need it for one night or two?'

'I'll see. Not sure yet.' Sam seems so unmoved, I feel a stab of frustration.

'Don't you *answer* your emails?'

'I prioritize.' He calmly taps at his screen.

'Ooh, it's Lindsay Cooper's birthday!' Now I'm reading a round-robin email. 'Lindsay in marketing. Do you want to say Happy Birthday to her?'

'No, I do not.' He sounds so adamant, I feel a bit affronted.

'What's wrong with saying Happy Birthday to a colleague?'

'I don't know her.'

'Yes, you do! You work with her.'

'I work with 243 people.'

'But isn't she the girl who came up with that website-strategy document the other day?' I say, suddenly remembering an old email correspondence. 'Weren't you all really pleased?'

'Yes,' he says blankly. 'What's that got to do with this?'

God, he's stubborn. Giving up on Lindsay's birthday, I scroll down to the next email.

'Peter has finalized the Air France deal. He wants to give you his full report on Monday straight after the team meeting. Is that OK?'

'Fine.' Sam barely glances up. 'Just forward it. Thanks.'

If I forward it, he'll just let it sit there all day without answering.

'Why don't I reply?' I offer. 'Since you're here and I've got the email open? It'll only take a minute.'

'Oh.' He seems surprised. 'Thanks. Just say "Yes".'

'Yes,' I carefully type. 'Anything else?'

'Put "Sam".'

I stare at the screen, dissatisfied. 'Yes, Sam'. It looks so bare. So curt.

'What about adding something like, "Well done"?' I suggest. 'Or "You did it! Yay!" Or just "Best wishes and thanks for everything"?'

Sam looks unimpressed. '"Yes, Sam" will be plenty.'

'Typical,' I mutter under my breath. Except perhaps it wasn't *quite* as submerged under my breath as I'd intended, because Sam looks up.

'Excuse me?'

I know I should bite my tongue. But I'm so frustrated I can't stop myself.

'You're so abrupt! Your emails are so short! They're awful!'

There's a long pause. Sam looks as astonished as if the chair had started to speak.

'Sorry,' I add at last, giving an awkward shrug. 'But it's true.'

'OK,' says Sam at last. 'Let's just get things straight. In the first place, borrowing this phone does *not* give you a licence to read and critique my emails.' He hesitates. 'In the second place, short is good.'

I'm already regretting having spoken. But I can't back down now.

'Not *that* short,' I retort. 'And you ignore most people completely! It's rude!'

There. Said it.

Sam is glowering at me. 'Like I said, I prioritize. Now, since your ring situation is sorted, maybe you'd like to hand the phone back and my emails won't have to bother you any more.' He holds out his hand.

Oh God. Is *that* why he's helping me? So I give the phone back?

'No!' I clutch the phone. 'I mean . . . please. I still need it. The hotel might phone me any minute, Mrs Fairfax will have this number . . .'

I know it's irrational, but I feel like the moment I give this phone up, I'm saying goodbye to any chance of finding the ring.

I put it behind my back for good measure and gaze beseechingly at him.

'Jesus.' Sam exhales. 'This is *ridiculous*. I'm interviewing for a new PA this afternoon. That's a company phone. You can't just keep it!'

'I won't! But can I have it just a few more days? I won't

critique your emails any more,' I add tamely. 'Promise.'

'OK, guys!' Mark interrupts us. 'Good news. I've found a mount. Now I'll select some stones for you to look at. Excuse me a moment . . .'

As he heads out of the room, my phone bleeps with a new text.

'It's from Willow,' I say, glancing down. 'Look.' I gesture at my hands. 'Forwarding. Not passing any comment. None at all.'[51]

'Hrrmm.' Sam gives the same noncommittal growl he gave before when I mentioned Willow.

There's an odd little pause. What *should* happen now is I ask something polite like, 'So, how did you two meet?' and 'When are you getting married?' and we start a conversation about wedding lists and the price of caterers. But for some reason I can't bring myself to. Their relationship is so peculiar, I just don't want to go there.

I know he can be growly and curt, but I still can't see him with a self-obsessed, whingey bitch like Willow. Especially now I've met him in the flesh. She must be really, really, *really* attractive, I decide. Like, supermodel standard. Her dazzling looks have blinded him to everything else about her. It's the only explanation.

'Loads of people are replying to the email about Lindsay's birthday,' I observe, to fill the silence. '*They* obviously don't have a problem with it.'

'Round-robin emails are the work of the devil.' Sam barely misses a beat. 'I'd rather shoot myself than reply to one.'

Well, *that's* a nice attitude.

This Lindsay is obviously popular. Every twenty seconds some fresh, Reply All message arrives on the screen, like

51. Which is a shame, because what I'm dying to ask is: why does Willow keep sending messages via me when she must know I'm not Violet by now? And what's with all this communication through his PA, anyway?

'Happy Birthday Lindsay! Have a wonderful celebration, whatever you're doing.' The phone keeps buzzing and flashing. It's like a party in here. And only Sam is refusing to join in.

Oh, I can't stand it. How hard is it to type 'Happy Birthday'? Why wouldn't you? It's two words.

'Can't I write "Happy Birthday" from you?' I beg. 'Go on. You don't have to do anything. I'll type it.'

'Fuck's *sake*!' Sam looks up from his own phone. 'OK. Whatever. Say Happy Birthday. But no smiley faces or kisses,' he adds warningly. 'Just "Happy Birthday. Sam".'

'Happy Birthday, Lindsay!' I type defiantly. 'Hope you're having a great time today. Well done again on that website strategy, it was awesome. Best wishes, Sam.'

Hurriedly I send it, before he can wonder why I'm typing so much.

'What about the dentist?' I decide to push my luck.

'What *about* the dentist?' he echoes, and I feel an almighty surge of exasperation. Is he pretending he doesn't know what I'm talking about or has he genuinely forgotten?

'Here we are!' The door opens and Mark reappears, holding out a dark-blue velvet tray. 'These are our simulated emeralds.'

'Wow,' I breathe, my attention torn away from the phone.

In front of me are ten rows of gleaming emeralds. I mean, I know they're not real but quite frankly, I couldn't tell the difference.[52]

'Is there any stone which strikes you as having a particular resemblance to the one you've lost?'

'That one.' I point to an oval rock in the middle. 'It's almost exactly the same. It's amazing!'

'Great.' He picks it up with a pair of tweezers and places it

---

52. Which makes me wonder: if man can *make* emeralds these days, why do we all keep on spending loads of money on real ones? Also: should I get some earrings?

on a small plastic dish. 'The diamonds are obviously smaller and less noticeable, so I'm fairly confident of a match. You want a little distressing?' he adds. 'Take the shine off?'

'Can you do that?' I say in amazement.

'We can do anything,' he says confidently. 'We once made the Crown Jewels for a Hollywood movie. Looked absolutely genuine, although they never even used them in the end.'

'Wow. Well . . . yes, please!'

'No problem. We should get this knocked up in . . .' He glances at his watch. 'Three hours?'

'Great!'

As I stand up, I'm astounded. I can't believe this was so easy. In fact, I feel quite exhilarated with relief. This will see me through a couple of days and then I'll get the real thing back and it'll all be OK.

As we move back into the showroom, I sense a rustle of interest. Martha's head pops up from the book she was writing in, and a couple of girls in dove grey are whispering and nodding at me from their position by the door. Mark leads us over to Martha again, who beams at me even more widely than before.

'Look after these lovely people for me, Martha, will you?' he says, giving her a folded piece of paper. 'Here are the details. Bye, again.'

He and Sam shake hands warmly, then Mark disappears off to the rear of the shop.

'You look happy!' Martha says to me with a twinkle.

'I'm so happy!' I can't contain my delight. 'Mark's brilliant. I just can't *believe* what he can do!'

'Yes, he is rather special. Oh, I'm so pleased for you.' She squeezes my arm. 'What a *wonderful* day for you both!'

Oh . . . shit. Suddenly I realize what she means. I glance sharply at Sam but he's stepped aside to read something on his phone and is oblivious.

'So, we're all dying to know.' Martha's eyes are sparkling. 'What are you getting?'

'Err . . .'

This conversation has definitely lurched in the wrong direction. But I can't think how to steer it back.

'Martha told us about the vintage Cartier watch!' Another girl in dove grey joins the conversation, and I can see two other girls edging forward to listen.

'We've all been guessing, out here.' Martha nods. 'I think Mark will have made you something really special and bespoke. With some wonderful, romantic touch.' She clasps her hands. 'Maybe a flawless diamond—'

'Those princess-cut ones are exquisite,' one of the girls in dove grey gushes.

'Or an antique,' chimes in another girl eagerly. 'Mark has some *amazing* old diamonds with stories attached to them. There's an incredible pale-pink one, did he show you that?'

'No!' I say quickly. 'Um . . . you don't understand. I'm not— I mean—'

Oh God. What can I say? I'm *not* getting into the whole story.

'We love a beautiful ring.' Martha sighs happily. 'It doesn't matter what it is, really, as long as it's magical for *you*. Oh, come on.' She gives an impish smile. 'I *have* to know.' She opens the paper with a beaming flourish. 'And the answer is . . .'

As she reads the words on the page, Martha's voice cuts off in a sort of gasp. For a moment she seems unable to speak. 'Oh! A simulated emerald,' she manages at last, sounding strangled. 'Lovely. And simulated diamonds too. *So* pretty.'

There's nothing I can say. I'm aware of four crestfallen faces gazing at me. Martha looks most devastated of all.

'We thought it was a lovely ring,' I offer lamely.

'It is! It is!' Martha is obviously forcing herself to nod animatedly. 'Well . . . congratulations! *So* sensible of you to go for simulations.' She exchanges looks with the other girls in dove grey, who all hastily chime in.

'Absolutely!'

'Very sensible!'

'Lovely choice!'

The bright voices *so* don't match the faces. One girl almost looks like she wants to cry.

Martha seems slightly fixated by Sam's vintage gold Cartier. I can practically read her mind: *He can afford vintage Cartier for himself and he bought his girlfriend a FAKE?*

'Can I just see the price?' Sam has finished tapping at his phone and takes the paper from Martha. As he reads it, he frowns. 'Four hundred and fifty pounds. That's a lot. I thought Mark promised a discount.' He turns to me. 'Don't you think that's too much?'

'Maybe.'[53] I nod, a bit mortified.

'Why's it so expensive?' He turns to Martha and her eyes flick yet again to his Cartier watch before she addresses him with a professional smile.

'It's the platinum, sir. It's a precious, timeless material. Most of our customers value a material that will last a lifetime.'

'Well, can we have something cheaper? Silver-plate?' Sam turns to me. 'You agree, don't you, Poppy? As cheap as possible?'

Across the shop I hear a couple of stifled gasps. I catch a glimpse of Martha's horrified face and can't help flushing.

'Yes! Of course,' I mutter. 'Whatever's cheapest.'

'I'll just check with Mark,' says Martha after rather a long pause. She moves away and makes a brief phone call. As she returns to the till point, she's blinking fast and can't look me in the eye. 'I've spoken to Mark and the ring can be made in silver-plated nickel, which brings the price down to . . .' She taps again. 'To £112. Would you prefer that option?'

---

53. I *did* actually think it was quite a lot. But I figured that was the hit I had to take. I would certainly never query the price of a ring in a posh shop, never in a million years.

'Well, of course we would.' Sam glances at me. 'No-brainer, right?'

'I see. Of course.' Martha's bright smile has frozen solid. 'That's . . . fine. Silver-plated nickel it is.' She seems to gather control of herself. 'In terms of presentation, sir, we offer a deluxe leather ring box at £30, or a simpler, wooden box, for £10. Each option will be lined with rose petals and can have a personalization. Perhaps initials or a little message?'

'A *message*?' Sam gives an incredulous laugh. 'No, thanks. And no packaging. We'll just have it as it is. D'you want a carrier bag or something, Poppy?' He glances at me.

Martha is breathing harder and harder. Just for a moment I think she might lose it.

'Fine!' she says at last. 'Absolutely fine. No box, no rose petals, no message . . .' She taps at her computer. 'And how will you be paying for the ring, sir?' She's obviously mustering all her energies to stay pleasant.

'Poppy?' Sam nods at me expectantly.

As I pull out my purse, Martha's expression is so aghast, I nearly expire with embarrassment.

'So . . . *you'll* be paying for the ring, madam.' She can obviously barely get the words out. 'Wonderful! That's . . . wonderful. No problem at all.'

I tap in my PIN and take the receipt. Yet more girls in dove grey have appeared in the showroom, and they're standing in clusters, whispering and staring at me. My entire body is drenched in mortification.

Sam, of course, has noticed nothing.

'Will we see you both later?' Martha clearly makes a supreme effort to recover herself as she ushers us to the door. 'We'll have champagne waiting and we'll take a photo for your album, of course.' A tiny glow comes back into her eyes. 'It's *such* a special moment when you first take the ring, and slide it on to her finger . . .'

'No, I've spent far too long here already,' says Sam, absently glancing at his watch. 'Can't you just bike it round to Poppy?'

This seems to be the last straw for Martha. When I've given her my details and we're walking out, she suddenly exclaims, 'Could I have a little word about care and upkeep, madam? Just very quickly?' She grabs my arm and pulls me back into the shop, her grip surprisingly strong. 'In seven years of selling engagement rings, I've never done this before,' she whispers urgently into my ear. 'I know he's a friend of Mark's. And I know he's very handsome. But . . . are you *sure*?'

As I eventually emerge on to the street, Sam is waiting for me, looking impatient.

'What was that about? Everything OK?'

'Yes! All fine!'

My face is scarlet and I just want to get out of here. As I glance back towards the shop, I can see Martha talking animatedly to the other girls in dove grey and gesticulating towards Sam, a look of outrage on her face.

'What's going on?' Sam frowns. 'She didn't try to sell you the expensive ring, did she? Because I'll have a word with Mark—'

'No! Nothing like that.' I hesitate, almost too embarrassed to tell him.

'Then what?' Sam looks at me.

'She thought you were my fiancé and you were making me buy my own engagement ring,' I admit at last. 'She told me not to marry you. She was very worried for me.'

I won't go into Martha's theory about generosity in the jewellery shop and generosity in bed and how they relate.[54]

I can see the light slowly dawning on Sam's face.

'Oh, that's funny.' He bursts into laughter. 'That's very funny. Hey.' He hesitates. 'You didn't *want* me to pay for it, did you?'

'No, of course not!' I say, shocked. 'Don't be ridiculous! I just

54. 'I could draw you a graph, Poppy. A *graph*.'

feel terrible that the whole shop thinks you're a cheapskate, when you were actually doing me a massive favour. I'm really sorry.' I wince.

Sam looks baffled. 'What does that matter? I don't care what they think of me.'

'You must care a *bit*.'

'Not one bit.'

I peer at him closely. His face is calm. I think he means it. He doesn't care. How can you not care?

Magnus would care. He always flirts with shop assistants and tries to work out if they recognize him from TV. And one time, when his card was declined in our local supermarket, he made a point of going back in there the next day and telling them about how his bank *completely* cocked up yesterday.

Oh well. Now I don't feel quite so bad.

'I'm going to grab a Starbucks.' Sam starts heading off down the street. 'Want one?'

'I'll get them.' I hurry after him. 'I owe you one. Big time.'

I don't have to be back at the clinic till after lunch, because I got Annalise to swap her morning off with mine. For a hefty bribe.

'You remember I mentioned a man called Sir Nicholas Murray?' Sam says as he swings the coffee-shop door open. 'He's sending over a document. I've told him to use my own email address, but if by any chance he sends it your way by mistake, please let me know at *once*.'

'OK. He's quite famous, isn't he?' I can't resist adding. 'Wasn't he number 18 on the world's movers and shakers list in 1985?'

I did some Googling last night, and I'm totally on top of the whole subject of Sam's company. I know everything. I could go on *Mastermind*. I could do a PowerPoint presentation. In fact, I wish someone would ask me to do one! Facts I know about White Globe Consulting, in no particular order:

1. It was started in 1982 by Nicholas Murray and now it's been bought out by some big multinational group.
2. Sir Nicholas is still the CEO. Apparently he can smooth a meeting's atmosphere by just arriving, and stop a deal in its tracks with a single shake of the head. He always wears floral shirts. It's his thing.
3. The Finance Director was a protégé of Sir Nicholas, but he's recently left the company. His name is Ed Exton.[55]
4. Ed and Sir Nicholas's friendship has disintegrated over the years, and Ed didn't even attend the party when Sir Nicholas was knighted.[56]
5. They had this scandal recently when a guy called John Gregson made a politically incorrect joke at a lunch and had to resign.[57] Some people thought it was unfair, but the new chairman of the board apparently has 'zero tolerance for inappropriate behaviour'.[58]
6. Sir Nicholas is currently advising the Prime Minister on a new special 'Happiness and Wellbeing' committee which all the newspapers have been rude about. One even described Sir Nicholas as past his prime, and had a cartoon of him as a flower with straggly petals. (I won't mention that to Sam.)
7. They won an award for their paper-recycling programme last year.

---

55. Aha! Clearly the same Ed who was in the Groucho Club, the worse for wear. Just call me Poirot.
56. *Daily Mail* gossip column.
57. I actually half-remember seeing that story in the paper.
58. Good thing he isn't my boss, is all I can say.

'Well done on the recycling, by the way,' I add, eager to display my knowledge. 'I saw your statement about "environmental responsibility is a fundamental linchpin for any company that aspires to excellence". *So* true. We recycle, too.'

'What?' Sam seems taken aback; even suspicious. 'How did you see that?'

'Google. It's not against the law!' I add, at his expression. 'I was just *interested*. Since I'm sending on emails all the time, I thought I'd find out a bit about your company.'

'Oh, you did, did you?' Sam shoots me a dubious look. 'Double tall cappuccino, please.'

'So, Sir Nicholas is advising the Prime Minister! That's really cool!'

This time, Sam doesn't even answer. Honestly. He's not exactly a great ambassador.

'Have *you* been to Number Ten?' I persist. 'What's it like?'

'They're waiting for your coffee order.' Sam gestures at the barista.

Obviously he's going to give away absolutely nothing. Typical. You'd think he'd be *pleased* I'm interested in what he does.

'Skinny latte for me.' I haul out my purse. 'And a chocolate-chip muffin. You want a muffin?'

'No, thanks.' Sam shakes his head.

'Probably for the best,' I nod wisely. 'Since you refuse to go to the dentist.'

Sam gives me a blank look, which could mean, 'Don't go there', or 'I'm not listening', or, again, 'What do you mean, the dentist?'

I'm beginning to learn how he works. It's like he has an 'on' switch and an 'off' switch. And he only turns the 'on' switch on when he can be bothered.

I click on my browser, search for another revolting picture of many teeth and forward it to him silently.

'This Savoy reception, by the way,' I say as we go to pick up our drinks. 'You need to send your acceptance.'

'Oh, I'm not going to that,' he says, as though it's obvious.

'Why not?' I stare at him.

'I have no particular reason to.' He shrugs. 'And it's a heavy week for social events.'

I don't believe this. How can he not want to go to the Savoy? God, it's all right for top businessmen, isn't it? Free champagne, yawn, yawn. Goody bags, yet another party, yawn, how tedious and dull.

'Well, you should let them know, then.' I barely hide my disapproval. 'In fact, I'll do it right now. "Dear Blue, Thanks so much for the invitation,"' I read out as I type. '"Unfortunately Sam will be unable to attend on this occasion. Best wishes, Poppy Wyatt."'

'You don't have to do that.' Sam is staring at me, bemused. 'One of the PAs at the office is helping me out now. Girl called Jane Ellis. She can do that.'

Yes, but *will* she do it? I want to retort. I'm aware of this Jane Ellis, who has started making an occasional appearance in Sam's in-box. But her real job is working for Sam's colleague Malcolm. I'm sure the last thing she wants to be doing is wrangling with Sam's diary on top of her usual workload.

'It's OK.' I shrug. 'It's been really bugging me.' Our coffees have arrived on the counter and I hand him his. 'So . . . thanks again.'

'No trouble.' He holds the door open for me. 'Hope you find the ring. As soon as you've finished with the phone—'

'I know.' I cut him off. 'I'll bike it round. The same nanosecond.'

'Fine.' He allows me a half-smile. 'Well, I hope everything goes well for you.' He extends a hand and I shake it politely.

'Hope everything goes well for you too.'

I haven't even asked him when his wedding is. Perhaps it's a week tomorrow, like ours. In the same church, even. I'll arrive, and see him on the steps with Willow the Witch on his arm, telling him he's toxic.

He strides away and I hurry off towards the bus stop. There's a 45 disgorging passengers, and I climb on board. It'll take me to Streatham Hill and I can walk from there.

As I take my seat, I look out and see Sam walking swiftly along the pavement, his face impassive, almost stony. I don't know if it's the wind or if he's been knocked by a passer-by, but somehow his tie has gone skew-whiff, and he doesn't even seem to have noticed. Now *that's* bugging me. I can't resist sending him a text.

Your tie's crooked.

I wait about thirty seconds then watch his face jolt in surprise. As he's looking around, searching the pedestrians on the pavement, I text again:

On the bus.

The bus has moved off by now, but the traffic's heavy and I'm pretty much keeping pace with Sam. He looks up, straightening his tie, and flashes me a smile.

I'll have to admit, he really does have quite a smile. Kind of heart-stopping, especially as it comes out of nowhere.

I mean . . . you know. If your heart was in the kind of place to be stopped.

Anyway. An email has just come in from Lindsay Cooper and I briskly open it.

Dear Sam
Thank you so much! Your words mean a lot to me – it's so nice to know you are appreciated!! I've told the whole team who helped me with the strategy document, and it's really boosted morale!
Best
Lindsay

It's cc-ed to his other address too, so he'll have got it on his phone. A moment later my phone bleeps with a text from Sam.

What did you write to Lindsay??

I can't help giggling as I type back:

Happy birthday. Just like you said.

What else??

I don't see why I need to answer. Two can play at selective deafness. I counter:

Have you contacted the dentist yet?

I wait a while – but we're back to radio silence. Another email has just arrived in the phone, this time from one of Lindsay's colleagues, and as I read it I can't help feeling vindicated.

Dear Sam
Lindsay passed on your kind words about the website strategy. We were so honoured and delighted you took the time to comment. Thanks, and look forward to chatting about more initiatives, maybe at the next monthly meeting.
Adrian (Foster)

Ha. You see? *You see?*
It's all very well sending off two-word emails. It might be efficient. It might get the job done. But *no one likes you*. Now that whole website team will feel happy and wanted and work brilliantly. And it's all because of me! Sam should have me doing his emails all the time.

On a sudden impulse, I scroll down to Rachel's zillionth email about the Fun Run, and press Reply.

> Hi Rachel
> Count me in for the Fun Run. It's a great endeavour and I look forward to supporting it. Well done!
> Sam

He looks fit. He can do a Fun Run, for God's sake.

On a roll now, I scroll down to that guy in IT who's been politely asking about sending Sam his CV and ideas for the company. I mean, surely Sam should be *encouraging* people who want to get ahead?

> Dear James
> I would be very glad to see your CV and hear about your ideas. Please make an appointment with Jane Ellis and well done for being so proactive!
> Sam

And now I've started, I can't stop. As the bus chugs along, I email the guy wanting to assess Sam's workstation for health and safety, set up a time, then email Jane to tell her to put it in the diary.[59] I email Sarah who's been off with shingles and ask her if she's feeling better.

All those unanswered emails that have been nagging away at me. All those poor ignored people, trying to get in touch with Sam. Why *shouldn't* I answer them? I'm doing him such a service! I feel like I'm repaying him for his favour with the ring. At least, when I hand this phone back, his in-box will have been dealt with.

In fact, what about a round-robin email telling everyone

---

59. I know he's free a week on Wednesday for lunch because someone has just cancelled.

they're fab? Why not? Who can it hurt?

> Dear Staff
> I just wanted to say that you've all done a great job so far this year.

As I'm typing, an even better thought comes to me.

> As you know, I value the views and ideas of you all. We are lucky to have such talent at White Globe Consulting and want to make the most of it. If you have any ideas for the company you would like to share with me, please send them to me. Be honest!
> All best wishes and here's to a great rest of the year.
> Sam

I press Send with satisfaction. There. Talk about motivational. Talk about team spirit! As I sit back, my fingers are aching from so much typing. I take a sip of latte, reach for my muffin and stuff a massive chunk into my mouth, just as my phone starts ringing.

Shit. Of *all* the times.

I press Talk, lift the receiver to my ear and try to say, 'Just a moment', but it comes out as 'gobbllllllg'. My whole mouth is full of claggy muffin. What do they *put* in these things?

'Is that you?' A youthful, reedy male voice is speaking. 'It's Scottie.'

Scottie? *Scottie?*

Something suddenly sparks in my mind. Scottie. Wasn't that the name mentioned by Violet's friend who rang before? The one who was talking about liposuction?

'It's done. Like I said. It was a surgical strike. No trace. Genius stuff, though I say it myself. Adios, Santa Claus.'

I'm chewing my muffin as frantically as I can, but I still can't utter a sound.

'Are you there? Is this the right— Oh *fucking*—' The voice disappears as I manage to swallow.

'Hello? Can I take a message?'

He's gone. I check the caller ID, but it's Unknown Number.

You'd think all Violet's friends would know her new number by now. Clicking my tongue, I reach inside my bag for the *Lion King* programme, which is still there.

'Scottie rang,' I scribble next to the first message. 'It's done. Surgical strike. No trace. Genius stuff. Adios, Santa Claus.'

If I ever meet this Violet, I hope she's grateful for all my efforts. In fact, I hope I *do* meet her. I haven't been taking all these messages for nothing.

I'm about to put the phone away when a crowd of new emails arrives in a flashing bunch. Replies to my round robin already? I scroll down – and to my disappointment, most of them are standard company messages or adverts. But the second-to-last makes me stop in my tracks. It's from Sam's dad.

I've been wondering about him.

I hesitate – then click the email open.

Dear Sam

Just wondering if you got my last email? You know I'm not much of a technological expert, probably sent it off to the wrong place. But here goes again.

Hope all is well and you are flourishing in London as ever. You know how proud we are of your success. I see you in the business pages. Amazing. I always knew you were destined for big things, you know that.

As I said, there is something I'd love to talk to you about. Are you ever down Hampshire way? It's been so long and I do miss the old days.

Yours ever

Your old

Dad

As I get to the end I feel rather hot round the eyes. I can't quite believe it. Did Sam not even reply to that last email? Doesn't he *care* about his dad? Have they had a big row or something?

I have no idea what the story is. I have no idea what could have happened between them. All I know is, there's a father sitting at a computer, putting out feelers to his son and they're being ignored and I can't bear it. I just can't. Whatever's gone before, life's too short not to make amends. Life's too short to bear a grudge.

On impulse I press Reply. I don't dare reply in Sam's voice to his own father, that would be going too far. But I can make contact. I can let a lonely old man know that his voice is being heard.

> Hello
> This is Sam's PA. Just to let you know, Sam will be at his company conference at the Chiddingford Hotel in Hampshire next week, April 24th. I'm sure he'd love to see you.
> Best
> Poppy Wyatt

I press Send before I can chicken out, then sit back for a few moments, a bit breathless at what I've just done. I've masqueraded as Sam's PA. I've contacted his father. I've waded right into his personal life. He'd be livid if he knew – in fact the very thought of it makes me quail.

But sometimes you have to be brave. Sometimes you have to show people what's important in life. And I have this very strong gut instinct that what I've done is the right thing. Maybe not the easy thing – but the right thing.

I have a vision of Sam's dad sitting at his desk, his grey head bowed. The computer beeping with a new email, the light of hope in his face as he opens it . . . a sudden smile of joy . . .

turning to his dog, patting his head, saying, 'We're going to see Sam, boy!'[60]

Yes. It was the right thing to do.

Exhaling slowly, I open the last email, which is from Blue.

Hello
We're so sorry to hear that Sam can't make the Savoy reception. Would he like to nominate another person to attend in his place? Please email over the name and we will be sure to add them to the guest list.
Kind regards
Blue

The bus has come to a halt; it's juddering at a set of traffic lights. I take another bite of muffin and stare silently at the email.

Another person. That could be anybody.

I'm free on Monday night. Magnus has a late seminar in Warwick.

OK. Here's the thing. There's no way I'd *ever* be invited to anything glitzy like this in the normal way of things. Physiotherapists just aren't. And Magnus's events are all academic book launches or stuffy college dinners. They're never at the Savoy. There are never goody bags or cocktails or jazz bands. This is my one and only chance.

Maybe this is karma. I've come into Sam's life, I've made a difference for the good – and this is my reward.

My fingers are moving almost before I've made a decision.

'Thank you so much for your email,' I find myself typing. 'Sam would like to nominate Poppy Wyatt.'

---

60. I know he may not have a dog. I just feel pretty sure that he does.

SEVEN

The fake ring's perfect!

OK, not *perfect*. It's a tad smaller than the original. And a bit tinnier. But who's going to know without the other one to compare? I've worn it most of the afternoon and it feels really comfortable. In fact, it's lighter than the real thing, which is an advantage.

Now I've finished my last appointment of the day and am standing with my hands spread out on the reception desk. All the patients have gone, even sweet Mrs Randall, with whom I've just had to be quite firm. I told her not to come back here for two weeks. I told her she was *perfectly* capable of exercising at home alone, and there was no reason why she shouldn't be back on the tennis court.

Then, of course, it all came out. It turned out she was nervous of letting down her doubles partner, and that's why she was coming in so often: to give herself confidence. I told her she was absolutely ready and I wanted her to text me her next score before she came back to see me. I said if it came to it *I'd* play tennis with her, at which point she laughed and said I was right, she was being nonsensical.

Then, when she'd gone, Angela told me that Mrs Randall is some shit-hot player who once played in Junior Wimbledon. Yowzer. Probably a good thing we *didn't* play, since I can't even hit a backhand.

Angela's gone home too now. It's just me, Annalise and Ruby and we're surveying the ring in silence except for a spring storm outside. One minute it was a bright breezy day, the next, rain was hammering at the windows.

'Excellent.' Ruby is nodding energetically. Her hair is up in a ponytail today, and it bounces as she nods. 'Very good. You'd never know.'

'*I'd* know,' Annalise retorts at once. 'It's not the same green.'

'Really?' I peer at it in dismay.

'The question is, how observant is Magnus?' Ruby raises her eyebrows. 'Does he ever look at it?'

'I don't *think* so—'

'Well, maybe keep your hands away from him for a while, to be on the safe side.'

'Keep my hands away from him? How do I do that?'

'You'll have to restrain yourself!' says Annalise tartly. 'It can't be *that* hard.'

'What about his parents?' says Ruby.

'They're bound to want to see it. We're meeting at the church, so the lights will be pretty dim, but even so . . .' I bite my lip, suddenly nervous. 'Oh God. *Does* it look real?'

'Yes!' says Ruby at once.

'No,' says Annalise, equally firmly. 'Sorry, but it doesn't. Not if you look carefully.'

'Well, don't let them!' says Ruby. 'If they start looking too closely, create a diversion.'

'Like what?'

'Faint? Pretend to have a fit? Tell them you're pregnant?'

'*Pregnant?*' I stare at her, wanting to laugh. 'Are you nuts?'

'I'm just trying to help,' she says defensively. 'Maybe they'd *like* you to be pregnant. Maybe Wanda's gunning to be a granny.'

'No.' I shake my head. 'No way. She'd freak out.'

'Perfect! Then she won't look at the ring. She'll be too consumed with rage.' Ruby nods in satisfaction, as though she's solved all my problems.

'I don't want a raging mother-in-law, thanks very much!'

'She'll be raging either way,' Annalise points out. 'You just have to decide, which is worse? Pregnant daughter-in-law or flaky daughter-in-law who lost the priceless heirloom? I'd say go with pregnant.'

'Stop it! I'm *not* saying I'm pregnant!' I look at the ring again and rub the fake emerald. 'I think it'll be fine,' I say, as much to convince myself as anything. 'It'll be fine.'

'Is that Magnus?' says Ruby suddenly. 'Across the street?'

I follow her gaze. There he is, holding an umbrella against the rain, waiting for the traffic lights to change.

'Shit.' I leap to my feet and clasp my right hand casually over my left. No. Too unnatural. I thrust my left hand into my uniform pocket, but my arm is left sticking out at an awkward angle.

'Bad.' Ruby is watching. 'Really bad.'

'What shall I dooo?' I wail.

'Hand cream.' She reaches for a tube. 'Come on. I'm giving you a manicure. Then you can leave a bit of the cream on. Accidentally on purpose.'

'Genius.' I glance over at Annalise and blink in surprise. 'Err . . . Annalise? What are you *doing*?'

In the thirty seconds since Ruby spotted Magnus, Annalise seems to have applied a fresh layer of lipgloss, sprayed scent on, and is now pulling a few sexy strands of hair out of her ballerina's bun.

'Nothing!' she says defiantly, as Ruby starts rubbing cream into my hands.

I only have time to dart her a suspicious look before the door opens and Magnus appears, shaking water from his umbrella.

'Hello, girls!' He beams around as though we're an appreciative audience waiting for his entrance. Which I suppose we are.

'Magnus! Let me take your coat.' Annalise has rushed forward. 'It's OK, Poppy. You're having your manicure. I'll do it. And maybe a cup of tea?'

Ooh. *Typical.* I watch as she slides Magnus's linen jacket from his shoulders. Isn't she doing that a bit slowly and lingeringly? Why does he need to take his jacket off, anyway? We're about to go.

'We're nearly finished.' I glance at Ruby. 'Aren't we?'

'No hurry,' says Magnus. 'Plenty of time.' He looks around the reception area and breathes in, as though appreciating some beautiful vista. 'Mmm. I remember coming here the first time as though it were yesterday. You remember, Pops? God, that was amazing, wasn't it?' He meets my eye with a suggestive glint and I hastily telegraph back, *Shut up, you idiot.* He is going to get me in *so* much trouble.

'How's your wrist, Magnus?' Annalise is approaching him with a cup of tea from the kitchen. 'Did Poppy ever give you a three-month follow-up appointment?'

'No.' He looks taken aback. 'Should she have done?'

'Your wrist's fine,' I say firmly.

'Shall I take a look?' Annalise is ignoring me completely. 'Poppy shouldn't be giving you therapy now, you know. Conflict of interest.' She takes his wrist. 'Where was the pain exactly? Here?' She unbuttons his cuff, moving up his arm. 'Here?' Her voice deepens slightly and she bats her eyelashes at him. 'What about . . . here?'

OK. This is the limit.

'Thanks, Annalise!' I beam brightly at her. 'But we'd better be going to the church. For the meeting about our *wedding,*' I add pointedly.

'About that.' Magnus frowns briefly. 'Poppy, can we have a quick chat? Maybe go into your room a moment?'

'Oh.' I feel a flicker of foreboding. 'OK.'

Even Annalise looks taken aback, and Ruby raises her eyebrows.

'Cuppa, Annalise?' she says. 'We'll just be out here. No rush.'

As I usher Magnus in, my mind is skittering in panic. He knows about the ring. The Scrabble. Everything. He's having cold feet. He wants a wife he can talk to about Proust.

'Does this door lock?' He fiddles with the catch and after a moment has secured it. 'There. Excellent!' As he turns, there's an unmistakable light in his eyes. 'God, Poppy, you look hot.'

It takes about five seconds for the penny to drop.

'*What?* No. Magnus, you have to be joking.'

He's heading towards me with an intent, familiar expression. No way. I mean, *no way*.

'Stop!' I bat him away as he reaches for the top button of my uniform. 'I'm at work!'

'I know.' He closes his eyes briefly as though in some paroxysm of bliss. 'I don't know what it is about this place. Your uniform, maybe. All that white.'

'Well, too bad.'

'You know you want to.' He nibbles one of my earlobes. 'Come on . . .'

Damn him for knowing about my earlobes. For a moment – just a moment – I slightly lose my focus. But then, as he makes another salvo on my uniform buttons, I snap back into reality. Ruby and Annalise are three feet away on the other side of the door.[61] This *cannot happen.*

'No! Magnus, I thought you wanted to talk about something serious! The wedding or something!'

'Why would I want to do that?' He's pressing the button which reclines the couch all the way down. 'Mmm. I remember this bed.'

---

61. In fact, probably pressing a glass up to it.

'It's not a bed, it's a professional couch!'

'Is that massage oil?' He's reached for a nearby bottle.

'Sssh!' I hiss. 'Ruby's only just outside! I've already had one disciplinary hearing—'

'What's this thing? Ultrasound?' He's grabbed the ultrasound wand. 'I bet we could have some fun with this. Does it heat up?' His eyes suddenly glint. 'Does it *vibrate*?'

This is like having a toddler to control.

'We can't! I'm sorry.' I step away, putting the couch between him and me. 'We can't. We just *can't*.' I smooth down my uniform.

For a moment Magnus looks so sulky I think he might shout at me.

'I'm sorry,' I say again. 'But it's like asking you to have sex with a student. You'd get fired. Your career would be over!'

Magnus seems about to contradict me – then thinks better of whatever he was going to say.

'Well, great.' He gives a grumpy shrug. 'Just great. What are we supposed to do instead?'

'We could do loads of things!' I say brightly. 'Have a chat? Go through wedding stuff? Only eight more days to go!'

Magnus doesn't reply. He doesn't need to. His lack of enthusiasm is emanating from him like some kind of psychic force.

'Or have a drink?' I suggest. 'We've got time to go to the pub before the rehearsal.'

'All right,' he says heavily at last. 'Let's go to the pub.'

'We'll come back here,' I say coaxingly. 'Another day. Maybe at a weekend.'

What the hell am I promising? Oh God. I'll cross that bridge when I come to it.

As we head out of the room, Ruby and Annalise look up artificially from magazines they obviously *haven't* been reading.

'Everything OK?' says Ruby.

'Yes, great!' I smooth my skirt again. 'Just . . . wedding chit-chat. Veils, almonds, that kind of thing . . . anyway, we'd better be off . . .'

I've just glimpsed my reflection in the mirror. My cheeks are bright scarlet and I'm talking nonsense. Total give-away.

'Hope it goes well.' Ruby glances meaningfully at the ring, then at me.

'Thanks.'

'Text us!' chips in Annalise. 'Whatever happens. We'll be *dying* to know!'

The thing to remember is, the ring fooled Magnus. And if it fooled him, surely it'll fool his parents? As we arrive at St Edmund's Parish Church, I feel more optimistic than I have for ages. St Edmund's is a big, grand church in Marylebone, in fact we chose it because it's so beautiful. As we head inside, some-one's practising a flashy piece on the organ. There are pink and white flowers for another wedding decorating all the pews, and a general air of expectancy.

I suddenly feel a tingle of excitement. In eight days, that'll be us! A week tomorrow, the place will be festooned with white silk and posies. All my friends and family will be waiting excitedly. The trumpeter will be in the organ loft and I'll be in my dress and Magnus will be standing at the altar in his designer waistcoat.[62] It's really, really happening!

I can already see Wanda inside the church, peering at some old statue. As she turns, I force myself to wave confidently, as though everything's great and we're the best of friends and they don't intimidate me at all.

Magnus is right, I tell myself. I've been overreacting. I've let them get to me. They probably can't *wait* to welcome me into the family.

After all, I beat them all at Scrabble, didn't I?

62. His waistcoat cost nearly as much as my dress.

'Just think.' I clutch Magnus's arm. 'Not long now!'

'Hello?' Magnus answers his phone, which must be on Vibrate. 'Oh, hi, Neil.'

Great. Neil is Magnus's keenest undergraduate, and is writing a dissertation on 'Symbols in the Work of Coldplay'.[63] They'll be on the phone for hours. Mouthing apologetically, he disappears out of the church.

You'd think he could have turned his phone off. I've turned *mine* off.

Anyway, never mind.

'Hello!' I exclaim as Wanda comes down the aisle. 'Good to see you! Isn't this exciting?'

I'm not exactly proffering my ring hand. But nor am I hiding it. It's neutral. It's the Switzerland of hands.

'*Poppy.*' Wanda does her usual dramatic swoop towards my cheek. 'Dear girl. Now, let me introduce Paul. Where's he got to? How *is* your burn, by the way?'

For a moment I can't move.

Paul. The dermatologist. Shit. I forgot about the dermatologist. How could I forget about the dermatologist? How could I be so *stupid*? I was so relieved to get a substitute ring I forgot I was supposed to be mortally injured.

'You've taken your bandage off,' observes Wanda.

'Oh.' I swallow. 'Yes. I did. Because ... my hand's much better, actually. *Much* better.'

'Can't be too careful, though, even with these small injuries.' Wanda is ushering me up the aisle and there's nothing I can do except walk obediently. 'Colleague of ours in Chicago stubbed his toe and just soldiered on, next thing we know, he's in hospital with gangrene! I said to Antony—' Wanda interrupts herself. 'Here she is. The fiancée. The betrothed. The patient.'

Antony and an elderly man in a purple V-neck both turn

63. I think 'Cymbals in the Work of Coldplay' would make more sense, but what do I know?

from examining a painting hanging on a stone pillar, and peer at me instead.

'Poppy,' says Antony. 'Let me introduce our neighbour, Paul McAndrew, one of the most eminent professors of dermatology in the country. Specialist in burns, isn't that fortunate?'

'Great!' My voice is a nervous squeak and my hands have crept behind my back. 'Well, like I say, it's a *lot* better . . .'

'Let's take a look,' says Paul, in a pleasant, matter-of-fact way.

There's no way out. Squirming with mortification, I slowly extend my left hand. Everybody looks at my smooth, unblemished skin in silence.

'*Where* was the burn, exactly?' asks Paul at last.

'Um . . . here.' I gesture vaguely at my thumb.

'Was it a scald? A cigarette burn?' He's taken hold of my hand and is feeling it with an expert touch.

'No. It was . . . um . . . on a radiator.' I swallow. 'It was really sore.'

'Her whole hand was bandaged.' Wanda sounds bemused. 'She looked like a war victim! That was only yesterday!'

'I see.' The doctor relinquishes my hand. 'Well, it seems OK now, doesn't it? Any pain? Any tenderness?'

I shake my head mutely.

'I'll prescribe some aqueous cream,' he says kindly. 'In case the symptoms return. How about that?'

I can see Wanda and Antony exchanging looks. Great. They obviously think I'm a total hypochondriac.

Well . . . OK. Fine. I'll go with that. I'll be the family hypochondriac. It can be one of my little quirks. Could be worse. At least they haven't exclaimed, 'What the hell have you done with our priceless ring, and what's that piece of junk you're wearing?'

As though reading my mind, Wanda glances again at my hand.

'My mother's emerald ring, do you see, Antony?' She points

at my hand. 'Magnus gave it to Poppy when he proposed.'

OK. I'm definitely not making this up: there's a pointed edge to her voice. And now she's shooting Antony a significant look. What's going on? Did she want the ring herself? Was Magnus *not* supposed to give it away? I feel like I've blundered into some tricksy family situation which is invisible to me, but they're all too polite to mention it, and I'm never going to know what anybody really thinks.

But then, if it's so special, how come she hasn't noticed it's a fake? Perversely, I feel a teeny bit disappointed in the Tavishes for not realizing. They think they're so clever – and then they can't even spot a false emerald.

'Super engagement ring,' says Paul politely. 'That's a real one-off, I can tell.'

'Absolutely!' I nod. 'It's an antique. Totally unique.'

'Ah, Poppy!' chimes in Antony, who has been examining a nearby statue. 'Now, that reminds me. There's something I was going to ask you.'

Me?

'Oh, right,' I say in surprise.

'I *would* ask Magnus, but I gather it's more your area than his.'

'Fire away.' I smile up at him politely, expecting some weddingy question along the lines of, 'How many bridesmaids will there be?' or 'What flowers are you having?' or, even, 'Were you surprised when Magnus proposed?'

'What do you think of McDowell's new book on the Stoics?' His eyes are fixed beadily on mine. 'How does it compare to Whittaker?'

For a moment I'm too pole-axed to react. What? What do I think of *what*?

'Ah yes!' Wanda is nodding vigorously. 'Poppy is somewhat of an *expert* on Greek philosophy, Paul. She foxed us all at Scrabble with the word "aporia", didn't you?'

Somehow I manage to keep smiling.

Aporia.

That was one of the words Sam texted me. I'd had a few glasses of wine and was feeling pretty confident by then. I have a hazy memory of laying down the tiles and saying that Greek philosophy was one of my great interests.

Why? Why, why, why? If I could go back in time, *that's* the moment I'd go up to myself and say, 'Poppy! Enough!'

'That's right!' I attempt an easy smile. 'Aporia! Anyway, I wonder where the vicar is—'

'We were reading the *TLS* this morning' – Antony ignores my attempt to divert the conversation – 'and there was a review of this new McDowell book and we thought, now *Poppy* will know about this subject.' He looks expectantly at me. 'Is McDowell correct about fourth-century virtues?'

I give an internal whimper. Why the hell did I pretend I knew about Greek philosophy? What was I *thinking*?

'I haven't *quite* got to the McDowell book yet.' I clear my throat. 'Although obviously it's on my reading list.'

'I believe Stoicism has often been misunderstood as a philosophy, isn't that right, Poppy?'

'Absolutely,' I nod, trying to look as knowledgeable as possible. 'It's completely misunderstood. Very much so.'

'The Stoics weren't *emotionless*, as I understand it.' He gestures with his hands as though lecturing to three hundred people. 'They simply valued the virtue of fortitude. Apparently they displayed such impassiveness to hostility that their aggressors wondered if they were made of stone.'

'Extraordinary!' says Paul, with a laugh.

'That's correct, isn't it, Poppy?' Antony turns to me. 'When the Gauls attacked Rome, the old senators sat in the forum, calmly waiting. The attackers were so taken aback by their dispassionate attitude, they thought they must be statues. One Gaul even tugged the beard of a senator, to check.'

'Quite right.' I nod confidently. 'That's exactly it.'

As long as Antony just keeps talking and I keep nodding then I'll be OK.

'Fascinating! And what happened next?' Paul turns expectantly to me.

I glance at Antony for the answer – but he's waiting for me, too. And so is Wanda.

Three eminent professors. All waiting for *me* to tell them about Greek philosophy.

'Well!' I pause thoughtfully, as though wondering where to begin. 'Well, now. It was . . . interesting. In many, many ways. For philosophy. And for Greece. And for history. And humanity. One could, in fact, say that this was *the* most significant moment in Greek . . . ness.' I come to a finish, hoping no one will realize I haven't actually answered the question.

There's a puzzled pause.

'But what *happened*?' says Wanda, a little impatiently.

'Oh, the senators were massacred, of course,' says Antony with a shrug. 'But what I wanted to ask you, Poppy, was—'

'That's a lovely painting!' I cry desperately, pointing to a picture hanging on a pillar. 'Look over there!'

'Ah, now, that *is* an interesting piece.' He wanders over to have a look.

The great thing about Antony is, he's so curious about everything, he's quite easily distracted.

'I just need to check something in my diary . . .' I say hastily. 'I'll just . . .'

My legs are shaking slightly as I escape to a nearby pew. This is a disaster. Now I'll have to pretend to be a Greek-philosophy expert for the rest of my life. Every Christmas and family gathering, I'll have to have a view on Greek philosophy. Not to mention be able to recite Robert Burns' poetry.

I should never, *ever* have cheated. This is karma. This is my punishment.

Anyway, too late. I did.

I'm going to have to start taking notes. I pull out my

phone, create a new email and start typing notes to myself.

THINGS TO DO BEFORE WEDDING
1. *Become expert on Greek philosophy.*
2. *Memorize Robert Burns poems.*
3. *Learn long Scrabble words.*
4. *Remember: am HYPOCHONDRIAC.*
5. *Beef Stroganoff. Get to like. (Hypnosis?)*[64]

I look at the list for a few moments. It's fine. I can be that person. It's not *that* different from me.

'Well, of course, you know *my* views on art in churches . . .' Antony's voice is ringing out. 'Absolutely *scandalous* . . .'

I shrink down out of view, before anyone can drag me into the conversation. Everyone knows Antony's views on art in churches, mostly because he's the founder of a national campaign to turn churches into art galleries and get rid of all the vicars. A few years ago he was on TV and said, 'Treasures such as these should not be left in the hands of Philistines.' It got repeated everywhere and there was a big fuss and headlines like 'Professor Dubs Clerics Philistines' and 'Prof Disses Revs' (that one was in the *Sun*).[65]

I just wish he'd keep his voice down. What if the vicar hears him? It's not exactly tactful.

Now I can hear him laying into the Order of Service.

'"Dearly beloved."' He gives that sarcastic little laugh. 'Beloved by whom? Beloved by the stars and the cosmos? Does

64. Wanda made beef Stroganoff for us, the first time I met her. How could I tell her the truth, which is that it makes me gag?
65. He was on *Newsnight* and everything. According to Magnus, Antony loved all the attention, although he pretended he didn't. He's been saying even more controversial things ever since, but none have ever taken off like the Philistines thing.

anyone expect us to believe that some beneficent being is up there, *loving* us? "In the sight of God." I ask you, Wanda! Absolute weak-minded nonsense.'

I suddenly see the vicar of the church walking up the aisle towards us. He's obviously heard Antony, from his glowering expression. Yikes.

'Good evening, Poppy.'

I hastily leap up from my pew. 'Good evening, Reverend Fox! How are you? We were just saying . . . how lovely the church looks.' I smile lamely.

'Indeed,' he says frostily.

'Have you . . .' I swallow. 'Have you met my future father-in-law? Professor Antony Tavish.'

Thankfully Antony shakes hands quite pleasantly with Reverend Fox, but there's still a prickly atmosphere in the air.

'So, you're doing a reading, Professor Tavish,' says Reverend Fox after he's checked a few other details. 'From the Bible?'

'Hardly.' Antony's eyes glitter at the vicar.

'I thought not.' Reverend Fox smiles back aggressively. 'Not really your "bag", shall we say.'

Oh God. You can *feel* the animosity crackling through the air between them. Should I try a joke, lighten the atmosphere?

Maybe not.

'And, Poppy, you'll be given away by your brothers?' Reverend Fox checks his notes.

'That's right.' I nod. 'Toby and Tom. They're going to lead me down the aisle, either side.'

'Your brothers!' chimes in Paul with interest. 'That's a nice idea. But why not your father?'

'Because my father is . . .' I hesitate. 'Well, actually, both my parents are dead.'

And like night follows day, here it is. The awkward pause. I stare at the stone floor, counting down the seconds, waiting patiently for it to pass.

How many awkward pauses have I caused in the last ten years? It's always the same. No one knows where to look. No one knows what to say. At least this time no one's trying to give me a hug.

'My dear girl,' says Paul, in consternation. 'I'm *so* sorry—'

'It's fine!' I cut him off brightly. 'Really. It was an accident. Ten years ago. I don't talk about it. I don't think about it. Not any more.'

I smile at him as off-puttingly as I can. I'm not getting into this. I never do get into it. It's all folded up in my mind. Packaged away.

No one wants to hear stories about bad things. That's the truth. I remember my tutor at college once asked me if I was all right and if I wanted to talk. The moment I started, he said, 'You mustn't lose your confidence, Poppy!' in this brisk way that meant, 'Actually I don't want to hear about this, please stop now.'

There was a counselling group. But I didn't go. It clashed with hockey practice. Anyway, what's there to talk about? My parents died. My aunt and uncle took us in. My cousins had left home already, so they had the bedrooms and everything.

It happened. There's nothing else to say.

'*Beautiful* engagement ring, Poppy,' says Reverend Fox at last, and everyone seizes on the distraction.

'Isn't it lovely? It's an antique.'

'It's a family piece,' puts in Wanda.

'Very special.' Paul pats my hand kindly. 'An absolute one-off.'

The church door opens with a clang of iron bolts. 'Sorry I'm late,' comes a familiar, piercing voice. 'It's been a *bugger* of a day.'

Striding up the aisle, holding several bags full of silk, is Lucinda. She's wearing a beige shift dress and massive sunglasses on her head and looks hassled. 'Reverend Fox! Did you get my email?'

'Yes, Lucinda,' says Reverend Fox wearily. 'I did. I'm afraid the church pillars cannot be sprayed silver, under any circumstances.'

Lucinda stops dead and a bolt of grey silk starts unravelling, all the way up the aisle.

'They *can't*? Well, what am I supposed to do? I promised the florist silver columns!' She sinks down on a nearby pew. 'This bloody wedding! If it's not one thing it's another—'

'Don't worry, Lucinda, dear,' says Wanda, swooping down on her fondly. 'I'm sure you're doing a *marvellous* job. How's your mother?'

'Oh, she's fine.' Lucinda waves a hand. 'Not that I ever see her, I'm up to my *eyes* with it— Where is that dratted Clemency?'

'I've booked the cars, by the way,' I say quickly. 'All done. And the confetti, and I was wondering, shall I book some buttonholes for the ushers?'

'If you could,' she says a little tetchily. 'I would appreciate it.' She looks up and seems to take me in properly for the first time. 'Oh, Poppy. *One* piece of good news, I've got your ring! It was caught on the lining of my bag.'

She pulls out the emerald ring and holds it out. I'm so blindsided, all I can do is blink.

The real ring. My real, antique, priceless emerald engagement ring. Right there, in front of my eyes.

How did she—

What the hell—

I can't bring myself to look at anybody else. But even so, I'm aware of glances of astonishment all around me, criss-crossing like laser beams, moving from my fake ring to the real one and back again.

'I don't quite understand—' begins Paul at last.

'What's up, everyone?' Magnus is striding up the aisle, taking in the tableau. 'Someone seen a ghost? The Holy Ghost?' He laughs at his own joke but no one joins in.

'If *that's* the ring . . .' Wanda seems to have found her voice.

'Then what's that?' She points at the fake on my finger, which of course now looks like something out of a cracker.

My throat is so tight I can hardly breathe. Somehow I have to save this situation. Somehow. *They must never know I lost the ring.*

'Yes! I . . . *thought* you'd be surprised!' Somehow I find some words; somehow I muster a smile. I feel as though I'm walking over a bridge which I'm having to construct myself as I go, out of playing cards. 'I actually . . . had a replica made!' I try to sound casual. 'Because I lent the original to Lucinda.'

I look at her desperately, willing her to go along with this. Thankfully she seems to have realized what a faux pas she's committed.

'Yes!' she joins in quickly. 'That's right. I borrowed the ring for . . . for . . .'

'. . . for design reasons.'

'Yes! We thought the ring could be inspiration for . . .'

'The napkin rings,' I grasp from nowhere. 'Emerald napkin rings! Which we *didn't* go with in the end,' I add carefully.

There's silence. I pluck up the courage to look around.

Wanda's face is creased deeply with a frown. Magnus looks perplexed. Paul has taken a step backwards from the group as though to say, 'Nothing to do with me.'

'So . . . thanks very much.' I take the ring from Lucinda with trembling hands. 'I'll just . . . put that back on.'

I've crashed on to the far bank and am clinging to the grass. Made it. Thank God.

But as I rip the fake ring off, drop it into my bag and slide the real thing on, my mind is in overdrive. How come Lucinda had the ring? What about Mrs Fairfax? *What the fuck is going on?*

'*Why* exactly did you have a replica made, sweets?' Magnus still looks totally baffled.

I stare at him, desperately trying to think. Why would I have gone to all the trouble and expense of making a fake ring?

'Because I thought it would be nice to have two,' I venture feebly after a pause.

Oh God. No. *Bad*. I should have said, 'For travel.'

'You wanted *two* rings?' Wanda seems almost speechless.

'Well, I hope that desire won't apply to your husband as well as your engagement ring!' Antony says, with heavy humour. 'Eh, Magnus?'

'Ha ha ha!' I give a loud, sycophantic laugh. 'Ha ha ha! Very good! Anyway.' I turn to Reverend Fox, trying to hide my desperation. 'Shall we crack on?'

Half an hour later my legs are still shaking. I've never experienced such a near-miss in my life. I'm really not sure Wanda believes me. She keeps shooting me suspicious looks, plus she's asked me how much the replica ring cost and where I had it made, and all sorts of questions I really didn't want to answer.

What does she think? That I was going to sell the original, or something?

We've practised me coming up the aisle, and going back down the aisle together, and worked out where we'll kneel and sign the register. And now the vicar has suggested a run-through of the vows.

But I can't. I just can't say those magical words with Antony there, making clever-clever comments and mocking every phrase. It'll be different during the wedding. He'll have to shut up.

'Magnus.' I pull him aside with a whisper. 'Let's not do our vows today after all. Not with your father here. They're too special to ruin.'

'OK.' He looks surprised. 'I don't mind either way.'

'Let's just say them once. On the day.' I squeeze his hand. 'For real.'

Even regardless of Antony, I don't want to pre-empt the big moment, I realize. I don't *want* to rehearse. It'll take the specialness out of it all.

'Yes, I agree.' Magnus nods. 'So . . . are we done now?'

'No, we're not done!' says Lucinda, sounding outraged. 'Far from it! I want Poppy to walk up the aisle again. You went *far* too fast for the music.'

'OK.' I shrug, heading to the back of the church.

'Organ, please!' shrieks Lucinda. 'Or-gan! From the top! Glide *smoothly*, Poppy,' she orders as I pass. 'You're wobbling! Clemency, where are those cups of tea?'

Clemency is just back from a Costa run and I can see her out of the corner of my eye, hastily tearing open sachets of sugar.

'I'll help!' I say, and break off from gliding. 'What can I do?'

'Thanks,' whispers Clemency as I come over. 'Antony wants three sugars, Magnus's is the cappuccino, Wanda has the biscotti . . .'

'Where's my double-chocolate extra-cream muffin?' I say with a puzzled frown and Clemency jumps sky-high.

'I didn't – I can go back—'

'Joke!' I say. 'Just joking!'

The longer Clemency works for Lucinda, the more like a terrified rabbit she looks. It really can't be good for her health.

Lucinda takes her tea (milk, no sugar) with the briefest of nods. She seems totally hassled again, and has laid a massive spreadsheet across the pews. It's such a mess of highlighter and scribbles and Post-it notes, I'm amazed she's organized anything.

'Oh God, oh God,' she's saying under her breath. 'Where's the fucking *florist's* number? She riffles through a bundle of papers, then clasps her hair despairingly. 'Clemency!'

'Shall I Google it for you?' I suggest.

'Clemency will Google it. *Clemency!*' Poor Clemency starts so badly, tea slops out of one of the cups.

'I'll take that,' I say hastily, and relieve her of the Costa tray.

'If you could, that *would* be helpful.' Lucinda exhales sharply. 'Because you know, we *are* all here for your benefit,

Poppy. And the wedding *is* only a week away. And there is still an *awful* lot to do.'

'I know,' I say awkwardly. 'Um . . . sorry.'

I have no idea where Magnus and his parents have got to, so I head towards the back of the church, holding the Costa tray full of cups, trying to glide, imagining myself in my veil.

'Ridiculous!' I hear Wanda's muffled voice first. '*Far* too fast.'

I look around uncertainly – then realize it's coming from behind a heavy, closed wooden door to the side of the aisle. They must be in the antechapel.

'Everyone knows . . . Attitude to marriage . . .' That's Magnus speaking – but the door is so thick I can only catch the odd word.

'. . . *not* about marriage *per se*!' Wanda's voice is suddenly raised. '. . . *pair* of you! . . . just *can't* understand . . .'

'*Quite* misguided . . .' Antony's voice is like a bassoon suddenly thundering in.

I'm rooted to the spot, ten yards away from the door, holding the Costa Coffee tray. I know I shouldn't eavesdrop. But I can't stop myself.

'. . . admit it, Magnus . . . complete mistake . . .'

'. . . cancel. Not too late. Better now, than a messy divorce . . .'

I swallow hard. My hands are trembling around the tray. What am I hearing? What was that word, *divorce*?

I'm probably misinterpreting, I tell myself. It's just a few stray words . . . they could mean anything . . .

'*Well, we're getting married whatever you say! So you might as well bloody like it!*' Magnus's voice suddenly soars out, clear as a bell.

A chill settles on me. It's quite hard to find an alternative interpretation of that.

There's some rumbling reply from Antony, then Magnus yells again, '. . . will *not* end in bloody disaster!'

I feel a swell of love for Magnus. He sounds so furious. A moment later there's a rattling at the door and in a flash I backtrack about ten steps. As he emerges, I walk forward again, trying to look relaxed.

'Hi! Cup of tea?' Somehow I manage a natural tone. 'Everything all right? I wondered where you'd got to!'

'Fine.' He smiles affectionately and snakes an arm round my waist.

He's giving no hint that he was just yelling at his parents. I never realized he was such a good actor. He should go into politics.

'I'll take those in to my parents, actually.' He quickly removes the tray from my grasp. 'They're just . . . err . . . looking at the art.'

'Great!' I manage a smile, but my chin is wobbling. They're not looking at the art. They're telling each other what a terrible choice their son has made for a wife. They're making bets that we'll be divorced within a year.

As Magnus emerges from the antechapel again, I take a deep breath, feeling sick with nerves.

'So . . . what do your parents make of all this?' I say as lightly as I can manage. 'I mean, your father's not really into church, is he? Or . . . or . . . marriage, even.'

I've given him the perfect cue to tell me. It's all set up. But Magnus just shrugs sulkily.

'They're OK.'

I sip my tea a few times, staring gloomily at the ancient stone floor, willing myself to pursue the matter. I should contradict him. I should say, 'I heard you arguing just now.' I should have it out with him.

But . . . I can't do it. I'm just not brave enough. I don't want to hear the truth – that his parents think I'm crap.

'Just got to check an email.' Is it my imagination or is Magnus avoiding my gaze?

'Me too.' I peel away from him miserably and go to sit by

myself on a side pew. For a few moments I just sit, shoulders hunched, trying to resist the urge to cry. At last I reach for my phone and switch it on. I might as well catch up with some stuff. I haven't looked at it for hours. As I switch it on, I almost recoil at the number of buzzes and flashes and bleeps which greet me. How many messages have I missed? I quickly text the concierge at the Berrow Hotel, telling him he can call off the search for the ring, and thanking him for his time. Then I turn my attention to the messages.

Top of the pile is a text from Sam, which arrived about twenty minutes ago:

On way to Germany over weekend. Heading to mountainous region. Will be off radar for a bit.

Seeing his name fills me with a longing to talk to someone, and I text back:

Hi there. Sounds cool. Why Germany?

There's no reply, but I don't care, it's cathartic just to type.

So much for fake ring. Did not work. Was found out and now M's parents think I'm a weirdo.

For a moment I wonder whether to tell him that Lucinda had the ring and ask him what he thinks. But . . . no. It's too complicated. He won't want to get into it. I send the text – then realize he might think I'm having a go at him. Quickly I type a follow-up:

Thx for help, anyway. Appreciate it.

Maybe I should have a look at his in-box. I've been neglecting it. There are so many emails with the same subject heading, I find myself squinting at the screen in puzzlement – till it dawns on me. Of course. Everyone's responded to my invitation to send ideas in! These are all the replies!

For the first time this evening, I feel a small glow of pride in myself. If one of these people has come up with a ground-breaking idea and revolutionizes Sam's company, then it will all be down to me.

I click on the first one, full of anticipation.

Dear Sam
I think we should have yoga at lunchtimes, funded by the company, and several others agree with me.
Best
Sally Brewer

I frown uncertainly. It's not exactly what I was expecting, but I suppose yoga *is* a good idea.

OK, next one.

Dear Sam
Thanks for your email. You asked for honesty. The rumour among our department is that this so-called ideas exercise is a weeding-out process. Why not just be honest yourself and tell us if we're going to be fired?
Kind regards
Tony

I blink in astonishment. What?

OK, that's just a ridiculous reaction. He's got to be a nutter. I quickly scroll down to the next one.

Dear Sam
Is there a budget for this 'New Ideas' programme you've launched? A few team leaders are asking.
Thanks
Chris Davies

That's another ridiculous reaction. A *budget*? Who needs a budget for ideas?

Sam
What the fuck is going on? Next time you feel like announcing a new staff initiative would you mind consulting the other Directors?
Malcolm

The next is even more to the point:

Sam
What's this all about? Thanks for the heads-up. Not.
Vicks

I feel a twinge of guilt. It never occurred to me that I might get Sam into trouble with his colleagues. But surely everyone will see the beneficial side as soon as the ideas start flooding in?

Dear Sam
The word is that you're appointing a new 'Ideas Czar'. You may recall that this was *my* idea, which I raised in a department-mental meeting three years ago. I find it a little rich that my initiative has been appropriated, and very much hope that when the appointment is made, I will be at the top of the shortlist.
Otherwise, I fear I will have to make a complaint to a more senior level.
Best
Martin

What? Let's try another one:

Dear Sam
Will we be having a special presentation of all our ideas? Could you please let me know the time limit on a PowerPoint presentation? May we work as teams?
Best wishes
Mandy

There. You see? A brilliant, positive reaction. Teamwork! Presentations! This is fantastic!

Dear Sam
Sorry to bother you again.
If we *don't* want to work in a team after all, will we be penalized? I have fallen out with my team, but now they know all my ideas, which is totally unfair.
Just so you know, *I* had the idea about restructuring the marketing department first. Not Carol.
Best
Mandy

OK. Well, obviously you have to expect a few glitches. It doesn't matter. It's still a positive result . . .

Dear Sam
I'm sorry to do this, but I wish to make a formal complaint about the behaviour of Carol Hanratty.
She has behaved totally unprofessionally in the 'new ideas exercise', and I am forced to take the rest of the day off, due to my great distress. Judy is also too distressed to work for the rest of the day and we are thinking of contacting our union.
Best
Mandy

What? *What?*

Dear Sam
Forgive the long email. You ask for ideas.
Where to start?
I have worked at this company for fifteen years, during which
time a long process of disillusionment has silted up my very
veins, until my mental processes . . .

This guy's email is about fifteen pages long. I drop my
phone into my lap, my jaw slack.

I can't believe all these replies. I never *ever* meant to cause all
this kerfuffle. Why are people so *stupid*? Why do they have to
fight? What on earth have I stirred up?

I've only read the first few emails. There are about thirty
more to go. If I forward all these to Sam, and he steps off the
plane in Germany and gets them in one fell swoop . . . I
suddenly hear his voice again: *Round-robin emails are the work of
the devil.*

And I sent one out in his name. To the whole company.
Without consulting him.

Oh God. I'm really wishing I could go back in time. It
seemed like such a great idea. What was I *thinking*? All I know
is, I can't land this on him out of the blue. I need to explain it
all to him first. Tell him what I was trying to achieve.

My mind is ticking over now. I mean, he's in a plane. He's
off-radar. And it's Friday night, after all. There's no *point* forwarding anything to him. Maybe everyone will have calmed
down by Monday. Yes.

The phone suddenly bleeps with a text and I jump,
startled.

Soon taking off. Anything I need to know about? Sam

I stare at the phone, my heart beating with slight paranoia.
Does he need to know about this right at this very
moment? Does he *need* to?

No. He does not.

Not right now. Have a good trip! Poppy

EIGHT

I don't know what to do about Antony and Wanda and Antechapelgate, as I've named it in my head. So I've done nothing. I've said nothing.

I know I'm avoiding it. I know it's weak. I know I should face the situation. But I can barely even take it in, let alone talk about it. Especially to Magnus.

All weekend, I've given nothing away. I've had dinner with the Tavish family. I've been out for a drink with Ruby and Annalise. I've laughed and talked and exclaimed and joked and had sex. And all the time there's been this little gnawing pain in my chest. I'm almost getting used to it.

If they'd *say* something to me, I might feel better. We could have a stand-up row and I could convince them that I love Magnus and I'm going to support his career and I do have a brain really. But they've said nothing. They've been outwardly charming and pleasant, politely enquiring about our house-hunting plans and offering me glasses of wine.

Which only makes it worse. It confirms that I'm an outsider. I'm not even allowed into the family powwow about how unsuitable this new girlfriend of Magnus's is.

It would even be OK if Magnus hated his parents and didn't respect their views and we could just write them off as loonies. But he does respect them. He likes them. They get on really well. They agree on most things, and when they don't agree it's good-natured and with banter. On every subject.

Every subject except me.

I can't think about it for too long because I get all upset and panicky, so I only allow myself a tiny snippet of worry at a time. I've had my quota for this evening. I sat in a Starbucks after work, nursing a hot chocolate, and got quite morose.

But right now, looking at me, you'd have no idea. I'm dressed up in my best LBD and high heels. My make-up is immaculate. My eyes are sparkling. (Two cocktails.) I caught a glimpse of myself in a mirror just now, and I look like a care-free girl, wearing an engagement ring, drinking Cosmos at the Savoy, with nothing to worry about.

And to be truthful, my mood *is* a lot better than it was. Partly because of the cocktails and partly because I'm so thrilled to be here. I've never been to the Savoy in my life before. It's amazing!

The party is in a stunning room with panelling and spectacular chandeliers everywhere and waiters handing round cocktails on trays. A jazz band is playing, and all around, smartly dressed people are chatting in clusters. There are lots of back-slaps and handshakes and high-fives going on, and everyone seems in a great mood. I don't know a single person, obviously, but I'm happy just to watch. Every time someone notices me standing on my own and starts to approach, I get out my phone to check my messages, and they turn away again.

This is the great thing about a phone. It's like an escort.

Lucinda keeps texting, telling me how she's in north London, looking at another variety of grey silk, and do I have any thoughts on texture? Magnus has texted from Warwick about some research trip he's cooking up with a professor there. Meanwhile I'm having quite a long conversation with Ruby about the blind date she's on. The only thing is, it's quite hard to text and hold a cocktail at the same time, so at last I put my Cosmo down on a nearby table and fire off some replies:

> Sure the grey slub silk will be fine. Thanks so much!! Love Poppy xxxxx

> Sounds fab, can I come too?! P xxxxx

> I don't think ordering two steaks is necessarily creepy . . . maybe he is on Atkins diet??? Keep me posted! P xxxxx

There are screeds of emails for Sam, too. Loads more people have replied to the new-ideas request. Many have enclosed long attachments and CVs. There are even a couple of videos. People must have been busy over the weekend. I wince as I catch sight of one entitled '1,001 Ideas for WGC – Part 1' and avert my eyes.

What I was *hoping* was that everything would calm down over the weekend and people would forget all about it. But at about 8 a.m. this morning, the avalanche of emails began, and they still keep flying back and forth. There are continued rumours that this is all some big audition for a job. There's a bitter dispute about which department had the idea of expanding to the States first. Malcolm keeps sending tetchy emails asking who approved this initiative and the whole thing is basically mayhem. Don't these people have *lives*?

It makes me hyperventilate slightly whenever I think about it. So I have a new coping technique: I'm not. It can wait till tomorrow.

And so can Willow's most recent email to Sam. I've now decided she must not only have supermodel good looks, but be amazing in bed *and* a gazillionairess, to make up for her foul temper.

159

Today she's sent him yet another long, tedious rant, saying that she wants Sam to find her a special brand of German exfoliator while he's over there, but he probably won't bother and that's just like him, after all that pâté she dragged back from France for him, it made her gag but she still did it, but that's the kind of person she is and he could really learn from that, but has he EVER wanted to learn from her? HAS HE???

Honestly. She does my head in.

I'm scrolling back up the endless stack of emails when one grabs my attention. It's from Adrian Foster, in marketing.

Dear Sam
Thanks for agreeing to present Lindsay's birthday flowers to her – they've arrived at last! As you weren't around today I've put them in your room. They're in water, so they should keep all right.
Best
Adrian

It wasn't actually Sam who agreed to present the flowers. It was me, on behalf of Sam.

Now I feel less confident this was a good idea. What if he's frantically busy tomorrow? What if he gets pissed off that he has to take time out of his schedule to go and present flowers? How could I make this easier for him?

I hesitate for a moment then quickly type an email to Lindsay.

Hi Lindsay
I want to give you something in my office. Something you'll like. ☺ Stop by tomorrow. Any time.
Sam xxxxx

I press Send without re-reading it and take a swig of Cosmo. For about twenty seconds I'm relaxed, savouring my drink, wondering when the canapés will start to arrive. Then, as though an alarm clock has gone off, I start.

Wait. I put kisses after Sam's name. I shouldn't have done that. People don't put kisses on professional emails.

Shit. I retrieve the email and re-read it, wincing. I'm just so used to kisses, they popped out automatically. But Sam never puts kisses. Ever.

Should I somehow try to *un*-send the kisses?

Dear Lindsay, Just to clarify, I did not mean to add kisses just now . . .

No. Awful. I'll have to leave it. I'm probably overreacting, anyway. She probably won't even notice—

Oh God. An email reply has already arrived from Lindsay. That was quick. I click it open and stare at the message.

See you then, Sam.
Lindsay xx ;)

Two kisses and a winky face. Is that normal?

I stare at it for a few moments, trying to convince myself that it is.

Yes. Yes, I think that's normal. It could definitely be normal. Just friendly office correspondence.

I put my phone away, drain my drink and look around for another. There's a waitress standing a few yards away and I start to thread my way through the crowds.

'. . . policy Sam Roxton's idea?' A man's voice attracts my attention. 'Fucking *ludicrous*.'

'You know Sam . . .'

I stop dead, pretending to fiddle with my phone. A group of men in suits has paused near me. They're all younger than Sam and very well dressed. They must be his colleagues.

I wonder if I can match the faces to the emails. I bet that one with the olive skin is Justin Cole, who sent the round robin telling everyone that casual dressing on Fridays was *compulsory* and could everyone please do it with *style*? He looks like the fashion police, in his black suit and skinny tie.

'Is he here?' says a blond guy.

'Haven't seen him,' replies the olive-skinned man, draining a shot glass.[66] 'Stubborn fuck.'

My head jerks in surprise. Well, *that's* not very nice.

My phone bleeps with a text and I click on it, grateful to have something to occupy my fingers. Ruby has sent me a photo of some brown hair, with the message:

Is this a toupee???

I can't suppress a snort of laughter. Somehow she's managed to snap a photo of her date's head from behind. How did she manage that? Didn't he notice?

I squint at the picture. It looks like normal hair to me. I've no idea why Ruby's so obsessed by toupees, anyway. Just because of that one disastrous blind date she had last year, where the guy turned out to be fifty-nine, not thirty-nine.[67]

Don't think so. Looks fine! xxxxxx

As I look up, the men who were talking have moved away, into the crowd. Damn. I was quite intrigued by that conversation.

I take another Cosmo, and a few delicious pieces of sushi (already this evening would have cost me about fifty quid if I was paying for it), and am about to head over towards the jazz band when I hear the screechy sound of a microphone being turned on. I swivel round – and it's only about five feet away on a small podium, which I hadn't noticed. A blonde girl in a black trouser suit taps the microphone and says, 'Ladies

---

66. Where did he get that? Why has nobody offered me a shot?

67. He claimed it was a typo. Yeah, I'm sure his finger just happened to slip two spaces to the left.

and gentlemen. May I have your attention, please?' After a moment, she says more loudly, 'People! It's time for the speeches! The quicker we start, the quicker they're over, OK?'

There's general laughter and the crowd starts to move towards this end of the room. I'm being pushed straight towards the podium, which is *really* not where I want to be – but I don't have much choice.

'So, here we are!' The blonde woman spreads her arms. 'Welcome to this celebration of the merger of ourselves, Johnson Ellison and the wonderful Greene Retail. This is a marriage of hearts and minds as much as companies, and we have many, *many* people to thank. Our MD, Patrick Gowan, showed the initial vision which led to us standing here now. Patrick, get up here!'

A bearded guy in a pale suit walks on to the podium, smiling modestly and shaking his head, and everyone starts clapping, including me.

'Keith Burnley . . . what can I say? He's been an inspiration to us all.'

The trouble with standing right at the front of the crowd is that you feel really conspicuous. I'm trying to listen attentively and look interested, but none of these names mean anything to me. Maybe I should have done some homework. I surreptitiously get my phone out and wonder if I can discreetly find the email about the merger.

'And I know he's here somewhere . . .' She's looking around, shading her eyes. 'He tried to wriggle out of coming tonight, but we had to have the man himself here, Mr White Globe Consulting, Sam Roxton!'

My head jerks up in shock. No. That can't be right, he can't be—

Fuck.

Fresh applause breaks out as Sam strides on to the podium, wearing a dark suit and a slight frown. I'm so stunned I can't even move. He was in Germany. He wasn't coming tonight. What's he *doing* here?

From the way his face jolts in surprise as he sees me, I guess he's wondering the same thing.

I am so busted. *Why* did I think I could get away with gate-crashing a big posh party like this?

My face is flaming with embarrassment. I quickly try to back away, but the mass of people pressing behind me is too heavy, so I'm stuck, staring mutely up at him.

'. . . when Sam's in the room you know things will reach a resolution,' the blonde woman is saying. 'Whether it's the resolution you *want* . . . eh, Charles?' There's a roar of laughter around the room, and I hastily join in with fake gusto. Clearly this is a massive in-joke, which I would know about if I weren't a gatecrasher.

The guy next to me turns and exclaims, 'She's a bit near the knuckle there!' and I find myself replying, 'I know, I know!' and giving another huge phoney laugh.

'Which brings me to another key player . . .'

As I lift my eyes, Sam is looking nowhere near me, thank God. This is excruciating enough as it is.

'Let's hear it for Jessica Garnett!'

As a girl in red steps on to the podium, Sam takes his phone out of his pocket and unobtrusively taps at it. A moment later a text bleeps in my phone.

Why were you laughing?

I feel a stab of mortification. He must know I was just trying to blend in. He's deliberately winding me up. Well, I'm not going to rise to the bait.

It was a good joke.

I watch as Sam checks his phone again. His face only

twitches the tiniest bit but I know he got it. He types again briefly – then a moment later my phone bleeps again.

I didn't know your name was on my invitation.

I glance up in trepidation, trying to gauge his expression, but again he's looking in the other direction, his face impassive. I think for a moment, then type:

Just stopped by to collect your goody bag for you. All part of the service. No need to thank me.

And my cocktails, I see.

Now he's looking right at my Cosmo. He raises his eyebrows and I suppress an urge to giggle.

I was going to put them in a hipflask for you. Obviously.

Obviously. Although mine's a Manhattan.

Ah, well now I know. I'll chuck all those Tequila shots I had saved up.

As he clocks this last message, Sam looks up from his phone and flashes me that sudden smile. Without meaning to I find myself beaming back, and even catch my breath a little. It really *does* something to me, that smile of his. It's disconcerting. It's . . .

Anyway. Concentrate on the speech.

'. . . and finally, have a great night tonight! Thanks, everyone!'

As a final round of applause breaks out, I try to find an escape route, but there isn't one. Within approximately ten seconds, Sam has stepped straight down off the podium and is standing in front of me.

'Oh.' I try to hide my discomfiture. 'Er . . . hi. Fancy seeing you here!'

He doesn't reply but just looks at me quizzically. There's no point trying to brazen this out.

'OK, I'm sorry,' I say in a rush. 'I know I shouldn't be here, it's just I've never been to the Savoy, and it sounded so amazing, and you didn't want to go, and—' I break off as he lifts a hand, looking amused.

'It's no problem. You should have told me you wanted to come. I would have put you on the list.'

'Oh!' The wind is taken out of my sails. 'Well . . . thanks. I'm having a really nice time.'

'Good.' He smiles and takes a glass of red wine from a passing waiter's tray. 'You know what?' He pauses thoughtfully, cradling his glass in his hands. 'I have something to say, Poppy Wyatt. I should have said it before. And that's "thank you". You've been a great help to me, these past few days.'

'It's fine, really. No problem.' I hurriedly make a brushing-off motion, but he shakes his head.

'No, listen, I want to say this. I know originally I was doing you the favour – but in the end, you've done me one. I haven't had any proper PA support at work. You've done a great job, keeping me up to date with everything. I appreciate it.'

'Honestly, it's nothing!' I say, feeling uncomfortable.

'Take the credit!' He laughs, then shrugs off his jacket and loosens his tie. 'Jesus, it's been a long day.' He slings his jacket over his shoulder and takes a gulp of wine. 'So, nothing up today? The airwaves have gone very quiet.' He gives another of those devastating little smiles. 'Or are all my emails coming through to Jane now?'

My phone contains 243 emails for him. And they're still coming in.

'Well . . .' I take a gulp of Cosmo, desperately playing for time. 'Funnily enough, you did get a *few* messages. I thought I wouldn't disturb you while you were in Germany.'

'Oh yes?' He looks interested. 'What?'

'Um . . . this and that. Or would you rather wait till tomorrow?' I clutch at a last hope.

'No, tell me now.'

I rub my nose. Where do I start?

'Sam! There you are!' A thin guy in glasses is approaching. He's blinking quite fast and holding a large black portfolio under his arms. 'They said you weren't coming tonight.'

'I wasn't,' Sam says wryly.

'Great. Great!' The thin guy is twitching with nervous energy. 'Well, I brought these along on the off-chance.' He thrusts the portfolio at Sam, who takes it, looking bemused. 'If you have a moment tonight, I'll be staying up till two or three, always happy to Skype from home . . . A *bit* radical, some of it, but . . . Anyway! I think it's a great thing you're doing. And if there *is* a job opportunity behind all this . . . count me in. Right. Well . . . I won't keep you any longer. Thanks, Sam!' He darts away again into the crowd.

For a moment neither of us speaks. Sam because he looks too baffled and me because I'm trying to work out what to say.

'What was all that about?' says Sam at last. 'Do you have any idea? Is there something I've missed?'

I lick my dry lips nervously. 'There *was* something I meant to tell you about.' I give a high-pitched laugh. 'It's quite funny actually, if you see it that way—'

'Sam!' A large woman with a booming voice interrupts me. '*So* delighted we've got you signed up for the Fun Run!' Oh my God. This must be Rachel.

'Fun Run?' Sam echoes the words as though they're complete anathema to him. 'No. Sorry, Rachel. I don't do Fun Runs. I'm happy to donate, let other people do the running, good for them . . .'

'But your email!' She stares at him. 'We were so thrilled you wanted to take part! No one could believe it! This year, we're all running in superhero costumes,' she adds enthusiastically. 'I've earmarked a Superman one for you.'

'Email?' Sam looks bewildered. 'What email?'

'That lovely email you sent! Friday, was it? Oh, and *bless* you for the e-card you sent young Chloe.' Rachel lowers her voice and pats Sam on the hand. 'She was so touched. Most directors wouldn't even *care* if an assistant's dog had died, so for you to send such a lovely e-card of condolence, with a poem and everything . . .' She opens her eyes wide. 'Well. We were all amazed, to be honest!'

My face is getting hotter. I'd forgotten about the e-card.

'An e-card of condolence for a dog,' says Sam at last, in a strange voice. 'Yes, I'm pretty amazed at myself.'

He's staring straight at me. It's not the most friendly of expressions. In fact, I feel like backing away, only there's nowhere to go.

'Oh, Loulou!' Rachel suddenly waves a hand across the room. 'Do excuse me, Sam . . .' She heads off, pushing her way through the throng, leaving us alone.

There's silence. Sam regards me evenly, without a flicker. He's waiting for me to start, I realize.

'I thought . . .' I swallow hard.

'Yes?' His voice is curt and unforgiving.

'I thought you might *like* to do a Fun Run.'

'You did.'

'Yes. I did.' My voice is a little husky with nerves. 'I mean . . . they're fun! So I thought I'd reply. Just to save you time.'

'You wrote an email and signed it as *me*?' He sounds thunderous.

'I was trying to help!' I say hurriedly. 'I knew you didn't have time, and they kept asking you, and I thought—'

'The e-card was you too, I take it?' He shuts his eyes briefly. 'Jesus. Is there anything *else* you've been meddling in?'

I want to bury my head like an ostrich. But I can't. I have to tell him, quickly, before anyone else accosts him.

'OK, I had this . . . this other idea,' I say, my voice barely above a whisper. 'Only, everyone got a bit carried away, and now everyone's emailing about it, and they think there's a job involved—'

'A job?' He stares at me. 'What are you talking about?'

'Sam.' A guy claps him on the back as he passes. 'Glad you're interested in coming to Iceland. I'll be in touch.'

'*Iceland?*' Sam's face jerks in shock.

I'd forgotten about accepting the Iceland trip, too.[68] But I only have time to make another apologetic smile before someone else is accosting Sam.

'Sam, OK, I don't know what's going on.' It's a girl with glasses and a very intense way of speaking. 'I don't know if you're playing us for fools, or what . . .' She seems a bit stressed out and keeps pushing her hair back off her brow. 'Anyway. Here's my CV. You *know* how many ideas I've had for this company, but if we all have to keep jumping through even *more* bloody hoops, then . . . whatever, Sam. Your call.'

'Elena . . .' Sam breaks off in bafflement.

'Just read my personal statement. It's all in there.' She stalks off.

There's a silent beat, then Sam wheels round, his face so ominous I feel a quailing inside.

'Start from the beginning. What did you do?'

'I sent an email.' I scuff my foot, feeling like a naughty child. 'From you.'

'To whom?'

'Everyone in the company.' I cringe as I say the words. 'I just wanted everyone to feel . . . encouraged and positive. So I said everyone should send their ideas in. To you.'

'You *wrote* that? Under *my name?*'

68. Doesn't everyone want to go to Iceland? Why would you say no to Iceland?

He looks so livid I actually back away, feeling a bit petrified.

'I'm sorry,' I say breathlessly, 'I thought it was a good idea. But some people thought you were trying to sack them, and other people think you're secretly interviewing for a job, and everyone's got into a tizz about it . . . I'm sorry,' I end lamely.

'Sam, I got your email!' A girl with a ponytail interrupts us eagerly. 'So, I'll see you at dance classes.'

'Wh—' Sam's eyes swivel in his head.

'Thanks *so* much for the support. Actually, you're my only pupil so far! Bring comfortable clothes and soft shoes, OK?'

I glance at Sam and gulp at his expression. He seems literally unable to speak. What's wrong with dance classes? He's going to need to dance at his wedding, isn't he? He should be *grateful* I signed him up.

'Sounds great!' I say encouragingly.

'See you next Tuesday evening, Sam!'

As she disappears into the hubbub, I fold my arms defensively, all ready to tell him that I've done him a huge favour. But as he turns back, his face is so stony, I lose my nerve.

'Exactly how many emails have you sent in my name?' He sounds calm, but not in a good way.

'I . . . not many,' I flounder. 'I mean . . . just a few. I only wanted to help—'

'If you were my PA I'd have you fired on the spot and quite possibly prosecuted.' He spits the words out as though he's a machine gun. 'As it is, I can only ask for my phone back and request that you—'

'Sam! Thank God for a friendly face!'

'Nick.' Sam's demeanour instantly changes. His eyes light up and his icy expression seems to melt. 'Good to see you. I didn't know you were coming.'

A man in his sixties, wearing a pinstriped suit over a groovy floral shirt, is raising a glass to us. I raise mine back, feeling awestruck. Sir Nicholas Murray! When I was Googling the company I saw pictures of him with the Prime Minister, and Prince Charles, and everybody.

'Never turn down a bash, if I can help it,' Sir Nicholas says cheerfully. 'Missed the speeches, have I?'

'Spot-on timing.' Sam grins. 'Don't tell me you sent your driver in to see if they were over.'

'I couldn't possibly comment.' Sir Nicholas winks at him. 'Did you get my email?'

'Did you get *mine*?' counters Sam, and lowers his voice. 'You've nominated Richard Doherty for this year's Dealmaker Award?'

'He's a bright young talent, Sam,' says Sir Nicholas, looking a little caught out. 'Remember his work with Hardwicks last year? He deserves recognition.'

'*You* put the FSS Energy deal together. Not him.'

'He helped,' Sir Nicholas retorts. 'He helped in many ways. Some of them . . . intangible.'

For a moment they stare at each other. They both look as though they're suppressing laughter.

'You're incorrigible,' says Sam at last. 'I hope he's grateful. Now, you know I'm just back from Germany? Few things we should discuss.'

He's totally frozen me out of the conversation, but I really don't mind. Really. In fact, maybe I'll just creep away while I have the chance.

'Sam, do introduce me to your friend.' Sir Nicholas cuts into my thoughts, and I smile back nervously.

Sam obviously has no desire at all to introduce me to Sir Nicholas. But he's obviously also a polite man, because after about thirty seconds of what is clearly an internal struggle,[69] he says, 'Sir Nicholas, Poppy Wyatt. Poppy, Sir Nicholas Murray.'

'How do you do.' I shake his hand, trying not to give away my excitement. Wow. Me and Sir Nicholas Murray. Chatting at

---

69. So not *that* polite.

the Savoy. I'm already thinking of ways I could casually drop this into conversation with Antony.

'Are you at Johnson Ellison or Greene Retail?' enquires Sir Nicholas politely.

'Neither,' I say awkwardly. 'Actually, I'm a physiotherapist.'

'A physiotherapist!' His face lights up. 'How wonderful! The most underrated of all the medical arts, I always think. I've been going to a super man in Harley Street for my back, although he hasn't *quite* cracked it . . .' He winces slightly.

'You want Ruby,' I say, nodding wisely. 'My boss. She's amazing. Her deep-tissue massage makes grown men *weep*.'

'I see.' Sir Nicholas looks interested. 'Do you have a card?'

Yessss! Ruby made us all cards when we first started out, and I have never been asked for mine before. Not once.

'Here you are.' I reach in my bag and produce a card nonchalantly, as though I do it all the time. 'We're in Balham. It's south of the river, you may not know it . . .'

'I know Balham well.' He twinkles at me. 'My first flat in London was on Bedford Hill.'

'No way!' My canapé nearly falls out of my mouth. 'Well, you'll definitely have to come and see us now.'

I can't believe it. Sir Nicholas Murray, living on Bedford Hill. God, it just shows. You start off in Balham and you end up knighted. It's quite inspiring, really.

'Sir Nicholas.' The guy with olive skin has materialized from nowhere to join the group. 'Delighted to see you here. Always a pleasure. How are things going at Number Ten? Found the secret to happiness yet?'

'The wheels turn.' Sir Nicholas gives him an easy smile.

'Well, it's an honour. Absolute honour. And Sam.' The olive-skinned guy claps him on the back. 'My main man. Couldn't do what we do without you.'

I stare at him indignantly. He was calling Sam a 'stubborn fuck' a moment ago.

'Thanks, Justin.' Sam smiles tightly.

It *is* Justin Cole. I was right. He looks as sneery in real life as he does in his emails.

I'm about to ask Sir Nicholas what the Prime Minister's really like, when a young guy approaches us nervously.

'Sam! Sorry to interrupt. I'm Matt Mitchell. Thanks *so* much for volunteering. It's going to make such a difference to our project to have you on board.'

'Volunteering?' Sam shoots a sharp look at me.

Oh God. I have no idea. My mind is working overtime, trying to recall. Volunteering . . . volunteering . . . what was it again . . .

'For the expedition to Guatemala! The exchange programme!' Matt Mitchell is glowing. 'We're so excited that you want to sign up!'

My stomach flips over. Guatemala. I'd *totally* forgotten about Guatemala.

'Guatemala?' echoes Sam, with a kind of rictus smile on his face.

Now I remember. I sent that email quite late at night. I think I'd had a glass of wine or two. Or . . . three.

I risk a tiny peek at Sam, and his expression is so thunderous, I want to slink away. But the thing is, it sounded like an amazing opportunity. And from what I've seen of his diary, he never takes a holiday. He *should* go to Guatemala.

'We were all really touched by your email, Sam.' Matt grasps Sam's hand earnestly in both of his. 'I never knew you felt that way about the developing world. *How* many orphans do you sponsor?'

'Sam! Oh my God!' A dark-haired girl, quite drunk, lurches up to the group and elbows Matt out of the way, making him drop Sam's hand. She's looking highly flushed and her mascara is smudged, and she grabs Sam's hand herself. 'Thank you *so much* for your e-card about Scamper. You made my day, you know that?'

'It's quite all right, Chloe,' Sam says tightly. He darts an incandescent glance of fury at me, and I flinch.

'Those beautiful things you wrote,' she gulps. 'I knew when I read them you must have lost a dog yourself. Because you understand, don't you? You *understand*.' A tear suddenly rolls down her cheek.

'Chloe, do you want to sit down?' says Sam, extricating his hand, but Justin cuts in, a malicious grin playing on his lips.

'I've heard about this famous e-card. Could I see it?'

'I've got a print-out.' Wiping her nose, Chloe drags a crumpled piece of paper from her pocket, and Justin immediately grabs it.

'Oh, now, this is beautiful, Sam,' he says, scanning it with mock admiration. 'Very moving.'

'I've shown everybody in the department.' Chloe nods, tearfully. 'They all think you're *amazing*, Sam.'

Sam's hand is clenching his glass so hard, it's turning white. He looks like he wants to press an ejector button and escape. I'm feeling really, really bad now. I didn't realize I'd sent *quite* so many emails. I'd forgotten about Guatemala. And I shouldn't have sent the e-card. If I could go back in time, that's the moment I'd go up to myself and say, 'Poppy! Stop! No e-card!'

'"Young Scamper's joined his friends in heaven, but we are left to weep,"' Justin reads aloud in a stagy voice. '"His furry fur, his eyes so bright, his bone upon the seat."' Justin pauses. 'Not sure "seat" exactly rhymes with "weep", Sam. And why is his bone on the seat, anyway? Hardly hygienic.'

'Give that here.' Sam makes a swipe for it, but Justin dodges, looking delighted.

'"His blanket empty in his bed, the silence in the air. If Scamper now is looking down, he'll know how much we cared."' Justin winces. '"Air"? "Cared"? Do you know what a rhyme *is*, Sam?'

'I think it's very touching,' says Sir Nicholas cheerfully.

'Me too,' I say hurriedly. 'I think it's brilliant.'[70]

'It's so true.' Tears are now streaming down Chloe's face. 'It's beautiful because it's *true*.'

She's absolutely plastered. She's completely fallen out of one of her stilettos and doesn't even seem to have noticed.

'Justin,' says Sir Nicholas kindly. 'Maybe you could get Chloe a glass of water?'

'Of course!' Justin deftly pockets the sheet. 'You don't mind if I keep this poem of yours, do you, Sam? It's just so *special*. Have you ever thought of working for Hallmark?' He escorts Chloe away and practically dumps her on a chair. A moment later I see him gleefully beckoning to the group he was with earlier, and pulling the paper out of his pocket.

I almost don't dare look at Sam, I feel so guilty.

'Well!' says Sir Nicholas, looking amused. 'Sam, I had no idea you were such an animal-lover.'

'I'm not . . .' Sam seems barely able to operate his voice. 'I . . .'

I'm trying frantically to think of something I can say to redeem the situation. But what can I do?

'Now, Poppy, please do excuse me.' Sir Nicholas cuts into my thoughts again. 'Much as I would prefer to stay here, I must go over and talk to that *interminably* boring man from Greene Retail.' He makes such a comical face at me, I can't help giggling. 'Sam, we'll talk later.' He presses my hand in his and heads off into the crowd, and I quell an urge to run away with him.

'So!' I turn back to Sam and swallow several times. 'Um . . . sorry about all that.'

Sam says nothing, just holds out his hand, palm up. After five seconds I realize what he means.

'*What?*' I feel a swoop of alarm. 'No! I mean . . . can't I keep

---

70. OK, I know it's not brilliant. In my defence I chose it in a hurry from some e-card site, and the picture was really good. It was a line drawing of an empty dog basket and it nearly made *me* cry.

it till tomorrow? I've got all my contacts on it now, all my messages . . .'

'Give it.'

'But I haven't even been to the phone shop yet! I haven't got a replacement, this is my only number, I *need* it—'

'Give it.'

He's implacable. In fact, he looks quite scary.

On the other hand . . . he can't *force* it off me, can he? Not without causing a scene, which I'm sensing is the last thing he wants to do.

'Look, I know you're angry.' I try to sound as grovelly as possible. 'I can understand that. But wouldn't you like me to forward all your emails first? And give it back tomorrow when I've tied up all the loose ends? Please?'

At least that'll give me a chance to make a note of some of my messages.

Sam is breathing hard through his nose. I can tell he's realizing he doesn't have a choice.

'You don't send a single further email,' he snaps at last, dropping his hand.

'OK,' I say humbly.

'You detail for me a list of the emails you *did* send.'

'OK.'

'You hand the phone back tomorrow and that is the last I ever hear from you.'

'Shall I come to the office?'

'No!' He almost recoils at the idea. 'We'll meet at lunchtime. I'll text you.'

'OK.' I heave a sigh, feeling quite downcast by now. 'I'm sorry. I didn't mean to mess up your life.'

I was half-hoping Sam might say something nice like, 'Don't worry, you didn't' or 'Never mind, you meant well.' But he doesn't. He looks as merciless as ever.

'Is there anything else I should know about?' he asks curtly. 'Be honest, please. Any more foreign trips you've signed me up to? Company initiatives you've started in my name? Inappropriate poetry you've written on my behalf?'

'No!' I say nervously. 'That's it. I'm sure.'

'You realize how much havoc you've caused?'

'I know.' I gulp.

'You realize how many embarrassing situations you've put me in?'

'I'm sorry, I'm really sorry,' I say desperately. 'I didn't mean to embarrass you. I didn't mean to create trouble. I thought I was doing you a favour.'

'A favour?' He stares at me incredulously. 'A *favour*?'

'Hey, Sam.' A breathy voice interrupts us, and I get a waft of perfume. I turn to see a girl in her late twenties, wearing sky-scraper heels and lots of make-up. Her red hair is tonged into curls and her dress is *really* low-cut. I mean, I can practically see her navel. 'Excuse me, could I have a quick moment with Sam?' She shoots me an antagonistic glance.

'Oh! Err . . . sure.' I move away a few steps, but not so far that I can't just about hear them.

'So. Can't wait to see you tomorrow.' She's gazing up at Sam and batting her false eyelashes.[71] 'In your office. I'll be there.'

Sam looks perplexed. 'Do we have an appointment?'

'That's the way you want to play it?' She gives a soft, sexy laugh and swooshes her hair, like actresses do on those American TV drama series set in beautiful kitchens. 'I can play it any way you like.' She lowers her voice to a throaty whisper. 'If you know what I mean, Sam.'

'I'm sorry, Lindsay . . .' Sam frowns, obviously at a loss.

Lindsay? I nearly spill my drink down my dress. This girl is Lindsay?

Oh no. Oh no, oh no. This isn't good. I knew I should have cancelled out Sam's kisses. I knew that winky face meant

---

71. What *is* the etiquette when someone's false eyelash is coming off a bit at the edge? Tell them or politely ignore?

something. I'm almost hopping with alarm. Can I warn Sam? Should I somehow semaphore to him?

'I knew,' she's murmuring now. 'The first time I saw you, Sam, I knew there was a special vibe between us. You're *hot*.'

Sam looks disconcerted. 'Well ... thanks. I guess. But Lindsay, this really isn't—'

'Oh, don't worry. I can be very discreet.' She runs a lacquered nail gently down his shirt. 'I'd almost given up on you, you know that?'

Sam takes a step backwards, looking alarmed. 'Lindsay—'

'All this time, no signs – then out of the blue you start contacting me.' She opens her eyes wide. 'Wishing me Happy Birthday, complimenting my work ... I knew what that was really about. And then tonight . . .' Lindsay moves even closer to Sam, speaking even more breathily. 'You have no idea what it did to me, seeing your email. Mmm. Bad boy.'

'*Email?*' echoes Sam. He slowly turns his head to meet my agonized gaze.

I should have run. While I had the chance. I should have run.

NINE

I am the sorriest sorry person there ever was.

I really screwed up. I can see that now. I've caused Sam a whole load of work and aggro and I've abused his trust and been a complete pain in the neck.

Today was supposed to be a fun day. A weddingy day. I've got the rest of this week booked off work for last-minute wedding preparations – and what am I doing instead? Trying to think of all the different words for 'sorry' that I can.

As I arrive for lunch I'm wearing a suitably penitent grey T-shirt and denim skirt combo. We're meeting at a restaurant round the corner from his office, and the first thing I see when I walk in is a group of girls I remember from the Savoy last night, clustered round a circular table. I'm sure they wouldn't recognize me, but I duck hurriedly past, anyway.

Sam described this as 'a second office cafeteria' on the phone. Some cafeteria. There are steel tables and taupe linen-covered chairs and one of those cool menus where everything's in lower case and each dish is described in the minimal amount of words.[72]

72. 'soup', 'duck', etc. Which I know looks all cool and streamlined, but what *sort* of soup? What *sort* of duck?

There aren't even any pound signs.[73] No wonder Sam likes it.

I've ordered some water and am trying to decide between soup and salad, when Sam appears at the door. Immediately all the girls start waving him over, and after a moment's hesitation, he joins them. I can't hear all the conversation, but I catch the odd word: '. . . amazing idea . . .', '. . . excited . . .' '. . . so supportive . . .'. Everyone's smiling and looking positive, even Sam.

Eventually he makes his excuses and heads over towards me.

'Hi. You made it.' No smile for *me*, I notice.

'Yes. Nice restaurant. Thanks for meeting me. I really appreciate it.' I'm trying to be as mollifying as possible.

'I practically live here.' He shrugs. 'Everyone at WGC does.'

'So . . . here's a list of all the emails I sent in your name.' I want to get this over with straight away. As I hand him the sheet I can't help wincing. It looks such a lot, written down. 'And I've forwarded everything.'

A waiter interrupts me with a jug of water and a 'Welcome back, sir' to Sam, then beckons over a waitress with the bread basket. As they leave, Sam folds my sheet and pockets it without comment. Thank God. I thought he was going to go through it item by item, like a headmaster.

'Those girls are from your company, aren't they?' I nod at the circular table. 'What were they talking about?'

There's a pause as Sam pours himself some water – then he looks up. 'They were talking about your project, as it happens.'

I stare at him. '*My* project? You mean, my email about ideas?'

'Yes. It's gone down well in Admin.'

'Wow!' I let myself bask in this thought for a moment. 'So . . . not *everyone* reacted badly.'

73. Isn't that illegal? What if I wanted to pay in dollars? Would they have to let me?

'Not everyone, no.'

'Has anyone come up with any good ideas for the company?'

'As it happens . . . yes,' he says grudgingly. 'Some interesting thoughts have emerged.'

'Wow! Great!'

'Though I still have several people convinced there's a conspiracy to sack everyone, and one threatening legal action.'

'Oh.' I feel chastened. 'Right. Sorry about that.'

'Hello.' A cheerful girl in a green apron approaches. 'May I explain the menu?[74] We have a butternut squash soup today, made with an organic chicken stock . . .'

She goes through each item and, needless to say, I stop concentrating immediately. So by the end I have no idea what's available except butternut squash soup.

'Butternut squash soup, please.' I smile.

'Steak baguette, rare, and a green salad. Thanks.' I don't think Sam was listening either. He checks something on his phone and frowns, and I feel a pang of guilt. I must have really increased his workload with all this.

'I just want to say, I'm really, really sorry,' I say in a rush. 'I'm sorry about the e-card. I'm sorry about Guatemala. I got carried away. I know I've caused you a lot of grief and if I can help in any way I will. I mean . . . shall I send some emails for you?'

'No!' Sam sounds like he's been scalded. 'Thank you,' he adds more calmly. 'You've done enough.'

'So, how are you managing?' I venture. 'I mean, processing everyone's ideas.'

'Jane's taken charge for now. She's sending out my brush-off email.'

I wrinkle my nose. 'Your "brush-off email"? What's that?'

'You know the sort of thing. "Sam is delighted to have

---

74. OK, this is ridiculous. You write a menu which no one understands and then you pay someone to explain it.

received your email. He'll get back to you as soon as he possibly can. Meanwhile thanks for your interest." Translation: "Don't expect to hear from me any time soon."' He raises his eyebrows. 'You must have a brush-off email. They come in pretty useful for fending off unwanted advances too.'

'No, I don't,' I say, a little offended. 'I never want to brush people off. I answer them!'

'OK, that explains a *lot*.' He tears off a chunk of bread and chews it. 'If I'd known that, I would never have agreed to share a phone.'

'Well, you don't have to any more.'

'Thank God. Where is it?'

I rummage in my bag, take the phone out and put it on the table between us.

'What the hell is *that*?' Sam exclaims, looking horrified.

'What?' I follow his gaze, puzzled, then realize. There were some diamanté phone stickers in the Marie Curie goody bag, and I stuck them on the phone the other day.

'Don't worry.' I roll my eyes at his expression. 'They come off.'

'They'd better.' He still seems stunned by the sight of it. Honestly. Doesn't anyone at his company bother to decorate their phone?

Our food arrives and for a while we're distracted with peppermills and mustard and some side dish of parsnip chips which they seem to think we ordered.

'You in a hurry?' enquires Sam as he's about to bite into his steak baguette.

'No. I took a few days off to do wedding stuff, but actually it turns out there's not a lot to do.'

The truth is, I was a bit taken aback when I spoke to Lucinda this morning. I'd told her *ages* ago that I was taking a few days off to help with the wedding. I'd thought we could go and sort out some of the fun stuff together. But she basically said no thanks. She had some long story about having to go and see the florist in Northwood and needing to drop in at another client first and basically implied I'd be in the way.[75] So I've had the morning off. I mean, I wasn't about to go to work just for the sake of it.

As I sip my soup I wait for Sam to volunteer some wedding talk of his own – but he doesn't. Men just aren't into it, are they?

'Is your soup cold?' Sam suddenly focuses on my bowl. 'If it's cold, send it back.'

It *is* a bit less than piping hot – but I really don't feel like making a fuss.

'It's fine, thanks.' I flash him a smile and take another mouthful.

The phone suddenly buzzes, and on reflex I pull it to me. It's Lucinda, telling me she's at the florist's and could I please confirm that I only want four strands of gypsophila per bouquet?

I have no idea. Why would I specify something like that? What does four strands look like, anyway?

Yes fine. Thanks so much Lucinda, I really appreciate it! Not long now!!! Love Poppy xxxxx

There's a new email from Willow, too, but I can't bring myself to read it in front of Sam. I forward it quickly and put the phone down.

'There was a message from Willow just now.'

'Uh-huh.' He nods with an off-putting frown.

I'm *dying* to find out more about her. But how do I start without sounding unnatural?

I can't even ask, 'How did you meet?' because I already know, from one of her email rants. They met at her job inter-

---

75. Why are all her suppliers in such odd places? Whenever I ask her she talks vaguely about 'sourcing'. Ruby reckons it's so she can charge more for driving hours.

view for White Globe Consulting. Sam was on the panel, and he asked her some tricky question about her CV and she should have known THEN that he was going to fuck her life up. She should have stood up and just WALKED AWAY. Because does he think a six-figure salary is what her life is about? Does he think everyone's like him? Doesn't he realize that to build a life together you have to 'KNOW WHAT THE BUILDING BLOCKS ARE, Sam????'

Etc., etc., etc. I have honestly given up reading to the end.

'Haven't you got yourself a new phone yet?' says Sam, raising his eyebrows.

'I'm going to the shop this afternoon.' It'll be a real hassle, starting afresh with a new phone, but there's not much I can do about it. Except . . .

'In fact, I was just wondering,' I add casually. 'You don't want to sell it, do you?'

'A company phone, full of business emails?' He gives an incredulous laugh. 'Are you nuts? I was mad letting you have access to it in the first place. Not that I had a choice, Ms Lightfingers. I should have set the police on you.'

'I'm not a thief!' I retort, stung. 'I didn't *steal* it. I found it in a *bin*.'

'You should have handed it in.' He shrugs. 'You know it and I know it.'

'It was common property! It was fair game!'

'"Fair game"? You want to tell that to the judge? If I drop my wallet and it falls momentarily into a bin, does that give Joe Bloggs the right to steal it?'

I can't tell if he's winding me up or not, so I take a drink of water, avoiding the issue. I'm turning the phone round and round in my hand, not wanting to relinquish it. I've got used to this phone now. I like the feel of it. I've even got used to sharing my in-box.

'So, what will happen to it?' At last I look up. 'The phone, I mean.'

'Jane will forward everything of any relevance to her account. Then it'll get wiped. Inside and out.'

'Right. Of course.'

The idea of all my messages being wiped makes me want to whimper. But there's nothing I can do. This was the deal. It was only a loan. Like he said, it's not my phone.

I put it down again, about two inches from my bowl.

'I'll let you know my new number as soon as I get it,' I say. 'If I get any texts or messages—'

'I'll forward them.' He nods. 'Or rather, my new PA will do it.'

'When does she start?'

'Tomorrow.'

'Great!' I smile a little wanly and take a sip of my soup, which really is the wrong side of tepid.

'She's great,' he says with enthusiasm. 'Her name's Lizzy, she's very bright.' He starts to attack his green salad. 'Now. While we're here, you have to tell me. What was the deal with Lindsay? What the hell did you write to her?'

'Oh. That.' I feel warm with embarrassment. 'I think she misunderstood the situation because . . . Well. It was nothing, really. I just complimented her and then I put some kisses from you. At the end of an email.'

Sam puts his fork down. 'You added kisses to an email of *mine*? A business email?' He looks almost more scandalized by this than by anything else.

'I didn't mean to!' I say defensively. 'They just slipped out. I always put kisses on emails. It's friendly.'

'Oh. I see.' He raises his eyes to heaven. 'You're one of *those* ridiculous people.'

'It's not ridiculous,' I retort. 'It's just being nice.'

'Let me see.' He reaches for the phone.

'Stop it!' I say in horror. 'What are you *doing*?'

I make a swipe, but it's too late. He's got the phone and he's scrolling through all the messages and emails. As he reads, he lifts an eyebrow, then frowns, then gives a sudden laugh.

'What are you looking at?' I try to sound frosty. 'You should respect my confidentiality.'

He totally ignores me. Does he have no idea of privacy? What's he reading, anyway? It could be anything.

I take another sip of soup, but it's so cold I can't face any more. As I look up, Sam's still reading my messages avidly. This is hideous. I feel like he's riffling through my underwear drawer.

'Now you know what it's like, having someone else critiquing your emails,' he says, glancing up.

'There's nothing to critique,' I say, a little haughtily. 'Unlike you, I'm charming and polite, and *don't* brush people off with two words.'

'You call it charming. I call it something else.'

'Whatever.' I roll my eyes. Of course he doesn't want to admit I have superior communication skills.

Sam reads another email, shaking his head, then looks up and surveys me silently.

'What?' I say, nettled. 'What is it?'

'Are you so scared people will hate you?'

'What?' I stare at him, not knowing how to react. 'What are you *talking* about?'

He gestures at the phone. 'Your emails are like one big cry. "Kiss, kiss, hug, hug, please like me, please like me!"'

'*What?*' I feel like he's slapped me round the face. 'That's absolute . . . crap.'

'Take this one. "Hi Sue! Can I possibly change my wedding updo consultation to a later time, like 5 p.m.? It's with Louis. Let me know. But if not, no worries. Thanks so much! I really appreciate it! Hope all is well. Love, Poppy, kiss, kiss, kiss, kiss, kiss, kiss, kiss." Who's Sue? Your oldest, dearest friend?'

'She's the receptionist at my hairdresser.' I glare at him.

'So she gets thanks and appreciation and a zillion kisses, just for doing her job?'

'I'm being *nice!*' I snap.

'It's not being nice,' he says firmly, 'it's being ridiculous. It's a business transaction. Be businesslike.'

'I love my hairdresser!' I say furiously. I take a spoonful of soup, forgetting how revolting it is, and quell a shudder.

Sam's still scrolling through my messages, as if he has every right to. I should never have let him get his hands on that phone. I should have wiped it myself.

'Who's Lucinda?'

'My wedding planner,' I answer reluctantly.

'That's what I thought. Isn't she supposed to be working for *you*? What *is* all this shit she's laying on you?'

For a moment I'm too flustered to reply. I butter a piece of my roll, then put it down without eating it.

'She *is* working for me,' I say at last, avoiding his eye. 'I mean, obviously I help out a little when she needs it . . .'

'You've done the cars for her.' He's counting off on his fingers incredulously. 'You've organized the confetti, the buttonholes, the organist . . .'

I can feel a flush creeping over my face. I know I've ended up doing more for Lucinda than I intended. But I'm not going to admit that to him.

'I wanted to! It's fine.'

'And her tone's pretty bossy, if you ask me.'

'It's only her manner. I don't mind . . .' I'm trying to throw him off this path, but he's relentless.

'Why don't you just tell her straight, "You're working for me, cut out the attitude"?'

'It's not as simple as that, OK?' I feel on the back foot. 'She's not just a wedding planner. She's an old friend of the Tavishes.'

'The Tavishes?' He shakes his head as though the name means nothing to him.

'My future in-laws! The *Tavishes*. Professor Antony Tavish?

Professor Wanda Brook-Tavish? Their parents are great friends and Lucinda's part of that whole world, and she's one of them and I can't . . .' I break off and rub my nose. I'm not sure where I was going with that.

Sam picks up a spoon, leans over, takes a sip of my soup and winces.

'Freezing. Thought so. Send it back.'

'No, really.' I flash him an automatic smile. 'It's fine.' I take the opportunity to grab the phone back.

'It's not fine. Send it back.'

'No! Look . . . it doesn't matter. I'm not hungry anyway.'

Sam is gazing at me, shaking his head. 'You are a big surprise, you know that? *This* is a big surprise.' He taps the phone.

'What?'

'You're pretty insecure, for someone who's so feisty on the outside.'

'I'm not!' I retort, rattled.

'Not insecure? Or not feisty?'

'I . . .' I'm too confused to answer. 'I dunno. Stop it. Leave me alone.'

'You talk about the Tavishes as if they're gods—'

'Well, of *course* I do! They're in a different *league*—'

I'm cut off mid-stream by a man's voice.

'Sam! My main man!' It's Justin, clapping Sam on the back. He's wearing a black suit, black tie and dark glasses. He looks like one of the Men in Black. 'Steak baguette again?'

'You know me too well.' Sam gets to his feet, and taps a passing waiter. 'Excuse me, could we have a fresh soup for my guest? This one's cold.' Sitting back down he asks Justin, 'Did you meet Poppy the other night? Poppy, Justin Cole.'

'*Enchanté*.' Justin nods at me and I catch a waft of Fahrenheit aftershave.

'Hi.' I manage to smile politely, but I still feel stirred up inside. I need to tell Sam how wrong he is. About everything.

'How was the meeting with P&G?' Sam's saying to Justin.

'Good! Very good! Although of course they miss you on the team, Sam.' He makes a reproving gesture with his finger.

'I'm sure they don't.'

'You know this man is the star of our company?' Justin says to me, nodding at Sam. 'Sir Nicholas's heir apparent. "One day, dear boy, all this will be yours."'

'Now, that's just bullshit,' Sam says pleasantly.

'Of course it is.'

There's a beat of silence. They're smiling at each other – but it's a bit more like animals baring teeth.

'So, I'll see you around,' says Justin at length. 'Going to the conference tonight?'

'Tomorrow, in fact,' Sam replies. 'Lot of stuff to catch up on here.'

'Fair enough. Well, we'll toast you tonight.' Justin raises his hand at me, then walks away.

'Sorry about that,' says Sam. 'This restaurant is just impossible at lunchtime. But it's the closest one that's any good.'

I've been distracted from my churning thoughts by Justin Cole. He really is a prick.

'You know, I heard Justin talking about you last night,' I say in a low voice, and lean across the table. 'He called you a "stubborn fuck".'

Sam throws back his head and roars with laughter. 'I expect he did.'

A fresh bowl of butternut squash soup arrives in front of me, steaming hot, and suddenly I feel ravenous.

'Thanks for doing that,' I say awkwardly to Sam.

'My pleasure.' He tilts his head. *'Bon appétit.'*

'So, why did he call you a stubborn fuck?' I take a spoonful of soup.

'Oh, we disagree pretty fundamentally about how to run the company,' he says carelessly. 'My camp had a recent victory so his camp are feeling sore.'

Camps? Victories? Are they all permanently at war?

'So, what happened?'

God, this soup is good. I'm ladling it in as though I haven't eaten for weeks.

'You're really interested?' He looks amused.

'Yes! Of course!'

'A member of staff left the company. For the better, in my opinion. But not in Justin's.' He takes a bite of baguette and reaches for his water.

That's *it*? That's all he's going to tell me? A member of staff left the company?

'You mean John Gregson?' I suddenly remember my Google search.

'What?' He looks taken aback. 'How do you know about John Gregson?'

'*Daily Mail* online, of course.' I roll my eyes. What does he think, that he works in a secret, private bubble?

'Oh. I see.' Sam seems to digest this. 'Well . . . no. That was something different.'

'Who was this one, then? C'mon,' I wheedle as he hesitates. 'You can tell me. I'm best friends with Sir Nicholas Murray, you know. We have drinks at the Savoy together. We're like this.' I cross my fingers and Sam gives a reluctant snort of laughter.

'OK. I don't suppose it's any great secret.' He hesitates and lowers his voice. 'It was a guy called Ed Exton. Finance Director. The truth is, he was fired. Turned out he'd been defrauding the company for a while. Nick wouldn't press charges, but that was a big mistake. Now Ed's suing for wrongful dismissal.'

'Yes!' I nearly squeak. 'I *knew* it! And that's why he was the worse for wear in the Groucho.'

Sam gives another short, incredulous laugh. 'You know about that. Of course you do.'

'And so . . . Justin was angry when Ed was fired?' I'm trying to get this clear.

'Justin was gunning for Ed to take over as CEO with himself as right-hand man,' says Sam wryly. 'So, yes, you could say he was fairly angry.'

'CEO?' I say in astonishment. 'But ... what about Sir Nicholas?'

'Oh, they would have ousted Nick if they'd got enough support,' says Sam matter-of-factly. 'There's a faction in this company that's more interested in creaming off short-term profits and dressing in Paul Smith than anything else. Nick's all about playing the long game. Not always the most popular position.'

I finish my soup, digesting all this. Honestly, these office politics are all so complicated. How does anyone get any work done? It's bad enough when Annalise has one of her little hissy fits about whose turn it is to buy the coffee and we all get distracted and forget to write up our reports.

If I worked at White Globe Consulting I wouldn't be able to do my job. I would spend *all day* texting the other people in the office, asking them what was going on today and had they heard anything new and what did they think was going to happen?

Hmm. Maybe it's a good thing I'm not in an office job.

'I can't believe Sir Nicholas Murray used to live in Balham,' I say, suddenly remembering. 'I mean, Balham!'

'Nick hasn't always been grand, by any means.' Sam shoots me a curious look. 'Didn't you come across his background story during your little Google-fest? He was an orphan. Brought up in a children's home. Everything he's got, he's worked his socks off for. Not a snobbish bone in his body. Not like some of these pretentious tossers trying to get rid of him.' He scowls, and stuffs a bundle of rocket into his mouth.

'Fabian Taylor must be in Justin's camp,' I observe thoughtfully. 'He's so sarcastic with you. I always wondered why.' I look up to see Sam regarding me with a lowered, furrowed brow.

'Poppy, be honest. How many of my emails have you read?'
I can't believe he's asking that.

'All of them, of course. What did you think?' His expression
is so funny I suddenly get the giggles. 'The minute I got my
hands on that phone I started snooping on you. Emails from
colleagues, emails from Willow . . .' I can't resist throwing out
the name casually to see if he bites.

Sure enough, he blanks the reference completely. It's as
though the name 'Willow' means nothing to him.

But this is our farewell lunch. It's my last chance. I'm going
to persevere.

'So. Does Willow work on a different floor to you?' I say
conversationally.

'Same floor.'

'Oh, right. And . . . you two met through work?'

He just nods. This is like getting blood out of a stone.

A waiter comes to clear my bowl and we order coffees. As
the waiter moves away, I see Sam studying me thoughtfully.
I'm about to ask another question about Willow, but he gets in
first.

'Poppy, slight change of subject. Can I say something to you?
As a friend?'

'Are we friends?' I reply dubiously.

'A disinterested spectator, then.'

Great. First of all, he's dodging the Willow conversation.
Secondly, what now? A speech on why you shouldn't
steal phones? Another lecture on being businesslike in
emails?

'What is it?' I can't help rolling my eyes. 'Fire away.'

He picks up a teaspoon, as though marshalling his thoughts,
then puts it down.

'I know this is none of my business. I haven't been married.
I haven't met your fiancé. I don't know the situation.'

As he speaks, blood creeps into my face. I don't know
why.

'No,' I say. 'You don't. So—'

He presses on without listening to me.

'But it seems to me you can't – you *shouldn't* – go into a marriage feeling inferior in any way.'

For a moment I'm too stunned to respond. I'm groping for the right reaction. Shout? Slap him? Storm out?

'OK, listen,' I manage at last. My throat is tight, but I'm trying to sound poised. 'First of all, you *don't* know me, like you said. Second of all, I *don't* feel inferior—'

'You do. It's obvious from everything you say. And it's baffling to me. Look at you. You're a professional. You're successful. You're . . .' He hesitates. 'You're attractive. Why should you feel the Tavishes are in a "different league" from you?'

Is he being *deliberately* obtuse?

'Because they're like, major, famous people! They're all geniuses and they'll all end up being knighted, and my uncle's just a normal dentist from Taunton—' I break off, breathing hard.

Great. Now I've walked straight into it.

'What about your dad?'

Here goes. He asked for it.

'He's dead,' I say bluntly. 'Both my parents are dead. Car crash ten years ago.' I lean back in my chair, waiting for the awkward pause.

It can go so many different ways. Silence. Hand over mouth. Gasp.[76] Exclamation. Awkward change of subject. Morbid curiosity. Story about bigger, more gruesome crash that friend of friend's aunt was in.

One girl I told actually burst into tears, right then and there. I had to watch her sobbing and find her a tissue.

But . . . it's weird. This time doesn't seem to be awkward.

---

76. Magnus was a gasper. Then he gripped me tight between both hands and said he'd known I was vulnerable and that just added to my beauty.

Sam hasn't looked away. He hasn't cleared his throat *or* gasped *or* changed the subject.

'Both at once?' he says at last, in a more gentle voice.

'My mother straight away. My father the day after.' I flash him a brittle smile. 'Never got to say goodbye to him, though. He was pretty much gone at the . . . at the time.'

Smiling is actually the only way to get through these conversations, I've learned.

A waiter arrives with our coffees, and for a moment the conversation's on hold. But as soon as he's moved away, the same mood is back. The same expression on Sam's face.

'I'm very, very sorry.'

'No need to be!' I say in my standard upbeat voice. 'It all worked out. We moved in with my uncle, he's a dentist, my aunt's a dental nurse. They looked after us, me and my little brothers. So . . . it's all good. All good.'

I can feel his eyes on me. I look one way and then the other, dodging them. I stir my cappuccino, a little too fast, and take a gulp.

'That explains a lot,' says Sam at last.

I can't bear his sympathy. I can't bear anyone's sympathy.

'It does not,' I say tightly. 'It does *not*. It happened years ago and it's over and I'm a grown-up and I've dealt with it, OK? So you're wrong. It doesn't explain anything.'

Sam puts down his espresso cup, picks up his amaretto biscuit and unwraps it unhurriedly.

'I meant it explains why you're obsessed with teeth.'

'Oh.'

Touché.

I give him a reluctant smile. 'Yes, I suppose I am fairly familiar with dental care.'

Sam crunches into his biscuit and I take another gulp of cappuccino. After a minute or two it seems as if we've moved on, and I'm wondering if we should get the bill, when Sam suddenly says, 'My friend lost his mother when we were at college. I spent a lot of nights talking with him. Lot of nights.' He pauses. 'I know what it's like. You don't just get over it. And it doesn't make any difference if you're supposedly a "grown-up". And it never goes away.'

He wasn't supposed to come back to the subject. We'd moved on. Most people gallop off to something else with relief.

'Well, I did get over it,' I say brightly. 'And it did go away. So.'

Sam nods as though my words don't surprise him. 'Yes, that's what he said. To other people. I know. You have to.' He pauses. 'Hard to keep up the façade, though.'

Smile. Keep smiling. Don't meet his eye.

But somehow I can't help it, I do.

And my eyes are suddenly hot. Shit. *Shit.* This hasn't happened for years. Years.

'Don't look at me like that,' I mutter fiercely, glaring at the table.

'Like what?' Sam sounds alarmed.

'Like you understand.' I swallow. 'Stop it. Just stop it.'

I take a deep breath and then a sip of water. *Idiot*, Poppy. Get a grip. I haven't let myself be caught off guard like that since . . . I can't even remember when.

'I'm sorry,' says Sam, in a low voice. 'I didn't mean—'

'No! It's fine. Let's just move on. Shall we get the bill?'

'Sure.' He summons a waiter, and I take out my lipgloss, and after about two minutes I feel back to normal.

I try to pay for lunch, but Sam point-blank refuses, so we compromise on going Dutch. After the waiter's taken the money and wiped away the crumbs I look at him across the empty table.

'Well.' Slowly, I slide the phone across the table to him. 'Here you are. Thanks. Nice knowing you and everything.'

Sam doesn't even look at it. He's gazing at me with the sort of kind, concerned expression that makes me prickle all over and want to throw things. If he says anything more about my parents, I'll just walk. I'll go.

'I was wondering,' he says at last. 'Out of interest, have you ever learned any methods of confrontation?'

'What?' I laugh out loud with surprise. 'Of course not. I don't want to *confront* anybody.'

Sam spreads his hands. 'There you go. There's your problem.'

'I don't have a problem! You're the one with a problem. At least I'm *nice*,' I can't help saying pointedly. 'You're ... miserable.'

Sam roars with laughter and I flush. OK, maybe 'miserable' was the wrong word.

'I'm fine.' I reach for my bag. 'I don't need any help.'

'Come on. Don't be a coward.'

'I'm not a coward!' I retort in outrage.

'If you can give it out, you can take it,' he says cheerfully. 'When you read my texts you saw a curt, miserable git. And you told me so. Maybe you're right.' He pauses. 'But you know what I saw when I read yours?'

'No.' I scowl at him. 'And I don't want to know.'

'I saw a girl who races to help others but doesn't help herself. And right now, you need to help yourself. No one should walk up the aisle feeling inferior, or in a different league, or trying to be something they're not. I don't know exactly who your issues are with, but . . .'

He picks up the phone, clicks a button and turns the screen to face me.

Fuck.

It's my list. The list I wrote in the church.

THINGS TO DO BEFORE WEDDING
1. *Become expert on Greek philosophy.*
2. *Memorize Robert Burns poems.*
3. *Learn long Scrabble words.*

4. *Remember: am HYPOCHONDRIAC.*
5. *Beef Stroganoff. Get to like. (Hypnosis?)*

I feel drenched in embarrassment. *This* is why people shouldn't share phones.

'It's nothing to do with you,' I mutter, staring at the table.

'I know,' he says gently. 'I also know that standing up for yourself can be hard. But you have to do it. You have to get it out there. *Before* the wedding.'

I'm silent for a minute or two. I can't bear him to be right. But deep down inside me, everything he's saying is feeling true. Like Tetris blocks falling one by one into place.

I let my bag drop down on to the table and rub my nose. Sam patiently waits, while I get my thoughts in order.

'It's all very well you telling me that,' I say finally. 'It's all very well saying "get it out there". What am I supposed to say to them?'

'"Them" being . . .'

'I dunno. His parents, I guess.'

I suddenly feel disloyal, talking about Magnus's family behind his back. But it's a bit late for that.

Sam doesn't hesitate for a minute.

'You say, "Mr and Mrs Tavish, you're making me feel inferior. Do you really think I'm inferior or is this just in my mind?"'

'What *planet* do you live on?' I stare at him. 'I can't say that! People don't say things like that!'

Sam laughs. 'Do you know what I'm about to do this afternoon? I'm about to tell an industry CEO that he doesn't work hard enough, that he's alienating his fellow board members and that his personal hygiene is becoming a management issue.'

'Oh my God.' I'm cringing at the thought. 'No way.'

'It's going to be fine,' says Sam calmly. 'I'll take him through, point by point, and by the end he'll be agreeing with me. It's just technique and confidence. Awkward conversations are kind of my specialism. I learned a lot from Nick,' he adds. 'He can tell people that their company is a pile of shit and they lap it out of his hand. Or even that their *country* is a pile of shit.'

'Wow.' I'm a bit awestruck.

'Come and sit in on the meeting. If you're not busy. There'll be a couple of other people.'

'Really?'

He shrugs. 'It's how you learn.'

I had no idea you could be a specialist in awkward conversations. I'm trying to picture myself telling someone that their personal hygiene is an issue. I can't imagine finding the words to do that in a million years.

Oh, come on. I *have* to see this.

'OK!' I find myself smiling. 'I will. Thanks.'

He hasn't picked up the phone, I suddenly notice. It's still lying on the table.

'So . . . shall I bring this along to your office?' I say casually.

'Sure.' He's shrugging on his jacket. 'Thanks.'

Excellent. I get to check my texts again. Result!

TEN

It must be so amazing to work in a place like this. Everything about Sam's building is a novelty to me – from the massive escalator, to the whizzy lifts, to the laminated card with my photo on it, which got made by a machine in about three seconds. When visitors come to First Fit Physio, we just sign them in, in a book from Staples.

We go up to the sixteenth floor and along a corridor with a bright-green carpet, black and white photos of London on the wall, and funky seating in random shapes. On the right are individual, glass-fronted offices and on the left is a big, open-plan area with multicoloured desks. Everything here is so *cool*. There's a water machine, like we have, but there's also a coffee station with a real Nespresso machine and a Smeg fridge and a massive bowl of fruit.

I am so talking to Ruby about staff conditions at First Fit Physio.

'Sam!' A man in a navy linen jacket greets Sam and as they talk, I peer all around at the open-plan office area, wondering if I might spot Willow. That girl with wavy blonde hair, talking into a headset, sitting with her feet up on a chair. Could that be her?

'OK.' Sam seems to be wrapping up the conversation. 'That's interesting, Nihal. I'll have a think.'

Nihal. My ears prick up. I know that name from somewhere. I'm sure I do. What was it, now? Nihal . . . Nihal . . .

'Thanks, Sam,' Nihal is saying. 'I'll just forward that document to you right now . . .' As he's tapping at his phone, I suddenly remember.

'Congratulate him on his baby!' I whisper to Sam. 'Nihal just had a baby last week. Yasmin. Seven pounds. She's gorgeous! Didn't you see the email?'

'Oh.' Sam looks taken aback, but recovers smoothly. 'Hey, Nihal, congrats on the baby, by the way. Fantastic news.'

'Yasmin's a lovely name.' I beam at Nihal. 'And seven pounds! What a good size! How is she doing?'

'How's Anita?' joins in Sam.

'They're both really well, thanks! I'm sorry . . . I'm not sure we've met?' Nihal glances at Sam for help.

'This is Poppy,' says Sam. 'She's here to do some . . . consulting.'

'Right.' Nihal shakes my hand, still looking puzzled. 'So, how did you know about the baby?'

'Because Sam mentioned it to me,' I lie smoothly. 'He was so thrilled for you, he couldn't help telling me. Isn't that right, Sam?'

Ha! Sam's face!

'That's right,' he says, finally. 'Delighted.'

'Wow.' Nihal's face suffuses with pleasure. 'Thanks, Sam. I didn't realize you'd be so . . .' He breaks off awkwardly.

'No problem.' Sam lifts a hand. 'Congratulations again. Poppy, we should really be getting on.'

As Sam and I walk away down the corridor, I want to giggle at his expression.

'Can you cut it out, please?' Sam murmurs without moving his head. 'First animals, now babies. What kind of reputation are you going to give me?'

'A good one!' I retort. 'Everyone will love you!'

'Hey, Sam.' A voice hails us from behind and we turn to see Matt Mitchell from last night, glowing with delight. 'I just heard the news! Sir Nicholas is joining the Guatemala trip! That's awesome!'

'Oh, yes.' Sam nods brusquely. 'We spoke about it last night.'

'Well, I just wanted to thank you,' he says earnestly. 'I know this was your influence. You two guys will add *so* much heft to the cause. Oh, and thanks for the donation. We really appreciate it.'

I stare in astonishment. Sam gave a donation to the Guatemala trip? He gave a *donation*?

Now Matt is beaming at me. 'Hello again. Are you interested in the Guatemala trip?'

Oh my God, I would *love* to go to Guatemala.

'Well—' I begin enthusiastically, before Sam cuts me off firmly, 'No. She's not.'

Honestly. What a spoilsport.

'Maybe next time,' I say politely. 'I hope it goes well!'

As Matt Mitchell heads back down the corridor and we walk on, I'm mulling hard on what I just heard.

'You never told me Sir Nicholas was going to Guatemala,' I say at last.

'No?' Sam doesn't sound remotely interested. 'Well, he is.'

'And you gave them a donation,' I add. 'So you do think it's a good cause. You think it's worth supporting.'

'I gave them a *small* donation.' He corrects me with a forbidding look, but I'm undeterred.

'So actually . . . that situation turned out really well. Not a disaster at all.' I count off thoughtfully on my fingers. 'And the girls in Admin think you're wonderful and the whole ideas initiative is brilliant. And you've got some interesting new thoughts for the company. And Nihal thinks you're the bee's knees, and so does Chloe and all her department, and Rachel *loves* you for doing the Fun Run . . .'

'Where exactly are you going with this?' Sam's expression is so ominous, I quail slightly.

'Err . . . nowhere!' I backtrack. 'Just saying.'

Maybe I'll keep quiet now, for a while.

After the lobby I was expecting to be impressed by Sam's office – but I'm more than impressed. I'm awestruck.

It's a huge corner space, with windows overlooking Blackfriars Bridge, a designer light sculpture hanging from the ceiling, and a massive desk. There's another, smaller desk outside which is I guess where Violet used to sit. At the side of the office is a sleek little bar area with a fridge and a granite counter and *another* Nespresso machine. By the windows is a sofa, which is where Sam ushers me to.

'The meeting's not for twenty minutes. I've just got to catch up with some stuff. Make yourself comfortable.'

I sit on the sofa quietly for a few minutes – but it's quite boring just sitting on a sofa – so at last I get up and look out of the windows, gazing down at all the little cars whizzing over the bridge. There's a bookshelf nearby with lots of business hardbacks and a few awards. No photo of Willow, though. Nor is there one on his desk. He must have a photo of her somewhere, surely?

As I'm looking around, trying to spot it, I notice another doorway and can't help peering at it curiously. Why does he have another door? Where does it lead to?

'Bathroom,' says Sam, spotting me. 'Do you want to use it? Go ahead.'

Wow. He has an executive bathroom!

I head inside, hoping to find some amazing palace of marble – but it's quite normal really, with a small shower and glass tiles. Still. Your own bathroom inside your office. That's pretty cool.

I take the opportunity to redo my make-up, brush my hair and tug my denim skirt back into place. I open the door and am about to step outside when I suddenly realize there's a soup splash on my shirt. Shit.

Maybe I can get that off.

I dampen a towel and give the stain a quick rub. No. Not wet enough. I'll have to lean down and get it right under the tap.

As I'm bending down, I see a woman in a smart black trouser suit in the mirror, and jump. It takes me a moment to realize I've got a reflected view of the whole office, and she's actually approaching Sam's glass door. She's tall and imposing-looking, in her forties, maybe, and is holding a piece of paper.

Her expression is fairly grim. Ooh, maybe she's the CEO with bad personal hygiene.

No. Surely not. Look at that perfectly crisp white shirt.

Oh my God, is this *Willow*?

I suddenly feel even more embarrassed about my soup stain. It hasn't come off at all, I've just got a big wet patch on my T-shirt. In fact, I look hideous. Should I tell Sam I can't come to the meeting after all? Or maybe he has a spare shirt I could borrow. Don't businessmen always keep spare shirts at the office?

No, Poppy. Don't be ridiculous. And anyway, there's no time. The woman in the black suit is already rapping at his door and pushing it open. I watch in the mirror, on tenterhooks.

'Sam. I need a word.'

'Sure. What is it?' He looks up and frowns at her expression. 'Vicks, what's up?'

Vicks! Of course this is Vicks, head of PR. I should have realized at once.

I feel I already know her, from all her emails, and she's just as I imagined. Short, sharp brown hair, businesslike manner, sensible shoes, expensive watch. And, right now, a look of massive stress on her face.

'Only a handful of people know about this,' she says as she

closes the door. 'An hour ago I had a call from a mate of mine at ITN. They've got hold of an internal memo from Nick which they're planning to splash across the ten o'clock bulletin.' She winces. 'It's . . . it's bad, Sam.'

'Memo?' He looks perplexed. 'What memo?'

'A memo he apparently sent to you and Malcolm? Several months ago now? When you were doing that advisory work with BP? Here. Have a read.'

After about ten seconds I peep round the side of the ajar bathroom door. I can see Sam reading a printed sheet, an expression of shock on his face.

'What the *fuck*—'

'I know.' Vicks lifts her hands. 'I know.'

'This is . . .' He seems speechless.

'It's a disaster,' Vicks says calmly. 'He's basically talking about accepting bribes. Put that together with the fact he's on a government committee right now . . .' She hesitates. 'You and Malcolm could be compromised too. We'll need to look at that.'

'But . . . but I've never seen this memo in my life!' Sam finally seems to have found his voice. 'Nick didn't send this to me! He didn't write these things. He would *never* have written these things. I mean, he sent us a memo which *began* the same way, but—'

'Yes, that's what I gather from Malcolm too. The memo he received wasn't word for word the same as this one.'

'Not "word for word"?' echoes Sam impatiently. 'It was totally fucking different! Yes, it was about BP, yes, it raised the same issues, but it did *not* say these things.' He hits the page. 'I don't know where the hell this has come from. Have you spoken to Nick?'

'Of course. He says the same thing. He didn't send this memo, he's never seen it before, he's as baffled as we are.'

'So!' Sam exclaims impatiently. 'Head this off! Find the original memo, phone your friend at ITN, tell them they've been sold a pup. The IT guys will be able to prove what was written when, they're good at that stuff . . .' He breaks off. 'What?'

'We've tried.' She exhales. 'We've looked. We can't find an original version of the memo anywhere.'

'*What?*' He stares at her. 'But . . . that's crazy. Nick must have saved it.'

'They're searching. Here and at his Berkshire office. So far, this is the only version they've managed to find on the system.' She taps the paper in turn.

'Bullshit!' Sam gives an incredulous laugh. 'Wait. I have it myself!'

He sits down and opens up a file. 'I would have put it . . .' He clicks a few more times. 'Here we are! You see . . . here it is . . .' He breaks off suddenly, breathing hard. 'What the—'

There's silence. I can hardly breathe.

'No,' expostulates Sam suddenly. 'No way. This is *not* the version I received.' He looks up, baffled. 'What's going on? I *had* it.'

'Not there?' Vicks's voice is tight with disappointment.

Sam is clicking frantically at his computer mouse again.

'This makes no bloody sense,' he's saying, almost to himself. 'The memo was emailed over. It came to me and Malcolm on the system. I had it. I read it with my own eyes. It *has* to be here.' He glowers at his screen. 'Where the *fuck* is that *fucking* email?'

'Did you print it out? Did you keep it? Do you still have that original version?' I can see the hope in Vicks's eyes.

There's a long silence.

'No.' Sam sighs. 'I read it online. Malcolm?'

'He didn't print it out either. And he can only find this version on his laptop. OK.' Vicks sags a little. 'Well . . . we'll keep trying.'

'It has to be there.' Sam sounds adamant. 'If the techies say they can't find it, they're wrong. Put more of them on to it.'

'They're all searching. We haven't told them why, obviously.'

'Well, if we can't find it, you'll just have to tell ITN it's a mystery to us,' says Sam energetically. 'We refute it. We make it crystal clear that this memo was *never* read by me, *never* written by Nick, has *never* been seen before by anyone in the company—'

'Sam, it's on the company system.' Vicks sounds weary. 'We can hardly claim that no one in the company has ever seen it. Unless we can *find* the other memo—' Her phone bleeps with a text and she glances at it. 'That's Julian from Legal. They're going to go for an injunction, but . . .' She gives a hopeless shrug. 'Now Nick's a government adviser, there's not much chance.'

Sam is peering at the sheet of paper again, a frown of distaste on his face.

'Who wrote this crap?' he says. 'It doesn't even *sound* like Nick.'

'God knows.'

I'm so rapt that when my phone suddenly buzzes I nearly expire in fright. I glance at the screen and feel another jolt of fright. I can't stay hiding here. I quickly press Talk, and hurry out of the bathroom, my legs a little wobbly.

'Um, sorry to disturb,' I say awkwardly, and hold out the phone. 'Sam, it's Sir Nicholas for you.'

Vicks's expression of horror almost makes me want to laugh – except she looks as though she might strangle someone. And that someone could be me.

'Who's *she*?' she snaps, eyeing the stain on my T-shirt. 'Is this your new PA?'

'No. She's . . .' Sam waves it off. 'Long story. Nick!' he exclaims into the receiver. 'I've just heard. Jesus.'

'Did you hear any of that?' says Vicks to me in a savage undertone.

'No! I mean yes. A bit.' I'm gabbling in fright. 'But I wasn't really listening. I didn't hear anything. I was brushing my hair. Really hard.'

'OK. I'll be in touch. Keep us posted.' Sam switches off the phone and shakes his head. 'When the hell will he learn to use the right number? Sorry.'

Distractedly, he puts the phone down on the desk. 'This is ridiculous. I'm going to speak to the techies myself. If they can't find a lost email, for fuck's sake, they should all be fired. They should be fired anyway. They're useless.'

'Could it be on your phone?' I suggest timidly.

Sam's eyes light up for a moment – then he shakes his head.

'No. This was months ago. The phone doesn't store emails beyond two months. Nice idea, though, Poppy.'

Vicks looks as though she can't believe what she's hearing.

'Again – *who's she*? Does she have a *pass*?'

'Yes.' I hurriedly produce my laminated card.

'She's . . . OK. She's a visitor. I'll deal with her. Come on. We need to talk to the techies.'

Without a word in my direction, Sam hurries out into the corridor. A moment later, looking absolutely livid, Vicks follows. I can hear a stream of low-pitched invective coming from her as they walk off.

'Sam, when exactly were you planning to tell me you had a fucking *visitor* in your bathroom, listening to our fucking *confidential crisis*? You do realize my job is to control the flow of information? *Control* it?'

'Vicks, relax.'

As they disappear from view I sink down on to a chair, feeling a bit unreal. Yowzer. I have no idea what to do now. Should I stay? Should I go? Is the meeting with the CEO still going to happen?

I'm not exactly in a *hurry* to go anywhere – but after about twenty minutes of sitting there alone, I start to feel distinctly uncomfortable. I've leafed through a magazine full of words I don't understand, and I've thought about getting myself a coffee (and decided against it). The CEO meeting must surely be off. Sam must be tied up. I'm gearing myself up to write him a note and leave, when a blond guy taps at the glass door. He looks about twenty-three and is holding a massive rolled-up piece of blue paper.

'Hi,' he says shyly. 'Are you Sam's new PA?'

'No. I'm just . . . err . . . helping him.'

'Oh, OK.' He nods. 'Well, it's about the competition. The ideas competition?'

Oh God. This again.

'Yes?' I say encouragingly. 'Do you want to leave Sam a message?'

'I want this to get to him. It's a visualization of the company? A restructuring exercise? It's self-explanatory, but I've attached some notes . . .'

He hands over the rolled-up paper, together with an exercise book, full of writing.

I already know there is no way Sam is going to look at any of this. I feel quite sorry for this guy.

'OK! Well . . . I'll make sure he sees it. Thanks!'

As the blond guy heads off, I unroll a corner of the paper out of curiosity – and I don't believe it. It's a collage! Like I used to do when I was about five!

I spread the whole thing out flat on the floor, anchoring the corners with chair legs. It's in the design of a tree, with photos of staff stuck on to the branches. God only knows what it's supposed to say about the structure of the company – I don't care. What's interesting for me is that under each photo is the person's name. Which means finally I can put faces to all the people who have sent an email through Sam's phone. This is riveting.

Jane Ellis is a lot younger than I expected, and Malcolm is fatter and Chris Davies turns out to be a woman. There's Justin Cole . . . and there's Lindsay Cooper . . . and there's—

My finger stops dead.

Willow Harte.

She's nestling on a lower branch, smiling out cheerfully. Thin and dark-haired, with very arched black eyebrows. She's quite pretty, I grudgingly admit, although *not* supermodel standard.

And she works on the same floor as Sam. Which means . . .

Oh, I've got to. Come on. I've *got* to have a quick peek at the psycho fiancée before I go.

I head to Sam's glass door and peer cautiously out at the whole floor. I have no idea if she'll be in the open-plan area or have her own office. I'll just have to wander around. If anyone stops me I'll be Sam's new PA.

I grab a couple of files as camouflage, and cautiously venture out. A couple of people typing at their computers lift their heads and give me an uninterested glance. Skirting round the edge of the floor, I glance through windows and at names on doors, trying to catch a glimpse of a girl with dark hair; listening out for a whiny, nasal voice. She has to have a whiny, nasal voice, surely. And lots of stupid, made-up allergies, and about ten therapists—

I freeze. *That's her! It's Willow!*

She's ten yards away. Sitting in one of the glass-walled offices. To be honest, I can't see much of her except her profile and a hank of long hair hanging down the back of her chair and some long legs ending in black ballet pumps – but it's definitely her. I feel as though I've stumbled on some mythological creature.

As I approach I start to tingle all over. I have a dreadful feeling I might suddenly giggle. This is so ridiculous. Spying on someone I've never met. I clutch my folders more tightly and edge forward a little more.

There are two younger women in the office with her, and they're all drinking tea, and Willow is talking.

Damn. She *doesn't* have a whiny, nasal voice. In fact, it's quite melodious and sane-sounding – except when you start listening to what she's actually saying.

'Of course this is all just to get back at me,' she's saying. 'This whole exercise is one big "Fuck You, Willow". You know it was actually *my* idea?'

'No!' says one of the girls. 'Really?'

'Oh yes.' She turns her head briefly and I catch sight of a sorrowful, pitying smile. 'New-idea generation is *my* thing. Sam ripped me off. I was planning to send out exactly the same email. Same words, everything. He probably saw it on my laptop one night.'

I'm listening, completely stunned. Is she talking about *my* email? I want to burst in and say, 'He couldn't have ripped you off, he didn't even send it!'

'That's the kind of move he pulls all the time,' she adds and takes a sip of tea. 'That's how he's made his career. No integrity.'

OK, I'm completely fogged now. Either I'm all wrong about Sam or she's all wrong about him, because in my opinion he's the last person in the world you could imagine ripping somebody else off.

'I just don't know why he has to *compete* with me,' Willow's saying now. 'What is it with men? What's wrong with facing the world together? Side by side? What's wrong with being a partnership? Or is that just too . . . *generous* for him to get his stupid male head around?'

'He wants control,' says the other girl, cracking a biscuit in half. 'They all do. He's never going to give you the credit you deserve in a million years.'

'But can't he see how *perfect* it could be if we could just get it fucking *right*? If we could get *beyond* this crappy bad patch?' Willow sounds suddenly impassioned. 'Working together, being together . . . the whole package . . . it could be sublime.' She breaks off and takes a gulp of tea. 'The question is, how long do I give him? Because I can't go on like this much longer.'

'Have you talked it through?' says the first girl.

'Please! You know Sam and "talking".' She makes quote marks with her fingers.

Well. I'm with her there.

'It makes me sad.' She shakes her head. 'Not for me, for *him*.

He can't see what's in front of his face and he doesn't know how to value what he has, and you know what? He's going to lose it. And *then* he's going to want it, but it'll be too late. Too late.' She bangs her tea cup down. 'Gone.'

I'm suddenly gripped. I'm seeing this conversation in a new light. I'm suddenly realizing that Willow has more insight than I thought. Because, if truth be told, this is just what I feel about Sam and his father. Sam can't see what he's losing, and when he does it may be too late. OK, I know I don't know the whole story between them. But I've seen the emails, I've got the idea—

My thoughts stop abruptly in their tracks. Alarm bells have started to ring in my head. At first distant, but now getting loud and clangy. Oh no, oh no, oh God . . .

Sam's father. The 24th of April. That's today. I'd *completely* forgotten. How could I be so *stupid*?

Horror is rising up me like chill water. Sam's dad's going to pitch up at the Chiddingford Hotel, expecting some lovely reunion. Today. He's probably on his way already. He'll be all excited. And Sam won't even *be* there. He's not going to the conference until tomorrow.

Shiiiiit. I've really messed up. I'd forgotten all about it, what with all the other emergencies going on.

What do I do? How do I solve this? I can't tell Sam. He'll go absolutely mad. And he's so stressed anyway. Do I cancel the dad? Send a quick raincheck apology email? Or will that make everything even worse between them?

There's only one tiny ray of hope. Sam's dad never sent any reply, which is why I forgot about it. So maybe he never even got the email. Maybe it's all OK—

I suddenly realize I'm nodding emphatically, as though to persuade myself. One of the girls with Willow looks up and eyes me curiously. Oops.

'Right!' I say out loud. 'So . . . I'll just . . . Good. Yes.' I hastily turn on my heel. If there's one thing I *don't* want, it's being busted by Willow. I scurry to the safety of Sam's office, and am about to grab the phone to email Sam's dad when I see Sam and Vicks marching back towards the office, apparently in the middle of a blazing argument. They look a bit terrifying, and I find myself backing hastily into the bathroom.

As they stride in, neither of them even notices me.

'We *cannot* release this statement,' Sam is saying furiously. He crumples the piece of paper he's holding and throws it in the bin. 'It's a travesty. You're completely shafting Nick, you do understand that?'

'That's not fair, Sam.' Vicks looks prickly. 'I'd say it's a reasonable and balanced official response. Nothing in our statement says he did or didn't write the memo—'

'But it should! You should be telling the world that he would never say these things in a million years! You *know* he wouldn't!'

'That's for him to say in his own personal statement. What *we* cannot do is look as though we condone these kinds of practices—'

'Hanging John Gregson out to dry was bad enough,' says Sam, his voice low, as though he's trying to keep control of himself. 'That should never have happened. He should never have lost his job. But Nick! Nick is everything to this company.'

'Sam, we're not hanging him out to dry. He's going to release his own statement. He can say what he likes in that.'

'Great,' says Sam sarcastically. 'But meanwhile, his own board won't stand by him. What kind of vote of confidence is that? Remind me *not* to hire you to represent me when I'm ever in a spot.'

Vicks flinches, but says nothing. Her phone buzzes, but she presses Ignore.

'Sam . . .' She stops – then takes a deep breath and starts again. 'You're being idealistic. I know you admire Nick. We all do. But he's not everything to this company. Not any more.'

She winces at Sam's glare, but carries on. 'He's one man. One brilliant, flawed, high-profile man. In his sixties.'

'He's our *leader*.' Sam sounds livid.

'Bruce is our chairman.'

'Nick *founded* this fucking company, if you remember—'

'A long time ago, Sam. A very long time ago.'

Sam exhales sharply and walks off a few paces, as though trying to calm himself. I'm watching, totally agog, not daring even to breathe.

'So you side with them,' he says at last.

'It's not a question of *siding*. You know my affection for Nick.' She's looking more and more uncomfortable. 'But this is a modern business. Not some quirky family firm. We owe it to our backers, our clients, our staff—'

'Jesus Christ, Vicks. Listen to yourself.'

There's a sharp silence. Neither of them is looking at the other. Vicks's face is creased and troubled-looking. Sam's hair is more rumpled than ever and he looks absolutely furious.

I feel a bit stunned by the intensity in the room. I always thought being in PR sounded like a *fun* job. I had no idea it was like this.

'Vicks.' The unmistakable drawl of Justin Cole hits the air, and a moment later he's in the room, wafting Fahrenheit and satisfaction. 'Got this under control, have you?'

'The lawyers are on it. We're just drafting a press statement.' She gives him a tight smile.

'Because for the sake of the company, we need to be careful that none of the other directors are tainted with these unfortunate . . . views. You know what I'm saying?'

'It's all in hand, Justin.'

From Vicks's sharp tone, I'm guessing she doesn't like Justin any more than Sam does.[77]

'Great. Of course, very unfortunate for Sir Nicholas. *Great*

---

77. Or me, for that matter. Not that anyone's asked me.

shame.' Justin looks delighted. 'Still, he is getting on now—'

'He is not *getting on*.' Sam scowls at Justin. 'You really are an arrogant little shit.'

'Temper, temper!' Justin says pleasantly. 'Oh, tell you what, Sam. Let's send him an e-card.'

'Fuck you.'

'Guys!' Vicks pleads.

I can totally understand now why Sam was talking about victories and camps. The aggression between these two is brutal. They're like those stags who fight every autumn until they wrench each other's antlers off.

Justin shakes his head pityingly – his expression changing briefly to surprise as he clocks me in the corner – then saunters out again.

'That memo is a smear,' Sam says in a low, furious voice. 'It's been planted. Justin Cole knows it and he's behind it.'

'*What?*' Vicks sounds at the end of her tether. 'Sam Roxton, you do *not* go around saying things like that! You'll sound like a conspiracy nutter.'

'It was a different. Fucking. Memo.' Sam sounds like he's beyond exasperation with the whole world. 'I saw the original version. Malcolm saw it. There was no talk of bribes. Now it's disappeared from the entire computer system. No trace. Explain that and *then* call me a conspiracy nutter.'

'I can't explain it,' says Vicks after a pause. 'And I'm not even going to try to. I'm going to do my job.'

'Someone did this. You know it. You're playing right into their hands, Vicks. They're smearing Nick and you're letting them.'

'No. No. Stop.' Vicks is shaking her head. 'I'm not playing this game. I don't get involved.' She walks over to the waste-paper basket, retrieves the crumpled statement and spreads it out.

'I can change a detail or two,' she says. 'But I've spoken to Bruce and we have to go with this.' She holds out a pen. 'You want to make any small amendments? Because Julian is on his way right now to approve it.'

Sam ignores the pen.

'What if we find the original memo? What if we can prove this one is a fake?'

'Great!' There's a sudden new edge to her voice. 'Then we release it, Nick's integrity is saved and we throw a party. Believe me, Sam, I would like nothing better than that. But we have to work with what we have. Which, right now, is a damaging memo we can't explain away.' Vicks rubs her face, then screws her fists into her eyes. 'This morning I was trying to cover up that embarrassment with the drunken post guy,' she mutters, almost to herself. 'I was worried about *that*.'

She really shouldn't do that. She's giving herself bags under her eyes.

'When does the statement go out?' says Sam at length. All his tempestuous energy seems to have dissipated. His shoulders have slumped and he sounds so low I almost want to go and give him a hug.

'That's the one bright ray.' Vicks's voice is softer now, as though she wants to treat him gently in his defeat. 'They're keeping it for the ten o'clock bulletin, so we have a good six hours or so to play with.'

'A lot can happen in six hours,' I volunteer timidly, and both of them jump as though scalded.

'*She's* still here?'

'Poppy.' Even Sam looks taken aback. 'I'm so sorry. I had no idea you'd still be here—'

'She *heard* all that?' Vicks looks like she wants to hit some-one. 'Sam, are you out of your *mind*?'

'I won't say anything!' I say hurriedly. 'Promise.'

'OK.' Sam breathes out. 'My mistake. Poppy, this isn't your fault, I was the one who invited you. I'll find someone to escort you out.' He leans his head out of his office door. 'Stephanie? Borrow you a sec?'

A few moments later a pleasant-looking girl with long blonde hair arrives at the office.

'Can you take our visitor down, sign her out, sort out the pass, all that?' says Sam. 'Sorry, Poppy, I'd do it myself, but—'

'No, no!' I say at once. 'Of course. You're tied up, I understand—'

'The meeting!' says Sam as though suddenly remembering. 'Of course. Poppy, I'm sorry. It was cancelled. But it'll be rearranged. I'll be in touch . . .'

'Great!' I muster a smile. 'Thanks.'

He won't. But I don't blame him.

'I hope it all works out well for you,' I add. 'And Sir Nicholas.'

Vicks's eyes are swivelling madly in her head. She's obviously totally paranoid that I'm about to spill the beans.

I don't know what to do about Sam's dad. I can't possibly tell Sam now – he'll explode from stress. I'll just have to get a message to the hotel or something. And then bow out.

Like maybe I should have done in the first place.

'Well . . . thanks again.' I meet Sam's eyes and feel a sudden strange pang. This really is the last goodbye. 'Here you are.' I proffer the phone.

'No problem.' He takes it from me and puts it down on his desk. 'Sorry about all this—'

'No! I just hope it all . . .' I nod several times, not daring to say any more in front of Stephanie.

It's going to be odd, not being in Sam's life any more. I'll never know how any of it turns out. Maybe I'll read about this memo in the papers. Maybe I'll read an announcement about Sam and Willow in a wedding column.

'Bye, then.' I turn and follow Stephanie down the corridor. A couple of people are walking along with overnight bags, and as we get into the lift they're in mid-conversation about the hotel and how crap the mini bars are.

'So it's your conference today,' I say politely as we arrive at the ground floor. 'How come you're not down there?'

'Oh, we stagger it.' She ushers me out into the lobby. 'A whole bunch of people are already there and the second coach is leaving in a few minutes. I'll be on that. Although actually, tomorrow's the main event. That's when we have the gala dinner and Santa Claus's speech. It's usually quite fun.'

'*Santa Claus?*' I can't help laughing.

'It's what we call Sir Nicholas. You know, just a silly in-house nickname. Sir Nick ... St Nick ... Santa Claus ... it's a bit lame, I know.' She smiles. 'If you can just give me your security pass?'

I hand over the laminated card and she gives it to one of the security personnel. He says something about 'nice photo', but I'm not listening. An odd feeling is creeping over me.

Santa Claus. Wasn't that bloke who called Violet's phone going on about Santa Claus? Is that a coincidence?

As Stephanie leads me across the marble floor to the main doors, I'm trying to remember what he said. It was all about surgery. Incisions. Something about 'no trace'—

I stop dead, my heart suddenly thumping. That's the same phrase Sam used, just now. *No trace.*

'OK?' Stephanie notices I've stopped.

'Fine! Sorry.' I shoot her a smile and resume walking along, but my mind is wheeling. What else did that guy say? What exactly was it about Santa Claus? Come on, Poppy, *think.*

'Well, bye! Thanks for visiting!' Stephanie smiles once more.

'Thank you!' And as I step outside on to the pavement, I feel a jolt inside. I have it. *Adios, Santa Claus.*

More people are coming out of the building and I step aside, to where a window cleaner is swooshing suds all over the glass. I reach into my bag and start scrabbling around for the *Lion King* programme. *Please* don't say I've lost it, *please*—

I haul it out and stare at my scribbled words:

18 April – Scottie has a contact, keyhole surgery, no trace, be fucking careful.
20 April – Scottie rang. It's done. Surgical strike. No trace. Genius stuff. Adios, Santa Claus.

It's as though the voices are playing back in my mind. It's as though I'm listening to them again. I'm hearing the young, reedy voice and the older, sophisticated drawl.

And suddenly I know without a shadow of a doubt who left the first message. It was Justin Cole.

Oh. My God.

I'm quivering all over. I have to get back in and show these messages to Sam. They mean something, I don't know what, but it's *something*. I push the big glass doors open, and the concierge girl immediately appears in front of me. When I was with Sam she waved us through, but now she smiles at me remotely as though she hasn't just seen me walking along with Stephanie.

'Hello. Do you have an appointment?'

'Not exactly,' I say breathlessly. 'I need to see Sam Roxton at White Globe Consulting. Poppy Wyatt.'

I wait while she turns away and makes a call on her cell phone. I'm trying to stand there patiently but I'm barely able to contain myself. Those messages are something to do with this whole memo thing. I *know* they are.

'I'm sorry.' The girl faces me with professional pleasantness. 'Mr Roxton is unavailable right now.'

'Could you tell him it's urgent?' I shoot back. 'Please?'

Clearly restraining a desire to tell me to get lost, the girl turns away and makes another call, which lasts all of thirty seconds.

'I'm sorry.' Another frozen smile. 'Mr Roxton is busy for the remainder of the day, and most of the other staff are away at the company conference. Perhaps you should phone his assistant and make an appointment. Now, if you could please make way for our other guests?'

She's ushering me out of the main doors. 'Make way' clearly means 'Piss off'.

'Look, I need to see him.' I duck round her and start heading for the escalators. 'Please let me go up there. It'll be fine.'

'Excuse me!' she says, grabbing me by the sleeve. 'You can't just march in there! Thomas?'

Oh, you have to be *kidding*. She's calling over the security guard. What a wimp.

'But it's a real emergency.' I appeal to both of them. 'He'll *want* to see me.'

'Then call and make an appointment!' she snaps back, as the security guard leads me to the main doors.

'Fine!' I snap back. 'I will! I'll call right now! See you in two minutes!' I stomp on to the pavement and reach into my pocket.

And then the full horror hits me. I don't have a phone.

I don't have a phone.

I'm powerless. I can't get into the building and I can't ring Sam. I can't tell him about this. I can't do anything. Why didn't I buy a new phone earlier? Why don't I always walk around with a spare phone? It should be the *law*, like having a spare tyre.

'Excuse me?' I hurry over to the window cleaner. 'Do you have a phone I can borrow?'

'Sorry, love.' He clicks his teeth. 'I do, but it's out of battery.'

'Right.' I smile, breathless with anxiety. 'Thanks anyway – oh!'

I stop mid-stream, peering through the glass into the building. God loves me! There's Sam! He's standing twenty yards away in the lobby, talking animatedly to some guy in a suit holding a leather briefcase.

I push open the main doors, but Thomas the security guard is waiting for me.

'I don't think so,' he says, blocking my way.

'But I need to get in.'

'If you could step aside—'

'But he'll want to see me! Sam! Over here! It's Poppy! Saaam!' I yell, but someone's moving a sofa in the reception area and the scraping sound on the marble drowns me out.

'No you don't!' says the security guard firmly. 'Out you go.' His hands are around my shoulders and the next thing, I find myself back on the pavement, panting in outrage.

I can't believe that just happened. He threw me out! I've never been physically thrown out of anywhere in my life. I didn't think they were allowed to *do* that.

A crowd of people has arrived at the entrance and I stand aside to let them go in, my thoughts skittering wildly. Should I hurry down the street and try to find a payphone? Should I try to get in again? Should I make a run for it into the lobby and see how far I get before I'm tackled to the ground? Sam's standing in front of the lifts now, still talking to the guy with the leather briefcase. He'll be gone in a few moments. It's torture. If I could only attract his attention—

'No luck?' says the window cleaner sympathetically from the top of his ladder. He's covered an entire massive pane of glass with suds and is about to wipe them off with his scraper thing.

And then it comes to me.

'Wait!' I call urgently up to him. 'Don't wipe! Please!'

I've never written in soap suds in my life before, but luckily I'm not aiming for anything very ambitious. Just 'M A 2'. In six-foot-high letters. A bit wobbly – but who's fussing?

'Nice job,' says the window cleaner approvingly from where he's sitting. 'You could come into business with me.'

'Thanks,' I say modestly, and wipe my brow, my arm aching.

If Sam doesn't see that; if *someone* doesn't notice it and poke him on the shoulder and say, 'Hey, look at that—'

'*Poppy?*'

I turn and look down from my perch on the window cleaner's ladder. Sam's standing there on the pavement, looking up at me incredulously.

'Is that addressed to me?'

We take the lift upstairs in silence. Vicks is waiting in Sam's office and as she sees me she bangs her forehead with the heel of her hand.

'This had better be good,' says Sam tersely, closing the glass door behind us. 'I have five minutes. There's a bit of an emergency going on—'

I feel a flash of anger. Does he think I don't realize that? Does he think I wrote 'SAM' in six-foot sudsy letters just on a whim?

'I appreciate that,' I say, matching his curt tone. 'I just thought you might be interested in these messages which came into Violet's phone last week. This phone.' I reach for the phone, still lying on his desk.

'Whose phone is that?' says Vicks, eyeing me with suspicion.

'Violet's,' replies Sam. 'My PA? Clive's daughter? Shot off to be a model?'

'Oh, her.' Vicks frowns again and jerks a thumb at me. 'Well, what was *she* doing with Violet's phone?'

Sam and I exchange glances.

'Long story,' says Sam at last. 'Violet threw it away. Poppy was . . . babysitting it.'

'I got a couple of messages which I wrote down.' I put the *Lion King* programme down between them, and read the messages out for good measure, as I know my writing isn't that clear. ' "Scottie has a contact, keyhole surgery, no trace, be fucking careful." ' I point at the programme. 'This second message was two days later, from Scottie himself. "It's done. Surgical strike. No trace. Genius stuff. Adios, Santa Claus." ' I let the words sink in a moment before I add, 'The first message was from Justin Cole.'

'*Justin?*' Sam looks alert.

'I didn't recognize his voice at the time, but I do now. It was him talking about "keyhole surgery" and "no trace".'

'Vicks.' Sam is looking at her. 'Come on. You've got to see now—'

'I see nothing! Just a few random words. How can we even be sure it was Justin?'

Sam turns to me. 'Are these voice-mails? Can we still listen to them?'

'No. They were just . . . you know. Phone messages. They left them and I wrote them down.'

Vicks looks perplexed. 'OK, this makes no sense. Did you introduce yourself? Why would Justin have left a message with *you*?' She exhales angrily. 'Sam, I don't have time for this . . .'

'He didn't realize I was a person,' I explain, flushing. 'I pretended to be an answering machine.'

'*What?*' She stares at me, uncomprehending.

'You know.' I put on my voice-mail-lady voice. '"I'm afraid the person you've called is not available. Please leave a message." And then he left the message and I wrote it down.'

Sam gives a muffled snort of laughter, but Vicks looks speechless. She picks up the *Lion King* programme for a moment, frowning at the words, then flicks through to the inside pages, although the only information she'll find there is the actors' biographies. At last she puts it back down on the table. 'Sam, this means nothing. It changes nothing.'

'It does *not* mean nothing.' He shakes his head adamantly. 'This is it! Right here.' He jabs a thumb at the programme. '*This* is what's been going on.'

'But *what's* been going on?' Her voice rises in exasperation. 'Who's Scottie, for fuck's sake?'

'He called Sir Nicholas "Santa Claus".' Sam's face is screwed up in thought. 'Which means it's likely to be someone in the company. But where? In IT?'

'Is Violet anything to do with it?' I venture. 'It was her phone, after all.'

There's silence for a moment – then Sam shakes his head, almost regretfully.

'She was only here for about five minutes, her father's a good friend of Sir Nicholas ... I just can't believe she's involved.'

'So why did they leave messages for her? Did they have the wrong number or something?'

'Unlikely.' Sam wrinkles his nose. 'I mean, why *this* number?'

Automatically I look at the phone, flashing away on the desk. I wonder in a detached way if I've got any voice-mails. But somehow, right at this minute, the rest of my life seems a million miles away. The world has shrunk to this room. Both Sam and Vicks have sunk into chairs and I follow suit.

'Who had Violet's phone before her?' says Vicks suddenly. 'It's a company phone. She was only here for, what, three weeks? Could it have been someone else's number previously and those messages were left by mistake?'

'Yes!' I look up, galvanized. 'People are *always* calling the wrong number by mistake. And emailing the wrong address. I even do it myself. You forget to delete it and press the contact's name and the old number pops up and you don't realize. Especially if you go to some generic voice-mail.'

I can see Sam's mind working overtime.

'Only one way to find out,' he says, reaching for a landline phone on the desk. He jabs in a three-digit speed-dial and waits.

'Hi, Cynthia. Sam here,' he says easily. 'Just a quick question about the cell phone that was allocated to Violet, my PA. I was wondering: did anyone else have it before her? Did anyone else ever have that number?'

As he listens, his face changes. He makes a fierce, silent gesture at Vicks, who shrugs back helplessly.

'Great,' he says. 'Thanks, Cynthia—'

From the stream of tinny sound coming from the phone, it's clear this Cynthia likes to talk.

'I'd better go . . .' Sam is rolling his eyes desperately. 'Yes, I know the phone should have been delivered back. No, we haven't misplaced it, don't worry . . . Yes, very unprofessional. No warning. I know, company property . . . I'll pop it along . . . yes . . . yes . . .'

At last he manages to extricate himself. He puts the receiver down and is silent for an agonizing three seconds before turning to Vicks.

'Ed.'

'*No.*' Vicks breathes out slowly.

Sam has picked up the phone and is staring incredulously at it. 'This was Ed's company phone till four weeks ago. Then it was reassigned to Violet. I had no idea.' Sam turns to me. 'Ed Exton was—'

'I remember.' I nod. 'Finance Director. Fired. Suing the company.'

'Jesus.' Vicks seems genuinely shell-shocked. She's sagged back against her chair. '*Ed.*'

'Who else?' Sam seems absolutely wired by this discovery. 'Vicks, this isn't just an orchestrated plan, it's a bloody three-movement symphony. Nick is smeared. Bruce axes him, because he's a pusillanimous arsehole. The board needs another CEO, quick. Ed kindly announces he'll drop his lawsuit and step back in to save the day, Justin's nest is feathered . . .'

'They'd really go to all that trouble?' says Vicks sceptically.

Sam's mouth twists into a half-smile. 'Vicks, do you have any idea quite how much Ed loathes Nick? Some hacker was paid good money to change that memo and remove the old one from the system. I reckon Ed would spend a hundred grand to ruin Nick's reputation. Two hundred, even.'

Vicks's face twists with distaste.

'This would never happen if the company was run by women,' she says at last. 'Never. Bloody macho . . . twats.' She gets to her feet and heads over to the window, staring out at the traffic, her arms wrapped around her body.

'The question is: who made this happen? Who actually executed it?' Sam is sitting on his desk, tapping his pen against his knuckles in an urgent drumbeat, his face taut with concentration. ' "Scottie". Who's that? Someone Scottish?'

'He didn't actually *sound* Scottish,' I volunteer. 'Maybe his nickname's a joke?'

Sam suddenly focuses on me, the light dawning on his face. 'That's *it*. Of course. Poppy, would you know his voice again if you heard it?'

'Sam!' Vicks interjects sharply before I can answer. 'No way. You can't be serious.'

'Vicks, would you step out of denial for *just one second*?' Sam rises to his feet, erupting in fury. 'The faked memo wasn't an accident. The leak to ITN wasn't an accident. This is *happening*. Someone *did this* to Nick. This isn't just a matter of hushing up a little bit of embarrassing . . .' He gropes for a moment. 'I don't know. Facebook activity. It's a smear. It's *fraud*.'

'It's a *theory*.' She squares up to him. 'Nothing more, Sam. A few words on a fucking *Lion King* programme.'

I feel a bit hurt. It's not my fault all I had with me was a *Lion King* programme.

'We need to identify this guy Scottie.' Sam turns to me again. 'Would you know his voice again if you heard it?'

'Yes,' I say, a little nervous at his intensity.

'You're sure?'

'Yes!'

'Right. Well, let's do it. Let's go and find him.'

'Sam, stop right now!' Vicks sounds furious. 'You're insane! What are you going to do, just get her to listen to every staff member talk till she hears that voice?'

'Why not?' says Sam mutinously.

'Because it's the most ridiculous fucking idea I've ever heard!' Vicks explodes. 'That's why not!'

Sam regards her steadily for a moment, then turns to me. 'Come on, Poppy. We'll trawl the building.'

Vicks is shaking her head. 'And if she does recognize his voice? Then what? Citizen's arrest?'

'Then it'll be a start,' says Sam. 'Ready, Poppy?'

'Poppy.' Vicks comes over and faces me head-on. Her cheeks are pink and she's breathing hard. 'I have no idea who you are. But you don't have to listen to Sam. You don't have to do this. You owe him *nothing*. This is all *nothing* to do with you.'

'She doesn't mind,' says Sam. 'Do you, Poppy?'

Vicks ignores him. 'Poppy, I strongly advise you to leave. Now.'

'That's not the kind of girl Poppy is,' says Sam with a scowl. 'She doesn't bail out on people. Do you?' He meets my eye and his gaze is so unexpectedly warm, I feel an inward glow.

I turn to Vicks. 'You're wrong, I do owe Sam one. And Sir Nicholas is a potential patient at my physio practice, *actually*. So he is something to do with me, too.'

I quite liked dropping that in, although I bet Sir Nicholas never does make it down to Balham.

'And anyway,' I continue, lifting my chin nobly. '*Whoever* it was, whether I knew them or not, if I could help in some way, I would. I mean, if you can help, you have to help. Don't you think?'

Vicks stares at me for a moment, as though trying to work me out – then gives a strange, wry smile.

'OK. Well, you got me. I can't argue against that.'

'Let's go.' Sam makes for the door.

I grab my bag and wish yet again that my T-shirt didn't have a huge great splotch on it.

'Hey, Wallander,' Vicks chimes in sarcastically. 'Small point. In case you'd forgotten, everyone's either already at the conference or on their way to the conference.'

There's another silence apart from Sam tapping his pen furiously again. I don't dare speak. I certainly don't dare look at Vicks.

'Poppy,' says Sam at last. 'Do you have a few hours? Could you come down to Hampshire?'

ELEVEN

This is totally surreal. And thrilling. And a bit of a pain. All at the same time.

It's not that I'm *regretting* my noble gesture, exactly. I still mean what I said in the office. How could I possibly walk away? How could I not at least try to help Sam out? But on the other hand, I thought it would take about half an hour. Not a train journey down to Hampshire, and that's just for starters.

I'm supposed to be at the hairdresser's right now. I'm supposed to be talking about updos and trying on my tiara. Instead I'm on Waterloo station concourse, buying a cup of tea and clutching the phone, which, needless to say, I grabbed from the desk as we left. Sam could hardly complain. I've texted Sue to tell her that I'm really sorry, I'll have to miss the appointment with Louis but of course I'll pay the whole fee and please give Louis my love.

I looked at it after I'd finished typing it, and deleted half the kisses. Then I put them back in again. Then I took them out again. Maybe five *is* enough.

Now I'm waiting for Magnus to pick up. He's leaving for his stag trip to Bruges this afternoon, so it's not like I was going to see him, but still. I feel like if I don't at least ring him, it'll be wrong.

'Oh, hi, Magnus!'

'Pops!' The line is terrible, and I can hear a tannoy in the background. 'We're about to board. You OK?'

'Yes! I just wanted to . . .' I trail off, not sure where I want to go with this.

Just wanted to tell you that I'm off to Hampshire with a man you know nothing about, embroiled in a situation you know nothing about.

'I'll . . . be out tonight,' I say lamely. 'In case you call.'

There. That's honest. Kind of.

'OK!' He laughs. 'Well, you have fun. Sweets, I've got to go . . .'

'OK! Bye! Have a good time!' The phone goes dead and I look up to see Sam watching me. I tug my shirt self-consciously, wishing again that I'd popped to the shops. It turns out that Sam does keep a spare shirt in his office, and my T-shirt was so frightful that I borrowed it. But it makes the situation even stranger, wearing his stripy Turnbull & Asser.

'Just saying goodbye to Magnus,' I explain needlessly, as he's been standing there the whole time and must have heard every word.

'That'll be two pounds.' The woman at the sandwich shop hands me my cup.

'Thanks! Right . . . shall we go?'

As Sam and I walk down the concourse and get into the carriage I feel unreal. I'm stiff with awkwardness. We must look like a couple to anyone watching. What if Willow sees us?

No. Don't be paranoid. Willow was on the second coach to the conference. She sent an email to Sam, telling him. And anyway, it's not like Sam and I are doing anything illicit. We're just . . . friends.

No, 'friends' doesn't feel right. Not colleagues, either. Not really acquaintances . . .

OK. Let's face it. It's weird.

I glance over at Sam to see if he's thinking the same, but he's staring out of the train window with his usual blank stare. The train jolts and moves off down the tracks, and he comes to. As he catches me gazing at him, I quickly look away.

I'm trying to appear relaxed, but secretly I'm feeling more and more freaked out. What have I agreed to? Everything rests on my memory. It's up to me, Poppy Wyatt, to identify some voice I heard down a phone days ago, for about twenty seconds. What if I fail?

I take a sip of tea to calm myself and wince. First the soup was too cold. Now this is too hot. The train starts rushing along the tracks and a spot of tea jumps out of the lid, scalding my hand.

'OK?' Sam's noticed me wince.

'Fine.' I smile.

'Can I be honest?' he says bluntly. 'You don't look fine.'

'I'm good!' I protest. 'I'm just . . . you know. There's a lot going on at the moment.'

Sam nods.

'I'm sorry we never got to go through those confrontation techniques I promised.'

'Oh! That.' I brush his apology away with a hand. 'This is more important.'

'Don't just say, "Oh! That."' Sam shakes his head, looking exasperated. 'That's what I'm talking about. You automatically put yourself second.'

'I don't! I mean . . . you know.' I shrug awkwardly. 'Whatever.'

The train pulls into Clapham Junction and a group of people files into the carriage. For a while Sam is engrossed in texting. His phone has been constantly flashing and I can only imagine how many messages are flying around. Eventually, though, he puts the phone back in his pocket and leans forward, resting his elbows on the little table between us.

'Everything OK?' I ask timidly, immediately realizing what an inane question this is. To his credit, Sam totally ignores it.

'I have a question for you,' he says calmly. 'What is it about these Tavishes that makes you feel as though they're superior? Is it the titles? The doctorates? The brains?'

Not this again.

'Everything! It's obvious! They're just . . . I mean, you respect Sir Nicholas, don't you?' I throw back at him defensively. 'Look at all this effort you're making for him. It's because you respect him.'

'Yes, I respect him. Of course I do. But I don't feel as though I'm inherently inferior to him. He doesn't make me feel like a second-class citizen.'

'I don't feel like a second-class citizen! You don't know anything about it. So just . . . stop!'

'OK.' Sam lifts his hands up high. 'If I'm wrong, I apologize. It's only an impression I've got. I only wanted to help, as a . . .' I can sense him reaching for the word 'friend' then rejecting it, like I did. 'I just wanted to help,' he says finally. 'But it's your life. I'll butt out.'

There's silence for a while. He's stopped. He's given up. I've won.

Why don't I feel like I've won?

'Excuse me.' Sam puts his phone to his ear. 'Vicks. What's up?'

He heads out of the carriage and, without meaning to, I exhale a massive sigh. The gnawing pain is back, nestling beneath my ribs. But right now I can't tell if it's because the Tavishes don't want me to marry Magnus, or that I'm trying to deny it, or that I'm nervous about this whole escapade, or that my tea's too strong.

For a while I just sit there, gazing down at my steaming tea, wishing I'd never heard the Tavishes arguing in the church. That I knew nothing. That I could just blot that grey cloud out of my life and go back to 'Lucky, lucky me, isn't everything perfect?'

Sam takes his seat again and there's silence for a few moments. The train has come to a halt in the middle of nowhere, and it's oddly quiet without the sound of the wheels on the track.

'OK.' I stare down at the little Formica table. '*OK.*'

'OK, what?'

'OK, you're not wrong.'

Sam says nothing, just waits. The train jolts and lurches, like a horse deciding whether to behave, then slowly begins moving off again.

'But I'm not making this up in my head or whatever you think.' I hunch my shoulders miserably. 'I overheard the Tavishes, OK? They don't want Magnus to marry me. I've done everything I can. I've played Scrabble and I've tried making conversation and I've even read Antony's latest book.[78] But I'll never be like them. Never.'

'Why should you be?' Sam looks perplexed. 'Why would you *want* to?'

'Yeah right.' I roll my eyes. 'Why would anyone want to be a really brainy celebrity who goes on TV?'

'Antony Tavish has a big brain,' says Sam steadily. 'Having a big brain is like having a big liver or a big nose. Why do you feel insecure? What if he had a huge lower intestine? Would you feel insecure then?'

I can't help giggling.

'He's a freak, strictly speaking,' Sam presses on. 'You're marrying into a family of freaks. To be in the outermost percentile of anything is freakish. Next time you're intimidated by them, imagine a big neon sign over their heads, reading "FREAKS!"'

'That's not what you really think.' I'm smiling but shaking my head.

78. I've read four chapters, to be truthful.

'It is absolutely what I think.' He looks deadly serious now. 'These academic guys have to feel important. They give papers and present TV programmes to show they're useful and valuable. But you do useful, valuable work every day. You don't need to prove anything. How many people have you treated? Hundreds. You've reduced their pain. You've made hundreds of people happier. Has Antony Tavish ever made anyone happier?'

I'm sure there's something wrong with what he's saying, but right now I can't work out what it is. All I can do is feel a little glow. That had never occurred to me before. I've made hundreds of people happier.

'What about you? Have you?' I can't help saying, and Sam shoots me a wry smile.

'I'm working on it.'

The train slows as it passes through Woking and we both instinctively look out of the window. Then Sam turns back. 'The point is, it's not about them. It's about *you*. You and him. Magnus.'

'I know,' I say at last. 'I know it is.'

It sounds strange, hearing Magnus's name on his lips. It feels all wrong.

Magnus and Sam are so very different. It's like they're made out of different stuff. Magnus is so shiny, so mercurial, so impressive, so sexy. But just a teeny weeny bit self-obsessed.[79] Whereas Sam is so . . . straight and strong. And generous. And kind. You just know he'd always be there for you, whatever.

Sam looks at me now and smiles, as though he can read my thoughts, and my heart experiences that little tiny fillip it always does now when he smiles . . .

Lucky Willow.

I give a tiny inward gasp at my own thought, and take a gulp of tea to cover my embarrassment.

79. I can say that because he's my fiancé and I love him.

That thought popped into my head with *no warning*. And I didn't mean it. Or rather, yes, I *did* mean it, but simply in the sense that I wish them both well, as a disinterested friend . . . no, not friend . . .

I'm blushing.

I'm blushing at my own stupid, nonsensical, meaningless thought process, which, by the way, nobody knows about except me. So I can relax. I can stop this now, and drop the ridiculous idea that Sam can read my mind and knows I fancy him—

No. Stop. *Stop.* That's ridiculous.

This is just—

Erase the word 'fancy'. I do not. I do not.

'Are you OK?' Sam gives me a curious look. 'Poppy, I'm sorry, I didn't mean to upset you.'

'No!' I say quickly. 'You haven't! I appreciate it. Really.'

'Good. Because—' He breaks off to answer his phone. 'Vicks. Any news?'

As Sam moves away for another call, I gulp my tea again, staring fixedly out of the window, willing my blood to cool and my brain to go blank. I need to backtrack. I need to reboot. *Do not save changes.*

To establish a more businesslike atmosphere, I reach in my pocket for the phone, check it for messages, then put it on the table. There's nothing on general email about the memo crisis – clearly it's all going on between a select number of high-level colleagues.

'You do know you have to buy another phone at *some* point,' says Sam, raising an eyebrow as he returns. 'Or are you planning to purloin all your phones from bins from now on?'

'It's the only place.' I shrug. 'Bins and skips.'

The phone buzzes with an email and I automatically reach for it, but Sam gets there first. His hand brushes against mine and our eyes lock.

'Might be for me.'

'True.' I nod. 'Go ahead.'

He checks it, then shakes his head. 'Wedding trumpeter's fee. All yours.'

With a little grin of triumph I take the phone from him. I send a quick reply to Lucinda, then put it back on the table. As it buzzes again a few moments later, we both make a grab and I just beat him.

'Shirt sale.' I pass it to him. 'Not really my thing.' Sam deletes the email, then replaces the phone on the table.

'In the middle!' I shift it an inch. 'Cheat.'

'Put your hands on your lap,' he retorts. 'Cheat.'

There's silence. We're both sitting poised, waiting for the phone to buzz. Sam looks so deadly intent I feel a laugh rising. Someone else's phone suddenly rings across the carriage, and Sam makes a half-grab for ours before realizing.

'Tragic,' I murmur. 'Doesn't even know the ringtone.'

Ours suddenly bleeps with a text, and Sam's momentary hesitation is just enough for me to scoop the phone up out of his grasp.

'Haha! And I *bet* it's for me . . .'

I click on the text and peer at it. It's from an unknown number and only half the message has come in, but I can work out the gist—

I read it again. And again. I look up at Sam and lick my suddenly dry lips. Never in a million years was I expecting this.

'Is it for you?' says Sam.

'No.' I swallow. 'For you.'

'Vicks?' His hand is already outstretched. 'She shouldn't be using that number—'

'No, not Vicks. Not work. It's . . . it's . . . personal.'

Yet again I read it over, not wanting to relinquish the phone until I'm absolutely sure of what I'm seeing.

I'm not sure if this is the right number. But I had to let you know. Your fiancée has been unfaithful. It's with someone you know . . . (Incoming text)

I knew it, I *knew* she was a bitch and this proves she's even worse than I thought.

'What is it?' Sam bangs his hand impatiently on the table. 'Give. Is it to do with the conference?'

'No!' I knit my hands around the phone. 'Sam, I'm really sorry. And I wish I hadn't seen this first. But it says . . .' I hesitate, agonized. 'It says Willow's being unfaithful to you. I'm sorry.'

Sam looks absolutely shocked. As I hand the phone over I feel a wrenching sympathy for him. Who the hell sends that kind of news in a *text*?

I bet she's shagging Justin Cole. Those two would totally suit each other.

I'm scanning Sam's face for distress, but after that initial flash of shock, he seems extraordinarily calm. He frowns, flicks to the end of the text, then puts the phone back down on the table.

'Are you OK?' I can't help venturing.

He shrugs. 'Makes no sense.'

'I know!' I'm so stirred up on his behalf, I can't help throwing in my views. 'Why would she do that? And she gives you such a hard time! She's such a hypocrite! She's horrible!' I break off, wondering if I've gone too far. Sam is looking at me oddly.

'No, you don't understand. It makes no sense because I'm not engaged. I don't have a fiancée.'

'But you're engaged to Willow,' I say stupidly.

'No, I'm not.'

'But . . .' I stare at him blankly. How can he not be engaged? Of course he's engaged.

'Never have been.' He shrugs. 'What gave you that idea?'

'You told me! I *know* you told me!' My face is screwed up, trying to remember. 'At least . . . yes! It was in an email. Violet sent it. It said, "Sam's engaged." I know it did.'

'Oh that.' His brow clears. 'Occasionally I've used that as an excuse to get rid of persistent people.' He pauses, then adds, as though to make it clear, 'Women.'

'An *excuse*?' I echo incredulously. 'So, who's Willow, then?'

'Willow is my ex-girlfriend,' he says after a pause. 'We split up two months ago.'

Ex-girlfriend?

For a moment, I can't speak. My brain feels like a fruit machine, whirling round, trying to find the right combination. I can't cope with this. He's engaged. He's supposed to be *engaged*.

'But you— You should have said!' My agitation bursts out at last. 'All this time, you let me think you were engaged!'

'No, I didn't. I never mentioned it.' He looks perplexed. 'Why are you angry?'

'I . . . I don't know! It's all wrong.'

I'm breathing hard, trying to order my thoughts. How can he not be with Willow? Everything's different now. And it's all his fault.[80]

'We talked so much about everything.' I try to speak more calmly. 'I mentioned Willow several times and you never specified who she was. How could you be so secretive?'

'I'm not secretive!' He gives a short laugh. 'I would have explained who she was if the subject had come up. It's over. It doesn't matter.'

'Of *course* it matters!'

'Why?'

I want to scream with frustration. How can he ask why? Isn't it obvious?

'Because . . . because . . . she *behaves* as though you're

---

80. I don't quite know how. But I feel instinctively that it is.

together.' And suddenly I realize this is what's upsetting me the most. 'She behaves as though she has every right to rant at you. That's why I never doubted you were engaged. What's *that* all about?'

Sam flinches as though with irritation but says nothing.

'She cc-s your PA! She blurts everything out in public emails! It's just bizarre!'

'Willow's always been . . . an exhibitionist. She likes an audience.' He sounds reluctant to get into this. 'She doesn't have the same boundaries as other people—'

'Too right she doesn't! Do you know how possessive she is? I overheard her talking at the office.' A PA system starts broadcasting announcements about upcoming stations, but I raise my voice over the noise. 'You know she bitches about you to all the girls at the office? She told them you're just going through a bad patch and you need to wake up or you're going to realize what you're about to lose, i.e. her.'

'We're not going through a bad patch.' I hear a flash of real anger in his voice. 'We're over.'

'Does *she* know that?'

'She knows.'

'Are you sure? Are you totally positive that she realizes?'

'Of course.' He sounds impatient.

'It's not "Of course"! How exactly did you break up? Did you sit down and have a proper talk with her?'

There's silence. Sam's not meeting my eye. He so did not sit down and have a proper talk with her. I know it. He probably sent her a brief text, saying, '*Over. Sam.*'

'Well, you need to tell her to stop all this ridiculous emailing. Don't you?' I try to get his attention. 'Sam?'

He's checking his phone again. Typical. He doesn't want to know, he doesn't want to talk about it, he doesn't want to engage . . .

A thought strikes me. Oh my God, of *course*.

'Sam, do you ever actually *reply* to Willow's emails?'

He doesn't, does he? Suddenly it's all clear. That's why she starts a fresh one each time. It's like she's pinning messages to a blank wall.

'So if you never reply, how does she know what you really think?' I raise my voice still further over the tannoy. 'Oh, wait, she doesn't! That's why she's so deluded about everything! That's why she thinks you still somehow belong to her!'

Sam isn't even meeting my eye.

'God, you *are* a stubborn fuck!' I yell in exasperation, just as the announcement stops.

OK. *Obviously* I wouldn't have spoken so loudly if I'd realized that was about to happen. *Obviously* I wouldn't have used the F-word. So that mother with her children sitting three rows away can stop shooting me evil looks as though I'm personally corrupting them.

'You really are!' I continue in a furious undertone. 'You can't just blank Willow out and think she'll go away. You can't just press Ignore for ever. She won't go away, Sam. Take it from me. You need to talk to her and explain exactly what the situation is, and what is wrong with all this, and—'

'Look, leave it.' Sam sounds irate. 'If she wants to send pointless emails she can send pointless emails. It doesn't bother me.'

'But it's toxic! It's bad! It shouldn't happen!'

'You don't know anything about it,' he snaps. I think I've hit a nerve.

And by the way, that's a joke. *I* don't know anything about it?

'I know all about it!' I contradict him. 'I've been dealing with your in-box, remember? Mr Blank, No Reply, Ignore Everything and Everyone.'

Sam glares at me. 'Just because I don't reply to every email with sixty-five bloody smiley faces—'

He is not turning this against me. What's better, smiley faces or denial?

'Well, you don't reply to *anyone*,' I retort scathingly. 'Not even your own dad!'

'*What?*' He sounds scandalized. 'What the hell are you going on about now?'

'I read his email,' I say defiantly. 'About how he wants to talk to you and he wishes you'd come and visit him in Hampshire and he's got something to tell you. He said you and he hadn't talked for ages and he misses the old days. And you didn't even *answer* him. You're heartless.'

Sam throws his head back in a roar of laughter.

'Oh, Poppy. You really don't know what you're talking about.'

'I think I do.'

'I think you don't.'

'I think you'll find I have a little more insight into your own life than you do.'

I glare at him mutinously. Now I hope Sam's dad *did* get my email. Wait till Sam arrives at the Chiddingford Hotel and finds his father there, all dressed up and hopeful, with a rose in his buttonhole. Then maybe he won't be so flippant.

Sam has picked up our phone and is reading the text again.

'I'm not engaged,' he says, his brows knitted. 'I don't have a fiancée.'

'Yes, I got that, thanks,' I say sarcastically. 'You just have a psychotic ex who thinks she still owns you even though you broke up two months ago—'

'No, no.' He shakes his head. 'You're not following. The two of us are effectively sharing this phone right now, yes?'

'Yes.' Where's he going with this?

'So this message could have been meant for either of us. I don't have a fiancée, Poppy.' He raises his head, looking a little grim. 'But you do.'

I stare at him uncomprehendingly for a moment – then it's as though something icy trickles down my spine.

'No. You mean— No. *No.* Don't be stupid.' I grab the phone

from him. 'It says fiancée with an *e*.' I find the word and jab at it to prove my point. 'See? It's crystal clear. Fiancée, feminine.'

'Agreed.' He nods. 'But there *is* no fiancée, feminine. She doesn't exist. So . . .'

I stare back at him, feeling a little sick, rerunning the text in my mind with a different spelling. *Your fiancé has been unfaithful.*

No. It *couldn't* be—

Magnus would *never*—

There's a bleeping sound and we both start. It's the rest of the text coming in. I read the entire thing through silently:

I'm not sure if this is the right number. But I had to let you know. Your fiancée has been unfaithful. It's with someone you know. I'm sorry to do this to you so soon before your wedding, Poppy. But you should know the truth. Your friend.

I let the phone drop down on the table, my head spinning.

This can't be happening. It can't.

I'm dimly aware of Sam picking up the mobile and reading the text.

'Some friend,' he says at last, sounding grave. 'Whoever it is, they're probably just stirring. Probably no truth in it at all.'

'Exactly.' I nod several times. 'Exactly. I'm sure it's made up. Just someone trying to freak me out for no good reason.'

I'm trying to seem confident, but my trembling voice gives me away.

'When's the wedding?'

'Saturday.'

Saturday. Four days away and I get a text like that.

'There isn't anybody . . .' Sam hesitates. 'There's no one you'd . . . suspect?'

Annalise.

It's in my head before I even know I'm going to think it. Annalise and Magnus.

'No. I mean . . . I don't know.' I turn away, pressing my cheek to the train window.

I don't want to talk about it. I don't want to think about it – Annalise's my friend. I know she thought Magnus should have been hers, but surely . . .

Annalise in her uniform, batting her eyelashes at Magnus. Her hands lingering on his shoulders.

No. Stop it. *Stop* it, Poppy.

I bring my hands up to my face, screwing my fists into my eye-sockets, wanting to rip my own thoughts out. Why did whoever-it-is have to send that text? Why did I have to read it?

It can't be true. It can't. It's just scurrilous, hurtful, damaging, horrible . . .

A tear has escaped from beneath my fists and has snaked down my cheek to my chin. I don't know what to do. I don't know how to tackle this. Do I call Magnus in Bruges? Do I interrupt his stag do? But what if he's innocent and he gets angry and the trust between us is ruined?

'We're going to be there in a few minutes.' Sam's voice is low and wary. 'Poppy, if you're not up for this I'll totally understand—'

'No. I am up for it.' I lower my fists, reach for a paper napkin and blow my nose. 'I'm fine.'

'You're not fine.'

'No. I'm not. But . . . what can I do?'

'Text the bastard back. Write: "Give me a name."'

I stare at him in slight admiration. That would never even have occurred to me.

'OK.' I swallow hard, gathering my courage. 'OK. I'll do it.' As I reach for the phone I feel better already. At least I'm doing something. At least I'm not just sitting here, wondering in pointless agony. I finish the text, press Send with a tiny surge of adrenalin and slurp the last of my cold tea. Come on, Unknown Number. Bring it on. Tell me what you've got.

'Sent?' Sam has been watching me.

'Yup. Now I'll just have to wait and see what they say.'

The train is pulling into Basingstoke and passengers are heading for the doors. I dump my cup in the litter bin, grab my bag and stand up too.

'That's enough about my stupid problems.' I force myself to smile at Sam. 'Come on. Let's go and sort yours.'

TWELVE

The Chiddingford Hotel is large and impressive, with a beautiful main Georgian house at the end of a long drive and some less lovely glass buildings half-hidden behind a big hedge. But I seem to be the only one appreciating it as we arrive. Sam isn't in the best of moods. There was a problem getting a cab, then we got stuck behind some sheep, and then the taxi driver got lost. Sam has been texting furiously ever since we got into our taxi, and as we arrive, two men in suits who I don't recognize are waiting for us on the front steps.

Sam thrusts some notes at the driver and opens the taxi door almost before it brakes to a stop. 'Poppy, excuse me a moment. Hi guys . . .'

The three of them cluster into a huddle on the gravel and I get out more slowly. The taxi pulls away and I look around at the manicured gardens. There are croquet lawns and topiary and even a little chapel which I bet is lovely for weddings. The place seems empty and there's a freshness to the air which makes me shiver. Maybe I'm just nervous. Maybe it's delayed shock.

Or maybe it's standing in the middle of nowhere, not

knowing what the hell I'm doing here, with my personal life about to collapse in ruins around me.

I pull out my phone for companionship. Just the feel of it sitting in my hand comforts me a little, but not enough. I read the Unknown Number text a few more times again, just to torture myself, then compose a text to Magnus. After a few false starts I have it just right.

Hi. How are you doing? P

No kisses.

As I press Send, my eyes start to sting. It's a simple message, but I feel as though every word is freighted with double, triple, even quadruple meaning; with a heartbreaking subtext which he may or may not get.[81]

Hi means: *Hi, have you been unfaithful? Have you? Please, PLEASE don't let this be true.*

How means: *I really wish you'd ring me. I know you're on your stag do but it would reassure me so much just to hear your voice and know that you love me and you couldn't do such a thing.*

Are means: *Oh God, I can't bear it. What if it's true? What will I do? What will I say? But then, what if it's NOT true and I've suspected you for no good reason . . .*

'Poppy.' Sam is turning towards me and I jump.

'Yes! Here.' I nod, thrusting my phone away. I have to concentrate now. I have to put Magnus from my mind. I have to be useful.

'These are Mark and Robbie. They work for Vicks.'

'She's on her way down.' Mark consults his phone as we all head up the steps. 'Sir Nicholas is staying put for now. We think Berkshire's the best place for him to be if there's any chance of being doorstepped.'

'Nick shouldn't *hide*.' Sam's frowning.

81. OK, he won't get. I know.

'Not hiding. Staying calm. We don't want him rushing to London, looking like there's a crisis. He's speaking at a dinner tonight, we'll regroup tomorrow, see how things have played out. As for the conference, we keep going for now. Obviously Sir Nicholas was due to arrive here in the morning, but we'll have to see . . .' He hesitates, wincing slightly. '. . . what happens.'

'What about the injunction?' says Sam. 'I was talking to Julian, he's pulling out all the stops . . .'

Robbie sighs.

'Sam, we already know that won't work. I mean, we're not *not* going to apply for one, but—'

He stops mid-stream as we arrive in a big lobby. Wow. This conference is a lot more high-tech than our annual physiotherapists' one. There are massive White Globe Consulting logos everywhere, and big screens mounted all around the lobby. Someone is clearly using some kind of TV camera inside the hall, because images of an audience sitting in rows are being beamed out. There are two sets of closed double doors straight ahead of us, and the sound of an audience laughing suddenly emanates from behind them, followed, ten seconds later, by laughter from the screens.

The whole lobby is empty except for a table bearing a few lonely name badges, behind which a bored-looking girl is lolling. She stands up straighter as she sees us, and smiles uncertainly at me.

'They're having a good time,' says Sam, glancing at one of the TV screens.

'Malcolm's speaking,' says Mark. 'He's doing a great job. We're in here.' He ushers us into a side room and shuts the door firmly behind us.

'So, Poppy.' Robbie turns to me politely. 'Sam's filled us in on your . . . theory.'

'It's not *my* theory,' I say in horror. 'I don't know anything about it! I just got these messages, and I wondered if they could be relevant, and Sam worked it out . . .'

'I think she has something.' Sam faces up to Mark and Robbie as though daring them to disagree. 'The memo was planted. We all agree that.'

'The memo is . . . uncharacteristic,' amends Robbie.

'Uncharacteristic?' Sam looks like he wants to explode. 'He didn't bloody write it! Someone else wrote it and inserted it into the system. We're going to find out who. Poppy heard the voice. Poppy will recognize it.'

'OK.' Robbie exchanges wary glances with Mark. 'All I will say, Sam, is that we have to be very, very careful. We're still working on breaking this news to the company. If you go crashing in with accusations—'

'I won't crash in with anything.' Sam glowers at him. 'Have a little trust. Jesus.'

'So what are you planning to do?' Mark looks genuinely interested.

'Walk around. Listen. Find the needle in the haystack.' Sam turns to me. 'You up for that, Poppy?'

'Totally.' I nod, trying to hide how panicked I feel. I'm half-wishing I never took those messages down now.

'And then . . .' Robbie still looks dissatisfied.

'Let's cross that bridge.'

There's silence in the room.

'OK,' says Robbie at last. 'Do it. Go on. I guess it can't do any harm. And how will you explain away Poppy?'

'New PA?' suggests Mark.

Sam shakes his head. 'I've appointed a new PA and half the floor have met her this morning. Let's keep it simple. Poppy's thinking of joining the company. I'm showing her round. OK with that, Poppy?'

'Yes! Fine.'

'Got that personnel list?'

'Here.' Robbie hands it to him. 'But be discreet, Sam.'

Mark has opened the door a crack and is looking into the lobby.

'They're coming out,' he says. 'All yours.'

We head out of the room into the lobby. Both sets of double doors are open and people are streaming out of them, all wearing badges and chatting, some laughing. They all look pretty fresh, given it's 6.30 p.m. and they've been listening to speeches all afternoon.

'There are so *many*.' I stare at the groups of people, feeling totally daunted.

'It's fine,' says Sam firmly. 'You know it's a male voice. That already cuts it down. We'll just go round the room and rule them out, one by one. I have my suspicions but . . . I won't bias you.'

Slowly I follow him into the mêlée. People are grabbing drinks from waiters and greeting each other and shouting jokes across other people's heads. It's a cacophony. My ears feel as though they're radar sensors, straining this way and that to catch the sound of voices.

'Heard our guy yet?' Sam says, as he hands me a glass of orange juice. I can tell he's half-joking, half-hopeful.

I shake my head. I'm feeling overwhelmed. The sound in the room is like a melded roar in my head. I can barely distinguish any individual strands, let alone pick out the exact tones of a voice I heard for twenty seconds, days ago, on a mobile phone.

'OK, let's be methodical.' Sam is almost talking to himself. 'We'll go round the room in concentric circles. Does that sound like a plan?'

I flash him a smile but I've never felt so pressured in my life. No one else can do this. No one else heard that voice. It's down to me. Now I know how sniffer dogs must feel at airports.

We head to a group of women, who are standing together with two middle-aged men.

'Hi there!' Sam greets them all pleasantly. 'Having a good time? Let me introduce Poppy, who's having a look round – Poppy, this is Jeremy . . . and Peter . . . Jeremy, how many years have you been with us now? And Peter? Is it three years?'

OK. Now I'm listening properly, close up, this is easier. One man has a low growly voice and the other is Scandinavian. After about ten seconds I shake my head at Sam, and he moves us swiftly off to another group, discreetly ticking his list as we go.

'Hi there! Having a good time? Let me introduce Poppy, who's having a look round. Poppy, you've already met Nihal. Now Colin, what are you up to these days?'

It's amazing how different voices are, once you start to pay attention. Not only the pitch, but the accents, the timbres, the little speech impediments and slurs and quirks.

'What about you?' I join in, smiling at a bearded guy who hasn't uttered a syllable.

'Well, it's been a *tricky* year . . .' he begins ponderously.

No. Uh-huh. Nothing like. I glance at Sam, shaking my head, and he abruptly takes hold of my arm.

'Sorry, Dudley, we must dash . . .' He heads to the next group along and charges straight in, interrupting an anecdote. 'Poppy, this is Simon . . . Stephanie you've met, I think . . . Simon, Poppy was just admiring your jacket. Where's it from?'

I can't believe how blatant Sam's being. He's practically ignoring all the women, and being totally unsubtle about getting the men to talk. But I guess it's the only way.

The more voices I listen to, the more confident I feel. This is easier than I thought it would be, because they're all so *different* from the one on the phone. Except that we've already been to four groups and eliminated them. I scan the room anxiously. What if I get all the way round the room and I still haven't heard the guy from the message?

'Hi there, gang! Having a good time?' Sam is still in full flow as we approach the next group. 'Let me introduce Poppy who's having a look round – Poppy, this is Tony. Tony, why don't you tell Poppy about your department? And here's Daniel, and . . . this is . . . ah. Willow.'

She was turned away as we approached, so her face was averted, but now she faces us full-on.

Yowzer.

'Sam!' she says, after such a long pause I start to feel embarrassed for everybody. 'Who's . . . this?'

OK. If my text to Magnus was laden with meaning, that little two-word sentence of Willow's was collapsing under its weight. You don't have to be an expert in the Language of Willow to know what she *actually* meant was, 'Who the FUCK is this girl and WHAT is she doing here with YOU? Jesus, Sam, are you DELIBERATELY SCREWING AROUND WITH ME? Because believe me, you are going to regret that BADLY.'

You know. Paraphrasing.

I've never felt such overt hostility from anyone in my life. It's like an electric current between us. Willow's nostrils are flared and whitening. Her eyes are all stary. Her hand has gripped her glass so tightly her tendons are showing through her pale skin. But her smile is still soft and pleasant, and her voice is still mellifluous. Which is almost the most creepy of all.

'Poppy's thinking of joining the company,' says Sam.

'Oh.' Willow carries on smiling. 'Lovely. Welcome, Poppy.'

She's unnerving me. She's like some alien. Behind the soft smile and the dulcet voice is a lizard.

'Thanks.'

'Anyway, we must press on . . . See you later, Willow.' Sam takes my arm to guide me away.

Uh-oh. Bad idea. I can feel her laser eyes in my back. Does Sam not feel them too?

We head to a new group and Sam launches into his spiel, and I dutifully crane my neck to listen, but nobody sounds a bit like the phone guy. As we work our way round further I can tell Sam's getting dispirited, though he's trying to hide it. After we leave a group of youngish IT guys drinking beers, he says, 'Really? *None* of those guys?'

'No.' I shrug apologetically. 'Sorry.'

'Don't be sorry!' He gives a short, strained laugh. 'You heard what you heard. You can't . . . if it's not any of them . . .' He breaks off a moment. 'Definitely not the blond guy? The one talking about his car? He didn't sound at all familiar?'

And now the disappointment in his voice is evident.

'Is that who you thought it was?'

'I . . . don't know.' He spreads his hands, exhaling. 'Maybe. Yes. He'd have the IT contacts, he's new to the company, Justin and Ed could easily have talked him round . . .'

I don't know what to reply. Like he says, I heard what I heard.

'I think some people have gone out to the terrace,' I say, trying to be helpful.

'We'll try there.' He nods. 'Let's finish up here first.'

Even *I* can tell that none of the four grey-haired men standing by the bar will be the guy from the phone – and I'm right. As Sam is inveigled into a conversation about Malcolm's speech, I take the opportunity to edge away and see if Magnus has replied. Of course he hasn't. But flashing at the top of my in-box is an email sent to samroxton@whiteglobeconsulting. com, cc-ed to samroxtonpa@whiteglobeconsulting.com, which makes me splutter.

Sam
Nice try. I know EXACTLY what you're up to and you're PATHETIC. Where did you get her from, an agency? I would have thought you could do better than that.
Willow

As I'm staring at the screen in disbelief, a second email pops up.

I mean, Jesus, Sam. She isn't even DRESSED for the occasion. Or are cutesy denim skirts suddenly appropriate conference wear??

My skirt is *not* cutesy! And I wasn't exactly planning to come to a conference when I got dressed this morning, was I?

In outrage, I press Reply, and type an email:

Actually I think she's stunningly beautiful. And her denim skirt isn't cutesy. So there, Willow the Witch. Sam.

Then I delete it. Naturally. I'm about to put my phone away when a *third* email pops up from Willow. Honestly. Can't she give it a rest?

You want me to be jealous, Sam. Fine. I respect that. I even like it. We need sparks in our relationship. But TRY GIVING ME SOMETHING TO BE JEALOUS OF!!!

Because believe me, no one here is impressed by your little stunt. I mean, parading around some nondescript girl who clearly has NO IDEA HOW TO BLOW-DRY HER FUCKING HAIR . . . Well. It's tragic, Sam. TRAGIC.

Talk to you when you're a grown-up.

Willow

I touch my hair defensively. I *did* blow-dry it this morning. It's just hard to get to the back bits. I mean, not that I care what she thinks, but I can't help feeling a little stung—

My thoughts are interrupted mid-flow and I stare at the screen. I don't believe it. An email has just arrived in the phone from Sam. He's responded to Willow. He's actually replied to her! Except he's pressed Reply All, so it's come to me too.

I glance up in astonishment and see that he's still talking to the grey-haired men, apparently engrossed. He must have rattled it off very quickly. I open up the email and see a single line.

Cut it out, Willow. You're not impressing anyone.

I blink at the screen. She won't like that.

I wait for her to launch some further scathing attack on Sam – but no more emails arrive. Maybe she's as taken aback as I am.

'Great. We'll talk later.' Sam's voice rises above the hubbub. 'Poppy, a few more people I'd like you to meet.'

'OK.' I snap to attention, thrusting my phone away. 'Let's do it.'

We circulate around the rest of the room. Sam's list is covered with ticks. I must have listened to nearly every male voice in the company and I haven't heard anybody who sounds anything like the guy on the phone. I'm even starting to wonder whether I'm remembering him right. Or whether I hallucinated the whole thing.

As we head along a carpeted corridor towards the open terrace doors, I can tell Sam is low. I feel pretty low myself.

'Sorry,' I mutter.

'Not your fault.' He looks up, and seems to clock my mood. 'Poppy, seriously. I know you're doing your best.' His face crinkles for a moment. 'Hey, and I'm sorry about Willow.'

'Oh.' I brush it off. 'Don't worry about it.'

We walk in silence for a few moments. I want to say something like, 'Thanks for sticking up for me,' but I'm too awkward. I feel like I shouldn't really have been inside that email exchange.

The terrace is covered in lanterns and there are a few clusters of people, but not nearly as many as there were inside. I suppose it's too cold. But it's a shame, because there's actually quite a nice party-like atmosphere out here. There's a bar and a couple of people are even dancing. On the corner of the terrace a guy holding a TV camera seems to be interviewing a pair of giggling girls.

'So, maybe we'll strike lucky.' I try to sound upbeat.

'Maybe.' Sam nods, but I can tell he's given up.

'What happens if we don't find him out here?'

'Then . . . we tried.' Sam's face is taut, but for the briefest of moments his smile pops out. 'We tried.'

'OK. Well, let's do it.' I put on my best motivational, you-*can*-get-mobility-back-into-that-hip-joint voice. 'Let's try.'

We head out and Sam launches into the same old routine.

'Hi there, gang! Having a good time? Let me introduce Poppy, who's having a look round – Poppy, this is James. James, why don't you tell Poppy what your line is? And here's Brian, and this is Rhys.'

It's not James or Brian or Rhys. Or Martin or Nigel.

Every name on Sam's list is ticked off. I almost want to cry when I look at his face. At last we step away from a group of interns who weren't even on the list and can't possibly be Scottie.

We're done.

'I'll phone Vicks,' Sam says, his voice a little heavy. 'Poppy, thanks for giving up your time. It was a stupid plan.'

'It wasn't.' I put a hand on his arm. 'It . . . could have worked.'

Sam looks up and for a moment we just stand there.

'You're very kind,' he says at last.

'Hi Sam! Hi guys!' A girl's raised voice makes me flinch. Maybe I'm sensitive because I've been listening more carefully to the way people speak – but this voice is setting my teeth on edge. I turn to see a bubbly-looking girl with a pink scarf tied in her hair approaching us with the TV-camera guy, who has a dark crew-cut and jeans.

Uh-oh.

'Hi Amanda.' Sam nods. 'What's up?'

'We're filming all the conference guests,' she says cheerfully. 'Just a little shout-out, say hi, we'll show it at the gala dinner . . .'

The TV camera is pointing in my face and I flinch. I'm not supposed to be here. I can't do a 'little shout-out'.

'Anything you like,' Amanda prompts me. 'A personal message, a joke . . .' She consults her list, looking puzzled. 'I'm sorry, I don't know what department you're in . . .'

'Poppy's a guest,' says Sam.

'Oh!' The girl's brow clears. 'Lovely! Tell you what, since you're a special guest, why don't you do our Q and A interview? What do you think, Ryan? Do you know Ryan?' she adds to Sam. 'He's on a placement from the LSE for six months. He's been doing all our promotional filming. Hey Ryan, get a close-up. Poppy's a special guest!'

What? I'm not a 'special guest'. I want to escape, but somehow I feel pinned to the spot by the TV camera.

'Just introduce yourself and Ryan will ask the questions!' says the girl brightly. 'So, tell us your name . . .'

'Hi,' I say reluctantly to the camera. 'I'm . . . Poppy.' This is so stupid. What am I going to say to a conference of strangers? Maybe I'll do a shout-out to Willow.

Hey, Willow the Witch. You know how you think I'm parading around with your boyfriend? Well, here's the newsflash. He's not your boyfriend any more.

The thought makes me snort, and Amanda gives me an encouraging smile.

'That's right! Just enjoy yourself. Ryan, do you want to start the Q and A?'

'Sure. So, Poppy, what do you think of the conference so far?'

The high-pitched, reedy voice which comes from behind the camera hits my ears like a thousand-volt shock.

It's him.

That's the voice I heard down the phone. This person talking to me now. This guy, with a crew-cut and a camera on his shoulder. *This is him.*

'Having fun?' he prompts me, and my brain explodes with recognition again. The memory of his voice on the phone is running through my head like a TV sports replay.

It's Scottie. It's done. Like I said. It was a surgical strike.

'Which was your favourite speech of the conference so far?'
'She hasn't been to any of the speeches,' interjects Sam.
'Oh. OK.'

No trace. Genius stuff, though I say it myself. Adios, Santa Claus.
'On a scale of one to ten, how would you rate the drinks party?'

It's Scottie.

This is Scottie. No question.

'Are you all right?' He leans round the camera, looking impatient. 'You can talk. We're rolling.'

I stare at his thin, intelligent face, my heart thumping; willing myself not to give anything away. I feel like a rabbit being mesmerized by a snake.

'It's OK, Poppy.' Sam steps forward, looking sympathetic. 'Don't worry. A lot of people get stage fright.'

'No!' I manage. 'It's not— It's—'

I stare up at him helplessly. My voice won't work. I feel like I'm in one of those dreams where you can't shout out that you're being murdered.

'Guys, I don't think she's up for it,' Sam's saying. 'Could you . . .' He gestures with his hand.

'Sorry!' Amanda puts a hand over her mouth. 'Didn't mean to freak you out! Have a good evening!' They head off to accost another group of people and I stare after them, transfixed.

'Poor old Poppy.' Sam smiles ruefully. 'Just what you needed. Sorry about that, it's a new thing they're doing at the conferences, although I can't see what it adds—'

'Shut up.' Somehow I cut him off, although I can still barely speak. 'Shut up, shut up.'

Sam looks astonished. I move closer to him and reach up on tiptoe until my mouth is touching his ear, his hair brushing against my skin. I inhale, breathing in his warmth and smell, then murmur, as quietly as a breath, 'That's him.'

We stay outside for another twenty minutes. Sam has a long

telephone conversation with Sir Nicholas – none of which I can hear – then a brief, brusque call with Mark, of which I catch bits and pieces as he strides around, his hand to his head . . . *Well, company policy can fuck itself . . . The minute Vicks gets here . . .*

It's clear that tension levels are rising. I thought Sam would be happy that I'd helped but he looks even more grim than before. He ends the call by snapping, 'Whose side are you on, anyway? *Jesus*, Mark.'

'So . . . what are you going to do?' I say timidly as he rings off.

'Ryan's company email is being searched. But he's sharp. He won't have used the company system. He'll have set it all up by phone or with some private email account.'

'So what then?'

'That's the debate.' Sam screws up his face in frustration. 'Trouble is, we don't have *time* for a discussion on protocol. We don't have *time* to consult our lawyers. If it were me—'

'You'd have him arrested, all his personal property confiscated and a lie-detector test forcibly conducted,' I can't help saying. 'In a dark cellar somewhere.'

A reluctant smile passes across Sam's face. 'Something like that.'

'How's Sir Nicholas?' I venture.

'Acting chipper. You can imagine. He keeps his chin up. But he feels it far more than he's letting on.' Sam's face twists briefly and he wraps his arms around his chest.

'You do too,' I say, gently, and Sam looks up in a startled movement, as though I've caught him out.

'I suppose I do,' he says after a long pause. 'Nick and I go back a long way. He's a good guy. He's done some remarkable things over his lifetime. But if this smear gets out un-challenged, it'll be the only thing the wider world ever remembers about him. It'll be the same headline over and over, till he dies. "Sir Nicholas Murray, suspected of corruption". He doesn't deserve that. He especially doesn't deserve to be stitched up by his own board.'

There's a sombre moment, then Sam visibly pulls himself together. 'Anyway. Come on. They're waiting for us. Vicks is nearly here.'

We head back, past a group of girls clustered round a table, past an ornamental garden, towards the huge double doors leading into the hotel. My phone has been buzzing and I quietly take it out to check my in-box, just to see if Magnus has replied—

I blink at the screen. I don't believe it. I give a tiny, involuntary whimper and Sam shoots me an odd look.

There's a brand-new email right at the top of my in-box and I click on it, desperately hoping it won't say what I'm dreading—

Shit. *Shit.*

I stare at it in dismay. What am I going to do? We're nearly at the hotel. I have to speak. I have to tell him.

'Um, Sam.' My voice is a bit strangled. 'Um, stop a minute.'

'What?' He halts with a preoccupied frown and my stomach lurches with nerves.

OK. Here's the thing. In my defence, if I'd *known* Sam was going to be mired in a massive, urgent crisis involving leaked memos and senior government advisers and ITN News, I wouldn't have sent that email to his father. Of course I wouldn't.

But I didn't know. And I did send the email. And now . . .

'What's up?' Sam looks impatient.

Where on earth do I start? How do I soften him up?

'Please don't get angry,' I throw out as a first, pre-emptive sally, even though it feels a bit like chucking an ice cube into the path of a forest fire.

'About what?' There's an ominous tone to Sam's voice.

'The thing is . . .' I clear my throat. 'I thought I was doing the right thing. But I can see that you may not view it *exactly* that way . . .'

'What on earth are you—' He breaks off, his face suddenly clearing with appalled understanding. 'Oh Jesus. No. *Please* don't say you've been telling your friends about this—'

'No!' I say in horror. 'Of course not!'

'Then what?'

I feel slightly emboldened by his wrong suspicions. At least I haven't been blabbing everything to my friends. At least I haven't been selling my story to the *Sun.*

'It's a family thing. It's about your dad.'

Sam's eyes widen sharply, but he says nothing.

'I just felt really bad that you and he weren't in contact. So I emailed him back. He's desperate to see you, Sam. He wants to reach out! You never go down to Hampshire, you never see him—'

'For God's sake,' he mutters, almost to himself. 'I *really* don't have time for this.'

His words sting me. 'You don't have time for your own father? You know what, Mr Bigshot, maybe your priorities are a little screwed. I *know* you're busy, I *know* this crisis is important, but—'

'Poppy, stop right there. You're making a big mistake.'

He looks so impassive, I feel a surge of outrage. How *dare* he be so sure of himself all the time?

'Maybe you're the one who's making a big mistake!' The words burst out before I can stop them. 'Maybe you're the one who's just letting your life pass by without engaging in it! Maybe Willow's right!'

'*Excuse* me?' Sam looks thunderous at the mention of Willow.

'You're going to miss out! You're going to miss out on relationships which could give you so much, because you don't want to talk, you don't want to listen . . .'

Sam glances around, looking embarrassed. 'Poppy, cool it,' he mutters. 'You're getting too emotional.'

'Well, you're staying too calm!' I feel like exploding. 'You're too stoic!' An image suddenly comes to me of those Roman senators, all waiting in the arena to be massacred. 'You know something, Sam? You're turning into stone.'

'*Stone?*' He gives a burst of laughter.

'Yes, stone. You'll wake up one day and you'll be a statue but you won't know it. You'll be trapped inside yourself.' My voice is wobbling; I'm not sure why. It's nothing to me whether he turns into a statue or not.

Sam is eyeing me warily.

'Poppy, I've no idea what you're talking about. But we have to put this on pause. I have stuff I need to do.' His phone buzzes and he lifts it to his ear. 'Hey, Vicks. OK, on my way.'

'I know you're dealing with a crisis.' I grab his arm fiercely. 'But there's an old man waiting to hear from you, Sam. Longing to hear from you. Just for five minutes. And you know what? I envy you.'

Sam exhales sharply. 'For *fuck's sake*. Poppy, you've got this all wrong.'

'Have I?' I stare up at him, feeling all my buried emotions starting to bubble up. 'I just wish I had your chance. To see my dad. You don't know how lucky you are. That's all.'

A tear trickles down my cheek and I brush it away brusquely.

Sam is silent. He puts his phone away and faces me square-on. When he speaks, his voice is gentle.

'Listen, Poppy. I can understand how you feel. I don't mean to trivialize family relationships. I have a very good relationship with my father and I see him whenever I can. But it's not that easy, bearing in mind that he lives in Hong Kong.'

I gasp with horror. Are they *so* out of touch? Did he not even *know* his father had moved back to this country?

'Sam!' My words tumble out. 'You don't understand! He's moved back. He lives in Hampshire! He sent you an email. He wanted to see you. Don't you read *anything*?'

Sam throws back his head and roars with laughter, and I stare at him, affronted.

'OK,' he says at last, wiping his eyes. 'Let's start from the beginning. Let's get this straight. You're talking about the email from David Robinson, right?'

'No, I'm not! I'm talking about the one from—'

I break off mid-stream, suddenly uncertain. Robinson? *Robinson?* I grab my phone and check the email address. Davidr452@hotmail.com.

I just assumed he was David Roxton. It seemed *obvious* he was David Roxton.

'Contrary to your assumptions, I *did* read that email,' Sam is saying. 'And I chose to ignore it. Believe me, David Robinson is *not* my father.'

'But he called himself "Dad".' I'm totally bewildered. 'That's what he wrote. "Dad". Is he . . . your step-dad? Your half-dad?'

'He's not my dad in any shape or form,' says Sam patiently. 'If you must know, when I was at college I hung out with a group of guys. He was one of them. David Andrew Daniel Robinson. D. A. D. Robinson. We called him "Dad". OK? Got it, finally?'

He starts walking towards the hotel as though the subject is closed, but I'm rooted to the spot, my mind flitting around in shock. I can't get over this. 'Dad' *isn't* Sam's dad? 'Dad' is a *friend*? How was I supposed to know that? People shouldn't be allowed to sign themselves off 'Dad' unless they are your dad. It should be the *law*.

I've never felt so stupid in all my life.

Except . . . Except. As I'm standing there, I can't help replaying all David Robinson's emails in my head.

It's been a long time. I think of you often . . . Did you ever get any of my phone messages? Don't worry, I know you're a busy fellow . . . As I said, there is something I'd love to talk to you about. Are you ever down Hampshire way?

OK. So maybe I got it wrong about Sam's father and the

cottage and the faithful dog. But these words still touch a nerve in me. They sound so humble. So self-effacing. This David is clearly an old, old friend who wants to reach out. Maybe this is another relationship which Sam is leaving to wither. Maybe they'll see each other and the years will fall away and afterwards Sam will thank me, and tell me how he needs to value friendship more, he simply didn't realize it, and I've transformed his life . . .

Abruptly I hurry after Sam and catch up with him.

'So, is he a good friend?' I begin. 'David Robinson? Is he like, a really old, close chum?'

'No.' Sam doesn't break his stride.

'But you must have been friends once.'

'I suppose so.'

Could he sound any less enthusiastic? Does he realize how empty his life will be if he doesn't keep up with the people who were once important to him?

'So, surely he's someone you still have a bond with! If you saw him, maybe you'd rekindle that! You'd bring something positive into your life!'

Sam stops dead and stares at me. 'What business is this of yours, anyway?'

'Nothing,' I say defensively. 'I just . . . I thought you might like to get in touch with him.'

'I *am* in touch with him.' Sam sounds exasperated. 'Every few years we meet for a drink, and it's always the same story. He has some new entrepreneurial project he needs investors for, usually involving some ridiculous product or pyramid scheme. If it's not fitness equipment, it's double-glazing or time-shares in Turkey . . . Against my better judgement I give him some money. Then the business folds and I don't hear from him again for another year or so. It's a ridiculous cycle I need to break. Which is why I blanked his email. I'll call him in a month or two, maybe, but right now, frankly, the last thing I need in my life is David bloody Robinson . . .' He breaks off and peers at me. 'What?'

I gulp. There's no way round this. None.
'He's waiting for you in the bar.'

Maybe Sam hasn't turned into a statue *quite* yet. Because as we head back into the hotel, he says nothing, but I can easily read his feelings on his face, the entire range of them: from anger, to fury, to frustration, to . . .

Well. Back to anger again.[82]

'Sorry,' I say yet again. 'I thought . . .'

I peter out. I've already explained what I thought. It hasn't really helped, to be honest.

We push our way through the heavy double doors to see Vicks hurrying down the corridor towards us, holding a phone to her ear, struggling with a pile of stuff, looking harassed.

'Sure,' she's saying as she nears us. 'Mark, wait a minute. Just met Sam. I'll ring you back.' She looks up and launches in with no niceties. 'Sam, I'm sorry. We're going with the original statement.'

'*What?*' Sam's voice is so thunderous, I jump. 'You have to be kidding.'

'We have nothing on Ryan. No proof of anything untoward. There's no more time. I'm sorry, Sam. I know you tried, but . . .'

There's a tense silence. Sam and Vicks aren't even looking at each other, but the body language is obvious. Vicks's arms are now wrapped defensively around her laptop and a mass of papers. Sam is kneading both fists into his forehead.

Personally, I'm trying to blend into the wallpaper.

'Vicks, you know this is bollocks.' Sam sounds as though he's trying hard to control his impatience. 'We *know* what happened. What, we ignore all this new information?'

'It's not information, it's guesswork! We don't know what happened!' Vicks looks up and down the empty corridor and lowers her voice. 'And if we don't get a statement

82. Not such a huge range, then.

out to ITN pronto we are sitting fucking *ducks*, Sam.'

'We have time,' he says mutinously. 'We can talk to this guy Ryan. Interview him.'

'How long will that take? What will that achieve?' Vicks clutches her laptop closer to her. 'Sam, these are grave accusations. They have no substance. Unless we find some actual, solid proof . . .'

'So we stand back. We wash our hands. They win.' Sam's voice is calm, but I can tell he's simmering with rage.

'The techies are still investigating in London.' Vicks sounds weary. 'But unless they find *proof* . . .' She glances at a nearby clock. 'It's coming up to nine. Jesus. We have *no* time, Sam.'

'Let me speak to them.'

'OK.' She sighs. 'Not here. We've moved to a bigger room with a Skype screen.'

'Right. Let's go.'

They both start walking briskly along, and I follow, not sure if I should or not. Sam looks so preoccupied I don't dare utter a sound. Vicks leads us through a ballroom filled with banqueting tables, into another lobby, towards the bar . . .

Has he forgotten about David Robinson?

'Sam,' I mutter hastily. 'Wait! Don't go near the bar, we should go a different way—'

'Sam!' A throaty voice hails us. '*There* you are!'

My heart freezes in horror. That must be him. That's David Robinson. That guy with curly, receding dark hair and a pale-grey metallic suit which he's accessorized with a black shirt and white leather tie. He's striding towards us with a massive beam on his fleshy face and a whisky in his hand.

'Been far, far too long!' He envelops Sam in a bear hug. 'What can I get you, my old mucker? Or is it all on the house? In which case, mine's a double!' He gives a high-pitched laugh that makes me cringe.

I glance desperately at Sam's tight face.

'Who's this?' says Vicks, looking astonished.

'Long story. College friend.'

'I know all Sam's secrets!' David Robinson bangs Sam on the back. 'You want me to dish the dirt, cross my hand with a fifty. Only joking! I'll take a twenty!' He roars with laughter again.

This is officially unbearable.

'Sam.' Vicks can barely conceal her impatience. 'We have to go.'

'Go?' David Robinson makes a mock stagger backwards. '*Go?* When I've only just arrived?'

'David.' Sam's politeness is so chill I want to shiver. 'Sorry about this. Change of schedule. I'll try to catch up with you later.'

'After I've driven for forty minutes?' David shakes his head in a pantomime of disappointment. 'Can't even spare ten minutes for your old mate. What am I supposed to do, drink here like a muppet on my own?'

I'm feeling worse and worse. I've totally landed Sam in this. I have to do something about it.

'I'll have a drink with you!' I chime in hurriedly. 'Sam, you go. I'll entertain David. I'm Poppy Wyatt, hi!' I thrust my hand out and try not to wince at his clammy touch. 'Go.' I meet eyes with Sam. 'Go on.'

'OK.' Sam hesitates a moment, then nods. 'Thanks. Use the company tab.' Already he and Vicks are hurrying away.

'Well!' David seems a bit unsure how to react. 'That's a fine thing! Some people just get a bit too big for their boots, if you ask me.'

'He's very busy at the moment,' I say apologetically. 'I mean . . . *really* busy.'

'So where do you fit in? Sam's PA?'

'Not exactly. I've kind of been helping Sam out. Unofficially.'

'Unofficially.' David gives a great big wink. 'Say no more. All on expenses. Got to look kosher.'

OK, now I get it: this man is a nightmare. No wonder Sam spends his life avoiding him.

'Would you like another drink?' I say as charmingly as I can. 'And then maybe you could tell me what you do. Sam said you were an investor? In . . . fitness equipment?'

David scowls and drains his glass. 'I was in that line for a while. Too much health and safety, that's the problem with *that* game. Too many inspectors. Too many namby-pamby rules. Another double whisky, if you're buying.'

Rigid with mortification, I order the whisky and a large glass of wine for myself. I still can't believe how wrong I called this. I am never interfering in anyone's emails ever, *ever* again.

'And after fitness equipment?' I prompt him. 'What did you do then?'

'Well.' David Robinson leans back and cracks his knuckles. 'Then I went down the self-tanning route . . .'

Half an hour later my mind is numbed. Is there any business this man hasn't been in? Each story seems to follow the same pattern. The same phrases have been rolled out every time. *Unique opportunity, I mean, unique, Poppy . . . serious investment . . . on the brink . . . megabucks, I mean, megabucks, Poppy . . . events outside my control . . . damn stupid banks . . . short-sighted investors . . . bloody regulation . . .*

There's been no sign of Sam. No sign of Vicks. Nothing on my phone. I'm almost beside myself with tension, wondering what's going on. Meanwhile, David has sunk two whiskies, torn into three packets of crisps and is now scooping up a dish of hummus with taco chips.

'Interested in children's entertainment, are you, Poppy?' he suddenly says.

Why would I be interested in children's entertainment?

'Not really,' I say politely, but he ignores me. He's produced a brown furry-animal glove puppet from his briefcase and is dancing it around the table.

'Mr Wombat. Goes down a storm with the kids. Want to have a go?'

No, I do not want to have a go. But, in the interests of keeping the conversation going, I shrug. 'OK.'

I have no idea what to do with a glove puppet, but David seems galvanized as soon as I have it on my hand.

'You're a natural! You take these along to a kids' party, play-ground, whatever, they *fly*. And the beauty is the profit margin. Poppy, you would not believe it.' He smacks the table. 'Plus, it's flexible. You can sell them around your daytime job. I'll show you the whole kit . . .' He reaches into his briefcase again and produces a plastic folder.

I stare at him in bewilderment. What does he mean, *sell* them? He surely doesn't mean . . .

'Have I spelled your name right?' He looks up from writing on the folder, and I gape at it. Why is he writing my name on the front of a folder entitled 'Mr Wombat Official Franchise Agreement'?

'What you'd do is take a small consignment at first. Say . . . a hundred units.' He waves a hand airily. 'You'll sell that in a day, easy. Especially with our new free gift, Mr Magical.' He places a plastic wizard on the table and twinkles at me. 'The next step is the exciting one. Recruitment!'

'Stop!' I rip the glove puppet off. 'I don't want to sell glove puppets! I'm not doing this!'

David doesn't even seem to hear me. 'Like I say, it's totally flexible. It's all profit, direct to you, into your pocket—'

'I don't want any profit in my pocket!' I lean across the bar table. 'I don't want to join! Thanks anyway!' For good measure I take his pen and cross through 'Poppy Wyatt' on the folder, and David flinches as though I've wounded him.

'Well! No need for that! Just trying to do you a favour.'

'I appreciate it.' I try to sound polite. 'But I don't have time to sell wombats. Or . . .' I pick up the wizard. 'Who's this? Dumbledore?'

It's all so random. What's a magician got to do with a wombat, anyway?

'No!' David seems mortally offended. 'It's not Dumbledore. This is Mr Magical. New TV series. Next big thing. It was all lined up.'

'*Was?* What happened?'

'It's been temporarily cancelled,' he says stiffly. 'But it's still a very exciting product. Versatile, unbreakable, popular with both girls and boys . . . I could let you have five hundred units for . . . two hundred pounds?'

Is he nuts?

'I don't want any plastic wizards,' I say as politely as I can. 'Thanks anyway.' A thought suddenly crosses my mind. 'How many of these Mr Magicals have you got, then?'

David looks as though he doesn't want to answer the question. At last he says, 'I believe my current stock is ten thousand,' and takes a glug of whisky.

Ten thousand? Oh my God. Poor David Robinson. I feel quite sorry for him now. What's he going to do with ten thousand plastic wizards? I dread to ask how many wombats he's got.

'Maybe Sam will know someone who wants to sell them,' I say encouragingly. 'Someone with children.'

'Maybe.' David raises his eyes lugubriously from his drink. 'Tell me something. Does Sam still blame me for flooding his house?'

'He hasn't mentioned it,' I say honestly.

'Well, maybe the damage wasn't as bad as it looked. Bloody Albanian fish tanks.' David looks downcast. 'Absolute tat. And the fish weren't much better. Word of advice, Poppy. Steer clear of fish.'

I have an urge to giggle, and bite my lip hard.

'OK,' I nod as seriously as I can. 'I'll remember that.'

He polishes off the last taco chip, exhales noisily and looks around the bar. Uh-oh. He seems to be getting restless. I can't let him go wandering around.

'So, what was Sam like at college?' I ask, to spin out the conversation a little more.

'High-flyer.' David looks a little grouchy. 'You know the type. Rowed for the college. Always knew he'd end up doing well. Went off the rails a bit in his second year. Got in a bit of trouble. But that was understandable.'

'How come?' I frown, not following.

'Well, you know.' David shrugs. 'After his mum died.'

I freeze, my glass halfway to my lips. *What* did he just say?

'I'm sorry . . .' I'm trying not very well to conceal my shock. 'Did you just say Sam's mother died?'

'Didn't you know?' David seems surprised. 'Beginning of the second year. Heart disease, I think it was. She'd not been well, but no one was expecting her to peg it so soon. Sam took it badly, poor bloke. Though I always say to him, you're welcome to my old lady, any time you want . . .'

I'm not listening. My head is buzzing with confusion. He said it was a friend of his. I know he did. I can hear him now: *My friend lost his mother when we were at college. I spent a lot of nights talking with him. Lot of nights . . . And it never goes away . . .*

'Poppy?' David is waving his hand in front of my face. 'You all right?'

'Yes!' I try to smile. 'Sorry. I'm . . . I thought it was a friend of his who lost his mother. Not Sam himself. I must have got confused. Silly me. Um, do you want another whisky?'

David doesn't reply to my offer. He's silent a while, then shoots me an appraising look, cradling his empty tumbler in his hands. His fleshy thumbs are tracing a pattern on the glass, and I watch them, mesmerized.

'You weren't confused,' he says at last. 'Sam didn't tell you, did he? He said it was a friend.'

I stare at him, taken aback. I'd written this guy off as a boorish moron. But he's totally nailed it.

'Yes,' I admit at last. 'He did. How did you know?'

'He's private like that, Sam.' David nods. 'When it happened – the death – he didn't tell anyone at college for days. Only his two closest friends.'

'Right.' I hesitate doubtfully. 'Is that . . . you?'

'Me!' David gives a short, rueful laugh. 'No, not me. I'm not in the inner sanctum. It's Tim and Andrew. They're his right-hand men. All rowed in the same boat together. Know them?'

I shake my head.

'Joined at the hip, even now, those three guys are. Tim's over at Merrill Lynch, Andrew's a barrister in some chambers or other. And of course Sam's pretty close to his brother Josh,' David adds. 'He's two years older. Used to come and visit. Sorted Sam out when things went wrong for him. Spoke to his tutors. He's a good guy.'

I didn't know Sam had a brother, either. As I sit there, digesting all this, I feel a bit chastened. I've never even heard of Tim or Andrew or Josh. But then, why *would* I have heard of them? They probably text Sam directly. They're probably in touch like normal people. In private. Not like Willow the Witch and old friends trying to hustle some money.

All this time I've thought I could see Sam's entire life. But it wasn't his entire life, was it? It was one in-box. And I judged him on it.

He has friends. He has a life. He has a relationship with his family. He has a whole load of stuff I have no idea about. I was an idiot if I thought I'd got to know the whole story. I know a single chapter. That's all.

I take a swig of wine, numbing the strange wistfulness that suddenly washes over me. I'll never know all of Sam's other chapters. He'll never tell me and I'll never ask. We'll part ways and I'll just have the impression I've already got. The version of him that lives in his PA's in-box.

I wonder what impression he'll have of me. Oh God. Better not go there.

The thought makes me snort with laughter, and David eyes me curiously.

'Funny girl, aren't you?'

'Am I?'

My phone buzzes and I pull it to me, not caring if I'm rude. It's telling me I have a voice-mail from Magnus.

Magnus?

I missed a call from Magnus?

Abruptly my thoughts swoop away from Sam, away from David and this place, to the rest of my life. Magnus. Wedding. Anonymous text. *Your fiancée has been unfaithful* . . . A jumble of thoughts pile into my brain, all at once, as though they've been clamouring at the door. I leap to my feet, pressing Voice-mail, jabbing at the keys; impatient and nervous all at once. Although, what am I expecting? A confession? A rebuttal? Why would Magnus have any idea that I had received an anonymous message?

'Hey, Pops!' Magnus's distinctive voice is muffled by a background thump of music. 'Could you call Professor Wilson and remind her I'm away? Thanks, sweets. Number's on my desk. Ciao! Having a great time!'

I listen to it twice over, for clues, even though I have no idea what kind of clues I'm hoping to glean.[83] As I ring off, my stomach is churning. I can't bear it. I don't *want* this. If I'd never got that text message, I'd be happy now. I'd be looking forward to my wedding and thinking about the honeymoon and practising my new signature. I'd be *happy*.

I've run out of conversational gambits, so I kick off my shoes, draw my feet up on to the bench and hug my knees morosely. Around us, in the bar, I'm aware that the White Globe Consulting employees have started to cluster. I can hear snatches of low, anxious conversation and I've caught the word 'memo' a few times. The news must be seeping out. I glance at my watch and feel a clench of alarm. It's 9.40 p.m. Only twenty minutes till the ITN bulletin.

For the millionth time I wonder what Vicks and Sam are up

---

83. Magnus is doing it with Professor Wilson? No. Surely not. She has a beard.

to. I wish I could help. I wish I could do something. I feel powerless, sitting out here—

'OK!' A sharp female voice interrupts my thoughts and I look up to see Willow, standing in front of me, glaring down. She's changed into a halter-neck evening dress and even her shoulders are twitchy. 'I'm going to ask you this straight, and I hope you'll answer it straight. No games. No playing around. No little tricks.'

She's practically spitting the words at me. Honestly. What little tricks am I supposed to have played?

'Hello,' I say politely.

The trouble is, I can't see this woman without remembering all her screwy, capital-letter emails. It's as though they're emblazoned on her face.

'Who *are* you?' she bristles at me. 'Just tell me that. Who *are* you? And if you won't tell me, then believe me—'

'I'm Poppy,' I interrupt.

' "Poppy".' She sounds deeply suspicious, as though 'Poppy' must be my invented escort-agency name.

'Have you met David?' I add politely. 'He's an old university friend of Sam's.'

'Oh.' At these words I can see interest flash across her features. 'Hello, David, I'm Willow.' Her gaze swivels to focus on him, and I swear I feel a cooling on my face.

'Charmed, Willow. Friend of Sam's, are you?'

'I'm Willow.' She says it with slightly more emphasis.

'Nice name.' He nods.

'I'm Willow. *Willow*.' There's an edge to her voice now. 'Sam must have mentioned me. Wil-low.'

David wrinkles his brow thoughtfully. 'Don't think so.'

'But . . .' She looks as though she's going to expire with outrage. 'I'm *with* him.'

'Not right now you're not, are you?' says David jovially – then shoots me a tiny wink.

I'm actually warming to this David. Once you get

past the bad shirt and the dodgy investments, he's OK.

Willow looks incandescent. 'This is just ... The world is going insane,' she says, almost to herself. 'You don't know me, but you know *her*?' She jerks a thumb at me.

'I assumed she was Sam's special lady,' says David innocently.

'Her? *You?*'

Willow's eyeing me up and down in a disbelieving, supercilious sort of way that nettles me.

'Why not me?' I say robustly. 'Why shouldn't he be with me?'

Willow says nothing for a moment, just blinks very fast. 'So that's it. He's two-timing me,' she murmurs at last, her voice throbbing with intensity. 'The truth finally comes out. I should have known it. It explains ... a lot.' She exhales sharply, her fingers raking through her hair. 'So where do we go now?' She addresses some unknown audience. 'Where the *fuck* do we go now?'

She's a total fruit-loop. I want to burst out laughing. Where does she think she is, acting in her own private stage play? Who does she think is impressed by her performance?

And she's missed a crucial fact. How can Sam be two-timing her if *she's not his girlfriend*?

On the other hand, as much as I'm enjoying winding her up, I don't want to spread false rumours.

'I didn't say I *was* with him,' I clarify. 'I said, "Why shouldn't he be with me?" Are you Sam's girlfriend, then?'

Willow flinches, but *doesn't* answer, I notice.

'Who the hell *are* you?' She rounds on me again. 'You appear in my life, I have no idea who you are or where you came from ...'

She's playing to the gallery again. I wonder if she went to drama school and got chucked out for being too melodramatic.[84]

---

84. And by the way, in what sense have I appeared in *her* life?

'It's . . . complicated.'

The word 'complicated' seems to inflame Willow even more.

'Oh, "complicated".' She makes little jabby quote gestures. ' "Complicated". Wait a minute.' Her eyes suddenly narrow to disbelieving slits as she surveys my outfit. 'Is that Sam's shirt?'

Ah-ha-ha. She's *really* not going to like that. Maybe I won't answer.

'Is that Sam's shirt? Tell me right now!' Her voice is so hectoring and abrasive, I flinch. 'Are you wearing Sam's shirt? Tell me! Is that his shirt? Answer me!'

'Mind your own Brazilian!' The words fly out of my mouth before I can stop them. Oops.

OK. The trick when you've said something embarrassing by mistake is not to overreact. Instead, keep your chin up and pretend nothing happened. Maybe Willow didn't even notice what I said. I'm sure she didn't notice. Of course she didn't.

I dart a surreptitious look at her, and her eyes have widened so much, I think her eyeballs might pop out. All right, so she *did* notice. And from David's gleeful expression it's clear he did, too.

'I mean . . . business,' I amend, clearing my throat. 'Business.'

Over David's shoulder I suddenly see Vicks. She's striding through the clusters of White Globe Consulting employees and her grim expression makes my stomach turn over. I glance at my watch. Quarter to ten.

'Vicks!' Willow has noticed her too. She blocks Vicks's way, her arms folded imperiously. 'Where's Sam? Someone said he was with you.'

'Excuse me, Willow.' Vicks tries to get past.

'Just tell me where Sam is!'

'I have no idea, Willow!' Vicks snaps. 'Can you get out of my way? I need to speak to Poppy.'

'*Poppy*? You need to speak to *Poppy*?' Willow looks as if she's going to explode with frustration. 'Who *is* this fucking Poppy?'

I almost feel sorry for Willow. Completely ignoring her, Vicks comes round to my seat, bends down low and mutters, 'Do you know where Sam is?'

'No.' I look at her in alarm. 'What's happened?'

'Has he texted you? Anything?'

'No!' I check my phone. 'Nothing. I thought he was with you.'

'He was.' Vicks does her eye-rubbing thing with the heels of her hands, and I resist the temptation to grab her wrists.

'What happened?' I lower my voice further. 'Please, Vicks. I'll be discreet. I swear.'

There's a beat of silence, then Vicks nods. 'OK. We ran out of time. I guess you could say Sam lost.'

I feel a plunge of disappointment. After all that.

'What did Sam say?'

'Not a lot. He stormed out.'

'What will happen to Sir Nicholas?' I speak as quietly as I can.

Vicks doesn't reply, but her head turns away as though she wants to escape that particular thought.

'I have to go,' she says abruptly. 'Let me know if you hear from Sam. Please.'

'OK.'

I wait as Vicks walks away, then casually raise my head. Sure enough, Willow is fixated on me, like a cobra.

'So,' she says.

'So.' I smile back pleasantly, just as Willow's eyes land on my left hand. Her mouth opens. For an instant she seems incapable of speech.

'Who gave you that ring?' she utters at last.

What bloody business is it of hers?

'A girl called Lucinda,' I say, to wind her up. 'I'd lost it, you see. She gave it back.'

Willow draws breath and I swear she's about to launch her

fangs into me, when Vicks's voice comes blasting through the PA system, at top volume.

'I'm sorry to interrupt the party, but I have an important announcement to make. All employees of White Globe Consulting, please make your way back into the main conference hall immediately. That's back into the main conference hall, *immediately*. Thank you.'

There's an outbreak of chatter around us, and all the clusters of people start moving towards the double doors, some quickly refilling their glasses.

'Looks like my cue to leave,' says David, getting to his feet. 'You'll be needing to go. Give my regards to Sam.'

'I'm not actually an employee,' I say, for accuracy's sake. 'But, yes, I do need to go. Sorry about that.'

'Really?' David shakes his head, looking mystified. 'Then she's got a point.' He jerks his head at Willow. 'You're not Sam's girl-friend and you don't work for this company. Who the hell are you and what have you got to do with Sam?'

'Like I said.' I can't help smiling at his quizzical expression. 'It's . . . complicated.'

'I can believe it.' He raises his eyebrows, then produces a business card and presses it into my hand. 'Tell Sam. Exotic mini-pets. I've got a great opportunity for him.'

'I'll tell him.' I nod seriously. 'Thanks.' I watch him dis-appear towards the exit, then carefully put his card away for Sam.

'So.' Willow looms in front of me again, arms folded. 'Why don't you just start from the beginning?'

'Are you *serious*?' I can't hide my exasperation. 'Isn't there something *else* you need to be doing right now?' I gesture at the crowds surging into the conference room.

'Oh, nice try.' She doesn't even flicker. 'I'm hardly going to make some tedious corporate announcement my priority.'

'Believe me, this tedious corporate announcement is one you're going to want to hear.'

'You know all about it, I suppose,' Willow shoots back sarcastically.

'Yes.' I nod, suddenly feeling despondent. 'I know all about it. And . . . I think I'm going to get a drink.'

I stalk away to the bar. I can see Willow in the mirror, and after a few seconds she turns and heads towards the conference room, her expression murderous. I feel drained just from talking to her.

No, I feel drained by the whole day. I order myself another large glass of wine, then slowly walk towards the conference room. Vicks is standing on the stage, talking to a rapt, shocked audience. Behind her, the massive screen is on mute.

'. . . as I say, we don't know exactly what shape the report will take, but we have made our response, and that's the only thing we can do at this present time. Are there any questions? Nihal?'

'Where's Sir Nicholas now?' comes Nihal's voice from the crowd.

'He's in Berkshire. We'll have to see what happens about the rest of the conference. As soon as any decisions have been made, obviously you will all be informed.'

I'm looking around at the faces. Justin is a few feet away from me, gazing up at Vicks in a pantomime picture of shock and concern. Now he raises his hand.

'Justin?' says Vicks reluctantly.

'Vicks, bravo.' His smooth voice travels through the room. 'I can only imagine how difficult these last few hours have been for you. As a member of the senior management team, I'd just like to thank you for your sterling efforts. Whatever Sir Nicholas may or may not have said, whatever the truth of the matter, and of course none of us can *really* know that . . . your loyalty to the company is what we value. Well done, Vicks!' He leads a round of applause.

Ooh. Snake. Clearly I'm not the only one to think this, because another hand shoots straight up.

'Malcolm!' says Vicks in plain relief.

'I'd just like to make it clear to all employees that Sir Nicholas did *not* make these remarks.' Unfortunately Malcolm's voice is a bit rumbly and I'm not sure everyone can hear. 'I received the original memo he sent, and it was *completely* different . . .'

'I'm afraid I'll have to interrupt you now,' Vicks chimes in. 'The bulletin's starting. Volume up, please.'

Where's Sam? He should be here. He should be replying to Justin and crushing him. He should be watching the bulletin. I just don't get it.

The familiar ITN *News at Ten* music begins, and the swirling graphics fill the massive screen. I'm feeling ridiculously nervous, even though it doesn't have anything to do with me. Maybe they won't run the story, I keep thinking. You hear about items being bumped all the time . . .

Big Ben's chimes have begun. Any second they'll start announcing the headlines. My stomach clenches with nerves and I take a swig of wine. Watching the news is a completely different experience when it's something to do with you. This is what prime ministers must feel like all the time. God, I wouldn't be them for anything. They must spend every evening hiding behind the sofa, peering through their fingers.

Bong! 'Fresh attacks in the Middle East lead to fears of instability.' *Bong!* 'House prices make a surprise recovery – but will it last?' *Bong!* 'A leaked memo casts doubts on the integrity of a top government adviser.'

There it is. They're running it.

There's an almost eerie silence in the room. No one has gasped or even reacted. I think everyone's holding their breath, waiting for the full item. The Middle Eastern report has started and there are pictures of gunfire in a dusty street, but I'm barely taking it in. I've pulled out my phone and am texting Sam:

Are you watching? Everyone is in conference room. P

My phone remains silent. What's he doing? Why isn't he in here with everyone else?

I stare fixedly at the screen as the footage changes to house-price graphs and an interview with a family trying to move to Thaxted, wherever that is. I'm willing the presenters to speak more quickly; to get through it. Never have I been less interested in house prices in my life.[85]

And then suddenly both the first two items are done and we're back in the studio and the newsreader is saying, with her grave face on, 'Tonight, doubts were cast on the integrity of Sir Nicholas Murray, the founder of White Globe Consulting and a government adviser. In a confidential memo obtained exclusively by ITN, he refers to corrupt practices and the soliciting of bribes, apparently condoning them.'

Now there are a few gasps and whispers around the room. I glance at Vicks. Her face is amazingly composed as she watches the screen. I suppose she knew what to expect.

'But in a new twist, within the last few minutes ITN has discovered that another staff member at White Globe Consulting may in fact have written the words attributed to Sir Nicholas, something which official company sources deny all knowledge of. Our reporter Damian Standforth asks: is Sir Nicholas a villain . . . or the victim of a smear attempt?'

'*What?*' Vicks's voice rips across the hall. 'What the *fuck—*'

A babble has broken out, interspersed with 'Ssh!' and 'Listen!' and 'Shut up!' Someone has ramped the volume right up. I stare at the screen, utterly confused.

Did Sam find some proof? Did he pull it out of the bag? My phone suddenly bleeps and I yank it from my pocket. It's a text from Sam.

85. And we're not exactly starting from a high bar.

How did Vicks react?

I look at Vicks and flinch.

She looks like she wants to eat someone alive.

'White Globe Consulting has been a major influence in business for the last three decades . . .' a voice-over is saying, accompanied by a long-lens shot of the White Globe Consulting building.

My thumbs are so full of adrenalin the text almost writes itself:

Did you do this?

I did this.

You contacted ITN yourself?

Correct.

Thought the techies didn't find any proof. What happened?!

They didn't.

I swallow hard, trying to get my head round this. I know nothing about PR. I'm a physiotherapist, for God's sake. But even *I'd* say that you don't phone up ITN with a story of a smear without something to back it up.

How

As I start typing I realize I don't even know how to frame the question, so I send it as it is. There's silence for a little while – then a two-screen text arrives in my phone.

I blink at it in amazement. This is the longest text Sam has ever sent me, by approximately 2,000 per cent.

I went on the record. I stand by what I said. Tomorrow I give them an exclusive interview about original memo, directors washing hands of Nick, everything. It's a stitch-up. Corporate spin has gone too far. The true story needs to be out there. Wanted Malcolm to join me but he won't. He has three kids. Can't risk it. So it's just me.

My head is buzzing. Sam's put himself on the line. He's turned into a whistle-blower. I can't believe he's done something so extreme. But at the same time . . . I can.

That's a pretty big deal.

I have no idea what else to type. I'm in a state of shock.

Someone had to have the guts to stand by Nick.

I stare at his words, my brow crinkled, thinking this through.

Doesn't prove anything though, surely? It's only your word.

A moment later he replies:

Raises question mark over story. That's enough. Are you still in conference hall?

Yes.

Anyone know you're texting me?

I glance up at Vicks, who is talking volubly to some guy, while holding a phone to her ear too. She happens to glance my way and I don't know if it's my expression, but her eyes narrow a smidgen. She glances at my phone, then looks at my face again. I feel a dart of apprehension.

Don't think so. Yet.

Can you get away without anyone noticing?

I count to three, then casually scan the hall as though I'm interested in the light fittings. Vicks is in my peripheral vision. Now she's gazing straight at me. I lower my phone out of sight and text:

Where are you exactly?

Outside.

Doesn't help much.

All I've got. No idea where I am.

A moment later another one arrives:

It's dark, if that's a clue. Grass underfoot.

Are you in big trouble?

There's no reply. I guess that's a yes.

OK. I won't look at Vicks. I will simply yawn, scratch my nose – yes, good, unconcerned – turn on my heel and move behind this group of people. Then I'll duck down behind this big fat pillar.

Now I'll peek out.

Vicks is looking around with a frustrated expression. People are trying to get her attention but she's batting them away. I can almost *see* the calculation in her eyes – how much brain space does she allocate the strange girl who might know something but might also be a red herring?

Within five seconds I'm in the corridor. Ten seconds, through the deserted lobby, avoiding the eye of the disconsolate-looking barman. He'll be getting enough business in a minute. Fifteen seconds, I'm outside, ignoring the doorman, running over the gravel drive, round the corner until grass is underfoot and I feel as though I've got away.

I walk slowly, waiting for my breath to return. I'm still in shock over what's just happened.

Are you going to lose your job over this?

Another silence. I walk a little more, adjusting to the night sky, the cool air with a little breeze, the soft grass. The hotel is a good four hundred yards away by now, and I start to unwind.

Maybe.

He sounds quite relaxed about the fact. If a one-word text can sound relaxed.[86]

I'm outside now. Where should I head?

God knows. I went out back of hotel and walked into oblivion.

That's what I'm doing now.

So we'll meet.

---

86 I think it can. It's all in the timing.

You never said your mum had died.

I've typed it and pressed Send before I can stop myself. I stare at the screen, cringing at my own crassness. I can't believe I just said that. Of all the times. Like this is going to be his priority right now.

No. I never did.

I've reached the edge of what seems to be a croquet lawn. There's a wooded area ahead. Is that where he is? I'm about to ask him, when another text bleeps into my phone.

I just get tired of telling people. The awkward pause. You know?

I blink at the screen. I can't believe someone else knows about the awkward pause.

I understand.

I should have told you.

There's no way I'm guilt-tripping him over this. That's not what I meant. That's not what I wanted him to feel. As quickly as I can I type a reply:

No. No should. Never any should. That's my rule.

That's your rule for life?

Rule for life? That's not exactly what I meant. But I like the idea that he thinks I have a rule for life.

No, my rule for life is . . .

I pause, trying to think. A rule for life. That's quite a huge one. I can think of quite a few good rules, but for *life* . . .

On tenterhooks here.

Stop it, I'm thinking.

Then suddenly, inspiration hits. Confidently, I type:

If it's in a bin it's public property.

There's silence, then the phone bleeps again with his reply:

☺

I stare in disbelief. A smiley face. Sam Roxton typed a smiley face! A moment later he sends a follow-up.

I know. I don't believe it either.

I laugh out loud, then shiver as a breeze hits my shoulders. This is all very well. But I'm standing in a field in Hampshire with no coat and no idea where I'm going or what I'm doing. Come on, Poppy. Focus. There's no moon and all the stars must be hidden behind clouds. I can hardly see to type.

Where ARE you? In the wood? Can't see a thing.

Through the wood. Other side. I'll meet you.

Cautiously I start picking my way through the trees, cursing as a bramble catches my leg. There are probably stinging nettles and snake pits. There are probably man-traps. I reach for my phone, trying to text and avoid brambles at the same time.

My new rule for life: don't go into spooky dark woods on your own.

There's another silence – then my phone bleeps.

You're not on your own.

I clutch the phone more tightly. It's true, with him on the other end I do feel secure. I walk on a bit more, nearly tripping over a tree root, wondering where the moon's got to. Waxing, I suppose. Or waning. Whichever.

Look for me. I'm coming.

I stare at his text in disbelief. Look for him? How can I look for him?

It's pitch black, hadn't you noticed?

My phone. Look for the light. Don't call out. Someone might hear.

I peer into the gloom. I can't see anything at all except the dark shadows of trees and looming mounds of bramble bushes. Still, I guess the worst that can happen is I fall off a sudden cliff and break all my limbs. I take another few steps forward, listening to my own padding footfall, breathing in the musky, damp air.

OK?

Still here.

I've reached a tiny clearing and I hesitate for a moment, biting my lip. Before I go on I want to say the things I won't be able to when I see him. I'll be too embarrassed. It's different by text.

Just wanted to say I think you've done an amazing thing. Putting yourself on the line like that.

It had to be done.

That's typical of him to brush it off.

No. It didn't. But you did it.

I wait a little while, feeling the breeze on my face and listening to an owl hooting above me somewhere – but he doesn't reply. I don't care, I'm going to press on. I have to say these things, because I have a feeling no one else will.

You could have taken an easier path.

Of course.

But you didn't.

That's my rule for life.

And suddenly, with no warning, I feel a hotness behind my eyes. I have no idea why. I don't know why I suddenly feel affected. I want to type '*I admire you*', but I can't bring myself to. Not even by text. Instead, after a moment's hesitation, I type:

I understand you.

Of course you do. You'd do the same.

I stare at the screen, discomfited. *Me?* What have I got to do with it?

I wouldn't.

I've got to know you pretty well, Poppy Wyatt. You would.

I don't know what to say, so I start moving through the wood again, into what seems even blacker darkness. My hand is wrapped around the phone so tightly I'm going to get cramp. But somehow I can't loosen my fingers. I feel as though the harder I grip the more I'm connected to Sam. I feel as though I'm holding his hand.

And I don't want to let go. I don't want this to end. Even though I'm stumbling and cold and in the middle of nowhere. We're in a place that we won't ever be again.

On impulse I type:

I'm glad it was your phone I picked up.

A moment later his reply comes:

So am I.

I feel a tiny glow inside. Maybe he's just being polite. But I don't think so.

It's been good. Weird but good.

Weird but good would sum it up, yes. ☺

He sent another smiley face! I don't believe it!

What's happened to the man formerly known as Sam Roxton?

He's broadening his horizons. Which reminds me, where have all your kisses gone?

I look at my phone, surprised at myself.

Dunno. You've cured me.

I've never sent kisses to Sam, it occurs to me. Not once. Strange. Well, I can make up for that now. I'm almost giggling as I press the 'X' button down firmly.

Xxxxxxx

A moment later his reply arrives:

Xxxxxxxxx

Ha! With a snuffle of laughter I type an even longer row of kisses:

Xxxxxxxxxxxxxx

Xxxxxxxxxxxxxxxxx

Xoxoxoxoxoxoxoxoxoxoxoxo

Xoxoxoxoxoxoxoxoxoxoxoxoxoxox

☺ ☺ xxx ☺ ☺ xxx ☺ ☺ xxx

I see you.

I peer through the gloom again, but he must have better eyesight than me because I can't see anything.

Really?

Coming.

I lean forward, craning my neck, squinting for a glimpse of light, but there's nothing. He must have seen some other light.

Can't see you.

I'm coming.

You're nowhere near.

Yes I am. Coming.

And then suddenly I hear his footsteps approaching. He's *behind* me, thirty feet away, at a guess. No wonder I couldn't see him.

I should turn. Right now, I should turn. This is the moment that it would be natural to swivel round and greet him. Call out a hello; wave my phone in the air.

But my feet are rooted to the spot. I can't bring myself to move. Because as soon as I do, it will be time to be polite and matter-of-fact and back to normal. And I can't bear that. I want to stay right here. In the place where we can say anything to each other. Under the magic spell.

Sam pauses, right behind me. There's an unbearable, fragile beat as I wait for him to shatter the quiet. But it's as though he feels the same way. He says nothing. All I can hear is the gentle sound of his breathing. Slowly his arms wrap around me from behind. I close my eyes and lean back against his chest, feeling unreal.

I'm standing in a wood with Sam and his arms are around me and they really shouldn't be. I don't know what I'm doing. I don't know where I'm going with this.

Except . . . I do. Of course I do. Because as his hands gently hold my waist, I don't make a sound. As he swivels me round to face him, I don't make a sound. And as his stubble rasps my face I don't make a sound. I don't need to. We're still talking. Every touch he makes; every imprint of his skin is like another word, another thought; a continuation of our conversation. And we're not done yet. Not yet.

I don't know how long we're there. Five minutes, maybe. Ten minutes.

But the moment can't last for ever, and it doesn't. The bubble doesn't so much burst as evaporate, leaving us back in the real world. Realizing our arms are around each other; awkwardly stepping apart; feeling the chill night air rush between us. I look away, clearing my throat, rubbing his touch off my skin.

'So, shall we—'

'Yes.'

As we pad through the woods, neither of us speaks. I can't believe what just happened. Already it seems like a dream. Something impossible.

It was in the forest. No one saw it or heard it. So did it actually happen?[87]

Sam's phone is buzzing and this time he puts it to his ear.

'Hi. Vicks.'

And just like that, it's over. At the edge of the wood I can see a posse of people striding over the grass towards us. And the aftermath begins. I must be a little dazed from our encounter, because I can't engage with any of this. I'm aware of Vicks and Robbie and Mark all raising their voices, and Sam staying calm, and Vicks getting near to tears, which seems a bit unlikely for her, and talk of trains and cars and emergency press briefings and then Mark saying, 'It's Sir Nicholas for you, Sam,' and everyone moving back a step, almost respectfully, as Sam takes the call.

87. Another one for Antony Tavish. Not.

And then suddenly the cars are here to take everyone back to London, and we're heading out to the drive and Vicks is bossing everyone around and everyone's going to regroup at 7 a.m. at the office.

I've been allocated a car with Sam. As I get in, Vicks leans in and says, 'Thanks, Poppy.' I can't tell if she's being sarcastic or not.

'It's OK,' I say, just in case she's not. 'And ... I'm sorry. About...'

'Yup,' she says tightly.

And then the car moves off. Sam is texting intently, a deep frown on his face. I don't dare make a sound. I check my phone for a message from Magnus, but there's nothing. So I drop it down on the seat and stare out of the window, letting the street lamps blur into a stream of light, wondering where the hell I'm going.

I didn't even know I'd fallen asleep.

But somehow my head is on Sam's chest and he's saying, 'Poppy? Poppy?' and suddenly I wake up properly, and my neck is cricked and I'm looking out of a car window at a funny angle.

'Oh.' I scramble to a sitting position, wincing as my head spins. 'Sorry. God. You should have—'

'No problem. Is this your address?'

I peer blearily out of the window. We're in Balham. We're outside my block of flats. I glance at my watch. It's gone midnight.

'Yes,' I say in disbelief. 'This is me. How did you—'

Sam just nods at my phone, still on the car seat. 'Your address was in there.'

'Oh. Right.' I can hardly complain about him invading my privacy.

'I didn't want to wake you.'

'No. Of course. That's fine.' I nod. 'Thanks.'

Sam picks up the phone and seems about to hand it to me –
then he hesitates.

'I read your messages, Poppy. All of them.'

'Oh.' I clear my throat, unsure how to react. 'Wow. Well.
That's . . . that's a bit much, don't you think? I mean, I know I
read your emails, but you didn't need to—'

'It's Lucinda.'

'What?' I stare at him dumbly.

'For my money. Lucinda's your girl.'

Lucinda?

'But what— Why?'

'She's been lying to you. Consistently. She couldn't have
been in all the places she says she has at the times she said. It's
not physically possible.'

'Actually . . . I noticed that too,' I admit. 'I thought she was
trying to bill me for more hours, or something . . .'

'Does she bill by the hour?'

I rub my nose, feeling stupid. In fact, she doesn't. It's an
all-inclusive fee.

'Have you ever noticed that Magnus and Lucinda invariably
text you within ten minutes of each other?'

Slowly I shake my head. Why would I notice that? I get
zillions of texts every day, from all kinds of people. And anyway, how did *he* notice?

'I started off life as an analyst.' He looks a bit abashed. 'This
is my kind of thing.'

'What's your kind of thing?' I say, puzzled.

Sam produces a piece of paper and I clap a hand over my
mouth. I don't believe it. He's drawn a chart. Times and dates.
Calls. Texts. Emails. Has he been doing this while I've been
asleep?

'I analysed your messages. You'll see what's goingon.'

He analysed my messages. How do you analyse messages?

He hands me the paper and I blink at it.

'What . . .'

'You see the correlation?'

Correlation. I have no idea what he's talking about. It sounds like something from a maths exam.

'Um . . .'

'Take this date.' He points at the paper. 'They both email at around 6 p.m. asking how you're doing, being chatty. Then at 8 p.m. Magnus tells you he's working late at the London Library and a few minutes later Lucinda tells you she's working on garters for the bridesmaids at a fashion warehouse in Shoreditch. At eight at night? Please.'

I'm silent a few moments. I remember that email about the garters, now. It seemed a bit odd, even at the time. But you can't jump to conclusions from one weird email, surely?

'Who asked you to analyse my messages, anyway?' I know I sound all prickly, but I can't help it. 'Who said it was any of your business?'

'No one. You were asleep.' He spreads his hands. 'I'm sorry. I just started looking idly and then a pattern built up.'

'Two emails *aren't* a pattern.'

'It's not just two.' He gestures at the paper. 'Next day, Magnus has got a special evening seminar which he "forgot" to mention. Five minutes later, Lucinda tells you about a lace workshop in Nottinghamshire. But she was in Fulham two hours ago. Fulham to Nottinghamshire? In the rush hour? That's not real. My guess is it's an alibi.'

The word 'alibi' makes me feel a bit cold.

'Two days later, Magnus texts you, cancelling your lunch date. A moment later, Lucinda emails you, telling you she's frantically busy till 2 p.m. She doesn't give you any other reason for emailing. Why would she need to let you know that she's frantically busy over some random lunchtime?'

He looks up, waiting for a reply. Like I'll have one.

'I . . . I don't know,' I say at last. 'I don't know.'

As Sam continues, I knead my eyes briefly with my fists. I get why Vicks does this now. It's to block the world out, for just a second. Why didn't I see this? Why didn't I *see* any of this?

Magnus and Lucinda. It's like a bad joke. One of them's supposed to be organizing my wedding. The other's supposed to be *in* my wedding. To *me*.

But wait. My head jerks with a thought. Who sent me the anonymous text? Sam's theory can't be right, because someone must have sent that. It wouldn't have been any of Magnus's friends, and I don't know any of Lucinda's friends, so who on earth—

'Remember when Magnus told you he had to counsel some PhD student? And Lucinda suddenly pulled out of your drinks meeting? She sent Clemency along instead? If you look at the timings . . .'

Sam's still talking but I can barely hear him. My heart has constricted. Of course. Clemency.

Clemency.

Clemency is dyslexic. She would have spelled 'fiancée' wrong. She would have been too terrified of Lucinda to give her name. But she would have wanted me to know. If there was something to know.

My fingers are shaking as I grab my phone and find the text again. Now I read it over, I can hear the words in Clemency's sweet, anxious voice. It feels like her. It sounds like her.

Clemency wouldn't invent something like that. She must believe it's true. She must have seen something . . . heard something . . .

I sag back against the car seat. My limbs are aching. I feel parched and worn out and a little like I want to cry.

'Anyway.' Sam seems to realize I've stopped listening. 'I mean, it's a theory, that's all.' He folds the paper up and I take it.

'Thanks. Thanks for doing that.'

'I . . .' He shrugs, a bit awkward. 'Like I said. It's my thing.'

For a while we're both silent, although it feels like we're still communicating. I feel as though our thoughts are circling above our heads, interweaving, looping, meeting for a moment then diverging again. Him on his path, me on mine.

'So.' I exhale at last. 'I should let you go. It's late. Thanks for—'

'No,' he interrupts. 'Don't be ridiculous. Thank *you*.'

I nod simply. I think both of us are probably too drained to get into long speeches.

'It's been . . .'

'Yes.'

I look up and make the mistake of catching his eye, silvered in the light from the street lamp. And just for a moment I'm transported back—

No. *Don't*, Poppy. It never happened. Don't think about it. Blank it.

'So. Um.' I reach for the door handle, trying to force myself back into reality; into rationality. 'I still need to give you this phone back—'

'You know what? Have it, Poppy. It's yours.' He clasps my fingers over it and holds them tight for a moment. 'You earned it. And please don't bother to forward anything else. As from tomorrow all my emails will go to my new PA. Your work here is done.'

'Well, thanks!' I open the door – then on impulse turn around. 'Sam . . . I hope you're OK.'

'Don't worry about me. I'll be fine.' He flashes his wonder-smile and I suddenly feel like hugging him tight. He's about to lose his job and he can still smile like that. 'I hope *you're* OK,' he adds. 'I'm sorry about . . . it all.'

'Oh, *I'll* be OK!' I give a brittle laugh, even though I have no idea what I even mean by this. My husband-to-be is possibly shagging my wedding planner. In what sense will I be OK?

The driver clears his throat, and I start. It's the middle of the night. I'm sitting in a car on my street. Come on, Poppy. Get with it. Move. The conversation has to end.

So even though it's the last thing I feel like doing, I force myself to get out and bang the door shut and call, 'Goodnight!' then head to my front door and open it, because I know instinctively Sam won't drive away till he's seen I'm safely in. Then I come back out and stand on the doorstep, watching his car drive away.

As it rounds the corner I check my phone, half-hoping, half-expecting . . .

But it's dark and silent. It remains dark and silent. And for the first time in a long while, I feel utterly alone.

THIRTEEN

It's in every single paper the next morning. Front-page news. I headed out to the newsagent's as soon as I was up, and bought every paper they had.

There are pictures of Sir Nicholas, pictures of the Prime Minister, pictures of Sam, pictures of Ed Exton, even a picture of Vicks in the *Mail*. The headlines are full of 'corruption' and 'smear-attempt' and 'integrity'. The memo is printed in full, everywhere, and there's an official quote from Number Ten about Sir Nicholas, considering his position on the government committee.. There are even two different cartoons of Sir Nicholas holding up bags labelled 'Happiness' stuffed full of money.

But Sam's right: there's an air of confusion about it. Some journalists obviously think Sir Nicholas did write the memo. Others obviously think he didn't. One paper has run an editorial about how Sir Nicholas is an arrogant bighead and of course he's been taking bribes all along; another has written that Sir Nicholas is known for his quiet integrity and it couldn't possibly be him. If Sam wanted to throw up a question mark over everything, he's definitely succeeded.

I texted him this morning:

You OK?

But I got no reply. I guess he's busy. To say the least.

Meanwhile, I feel like a wreck. It took me hours to get to sleep last night, I was so wired – but then I woke at six, sitting up bolt upright, my heart racing, already grabbing for my phone. Magnus had texted four words:

Having a great time. M xxx

Having a great time. What does that tell me? Nothing.

He could be having a great time congratulating himself on how I have no idea about his secret mistress. Then again, he could be having a great time innocently looking forward to a life of faithful monogamy, with no idea that Clemency somehow got the wrong end of the stick about him and Lucinda.[88] Or possibly he could be having a great time deciding that he's never going to be unfaithful again and regrets it hugely and will confess everything to me as soon as he gets back.[89]

I can't cope. I need Magnus to be here, in this country, in this room. I need to ask him, 'Have you been unfaithful with Lucinda?' and see what he says and then maybe we can move forward and I can work out what I'm going to do. Until then, I feel like I'm in limbo.

As I go to make another cup of tea, I catch a glimpse of myself in the hall mirror, and wince. My hair is a mess. My hands are covered with newsprint from all the papers. My stomach is full of acid and my skin looks drawn. So much for my bridal-beauty regime. According to my plan, last night

88. OK, unlikely.
89. OK, even less likely.

I was supposed to apply a hydration mask. I didn't even take my make-up off.

I'd originally set today aside to do wedding preparation – but every time I even think about it, my insides clench and I feel like crying or shouting at someone. (Well, Magnus.) There's no point just sitting here all day, though. I have to go out. I have to do *something*. After a few sips of tea, I decide to go into work. I don't have any appointments, but I've got some admin I can catch up on. And at least it'll force me to have a shower and get myself together.

I'm the first to arrive, and I sit in the quiet calm, sorting through patient files, letting the monotony of the job soothe me. Which lasts about five minutes before Angela slouches in through the door and starts clattering around switching on her computer and making coffee and turning on the wall-mounted telly.

'Do we have to?' I wince at the noise. I feel as if I've got a hangover, even though I hardly drank excessively last night, and I could do without this blaring in my ears. But Angela stares at me as though I've just violated some basic human right.

'I always watch *Daybreak*.'

It's not worth arguing. I could always heft all the files into my consultation room but I don't have the energy for that either, so I just hunch my shoulders and try to block the world out.

'Parcel!' Angela dumps a jiffy bag in front of me. 'StarBlu. Is that your swimwear for the honeymoon?'

I stare at it blankly. I was a different person when I ordered that. I can remember myself now, going online one lunchtime, picking out bikinis and wraps. Never in a million years did I think that three days before the wedding I'd be sitting here, wondering if the whole thing should go ahead at all.

'. . . and in today's front-page story, we're talking possible corruption at government level.' The presenter's voice attracts my attention. 'Here in the studio, a man who has known Sir Nicholas Murray for thirty years, Alan Smith-Reeves. Alan, this is a confusing business. What's your take?'

'I know that guy,' Angela says self-importantly as Alan Smith-Reeves starts talking. 'He used to work in the same building at my last job.'

'Oh right.' I nod politely, as a picture of Sam appears on the screen.

I can't look. Just the sight of him sends shooting pains through my chest, but I don't even know why. Is it because he's in trouble? Is it because he's the only other person who knows about Magnus? Is it because last night I was standing in a wood with his arms around me and now I'll probably never see him again?

'He's quite good-looking,' says Angela, squinting at Sam critically. 'Is he Sir Nicholas Whatsit?'

'No!' I say, more vehemently than I mean to. 'Don't be stupid!'

'All right!' She scowls at me. 'What's it to you, anyway?'

I can't answer. I have to escape from all this. I get to my feet. 'Want a coffee?'

'I'm making one. Duh.' Angela shoots me an odd look. 'Are you OK? What are you doing here, anyway? Thought you had the day off.'

'I wanted to get ahead with stuff.' I grab my denim jacket. 'But maybe it was a bad idea.'

'She's here!' The door bursts open and Ruby and Annalise bustle in. 'We were just talking about you!' says Ruby, looking surprised. 'What are you doing here?'

'I thought I'd do some admin. But I'm going.'

'No, don't go! Wait a sec.' Ruby grabs my shoulder, then turns to Annalise. 'Now, Annalise. Why don't you *say* what we were talking about to Poppy? Then you won't have to write a letter.'

Uh-oh. She's wearing her headmistressy look. And Annalise's looking shamefaced. What's going on?

301

'I don't want to say it.' Annalise bites her lip like a six-year-old. 'I'll write a letter.'

'Say it. Then it's done.' Ruby is eyeing Annalise with the kind of stern gaze it's impossible to ignore.

'OK!' Annalise takes a breath, looking a little pink around the cheeks. 'Poppy, I'm sorry I behaved badly with Magnus the other day. It was wrong of me and I was just doing it to get back at you.'

'And?' prompts Ruby.

'I'm sorry I've given you a hard time. Magnus is yours, not mine. He belongs with you, not me. And I'm never going to mention the fact we switched appointments again,' she finishes in a rush. 'Promise.'

She looks so discomfited, I feel quite touched. I can't believe Ruby did that. They should put *her* in charge at White Globe Consulting. She'd sort out Justin Cole in no time.

'Well . . . thanks,' I say. 'I appreciate it.'

'I truly am sorry, you know, Poppy.' Annalise twists her fingers, looking abject. 'I don't want to spoil your wedding.'

'Annalise, take it from me. You won't spoil my wedding.' I smile, but to my horror I can feel tears welling up in my eyes.

If anything spoils my wedding it'll be the fact that it was called off. It'll be the fact that Magnus didn't really love me after all. It'll be the fact that I was a completely stupid, deluded fool . . .

Oh God. I *am* going to cry.

'Missus?' Ruby gives me a close look. 'You OK?'

'Fine!' I exclaim, blinking furiously.

'Wedding stress,' says Annalise. 'Oh my God, Poppy, are you turning into a bridezilla at last? Go on! I'll help. I'll be a bridesmaidzilla. Let's go and throw a hissy fit somewhere. That'll cheer you up.'

I raise a half-smile and wipe my eyes. I don't know how to respond. Do I tell them about Magnus? They're my friends after all, and I'm longing for someone to talk to.

But then, what if it *is* all a mix-up? I haven't heard anything further from Unknown Number.[90] The whole thing's guess-work. I can't start telling the world that Magnus has been unfaithful, based on one anonymous text. And then have Annalise putting it on Facebook and calling him a Love Rat and booing as we walk down the aisle.[91]

'I'm just tired,' I say at last.

'Slap-up breakfast!' exclaims Ruby. 'That's what you need.'

'No!' I say in horror. 'I won't fit into my dress!'

Assuming I'm still going to get married. I feel the rush of tears again. Preparing for a wedding is stressful enough. Preparing for a wedding *or* possible last-minute break-up/cancellation is going to turn my hair grey.

'You will,' Ruby contradicts me. 'Everyone knows brides lose two dress sizes before their wedding. You've got a massive margin to play with there, girl. Use it! Pig out! You'll never be in this position again!'

'*Have* you dropped two dress sizes?' asks Annalise, eyeing me a little resentfully. 'You can't have.'

'No,' I say gloomily. 'Maybe half a one.'

'Well that qualifies you for a latte and a doughnut, at any rate,' says Ruby, heading for the door. 'Come on. Comfort food's what you need. We've got half an hour. Let's cram it in.'

When Ruby gets an idea, she goes for it. She's already striding along the pavement and into the Costa two doors away. As Annalise and I push our way in, she's heading up to the counter.

'Hello there!' she begins cheerfully. 'I'd like three lattes, three doughnuts, three plain croissants, three almond croissants . . .'

'Ruby, stop!' I start giggling.

'Three pains au chocolat – we'll give them to the patients if we can't finish them – three apple muffins . . .'

---

90. A.k.a. Clemency. Possibly.
91. And if you think she wouldn't, you don't know Annalise.

'Three tins of breath mints,' chimes in Annalise.

'Breath mints?' Ruby turns to regard her scornfully. *'Breath mints?'*

'And some cinnamon swirls,' Annalise adds hurriedly.

'That's more like it. Three cinnamon swirls . . .'

My phone in my pocket rings and my stomach lurches. Oh God, who's this? What if it's Magnus?

What if it's Sam?

I haul it out, taking a step away from Ruby and Annalise, who are arguing about what kind of cookies they should buy. As I see the screen, I feel a dreadful squeezing sensation inside. It's Unknown Number. Whoever-it-is has finally phoned me back.

This is it. This is where I find out the truth. For good or for bad. I'm so petrified, my hand is actually shaking as I press Accept, and at first I can't catch my breath to speak.

'Hello?' a girl's voice is saying down the line. 'Hello? Can you hear me?'

Is that Clemency? I can't tell.

'Hi,' I manage to utter at last. 'Hello. This is Poppy speaking. Is this Clemency?'

'No.' The girl sounds surprised.

'Oh.' I swallow. 'Right.'

It's not Clemency? Who is it, then? My mind is scampering around frantically. Who else could have sent me that text? Does this mean Lucinda's *not* involved after all? I can see Annalise and Ruby watching me curiously from the till point and I swing away.

'So.' I try desperately to sound dignified, and not at all like someone who's about to be totally humiliated and have to call their entire wedding off. 'Was there something you wanted to say to me?'

'Yes. I'm urgently trying to get in touch with Sam Roxton.'

Sam?

The tension that's been growing inside me breaks with a

crash. It's not Unknown Number after all. At least, it's Different Unknown Number. I don't know if I'm disappointed or relieved.

'How did you get this number?' the girl is demanding. 'Do you know Sam?'

'Err . . . yes. Yes, I do.' I try to gather myself. 'Sorry. I misunderstood for a moment. I thought you were someone else. Can I take a message for Sam?'

I say it automatically before I realize that I'm not forwarding things to Sam any more. Still, I can get a message to him, can't I? Just for old times' sake. Just to be helpful.

'I've tried that.' She sounds quite high-handed. 'You don't understand. I need to speak to him. Today. Now. It's urgent.'

'Oh. Well, I can give you his email address—'

'That's a joke.' She cuts me off impatiently. 'Sam never reads his emails. But believe me, this is important. I *have* to speak to him, as soon as possible. It's about the phone, in fact. The phone you're holding right now.'

What?

I gape at the mobile, wondering if I've gone crazy. How does some strange girl know what phone I'm holding?

'Who *are* you?' I say in astonishment, and she heaves a sigh.

'No one remembers who I am, do they? I was Sam's PA. I'm Violet.'

Thank God I didn't eat the cinnamon swirls, is all I can say. Violet turns out to be about ten foot tall, with skinny legs clad in frayed denim shorts, and massive dark eyes with traces of make-up around them.[92] She looks like a cross between a giraffe and a bush-baby.

Luckily she lives in Clapham and it only took her about five minutes to get here. So here she is, in Costa, chomping on a

---

92. Either this is a very arty look, like you see in fashion magazines, or she didn't take her make-up off yesterday. (Still. Like I can talk.)

chicken wrap and swigging a smoothie. Ruby and Annalise have gone back to work, which is a good thing, because I couldn't cope with having to explain the whole saga to them. It's all too surreal.

As Violet has told me several times, if she hadn't *happened* to be in London, between jobs, and *happened* to see the headlines as she went to get a pint of milk, she would never have known about the scandal. And if she hadn't *happened* to have a brain in her head, she wouldn't have suddenly realized that she totally knew what had been going on the whole time. But are people grateful? Do they want to hear? No. They're all idiots.

'My parents are on this stupid *cruise*,' she's saying with disdain. 'I tried to look in their telephone book, but I don't know who's who, do I? So I tried ringing Sam's line, then Nick's line . . . but I only got snotty PAs. No one would listen to me. But I need to tell someone.' She bangs her hand on the table. 'Because I *know* something was going on. I even sort of knew it at the time? But Sam never listened to me? Do you find he never listens to you?' She focuses on me with interest for the first time. 'Who exactly are you, anyway? You said you'd been helping him. What does that mean?'

'It's kind of complicated,' I say after a pause. 'He was left in the lurch a bit.'

'Oh yeah?' She takes another bite of chicken wrap and regards me with interest. 'How come?'

Has she forgotten?

'Well . . . err . . . you left with no notice. Remember? You were supposed to be his PA?'

'*Riiiight.*' She opens her eyes wide. 'Yeah. That job didn't really work out for me. And the agency called and wanted me to get on a plane, so . . .' Her brow wrinkles in thought as though she's considering this for the first time. 'I guess he was a bit pissed off. But they've got loads of staff. He'll be all right.' She waves her hand airily. 'So, do you work there?'

'No.' How am I going to explain it? 'I found this phone and borrowed it, and got to know Sam that way.'

'I remember that phone. Yeah.' She peers at it, screwing up her nose. 'I never answered it.'

I suppress a smile. She must have been the crappest PA in the world.

'But *that's* why I know something was going on.' She finishes off her chicken wrap with a flourish. 'Because of all the messages. On that.' She jabs a finger at it.

OK. At last we're getting to it.

'Messages? What messages?'

'It had all these voice-mails on it. Not for Sam, for some guy called Ed. I didn't know what to do about them. So I listened to them and I wrote them down. And I didn't like the sound of them.'

'Why not?' My heart starts to thud.

'They were all from the same guy about altering a document. How they were going to do it. How long it would take. How much it would cost. That kind of thing. It didn't sound right, you know what I mean? But it didn't exactly sound *wrong*, either.' She crinkles her nose again. 'It just sounded . . . weird.'

My head is reeling. I can't take this in. Voice-mails for Ed about the memo. On this phone. *This phone.*

'Did you tell Sam?'

'I sent him an email and he said to ignore them. But I didn't *want* to ignore them. You know what I mean? I just had this instinct.' She swigs her smoothie. 'Then I open the paper this morning, and I see Sam talking about some memo and saying it must have been sexed up, and I think, yes!' She bangs her hand on the table again. '*That's* what was going on.'

'How many voice-mails were there in all?'

'Four? Five?'

'But there aren't any voice-mails on here now. At least, I haven't found any.' I can hardly bear to ask the question. 'Did you . . . delete them?'

'No!' She beams in triumph. 'That's the point! I saved them. At least my boyfriend Aran did. I was writing one out one night, and he was like, "Babe, just save it to the server." And I was like, "How do I save a *voice-mail*?" So he came into the office and put them all on a file. He can do amazing stuff, Aran,' she adds proudly. 'He's a model too but he writes games on the side.'

'A file?' I'm not following. 'So where's the file now?'

'It must still be there.' She shrugs. 'On the PA's computer. There's an icon called Voice-mails on the desktop.'

An icon on the PA's computer. Just outside Sam's office. All the time, it was right there, right in front of our faces—

'Will it still be there?' I feel a sudden blast of panic. 'Won't it have been deleted?'

'Don't know why it would have been.' She shrugs. 'Nothing was deleted when I arrived. There was just a big old pile of crap I was supposed to wade through.'

I almost want to laugh hysterically. All that panic. All that effort. We could have just gone to the computer outside Sam's office.

'Anyway, I'm going to the States tomorrow, and I had to tell someone, but it's impossible to get in touch with Sam at the moment.' She shakes her head. 'I've tried emailing, texting, phoning . . . I'm like, if you just *knew* what I had to tell you . . .'

'Let me have a go,' I say after a pause, and type a text to Sam:

Sam, you HAVE to call me. Now. It's about Sir Nicholas. Could be a help. Not a time-waster. Believe me. Call at once. Please. Poppy.

'Well, good luck with that.' Violet rolls her eyes. 'Like I told you, he's gone off radar. His PA said he's not responding to anybody. Not emailing, not answering calls . . .' She breaks off as the tinny sound of Beyoncé comes through the air. 'Sam Mobile' has already popped up on the display.

'OK.' Her eyes widen. 'I'm impressed.'

I press Accept and lift the phone to my ear. 'Hi. Sam.'

'Poppy.'

His voice feels like a blast of sunshine in my ear. There's so much I want to say. But I can't. Not now.

Maybe not ever.

'Listen,' I say. 'Are you in your office? Go to your PA's computer. Quickly.'

There's the briefest pause, then he says, 'OK.'

'Look on the desktop,' I instruct him. 'Is there an icon called "Voice-mails"?'

There's silence for a little while – then Sam's voice comes down the phone.

'Affirmative.'

'OK!' My breath comes out in a whoosh. I hadn't realized I'd been holding it. 'You need to look after that file carefully. And now you need to speak to Violet.'

'*Violet?*' He sounds taken aback. 'You don't mean Violet, my flaky ex-PA?'

'I'm with her now. Listen to her, Sam. Please.' I pass the phone over.

'Hey, Sam,' says Violet easily. 'Sorry about leaving you in the lurch and all that. But you've had Poppy to help you out, yeah?'

As she's talking, I head up to the counter and buy myself another coffee, even though I'm so wired I probably shouldn't. Just hearing Sam's voice has thrown me. I immediately wanted to talk to him about everything. I wanted to nestle up and hear what he had to say.

But that's impossible. Number one, because he's mired in massive problems of his own. Number two, because who is he? Not a friend. Not a colleague. Just some random guy who has no place in my life. It's over. The only place for us to go from here is goodbye.

Maybe we'll exchange the odd text. Maybe we'll meet up

awkwardly in a year's time. Both of us will look different and we'll say hello stiltedly, already regretting the decision to come. We'll laugh about how bizarre that whole phone business was. We'll never mention what happened in the woods. *Because it didn't happen.*

'You OK, Poppy?' Violet is standing in front of me, waving the phone in front of my face. 'Here.'

'Oh!' I come to and take it. 'Thanks. Did you speak to Sam?'

'He opened the file as I was talking to him. He's pretty stoked. He said to say he'd call you later.'

'Oh. Well . . . he doesn't have to.' I pick up my coffee. 'Whatever.'

'Hey, nice rock.' Violet grabs my hand.[93] 'Is that an emerald?'

'Yes.'

'Cool! So, who's the lucky guy?' She gets out an iPhone. 'Can I take a picture of it? I'm just getting ideas for when Aran becomes a gazillionaire. So, did you choose it yourself?' she presses, as we sit back down.

'No, he had it all ready when he proposed. It's a family ring.'

'Romantic.' Violet nods. 'Wow. So you didn't expect it?'

'No. Not at all.'

'Were you like, "Fuck!"?'

'Kind of.' I nod.

It seems a million years ago now, that evening when Magnus proposed. I was so giddy. I felt as if I'd entered a magic bubble where everything was shiny and perfect and nothing could ever go wrong again. *God*, I was a fool . . .

A tear splashes on to my cheek before I can stop it.

'Hey.' Violet looks at me with concern. 'What's up?'

'Nothing!' I smile, wiping at my eyes. 'It's just . . . things aren't exactly brilliant. My fiancé might be cheating on me and I don't know what to do.'

---

93. No one's ever grabbed my hand to look at the ring before. That is definitely an invasion of personal space.

Just letting the words out makes me feel better. I take a deep breath and smile at Violet. 'Sorry. Ignore that. You don't want to know.'

'No. It's fine.' She draws her feet up on to her chair and regards me intently. 'Why aren't you sure if he is or not? What makes you think he is?'

'Someone sent me an anonymous text. That's it.'

'So ignore it.' Violet gives me a close look. 'Or do you have a gut feeling? Does it seem like something he might do?'

I'm silent a moment. I *so* wish I could say, 'Never! Not in a million years!' But too many moments are sticking in my brain. Moments I haven't wanted to see; that I've tried to blank out. Magnus flirting with girls at parties. Magnus surrounded by all his female students, his arms casually draped around their shoulders. Magnus being practically molested by Annalise.

The thing is, girls like Magnus. And he likes them.

'I don't know,' I say, staring into my coffee. 'Maybe.'

'And do you have any idea who he's doing it with?'

'Maybe.'

'So!' Violet seems galvanized. 'Confront the situation. Have you spoken to him? Have you spoken to her?'

'He's in Bruges, on his stag do. I can't talk to him. And she's . . .' I break off. 'No. I can't. I mean, it's just a possibility. She's probably totally innocent.'

'Are you *sure* he's on his stag do?' says Violet, raising her eyebrows, then grins. 'No, I'm just winding you up.' She pushes my arm. 'I'm sure he is. Hey babe, I have to go and pack. Hope it all works out for you. Give my love to Sam.'

As she strides out of the coffee shop, about six male heads turn. I'm pretty sure that if Magnus were here, his would be one of them.

I stare morosely into my coffee for a little while longer. Why do people have to keep telling me to confront the situation? I *do* confront things. Loads of times. But it's not like I can march up to Magnus on his stag do, or accost Lucinda and accuse her out of the blue. I mean, you need *evidence*. You need *facts*. One anonymous text doesn't cut it.

My phone starts emitting Beyoncé and I stiffen, in spite of myself. Is that—

No. It's Unknown Number. But *which* bloody Unknown Number? I take a swig of coffee, to steel myself, and answer.

'Hi, Poppy Wyatt here.'

'Hello, Poppy. My name is Brenda Fairfax. I'm calling from the Berrow Hotel. I've been away on holiday for a few days, otherwise of course I should have called at once. I do apologize.'

Mrs Fairfax. After all this time. I almost want to burst out laughing.

To think how desperate I was to hear this woman's voice. And now it's all irrelevant. I've got the ring back. None of it matters. Why is she calling me, anyway? I told the concierge I'd got the ring safely. The whole thing is over.

'You don't need to apologize—'

'But of course I do! What a *dreadful* mix-up.' She sounds quite flustered. Maybe the concierge gave her a hard time. Maybe he told her to call me and apologize.

'Please don't worry. I had a bit of a fright, but it's all fine now.'

'And such a valuable ring, too!'

'It's fine,' I say soothingly. 'No harm done.'

'But I still can't understand it! One of the waitresses had handed it to me and I was going to put it in the safe, you see. That's what I was about to do.'

'Honestly, you don't have to explain.' I feel quite sorry for her. 'These things happen. It was a fire alarm, you got distracted—'

'No!' Mrs Fairfax sounds a mite offended. 'That's not what happened at all. I was about to put it in the safe, as I say. But before I could do so, another lady rushed up to me and told me it was hers. Another guest at the tea.'

'Another guest?' I say, after a puzzled pause.

'Yes! She said it was her engagement ring and that she'd been frantically searching high and low. She was very credible. The waitress vouched for the fact that she'd been sitting at your table. And then she put it on. Well, who was I to disbelieve her?'

I rub my eyes, wondering if I'm hearing this correctly.

'You're saying someone else took my ring? And said it was hers?'

'Yes! She was adamant that the ring belonged to her. She put it on straight away and it fitted. It looked very nice, as it happens. I know that strictly speaking I should have asked her for proof that she was the owner, and we *will* be reviewing our official procedures in the light of this unfortunate occurrence—'

'Mrs Fairfax.' I cut her off, not remotely interested in official procedures. 'Can I just ask you . . . did she have long dark hair, by any chance? And a little diamanté hairband?'

'Yes. Long dark hair, with a diamanté hairband, as you say, and a *wonderful* orange dress.'

I close my eyes in disbelief. Lucinda. It was Lucinda.

The ring didn't get caught on her bag lining. She deliberately took it. She knew how panicked I'd be. She knew how important it was. But she took it and pretended it was hers. God only knows why.

A pulse is beating in my head as I say goodbye to Mrs Fairfax. I'm breathing hard and my hands are balling into fists. Enough is enough. Maybe I don't have any evidence that she's sleeping with Magnus – but I can sure as hell confront her about this. And I'm going to do it right now.

I don't know what Lucinda's doing today. I haven't had any emails or messages from her for a couple of days, which is unusual. As I text, my hands are actually shaking.

Hi Lucinda! How's it going? What are you up to? Can I help? Poppy.

Almost immediately she replies:

Just polishing off some loose ends at home. Don't worry, nothing for you to help with. Lucinda

Lucinda lives in Battersea. Twenty minutes away by taxi. I'm not going to give her time to get her story straight. I'm going to take her by surprise.

I hail a cab and give her address, then sit back, trying to stay calm and steely, even though the more I think about this, the more flabbergasted I feel. Lucinda took my ring. Does that mean she's a *thief*? Did she make a copy and keep the real one and sell it? I glance at my left hand, suddenly doubtful. Am I so sure this is the real thing?

Or was she somehow meaning to be helpful? Did she forget she had it? Should I give her the benefit of the doubt—

No, Poppy. No chance.

As I arrive at her red-brick mansion block, a guy in jeans is opening the front door. I quickly dodge in behind him, and head up the three flights of stairs to Lucinda's flat. This way she'll get absolutely no warning that I'm here.

Maybe she'll open the door wearing the real ring, plus all the other jewellery she's stolen from unsuspecting friends. Maybe no one will answer because she's actually in Bruges. Maybe Magnus will open the door wrapped in a bedsheet—

Oh God. *Stop* it, Poppy.

I rap on the door, trying to sound like a delivery guy, and it must have worked, because she swings the door open, her face creased in annoyance, her phone to her ear, before stopping dead, her mouth in an 'O'.

I stare back, equally wordless. My eyes flick past Lucinda, to the huge suitcase in the hall, then to the passport in her hand and then back to the suitcase.

'As soon as possible,' she says. 'Terminal Four. Thanks.' She rings off and glares at me, as though daring me to ask what she's doing.

I'm racking my brains for something inspired and caustic to say, but my inner five-year-old is quicker off the mark.

'You took my ring!' As the words burst out, I can feel my cheeks turning pink, to add to the effect. Maybe I should stamp my foot, too.

'Oh, for God's sake.' Lucinda wrinkles her nose disparagingly, as though to accuse one's wedding planner of theft is a total etiquette no-no. 'You got it back, didn't you?'

'But you *took* it!' I step inside her flat, even though she hasn't invited me in, and can't help glancing around. I've never been to Lucinda's flat before. It's quite grand and has clearly been interior-decorated but is an absolute tip of cluttered surfaces and chairs, with wine glasses everywhere. No wonder she always wants to meet at hotels.

'Look, Poppy.' She sighs bad-temperedly. 'I've got things to do, OK? If you're going to come round and make offensive remarks, then I'm going to have to ask you to leave.'

Huh?

She's the one who did something wrong. She's the one who took a priceless engagement ring and pretended it was hers. How has she managed to leapfrog over that fact and make it look like *I'm* in the wrong for even mentioning it?

'Now, if that's all, I *am* rather busy—'

'Stop right there.' The force of my own voice takes me by surprise. 'That's not all. I want to know exactly why you took my ring. Were you planning to sell it? Did you need the money?'

'No, I didn't need the money.' She glares at me. 'You want to know why I took it, Miss Poppy? It's because it should have been *mine*.'

315

'*Yours?* Wh—'

I can't even finish the word, let alone the sentence.

'You know Magnus and I are old flames.' She throws the information out casually, like a swatch of material on to a table.

'What? No! No one ever told me that! Were you engaged?'

My mind is juddering with shock. Magnus was with Lucinda? Magnus was *engaged*? He never mentioned a previous fiancée, let alone that it was Lucinda. Why don't I know any of this? What is going *on*?

'No, we were never engaged,' she says reluctantly, then shoots me a murderous look. 'But we should have been. He proposed to me. With that ring.'

I feel a clench of disbelieving pain. Magnus proposed to another girl with *my ring*? With *our ring*? I want to turn on my heel and leave, escape, block my ears . . . but I can't. I have to get to the bottom of all this. Nothing seems to make sense.

'I don't understand. I don't get it. You said you *should* have been engaged. What happened?'

'He bottled it, is what happened,' she says furiously. 'The bloody coward.'

'Oh God. At what stage? Had you planned the wedding? He didn't *jilt* you, did he?' I say in sudden horror. 'He didn't leave you standing at the altar?'

Lucinda has closed her eyes as though reliving it. Now she opens them and gives me a vicious glare.

'*Far* worse. He chickened out halfway through the bloody proposal.'

'What?' I peer at her, not quite understanding. 'What do you—'

'We were on a skiing holiday, two years ago.' Her brow tightens at the memory. 'I wasn't stupid, I knew he'd brought the family ring. I knew he was going to propose. So we'd had dinner one night, and it was just us in the chalet. The fire was going, and he knelt down on the rug and brought out this little box. He opened it up, and there was this amazing, antique emerald ring.'

Lucinda pauses, breathing hard. I don't move a muscle.

'He took hold of my hand, and he said, "Lucinda, my darling, will you . . ."' She inhales sharply, as though she can hardly bear to carry on. 'And I was going to say yes! I was all poised! I was just waiting for him to get to the end. But then he stopped. He started sweating. And then he stood up and said, "Bugger. Sorry. I can't do this. Sorry, Lucinda."'

He didn't. He *didn't*. I stare at her in disbelief, almost wanting to laugh.

'What did you say?'

'I yelled, "Do *what*, you prick? You haven't even bloody proposed yet!" But he didn't have anything to say. He closed up the box and put the ring away. And that was that.'

'I'm sorry,' I say lamely. 'That's really awful.'

'He's such a commitment-phobe, he couldn't even commit to a fucking *proposal*! He couldn't even see *that* through!' She looks absolutely livid, and I don't blame her.

'So, why on earth did you agree to organize his wedding?' I say, incredulous. 'Isn't that rubbing it in your face, every day?'

'It was the least he could do to make amends.' She glowers at me. 'I needed a job. Although actually, I'm thinking of changing career. Arranging weddings is a bloody *nightmare*.'

No wonder Lucinda's been in such a bad mood this whole time. No wonder she's been so aggressive towards me. If I had known for one *second* that she was an old flame of Magnus's . . .

'I was never going to keep the ring,' she adds sulkily. 'I just wanted to give you a scare.'

'Well, you managed it all right.'

I can't believe I've let this woman into my life, confided in her, discussed all my hopes for my wedding day . . . and she's an ex of Magnus's. How could he have let this happen? How could he have thought it would ever work?

I feel like some kind of filter has been lifted from my eyes. I feel like I'm finally waking up to reality. And I haven't even tackled my main fear yet.

'I got the idea you were sleeping with Magnus,' I blurt out. 'I mean, not when you were going out together. Now. Recently. Last week.'

There's silence and I look up, hoping she'll launch into some stinging denial. But as I meet her eye, she turns away.

'Lucinda?'

She grabs her suitcase and starts wheeling it towards the door. 'I'm going away. I've had enough of this whole thing. I deserve a holiday. If I have to talk weddings for one more second—'

'*Lucinda?*'

'Oh, for Christ's sake!' she erupts impatiently. 'Maybe I slept with him once or twice for old times' sake. If you can't keep tabs on him, you shouldn't marry him.' Her phone rings and she answers. 'Hi. Yes. Coming down. Excuse me.' She ushers me out of the flat, slams the door and double-locks it.

'You can't just *leave*!' I'm shaking all over. 'You have to tell me what happened!'

'What do you want me to say?' She throws her hands up. 'These things happen. You weren't meant to find out, but there you go.' She manhandles her suitcase into the lift. 'Oh, and by the way. If you think you and I are the only girls he's hauled that emerald ring out of the bank safe for, think again. We're on the end of a list, sweetie.'

'*What?*' I'm starting to hyperventilate. 'What list? Lucinda, wait! What are you talking about?'

'Work it out, Poppy. It's your problem. I've sorted the flowers and the Order of Service and the almonds and the fucking . . . dessert spoons.' She jabs a button and the lift doors start to close. 'This one's all yours.'

FOURTEEN

After Lucinda's gone, I stand motionless for about three minutes solid, in a state of shock. Then, abruptly, I come to. I head for the stairwell and down the stairs. As I step out of the building I switch off my phone. I can't afford any distractions. I need to think. I need to be alone. Like Lucinda said, I need to work this out for myself.

I start walking along the pavement, not caring which direction I'm going. My mind is circling around all the facts, the guesses, the speculation, and back to the facts. But gradually, as I walk, thoughts seem to settle into place. My resolve hardens. I have a plan.

I don't know where my sudden determination has come from: whether Lucinda has spurred me on or whether I've just had enough of avoiding confrontation while my stomach ties itself in knots. But I'm going to face this one down. I'm going to do it. The weirdest thing is, I keep hearing Sam's voice in my ear, reassuring me and bolstering me and telling me I can do it. It's as if he's giving me a pep talk, even though he's not here. And it's making me stand taller. It's making me feel like I can do this. I'm going to be a Whole New Poppy.

As I reach the corner of Battersea Rise I feel ready. I haul out my phone, turn it on, and without reading a single new message, speed-dial Magnus. Of course he doesn't answer, but I expected that.

'Hi, Magnus,' I say in the most crisp, businesslike tones I can muster. 'Can you call me as soon as possible? We need to talk.'

OK. Good. That was dignified. A brief, cutting message that he will understand. Now ring off.

Ring *off*, Poppy.

But I can't. My hand feels welded to the phone. While I'm connected to him, or even just his voice-mail, I can feel my defences coming down. I want to talk. I want to hear from him. I want him to know how shocked and hurt I am.

'Because . . . I've heard some news, OK?' I hear myself continuing. 'I've been speaking to your great friend *Lucinda*.' I give 'Lucinda' an angry little emphasis. 'And what she told me was a bit of a shock, to say the least, so I think we need to talk as soon as possible. Because unless you've got some great, marvellous explanation, which I can't think how you would, because was Lucinda *lying*? Because *someone* must be lying, Magnus. Someone must be—'

Beep.

Damn, I got cut off.

As I turn off my phone again, I'm cursing myself. So much for the brief, cutting message. So much for a Whole New Poppy. That wasn't how it was supposed to go at all.

Still, never mind. At least I made the call. At least I didn't sit with my hands over my ears, avoiding the whole thing. And now, to the next thing on my mental list. I step into the road, lift my hand and flag down a cab.

'Hi,' I say as I get in. 'I'd like to go to Hampstead, please.'

I know Wanda's in today, because she said she was preparing for some radio show she's doing tonight. And sure enough, as I draw up to the house, music is blasting out of the windows. I have no idea if Antony is there too, but I don't care.

They can both hear this. As I approach the house, I'm trembling, like I was the other night – but in a different way. In a positive way. In a 'bring it on' way.

'Poppy!' As Wanda swings the door open she beams widely. 'What a lovely surprise!' She swoops in for a kiss, then studies my face again. 'Have you just dropped round to be sociable, or was there anything . . .'

'We need to talk.'

There's a brief moment of silence between us. I can tell she understands that I don't mean some jolly chit-chat.

'I see. Well, come in!' She smiles again but I can see anxiety in the downward slant of her eyes, and faint crinkling of her mouth. She has a very expressive face, Wanda: her English-rose skin is pale and fragile like tissue paper, and the lines round her eyes crease in a myriad different ways according to her mood. I guess that's what happens when you have no Botox, make-up or fake tan. You have expressions, instead. 'Shall I put on some coffee?'

'Why not?' I follow her into the kitchen, which is about ten times the tip it was when I was living here with Magnus. I can't help wrinkling my nose at a bad smell in the air – which I guess is the bunch of flowers still in paper, gently rotting on the counter. A man's shoe is in the sink, along with a hairbrush, and there are huge piles of old cardboard folders on every chair.

'Ah.' Wanda gestures vaguely around as though hoping one of the chairs might magically clear itself. 'We were just having a sort-out. To what extent does one archive? *That's* the question.'

Once upon a time I would have hastily cast around for something intelligent to say about archives. But now I face her square-on and say bluntly, 'Actually, there's something I want to talk to you about.'

'Indeed,' says Wanda after a pause. 'I rather thought there might be. Let's sit down.'

She grabs a pile of folders off a chair, to reveal a large fish wrapped in fishmonger's paper. OK. So that was the smell.

'*That's* where that went. Extraordinary.' She frowns, hesitates a moment, then puts the folders back on top of it. 'Let's try the drawing room.'

I sit down on one of the bumpy sofas and Wanda draws up an ancient chair covered in needlepoint opposite. The smell of old woodsmoke, musty kilim and pot-pourri is overwhelming. Golden light is streaming through the original stained-glass panels in the windows. This room is so Tavish. And so is Wanda. She's sitting in her usual uncompromising position, knees firmly apart, dirndl skirt draping around her legs, head tilted forward to listen, with her frizzy hennaed hair falling all around her face.

'Magnus—' I begin – then immediately come to a halt.

'Yes?'

'Magnus—'

I stop again. There's silence for a moment.

This woman is so significant in my life, but I barely know her. We've had a completely civilized, distant relationship where we haven't talked about anything except things that don't matter. Now it feels like I'm about to rip down the screen between us. But I don't know where to start. Words are buzzing around my head like flies. I need to catch one.

'How many girls has Magnus proposed to?' I didn't mean to start there, but then why not?

Wanda looks caught out. 'Poppy!' She swallows. 'Goodness. I really think Magnus . . . This is a matter . . .' She rubs her face and I notice her fingernails are filthy.

'Magnus is in Bruges. I can't talk to him. So I've come to talk to you.'

'I see.' Wanda's expression becomes grave.

'Lucinda told me there's a list and she and I are at the end of it. Magnus never mentioned anyone else. He never even told me he and Lucinda used to be an item. *Nobody* told me.' I can't keep the resentment out of my voice.

'Poppy. You mustn't . . .' I can tell Wanda's floundering. 'Magnus is very, very fond of you, and you really shouldn't worry about . . . about that. You're a lovely girl.'

She might be trying to be kind – but the way she says it makes me flinch. What does she mean by 'lovely girl'? Is that some patronizing way of saying, 'You may not have a brain but you look OK?'

I have to say something. I have to. It's now or never. Go, Poppy.

'Wanda, you're making me feel inferior.' The words rush out. 'Do you really think I'm inferior or is this just in my mind?'

Argh. I did it. I can't *believe* I said that out loud.

'*What?*' Wanda's eyes widen so far, I notice for the first time what a stunning periwinkle blue they are. I'm taken aback by how shocked she seems, but I can't back down now.

'I feel inferior when I'm here.' I pause. 'Always. And I just wondered if you really thought I was, or . . .'

Wanda has thrust both hands into her frizzy hair. She comes across a pencil, pulls it out and absent-mindedly puts it down on the table.

'I think we both need a drink,' she says at last. She heaves herself up out of the sagging chair and pours two glasses of Scotch from a bottle in the cabinet. She hands one to me, raises her own and takes a deep gulp. 'I feel a bit knocked for six.'

'I'm sorry.' Immediately I feel bad.

'No!' She raises a hand. 'Absolutely not! Dear girl! You do *not* have to apologize for a *bona fide* expression of your perception of the situation, be it a construct or not.'

I have no idea what she's going on about. But I think she's trying to be nice.

'It's up to me to apologize,' she continues, 'if you have ever felt uncomfortable, let alone "inferior". Although, this is such a ridiculous idea, that I can barely . . .' She trails off, looking baffled. 'Poppy, I simply don't understand. May I just ask what has given you this impression?'

'You're all so intelligent.' I shrug uncomfortably. 'You publish things in journals and I don't.'

Wanda looks perplexed.

'But why should you publish things in journals?'

'Because . . .' I rub my nose. 'I don't know. It's not *that*. It's . . . like, I don't know how to pronounce "Proust".'

Wanda looks even more baffled. 'You clearly do.'

'OK, I do now! But I *didn't*. The first time I met you I kept getting things wrong, and Antony said my physiotherapy degree was "amusing", and I felt so mortified . . .' I break off, my throat suddenly blocked.

'Ah.' A light dawns in Wanda's eye. 'Now, you must never take Antony seriously. Didn't Magnus warn you? His sense of humour can be, shall we say, a little "off"? He's offended so many of our friends with misplaced jokes, I can't count.' She raises her eyes briefly to heaven. 'He *is* a dear man underneath it all, though, as you'll get to know.'

I can't bring myself to reply so I take a gulp of my Scotch. I never usually drink Scotch but this is hitting the spot. As I look up, Wanda's sharp eyes are on me.

'Poppy, we're not the type to *gush*. But believe me, Antony thinks as highly of you as I do. He would be devastated to hear of your anxieties.'

'So what was the row in the church all about?' I fling the words at her furiously before I can stop myself. Wanda looks as though I've slapped her.

'Ah. You heard that. I'm sorry. I didn't realize.' She takes another mouthful of her Scotch, looking stressed out.

Suddenly I'm sick of being polite and talking around things. I want to cut to the chase.

'OK.' I put my glass down. 'The reason I've come here is, it turns out Magnus has been sleeping with Lucinda. So I'm calling off the wedding. So you might as well be honest and say how much you hated me from the start.'

'*Lucinda?*' Wanda claps a hand over her mouth, looking aghast. 'Oh, Magnus. That wretched, *wretched* boy. *When* will he learn?' She seems absolutely deflated by this piece of news. 'Poppy, I'm so sorry. Magnus is . . . what can I say? A flawed individual.'

'So . . . you guessed he might do this?' I stare at her. 'Has he done it before?'

'I was afraid he might do something stupid,' Wanda says after a pause. 'I'm afraid whatever gifts Magnus inherited from us, the gift of commitment was not among them. That's why we were concerned about the wedding. Magnus has a history of leaping into romantic ventures, backtracking, changing his mind, making things messy for everyone . . .'

'Then he *has* done it before.'

'In a way.' She winces. 'Although we've never got as far as the church before. There have been three previous fiancées, and I gather Lucinda was an almost-fiancée. When he announced yet *again* that he was marrying a girl we hardly knew, I'm afraid we didn't rush to celebrate.' She eyes me frankly. 'You're right. We *did* try to put him off the idea in the church, quite forcibly. We thought the two of you should spend a year getting to know each other better. The last thing we wanted was for you to be hurt by our son's idiocy.'

I feel dazed. I had no idea Magnus had proposed to anyone else. Let alone four girls including Lucinda (half). How can this be? Is this my fault? Did I ever actually ask him about his past?

Yes. Yes! Of *course* I did. The memory comes back to me in a fully composed picture. We were lying in bed, after that dinner at the Chinese place. We told each other about all our old flames. And OK, so I edited very slightly,[94] but I didn't leave out *four previous proposals*. Magnus never said a word. Not a word. But everyone else knew.

---

94. No one needs to know about that blond guy at the freshers' party.

Now, of course, all the odd looks and edgy voices between Antony and Wanda make sense. I was so paranoid. I assumed they were all about how crap I was.

'I thought you hated me,' I say, almost to myself. 'And I thought you were angry he'd used the family ring because . . . I dunno. I wasn't worthy of it.'

'Not *worthy*?' Wanda seems absolutely appalled. 'Who has put these ideas into your head?'

'What was the problem, then?' I feel the old hurt rising again. 'I know you weren't happy about it, so don't pretend.'

Wanda appears to debate internally for a moment. 'We're being frank with each other?'

'Yes,' I say firmly. 'Please.'

'Well then.' Wanda sighs. 'Magnus has taken that family ring out of the bank's safe so many times now, Antony and I have developed our own private theory.'

'Which is what?

'The family ring is so *easy*.' She spreads her hands. 'It requires no thought. He can do it on impulse. Our theory is that when he *really* wants to commit to someone, he'll find a ring for himself. He'll choose something carefully. Give it some thought. Perhaps even let his bride choose her own.' She gives me a rueful little smile. 'So when we learned that he'd used the family ring yet again . . . I'm afraid alarm bells rang.'

'Oh. I see.'

I twist the ring round my finger. It suddenly feels heavy and lumpish. I thought having a family ring was special. I thought it meant Magnus was *more* committed to me. But now I'm seeing it as Wanda sees it. A thoughtless, easy, no-brainer choice. I cannot believe how everything I thought has been turned on its head. I cannot believe how I misinterpreted everything.

'For what it's worth,' adds Wanda, a little despondently, 'I'm very sorry things have ended like this. You're a lovely girl, Poppy. Great fun. I was looking forward to having you as a daughter-in-law.'

I wait for my hackles to rise at the phrase 'great fun'; for my internal prickliness to put in an appearance . . . but somehow it doesn't. For the first time since I've met Wanda, I'm able to take her words at face value. By 'great fun' she doesn't mean 'low IQ and inferior degree'. She means 'great fun'.

'I'm sorry, too,' I say – and I'm speaking the truth. I do feel sad. Just as I work Wanda out, it's all over.

I thought Magnus was perfect and his parents were my only problem. Now I'm feeling like it's the other way round. Wanda's great; shame about her son.

'Here.' I wrench the ring off and hand it to her.

'Poppy!' She looks startled. 'Surely—'

'It's all over. I don't want to wear it any more. It belongs to you. To be honest, it never really felt like mine.' I grab my bag and stand up. 'I think I should go.'

'But . . .' Wanda seems bewildered. 'Please don't rush into anything. Have you spoken to Magnus?'

'Not yet.' I breathe out. 'But it's kind of irrelevant. It's over.'

That's pretty much the end of the conversation. Wanda sees me to the door and presses my hand as I leave, and I feel a sudden rush of affection for her. Maybe we'll stay in touch. Maybe I'll lose Magnus but gain Wanda.

The massive front door closes and I push my way through the overgrown rhododendrons down the path to the gate. I'm expecting to crumble into tears any moment. My perfect fiancé isn't perfect after all. He's a lying, unfaithful, commitment-phobic flake. I'm going to have to call off a whole wedding. My brothers won't get to walk me up the aisle after all. I should be in bits. But as I walk down the hill, all I can feel is numb.

I can't face the tube. Nor can I afford any more taxis. So I head towards an out-of-the-way bench in a patch of sunshine, sit down and stare blankly into space for a while. Random thoughts are floating around my brain, bouncing off each other as though in zero gravity.

So much for all that . . . I wonder if I'll be able to sell my wedding dress . . . I should have known it was too good to be true . . . I must tell the vicar . . . I don't think Toby and Tom ever liked Magnus, not that they admitted it . . . Did Magnus ever love me at all?

At last I heave a sigh and switch on my phone. I have to get back to real life. The phone is flashing with messages, about ten of them from Sam, and for a ridiculous instant I think, *Oh my God, he's psychic, he knows . . .*

But as I click on them, I immediately realize how stupid I'm being. Of course he's not texting about my personal life. This all is strictly business.

Poppy, are you there? It's incredible. File was on computer. Voice-mails were there. This confirms everything.

Are you around to talk?

Give me a call when you can. It's all kicking off here. Heads rolling. Press conference this afternoon, Vicks wants to talk to you too.

Hi Poppy, we need the phone. Can you call me asap?

I don't bother scrolling through the rest of the texts, but press Call. A moment later the line is ringing and I feel a sudden spasm of nerves. I have no idea why.

'Hi, Poppy! At last! It's Poppy.' Sam's ebullient voice greets me and I can hear a background hubbub of people. 'We're all whooping here. You have no *idea* what your little discovery means.'

'Not my discovery,' I say honestly. 'Violet's.'

'But if it hadn't been for you taking Violet's call and meeting her ... Vicks says, high-five! She wants to buy you a drink. We all do.' Sam sounds totally elated. 'So, did you get my message? The tech guys here want to look at the phone, just in case there's anything else on it.'

'Oh. Right. Sure. I'll bring it to your office.'

'Is that OK?' Sam sounds concerned. 'Am I disrupting your day? What are you up to?'

'Oh . . . nothing.'

Just cancelling my wedding. Just feeling like a total fool about everything.

'Because I can send a bike—'

'No, really.' I force a smile. 'It's fine. I'll come in straight away.'

FIFTEEN

This time I don't have any trouble getting into the building – there's practically a reception committee waiting for me. Sam, Vicks, Robbie, Mark and a couple more people I don't recognize are standing by the glass doors, ready with a badge and handshakes and lots of explanations which last all the way up in the lift and which I only half-follow as they keep interrupting each other. But the gist is as follows: the voice-mails are 100 per cent incriminating. Several members of staff were pulled in for questioning. Justin lost his cool and practically admitted everything. Another senior member of staff, Phil Stanbridge, is also involved, which everyone's gobsmacked by. Ed Exton has disappeared off the radar. Lawyers are having meetings. No one's sure yet whether criminal proceedings are likely, but the point is, Sir Nicholas's name is cleared. He's over the moon. Sam's over the moon.

ITN are slightly less over the moon as the story has turned from 'Government Adviser is Corrupt' into 'Internal Company Problem is Sorted' but they're still running a follow-up piece and claiming they were the ones who discovered everything.

'The whole company's going to be shaken up by this,' Sam

is saying enthusiastically as we stride along the corridor. 'The lines are going to be redrawn.'

'So you've won,' I venture, and he comes to a halt, smiling as widely as I've ever seen him smile.

'Yup. We've won.' He resumes walking, and ushers me into his office. 'Here she is! The girl herself. Poppy Wyatt.'

Two guys in jeans get up from the sofa, shake my hand and introduce themselves as Ted and Marco.

'So, you've got the famous phone,' says Marco. 'Might I take a look?'

'Of course.' I reach into my pocket, produce the phone and hand it over. For a few moments the guys examine it, pressing buttons, squinting at it, passing it from one to another.

There aren't any more incriminating voice-mails on there, I feel like saying. *Believe me, I would have mentioned them.*

'You mind if we keep this?' Marco says at last, looking up.

'*Keep* it?' The dismay in my voice is so obvious, he double-takes.

'Sorry. It's a company phone, so I assumed . . .' he hesitates.

'It's not any more,' says Sam, frowning. 'I gave it to Poppy. It's hers.'

'Oh.' Marco sucks air through his teeth. He seems a bit flummoxed. 'Thing is, we'd like to do a thorough examination of it. Could take a while. I could say we'll let you have it back afterwards, but who knows how long that'll be . . .' He glances at Sam for guidance. 'I mean, I'm sure we can get you a replacement, top of the range, whatever you want . . .'

'Absolutely.' Sam nods. 'Any budget.' He grins at me. 'You can get the highest-tech phone available.'

I don't want the highest-tech phone available. I want *that* phone. Our phone. I want to keep it safe, not give it up to be hacked about by technicians. But . . . what can I say?

'Sure.' I smile, even though there's a little wrenching in my stomach. 'Have it. It's just a phone.'

'As for your messages, contacts, all the rest of it . . .' Marco exchanges doubtful looks with Ted.

'I need my messages.' I'm alarmed at how shaky my voice is. I feel almost violated. But there's nothing I can do. It would be unreasonable and unhelpful to refuse.

'We could print them out.' Ted brightens. 'How's that? We print everything out for you, then you've got a record.'

'Some of them are *my* messages,' points out Sam.

'Yes, some are his.' I nod.

'What?' Marco looks from me to Sam. 'Sorry, I'm confused. Whose phone is this?'

'It's his phone really, but I've been using it—'

'We've both been using it,' explains Sam. 'Jointly. Sharing.'

'*Sharing?*' Marco and Ted both seem so appalled, I almost want to giggle.

'I've never come across anyone sharing a phone before,' says Marco flatly. 'That's sick.'

'Me neither.' Ted shudders. 'I wouldn't even share a phone with my girlfriend.'

'So . . . how did that work out for you?' says Marco, looking curiously from Sam to me.

'It had its moments,' says Sam, raising his eyebrows.

'There were definitely some moments.' I nod. 'But actually, I recommend it.'

'Me too. Everyone should try it at least once.' Sam grins at me, and I can't helping smiling back.

'O . . . kay.' Marco sounds as though he's realized he's dealing with a pair of nutters. 'Well, we'll get to it. Come on, Ted.'

'How long will you be?' asks Sam.

Ted wrinkles his face. 'Could be a while. An hour?'

They disappear out of Sam's office, and he closes the door. For a minute we just look at each other, and I notice a tiny nick on his cheek. He didn't have that last night.

Last night. In an instant I'm transported back to the forest. I'm standing in the dark, with the smell of the peaty ground in my nostrils, with woodland sounds in my ears, with his arms wrapped around me, with his mouth—

No. *Stop* it, Poppy. *Don't* go there. Don't remember, or wonder, or . . .

'What a day,' I say at last, groping for some nice bland words.

'You said it.' Sam ushers me to the sofa and I sit down awkwardly, feeling like someone who's having a job interview. 'So. Now we're alone . . . How are you doing? What about the other stuff?'

'Nothing much to report.' I give a deliberately careless shrug. 'Oh, except I'm calling my wedding off.'

As I say the words aloud I feel slightly sick. How many times am I going to have to utter those words? How many times am I going to have to explain myself? How am I going to cope over the next few days?

Sam nods, wincing. 'OK. That's pretty grim.'

'Not brilliant.'

'You speak to him?'

'Wanda. I went to see her at her house. I said, "Wanda, do you really think I'm inferior or is this just in my mind?"'

'You didn't!' exclaims Sam, looking delighted.

'Word for word.' I can't help laughing at his expression, even though I half-want to cry, too. 'You would have been proud of me.'

'Go, Poppy!' He lifts a hand to high-five me. 'I know that took guts. And what was the answer?'

'It was all in my head,' I admit. 'She's actually quite a sweetie. Shame about her son.'

There's silence for a while. I feel so surreal. The wedding's off. I've said it aloud, so it must be true. But it feels about as real as saying, 'Aliens have invaded.'

'So, what are your plans now?' Sam meets my gaze and I think I can see another question in his eyes. A question about him and me.

333

'Dunno,' I say after a pause.

I'm trying to answer his question, silently – but I don't know if my eyes are doing their job. I don't know if Sam can understand. After a moment I can't bear looking at him any longer, and quickly lower my head. 'Take things slowly, I guess. There'll be a lot of crap to deal with.'

'I'm sure.' He hesitates. 'Coffee?'

I've had so much coffee today I'm like a jumping bean . . . but on the other hand, I can't stand this heightened atmosphere. I can't gauge anything. I can't read Sam. I don't know what I expect or want. We're two people who were briefly thrown together by chance and are now conducting a business transaction. That's all.

So why does my stomach lurch every time he opens his mouth to speak? What on earth am I expecting him to *say*?

'Coffee would be great, thanks. Do you have decaf?' I watch as Sam fiddles with the Nespresso machine, trying to get the milk frother to work. I think it's a welcome distraction for both of us.

'Don't worry,' I say at last, as he jiggles the frother, looking frustrated. 'I can have it black.'

'You hate black coffee.'

'How do you know that?' I laugh in surprise.

'You told Lucinda once in an email.' He turns, his mouth twisting a little. 'You think you were the only one who did a little spying?'

'You have a good memory.' I shrug. 'What else do you remember?'

There's silence. As his gaze meets mine, my heart starts a little drumbeat inside. His eyes are so rich and dark and serious. The more I stare at them, the more I *want* to stare at them. If he's thinking what I'm thinking, then . . .

No. Stop it, Poppy. Of course he's not. And I don't even know what I'm thinking, not exactly . . .

'Actually, don't worry about the coffee.' I get abruptly to my feet. 'I'll head out for a bit.'

'You sure?' Sam sounds taken aback.

'Yes, I don't want to get in your way.' I avoid his eye as I pass him. 'I've got errands to run. See you in an hour.'

I don't run any errands. I just don't have the impetus. My future's been derailed and I know I'm going to have to take some action – but just at the moment I can't face dealing with it. From Sam's office I wander as far as St Paul's Cathedral. I sit on the steps in a shaft of sunshine, watching the tourists, pretending I'm on holiday from my own life. Then, at last, I make my way back. Sam is on a call as I'm shown into his office, and he nods at me, gesturing apologetically at the phone.

'Knock, knock!' Ted's head appears around the door, and I start. 'All done. We had three operatives on it.' He comes into the room, holding a massive sheaf of A4 papers. 'Only trouble is, we've had to print each text on a separate piece of paper. It's like ruddy *War and Peace*.'

'Wow.' I can't believe how many pieces of paper he's holding. I surely can't have sent *that* many texts and emails? I mean, I've only had the phone for a matter of days.

'So.' Ted puts the sheets down on the table with a businesslike air, and separates them into three bundles. 'One of the lads has been sorting them as we've gone along. These are all Sam's. Business emails, so forth. In-box, out-box, drafts, everything. Sam, here you go.' He holds them out as Sam gets up from his desk.

'Great, thanks,' says Sam, flipping through them.

'We've printed out all the attachments too. They should all be on your computer as well, Sam, but just in case . . . And these are yours, Poppy.' He pats a second bundle. 'Everything should be there.'

'Right. Thanks.' I leaf through the papers.

'Then there's this third pile.' Ted wrinkles his brow as though in puzzlement. 'We weren't sure what to do about this. It's . . . it's both of yours.'

'What do you mean?' Sam looks up.

'It's your correspondence to each other. All the texts and emails and whatnot that you sent backwards and forwards. In chronological order.' Ted shrugs. 'I don't know which of you wants it, or whether we should chuck them ... are they important at all?'

He puts the pile of papers down and I stare at the top sheet in disbelief. It's a grainy photograph of me in a mirror, holding the phone and making the Brownie sign. I'd forgotten I ever did that. I turn to the next page to find a single printed text from Sam:

I could send this to the police and have you arrested.

Then, on the following page is my answer:

I really, really appreciate it. Thx ☺ ☺ ☺

That feels like a million years ago now. When Sam was just a stranger at the other end of a phone line. When I hadn't met him properly, had no idea what he was like ... I sense a movement at my shoulder. Sam has come over to look, too.

'Strange, seeing it all printed out,' he says.

'I know.' I nod.

I come to a picture of manky teeth and we simultaneously snort with laughter.

'Quite a few pictures of teeth, aren't there?' says Ted, eyeing us curiously. 'We wondered what that was all about. In dental care, are you, Poppy?'

'Not exactly.' I leaf through the pages, mesmerized. It's everything we said to each other. Page after page of messages, back and forth, like a book of the last few days.

WHAIZLED. Use the D from OUTSTEPPED. Triple word score, plus 50 point bonus.

Have u booked dentist yet? U will get manky teeth!!!

What are you doing up so late?

My life ends tomorrow.

I can see how that might keep you up. Why does it end?

Your tie's crooked.

I didn't know your name was on my invitation.

Just stopped by to collect your goody bag for you. All part of the service. No need to thank me.

How did Vicks react?

As I reach the texts from last night, I catch my breath. Seeing those words, it's as though I'm back there.

I don't dare look at Sam, nor give away any hint of emotion, so I calmly flick through as though I'm really not bothered, catching just the odd text here and there.

Anyone know you're texting me?

Don't think so. Yet.

My new rule for life: don't go into spooky dark woods on your own.

You're not on your own.

I'm glad it was your phone I picked up.

So am I.

Xoxoxoxoxoxoxoxoxoxoxoxo

You're nowhere near.

Yes I am. Coming.

And suddenly there's a lump in my throat. Enough. Stop.
I slap the papers back on the pile and look up with a light-
hearted smile.

'Wow!'

'Yeah well, like I say,' Ted shrugs, 'we didn't know what to
do with them.'

'We'll sort it,' says Sam. 'Thanks, Ted.'

His face is impassive. I have no idea if he felt anything,
reading those texts.

'So we can do what we like with the phone, yeah?' says Ted.

'No problem.' Sam nods. 'Cheers, Ted.'

As Ted disappears, Sam heads over to the Nespresso
machine again and starts making a new cup.

'Come on, let me make you a coffee. I've worked it out now.'

'Really, I'm fine,' I begin, but the frother suddenly starts
emitting hot milk with such a loud hissing, there's no point
even trying to speak.

'Here you go.' He hands me a cup.

'Thanks.'

'So ... you want these?' He gestures at the pile of
papers.

I feel a kind of hotness rising from my feet and take a sip of
coffee, playing for time. The phone's gone. These print-outs are
the only record of that weird and wonderful time. Of course I
want them.

But for some reason I can't admit that to Sam.

'I'm easy.' I try to sound nonchalant. 'You want them?'

Sam says nothing, just shrugs.

'I mean, I don't *need* them for anything . . .' I hesitate.

'No.' He shakes his head. 'It's all pretty inconsequential stuff . . .' His phone bleeps with a text and he pulls it out of his pocket. He scans the screen, then scowls. 'Oh Jesus. Oh bloody hell. This is *all* I need.'

'What's wrong?' I say in alarm. 'Is it about the voice-mails?'

'It's not that.' He regards me from under lowered brows. 'What the hell did you send to Willow?'

'What?' I stare at him, bewildered.

'She's on the warpath about some email from you. Why the hell were you emailing Willow, anyway?'

'I didn't!' I stare at him, perplexed. 'I would never email her! I don't even know her!'

'Well, that's not what she says—' He breaks off as his phone bleeps again. 'OK. Here we are . . . recognize that?' He passes it to me and I start reading.

FFS, Willow the Witch, can't you LEAVE SAM ALONE AND STOP WRITING IN OBNOXIOUS CAPITALS? And just FYI: you are not Sam's girlfriend. So who cares what he was doing with some 'cutesy' girl last night? Why don't you get a life?????

A cold feeling is creeping over me.

OK. Maybe I did type something like that this morning, while I was on the tube to Sam's office. Just out of irritation at yet another rant from Willow. Just to vent a little. But I didn't *send* it. I mean, of course I didn't *send* it. I would never, ever have *sent* it . . .

Oh God . . .

'I . . . um . . .' My mouth is a little dry as I finally raise my head. 'I might possibly have written that as a joke. And accidentally pressed Send. Totally by mistake. I mean, I didn't *intend* to,' I add, just to make it crystal clear. 'I never would have done it on *purpose*.'

I scan the words again and imagine Willow reading them.

She must have hit the roof. I almost wish I'd been there to see it. I can't help a tiny snuffle of mirth as I imagine her eyes widening, her nostrils flaring, fire coming from her mouth . . .[95]

'You think this is funny?' snaps Sam.

'Well, no,' I say, shocked by his tone. 'I mean, I'm really sorry. Obviously. But it *was* just a mistake—'

'What does it matter whether it was a mistake or not?' He grabs the phone from me. 'It's a headache and it's the last thing I need on my plate—'

'Wait a minute!' I lift a hand. 'I don't understand. Why is it on *your* plate? Why is it *your* problem? It was me who sent the email, not you.'

'Believe me.' He gives me a savage look. 'It'll somehow end up being my problem.'

OK, this makes no sense. Why will it be his problem? And why is he so irate? I know I shouldn't have sent that email, but nor should Willow have sent him ninety-five million nutty rants. Why is he taking *her* side?

'Look.' I try to sound calm. 'I'll send her an email and apologize. But I think you're overreacting. She's not your girlfriend any more. This isn't anything to do with you.'

He isn't even looking at me. He's typing on his phone. Is he typing to Willow?

'You're not over her, are you?' I feel a raw hurt as the truth hits me. Why didn't I realize this before? 'You're not over Willow.'

'Of course I am.' He frowns impatiently.

'You're not! If you were over her you wouldn't care about this email. You'd think it served her right. You'd think it was funny. You'd take *my* side.' My voice is trembling and I have a dreadful feeling that my cheeks are turning pink.

Sam looks baffled. 'Poppy, why are you so upset?'

'Because . . . because . . .' I break off, breathing hard.

95. Artistic licence.

Because of reasons I could never tell him. Reasons I can't even admit to myself. My stomach is churning with humiliation. Who was I *kidding*?

'Because . . . you weren't honest!' The words burst from me at last. 'You gave me all this rubbish about "It's over and Willow should understand that." How can she understand anything if you react like this? You're acting as if she's still a major part of your life and you're still responsible for her. And that tells me, you're not over her.'

'This is all absolute bullshit.' He looks livid.

'So why not tell her to stop pestering you? Why not finish it once and for all and get closure? Is it because you don't *want* closure, Sam?' My voice rises in agitation. 'Do you *enjoy* your weirdo, stand-off relationship?'

Now Sam is breathing hard too. 'You have *no* right to comment on something you understand nothing about—'

'Oh, I'm sorry!' I give a sarcastic little laugh. 'You're right. I don't even begin to understand you two. Maybe you'll get back together, and I hope you'll be very happy.'

'Poppy, for Christ's sake—'

'What?' I put my cup down with a small bang, spilling coffee over the pile of our back-and-forth texts. 'Oh, I've ruined them now. Sorry. But I guess they don't have anything important in them, so it doesn't matter.'

'*What?*' Sam looks as though he's having trouble keeping up. 'Poppy, can we sit down calmly and just . . . regroup?'

I don't think I'm capable of calm. I feel erratic and out of control. All sorts of deep dark feelings are coming to the surface. I hadn't fully admitted my hopes to myself. I hadn't realized quite how much I'd assumed . . .

Anyway. I've been a deluded fool and I need to get out of here as quickly as possible.

'Sorry.' I take a deep breath and somehow muster a smile. 'Sorry. I'm just a bit stressed. With the wedding and every- thing. It's fine. Look, thanks for lending me the phone. It was nice knowing you and I hope you'll be very happy. With Willow or without.' I grab my bag, my hands still shaky. 'So, err . . . hope everything goes well with Sir Nicholas and I'll look out for the news stories . . . Don't worry, I'll see myself out . . .' I can barely meet his eye as I head to the door.

Sam looks utterly baffled. 'Poppy, don't go like that. Please.'

'I'm not going like anything!' I say brightly. 'Really. I've got things to do. I've got a wedding to cancel, people to give minor heart attacks to . . .'

'Wait. Poppy.' Sam's voice stops me and I turn round. 'I just want to say . . . thanks.'

His dark eyes meet mine and just for a moment my prickly, defensive shell is pierced.

'Same.' I nod, a lump in my throat. 'Thanks.'

I lift a hand in final farewell and walk away down the corridor. Head high. Keep going. Don't look back.

By the time I reach the street, my face is lightly spattered with tears and I'm fizzing with furious, agitated thoughts – although who I'm most furious at, I'm not sure. Maybe myself.

But there's one way I can make myself feel better. Within half an hour I've visited an Orange shop, signed up for the most expensive, full-on contract going, and am in possession of a slick, state-of-the-art smart phone. Ted said 'any budget' – well, I've taken him at his word.

And now I've got to christen it. I head out of the shop to an open, paved area away from the traffic. I dial Magnus's number, and give a satisfied nod when it goes straight to voice-mail. That's what I wanted.

'OK, you little *shit*.' I imbue the word with as much venom as I can manage. 'I've spoken to Lucinda. I know it all. I know you slept with her, I know you proposed to her, I know this ring has been round the houses, I know you're a lying scum-bag and just so you know . . . the wedding's off. Did you hear that? *Off*. So I hope you can find another good use for your waistcoat. And your life. See you, Magnus. Not.'

*

There are some moments in life that the white chocolate Magnum ice-cream was invented for and this is one of them.[96]

I can't face the phone calls yet. I can't face telling the vicar, or my brothers, or any of my friends. I'm too battered. I need to restore my energies first. And so by the time I've reached home, I have a plan.

Tonight: watch comfort-DVDs, eat Magnums, cry a lot. Hair mask.[97]

Tomorrow: break news to world that wedding is cancelled, deal with fall-out, watch Annalise try not to whoop with joy, etc., etc.

I've been texting my new mobile number to everyone I know, and a few friendly texts have already come back – but I haven't mentioned the wedding to anyone. It can all wait till tomorrow.

I don't want to watch anything with weddings in it, obviously,[98] so in the end I plump for cartoons, which turn out to be the biggest tear-jerkers of the lot. I watch *Toy Story 3*,[99] *Up*[100] – and by midnight I'm on *Finding Nemo*. I'm curled up on the sofa in my ancient pyjamas and furry throw, with the white wine within easy reach, my hair all oily with the conditioning mask, and the puffiest eyes in the universe. *Finding Nemo* always makes me cry anyway, but this time I'm a snivelling wreck before Nemo's even lost.[101] I'm just wondering if I should find something else to watch which is less savage and brutal, when the buzzer sounds.

96. Even the fact that its name reminds me of the very person I want to forget doesn't put me off.
97. I might as well stick to the regime.
98. Which rules out most of my DVDs, it turns out.
99. Weepfest.
100. Total weepfest.
101. What kind of movie starts with a mother fish and all her little glowy eggs being eaten by a shark, FFS? It's supposed to be for *children*.

Which is weird. I'm not expecting anyone. Unless . . . are Toby and Tom two days early? It would be just like them to arrive at midnight, straight off some cheapie coach. The entryphone is conveniently within reach from the sofa, so I pull the receiver down, pause *Finding Nemo* and tentatively say, 'Hi.'

'It's Magnus.'

Magnus?

I sit up straight on the sofa as though I've had an electric shock. Magnus. Here. On my doorstep. Has he heard the message?

'Hi.' I swallow, trying to pull myself together. 'I thought you were in Bruges.'

'I'm back.'

'Right. So why didn't you use your key?'

'I thought you might have changed the locks.'

'Oh.' I brush a lock of oily hair out of my tear-stained eyes. So he *has* heard the message. 'Well . . . I haven't.'

'Can I come up, then?'

'I suppose.'

I put the receiver down and look around. Shit. It's a pigsty in here. For one panicked instant I feel an urge to jump up, dispose of the Magnum wrappers, wash off my hair mask, plump up the cushions, shove on some eyeliner and find some attractive matching lounge wear. That's what Annalise would do.

And maybe that's what stops me. Who cares if I've got puffy eyes and a hair mask? I'm not marrying this man, so it's irrelevant what I look like.[102]

I hear his key in the lock and defiantly put *Finding Nemo* back on. I'm not pausing my life for him. I've done enough of that already. I turn the volume up slightly and refill my wine glass. I'm not offering him any, so he needn't expect it. *Or* a Magnum.[103]

102. NB: shouldn't it be irrelevant anyway, what I look like?
103. Because I've eaten them all.

The door makes a familiar squeaking sound and I know he's in the room, but I keep my gaze resolutely fixed on the screen.

'Hi.'

'Hi.' I shrug, as though to say, 'Whatever'.

In my peripheral vision I can see Magnus exhale. He looks a teeny bit nervous.

'So.'

'So.' I can play this game too.

'Poppy.'

'Poppy. I mean, Magnus.' I scowl. He caught me out. By mistake I lift my eyes to his, and he immediately rushes over and grabs my hands, just like he did that first time we met.

'Stop it!' I practically snarl at him, pulling them away. 'You don't get to do that.'

'I'm sorry!' He lifts his hands as though I've scalded him.

'I don't know who you are.' I gaze miserably at Nemo and Dory. 'You lied about everything. I can't marry someone who's a lying cheat. So you might as well go. I don't even know what you're doing here.'

Magnus heaves another huge sigh.

'Poppy . . . OK. I made a mistake. Hands up. I'll admit it.'

'A "mistake"?' I echo sarcastically.

'Yes, a mistake! I'm not perfect, OK?' He thrusts his fingers through his hair in a gesture of frustration. 'Is that what you expect out of a man? Perfection? You want a flawless man? Because believe me, that man doesn't exist. And if that's why you're calling off this wedding, because I made one simple error . . .' He holds his hands out, his eyes reflecting the coloured light of the TV. 'I'm *human*, Poppy. I'm a flawed, imperfect human being.'

'I don't want a flawless man,' I snap. 'I want a man who doesn't sleep with my wedding planner.'

'We don't choose our flaws, unfortunately. And I've regretted my weakness over and over again.'

How is he managing to sound all noble, like he's the victim here?

'Well, poor old you.' I turn up the volume of *Finding Nemo* again, but to my surprise, Magnus grabs the remote and switches it off. I blink at him in the sudden silence.

'Poppy, you can't be serious. You can't want to call everything off for one tiny . . .'

'It's not only that.' I feel an old, burning hurt in my chest. 'You never told me about all your other fiancées. You never told me you'd proposed to Lucinda. I thought that ring was *special*. Your mum's got it, by the way.'

'I have proposed to other girls,' he says slowly. 'But now I can't think why.'

'Because you loved them?'

'No,' he says with a sudden fierceness. 'I didn't. I was nuts. Poppy, you and me . . . we're different. We could make it. I know we could. We just have to get through the wedding . . .'

'Get *through* it?'

'That's not what I mean.' He breathes out impatiently. 'Look, come on, Poppy. The wedding's all set up. It's all arranged. It's not about what happened with Lucinda, it's about you and me. We can do it. I want to do it. I really want to do this.' He's speaking with such fervour, I stare at him in surprise.

'Magnus—'

'Will this change your mind?' To my astonishment he sinks down on one knee beside the sofa and reaches in his pocket. I stare speechlessly as he opens a little jewellery box. Inside is a ring made of twisted golden strands, with a tiny diamond perched at the side.

'Where . . . where did that come from?' I can hardly find my voice.

'I bought it for you in Bruges.' He clears his throat, as though embarrassed to admit it. 'I was just walking along the street earlier today. Saw it in a window, thought of you.'

I can't believe it. Magnus bought a ring for me. Specially for me. I can hear Wanda's voice in my head: *When he really wants to commit to someone, he'll find a ring for himself. He'll choose something carefully. Give it some thought.*

But I still can't relax.

'Why did you choose *this* ring?' I probe. 'Why did it make you think of me?'

'The strands of gold.' He gives an abashed smile. 'They reminded me of your hair. Not the colour, obviously,' he amends quickly. 'The shine.'

That was a good answer. Quite romantic. I raise my eyes and he gives me a hopeful, lopsided smile.

Oh God. When Magnus is sweet and puppy-dog like, he's almost irresistible.

Thoughts are still spinning round my head. So he made a mistake. A big, big mistake. Am I going to throw away everything for that? Am I so perfect myself? Let's face it, twenty-four hours ago my arms were wrapped around another man in a wood.

I feel a tiny pang in my chest at the thought of Sam, and give myself a mental shakedown. Stop. Don't go there. I got carried away by the situation, that's all. Maybe Magnus did too.

'What do you think?' Magnus is watching me eagerly.

'I love it,' I whisper. 'It's amazing.'

'I know.' He nods. 'It's exquisite. Like you. And I want you to wear it. So, Poppy . . .' He puts his warm hand on mine. 'Sweetest Poppy . . . will you?'

'Oh God, Magnus,' I say helplessly. 'I don't know . . .' My new phone is flashing with messages and I pick it up, just to buy myself some time. There's a brand-new email from samroxtonpa@whiteglobeconsulting.com.

My heart skips a beat. I sent Sam my new number earlier, just so that he had it. And at the last minute I added, 'Sorry about this afternoon', with a couple of kisses. Just to clear the air. Now he's answering me. At midnight. What does he want to say? With trembling fingers, my thoughts veering on to wild possibilities, I click on the message.

'Poppy?' Magnus sounds a little affronted. 'Sweets? Could we focus?'

Sam is delighted to have received your email. He'll get back to you as soon as he possibly can. Meanwhile, thanks for your interest.

I feel a sting of humiliation as I read the words. The brush-off email. He got his PA to send me the brush-off email.

I suddenly remember him, that time in the restaurant: *You must have a brush-off email . . . They come in pretty useful for fending off unwanted advances, too.* Well, he couldn't be any clearer than that, could he?

And now there's more than a tiny pang in my chest – there's a real wrenching pain. I was so stupid. What did I *think*? At least Magnus didn't delude himself that he and Lucinda were anything more than a casual fling. In some ways he stayed more faithful than I did. I mean, if Magnus ever knew the *half* of what's been going on these last few days . . .

'Poppy?' Magnus is peering at me. 'Bad news?'

'No.' I toss the phone on to the sofa and somehow find a dazzling smile. 'You're right. We all make stupid mistakes. We all get carried away. We all get distracted by things which aren't . . . which aren't real. But the point is . . .' I'm running out of steam here.

'Yes?' prompts Magnus gently.

'The point is . . . you bought me a ring. Yourself.'

As I say the words, my thoughts seem to come together and consolidate into something firm. All my deluded dreams fall away. This is reality, right here in front of me. I know what I want now. I take the ring out of the box and examine it a moment, the blood beating hard in my head. 'You chose it for me yourself. And I love it. And, Magnus . . . yes.'

I meet Magnus's gaze head-on, suddenly not caring about Sam; wanting to take my life forward, away from here, to somewhere new.

'Yes?' He stares at me as though not sure what he's hearing.

'Yes.' I nod.

In silence, Magnus takes the ring from me. He lifts up my left hand and slides it on to my ring finger.

I can't quite believe it. I'm getting married.

SIXTEEN

Magnus doesn't believe in superstitions. He's just like his father. So even though it's our wedding day today – even though *everyone* knows it's bad luck – he stayed at my place last night. When I told him he should go to his parents' house he got all sulky and said I couldn't be so ridiculous and why would he pack up all his stuff for one night? Then he added, surely the only people who believe in that kind of stuff are people with—

At which point he stopped himself. But I know he was going to say 'weak minds'. It's a good thing he didn't continue, or there would have been a *major* bust-up. As it is, I'm still feeling quite stroppy with him. Which isn't exactly ideal on your wedding day. I should be feeling all starry-eyed. I shouldn't be leaning round the kitchen door every five minutes saying, 'And *another* thing you always do . . .'

I now know exactly why they started the tradition of being apart the night before your wedding. It's not about romance, or sex, or being chaste or whatever. It's so you don't have a row and stomp up the aisle seething at your bridegroom, planning all the home truths you're going to tell him as soon as you get this wedding bit out of the way.

I was going to make him sleep in the sitting room, but Toby and Tom were in there in sleeping bags.[104] At least I've made him promise to leave the house before I get into my wedding dress. I mean, that would be the limit.

As I pour myself a cup of coffee, I can hear him declaiming in the bathroom, and feel another flinch of irritation. He's practising his speech. Here. In the flat. Isn't his speech supposed to be a *surprise*? Does he know *anything* about weddings? I approach the bathroom door, ready to give him an earful – then pause. I might as well listen to a snippet.

The door is slightly ajar and I peep through the gap to see him addressing himself in the mirror in his dressing gown. To my surprise, he looks quite worked up. His cheeks are red and he's breathing heavily. Maybe he's getting into the part. Maybe he's going to make a really passionate speech about how I've completed his life and everyone will cry.

'Everyone said I'd never get married. Everyone said I'd never do it.' Magnus pauses for so long, I wonder if he's lost his way. 'Well, look. Here I am. OK? Here I am.'

He takes a swig of something which looks like a gin and tonic and gazes belligerently at himself.

'Here I am. Married, OK? *Married.*'

I watch him uncertainly. I don't know quite what's wrong about this speech, but something is. There's some small detail that feels wrong ... something amiss ... something that jars ...

I've got it. He doesn't look happy.

Why doesn't he look happy? It's his wedding day.

'I've done it.' He raises his glass at the mirror, glowering. 'So all you people who said I couldn't, can fuck off.'

'Magnus!' I can't help exclaiming in shock. 'You can't say "fuck off" in your wedding speech!' Magnus's face jolts and his

104. They're still there, totally comatose.

belligerent air instantly vanishes as he whips round. 'Poppy! Sweets! I didn't know you could hear me.'

'Is that your speech?' I demand.

'No! Not exactly.' He takes a deep swig of his drink. 'It's a work in progress.'

'Well, haven't you written it yet?' I eye his glass. 'Is that a gin and tonic?'

'I think I'm allowed a gin and tonic on my wedding day, don't you?'

The belligerent air is creeping back. What is *wrong* with him?

If I was in one of those glossy, luxury-kitchen American TV dramas, I'd go up to him now and take his arm and say gently, 'It's going to be a great day, honey.' And his face would soften and he'd say, 'I know', and we'd kiss, and I would have diffused the tension with my loving tact and charm.

But I'm not in the mood. If he can be belligerent, so can I.

'Fine.' I scowl. 'Get pissed. Great idea.'

'I'm not going to get pissed. Jesus. But I've got to have *something* to take the edge off the—' He stops abruptly, and I stare at him in shock. Where exactly was he heading with that sentence?

Off the *ordeal*? Off the *pain*?

I think his mind is working the same way, because he quickly finishes the sentence: '. . . the *thrill*. I need to take the edge off the thrill, or I'll be far too hyper to concentrate. Sweets, you look beautiful. Gorgeous hair. You'll look spectacular.'

His old, engaging manner has returned, in full force, like the sun coming out from behind a cloud.

'My hair hasn't even been done yet,' I say, with a grudging smile. 'The hairdresser's on his way.'

'Well, don't let him ruin it.' He gathers the ends together and kisses them. 'I'll get out of your way. See you at the church!'

'OK.' I stare after him, feeling a bit unsettled.

And I'm unsettled for the rest of the morning. It's not exactly that I'm worried. It's more that I don't know if I *should* be worried. I mean, let's look at the facts. One moment Magnus is all over me, begging me to marry him – then he gets stroppy, as though I'm forcing him into it with a shotgun. Is it just jitters? Is this what men are always like on their wedding day? Should I tolerate it as normal male behaviour, like when he gets a cold and starts Googling *nose cancer symptoms discharge nostrils?*[105]

If Dad were alive I could ask him.

But that's a thought-path I *really* can't let myself go down, not today, or I'll be a mess. I blink hard and scrub at my nose with a tissue. Come on, Poppy. Brighten up. Stop inventing problems that don't exist. I'm getting married!

Toby and Tom emerge from their cocoons just as the hairdresser arrives, and make monster cups of tea in mugs which they brought with them.[106] They instantly start bantering with the hairdresser and putting rollers in their hair and making me fall about with laughter, and I wish for the zillionth time that I saw more of them. Then they disappear off to have breakfast at a café, and Ruby and Annalise arrive two hours early because they couldn't wait, and the hairdresser announces he's ready to start, and my Aunt Trudy rings from her mobile saying they're nearly here and her tights have laddered, is there anywhere she can buy a new pair?[107]

And then we're into a blur of hairdryers blasting, nails being painted, make-up being done, hair being put up, flowers arriving, dresses being put on, dresses being taken off to go to the loo, sandwiches being delivered, a spray-tan near-disaster (it was actually just a blotch of coffee on Annalise's knee) and somehow it's two o'clock before I realize it, and the cars are here and I'm standing in front of the mirror in my dress and

105. True.
106. Apparently my mugs are 'girly'.
107. My Aunt Trudy doesn't believe shops exist outside Taunton.

veil. Tom and Toby are standing either side of me, so handsome in their morning coats I have to blink away the tears again. Annalise and Ruby have already left for the church. This is it. My last few moments as a single girl.

'Mum and Dad would have been so proud of you,' says Toby gruffly. 'Amazing dress.'

'Thanks.' I try to shrug nonchalantly.

I suppose I look OK, as brides go. My dress is really long and slim with a low back and tiny bits of lace on the sleeves. My hair's in a chignon.[108] My veil is gossamer light and I've got a beaded headdress and a gorgeous posy of lilies. But somehow, just like Magnus this morning, something seems amiss . . .

It's my expression, I suddenly realize with dismay. It isn't right. My eyes are tense and my mouth keeps twitching downwards and I'm not radiant. I try baring my teeth at myself in a broad smile – but now I just look freaky, like some kind of scary clown-bride.

'You OK?' Tom is watching me curiously.

'Fine!' I pull at my veil, trying to bunch it round my face more. The point is, it doesn't matter what my expression is like. Everyone will be looking at my train.

'Hey, Sis.' Toby glances at Tom as though for approval. 'Just so you know, if you *did* change your mind, we'd be totally cool. We'd help you do a runner. We've discussed it, haven't we, Tom?'

'The 4.30 from St Pancras.' Tom nods. 'Gets you to Paris in time for dinner.'

'Do a runner?' I stare at him in dismay. 'What do you mean? Why would you plan a runner? Don't you like Magnus?'

'No! Whoa! Never said that.' Toby lifts his hands defensively. 'Just . . . putting it out there. Giving you the options. We see it as our job.'

---

108. It *was* long enough, in the end. Just about.

'Well, *don't* see it as your job.' I speak more sharply than I mean to. 'We've got to get to the church.'

'I got the papers when I was out, by the way,' adds Tom, proffering a stack of newspapers. 'You want to have a read in the car?'

'No!' I recoil in horror. 'Of course not! I'll get newsprint on my dress!'

Only my little brother could suggest reading the newspaper on the way to my own wedding. Like, it'll be so boring we'd better have some entertainment.

Having said that, I can't help flicking through the *Guardian* quickly as Toby goes for a quick, final bathroom break. There's a picture of Sam on page 5, under a headline 'Scandal Rocks Business World', and as soon as I see it, my stomach clenches tightly.

But less tightly than before. I'm sure of it.

The car is a black Rolls-Royce, which looks pretty amazing in my nondescript Balham street, and a small crowd of neighbours has gathered to watch as I come out. I do a little twirl and everyone claps as I get into the car. We set off, and I feel like a proper, glowing, radiant bride.

Except I can't look *that* radiant and glowing, because as we're driving along Buckingham Palace Road, Tom leans forward and says, 'Poppy? Are you car-sick or something?'

'What?'

'You look ill.'

'No I don't.' I scowl at him.

'You do,' says Toby, peering at me dubiously. 'Kind of . . . green.'

'Yeah, green.' Tom's face lights up. 'That's what I meant. Like you're about to hurl. *Are* you about to hurl?'

That is so typical of brothers. Why couldn't I have had sisters, who would tell me I looked beautiful and lend me their blusher?

'No, I'm not about to hurl! And it doesn't matter what I look like.' I turn my face away. 'No one will be able to see through my veil.' My phone beeps and I haul it out of my little bridal bag. It's a text from Annalise:

Don't go up Park Lane! Accident! We're stuck!

'Hey.' I lean forward to the driver. 'There's an accident on Park Lane.'

'Right you are,' he nods. 'We'll avoid that route then.'

As we swing round into a little side road, I'm aware of Tom and Toby exchanging glances.

'What?' I say at last.

'Nothing,' Toby says soothingly. 'Just sit back and relax. Shall I tell you some jokes, take your mind off it?'

'*No*. Thanks.'

I stare out of the window, watching the streets go by. And suddenly, before I feel quite ready, we've arrived. The church bells are pealing with a single, rhythmic tone as we get out of the car. A couple of late guests I don't recognize are running up the steps, the woman clutching at her hat. They smile at me, and I give a self-conscious nod.

It's for real. I'm actually doing this. This is the happiest day of my life. I should remember every moment. Especially how happy I am.

Tom surveys me and grimaces. 'Pops, you look awful. I'll just tell the vicar you're ill.' He barges straight past me into the church.

'No, don't! I'm not ill!' I exclaim furiously, but it's too late. He's on a mission. Sure enough, a few moments later Reverend Fox is hurrying out of the church, an anxious look on his face.

'Oh my goodness, your brother's right,' he says as soon as he sees me. 'You don't look well.'

'I'm fine!'

'Why don't you take a few minutes to compose yourself alone before we begin the service?' He's ushering me into a little side room. 'Sit down a moment, have a glass of water, perhaps eat a biscuit? There are some in the church hall. We need to wait for the bridesmaids anyway. I gather they've been held up in traffic?'

'I'll look out for them on the street,' says Tom. 'They won't be long.'

'I'll get the biscuits,' chimes in Toby. 'Will you be all right, Sis?'

'Fine.'

They all head out and I'm left alone in the silent room. A tiny mirror is perched on a shelf, and as I look into it I wince. I do look sick. What's *wrong* with me?

My phone dings and I glance at it in surprise. I've got a text from Mrs Randall.

6–4, 6–2. Thank you, Poppy!

She did it! She got back on the tennis court! This is the best thing I've heard all day. And all of a sudden I wish I were at work, away from here, absorbed in the process of treating someone, doing something useful—

No. Stop. Don't be *stupid*, Poppy. How can you wish you were at work on your wedding day? I must be some sort of freak. No other brides wish they were at the office. None of the bridal magazines carry articles on 'How to Look Radiant, Rather than Like You Want to Vomit'.

Another text has just dinged into my phone, but this one is from Annalise.

Finally!!!! We're on the move! Are you there already?

OK. Let's focus on the here and now. The simple act of texting a reply makes me feel more relaxed.

Just arrived.

An instant later she replies:

Argh! Going as quick as we can. Anyway you're supposed to be late. It's good luck. Have you still got your blue garter on?

Annalise was so obsessed by me wearing a blue garter that she brought along three different choices this morning. I'm sorry, *what* are garters all about? To be frank, I could really do without a length of tight elastic cutting off my leg circulation right now – but I promised her faithfully I'd keep it on.

Of course! Even though my leg will probably fall off now. Nice surprise for Magnus on the wedding night.

I smile as I send the text. It's cheering me up, having this stupid conversation. I put my phone down, have a drink of water and take a deep breath. OK. I'm feeling better. The phone dings with a new text, and I pick it up to see what Annalise has replied—

But it's from Sam Mobile.

For a few instants I can't move. My stomach is instantly moiling around as though I'm a teenager. Oh God. This is *pathetic*. It's mortifying. I see the word 'Sam' and I go to pieces.

Half of me wants to ignore it. What do I care what he's got to say? Why should I give one iota of head-space or time to him, when it's my wedding day and I have other things to focus on?

But I know I'll never get through the wedding with an unopened text burning a hole in my phone. I open it as calmly as I can, bearing in mind my fingers can hardly function – and it's a one-word Sam special.

Hi.

Hi? What's that supposed to mean, for God's sake?

Well, I'm not going to be rude. I'll text back a similarly effusive response:

Hi.

A moment later there's another ding:

This a good time?

What?

Is he for real? Or is he being sarcastic? Or—

Then I realize. Of course. He thinks I cancelled the wedding. He doesn't know. He has no idea.

And suddenly I see his text in a new light. He's not making a point. He's just saying 'Hi'.

I swallow hard, trying to work out what to put. Somehow I can't bear to tell him what I'm doing. Not straight out.

Not really.

I'll be brief then. You were right and I was wrong.

I stare at his words, perplexed. Right about what? Slowly I type:

What do you mean?

Almost immediately his reply dings into the phone.

About Willow. You were right and I was wrong. I'm sorry I reacted badly. I didn't want you to be right, but you were. I spoke to her.

What did you say?

Told her it was over, finito. Stop the emails or I'll take out a stalking injunction.

He *didn't*. I can't believe it.

How did she react?

She was pretty shocked.

I bet.

There's silence for a while. A fresh text from Annalise has arrived on my phone, but I don't open it. I can't bear to break the thread between me and Sam. I'm gripping my phone tightly, my eyes on the screen, waiting to see if he'll text again. He *has* to text again . . .

And then there's a beep.

Can't be an easy day for you. Today was supposed to be the wedding day, right?

My insides seem to plunge. What do I answer? What?

Yes.

Well, here's something to cheer you up.

Cheer me up? I'm peering at the screen, puzzled, when a photo text suddenly arrives which makes me laugh in surprise. It's a picture of Sam sitting in a dentist's chair. He's smiling widely and wearing a cartoon sticker on his lapel that says, 'I was a good dental patient!!'

He did that for me, flashes through my head before I can stop it. *He went to the dentist for me.*

No. Don't be stupid. He went for his teeth. I hesitate, then type:

You're right, that did cheer me up. Well done. About time!

An instant later he replies:

Are you free for a cup of coffee?

And to my horror, with no warning, tears start pressing at my eyes. How can he call *now* and ask me for a cup of coffee? How can he not realize that things have moved on? What did he *think* I would do? As I type, my thumbs are jerky and agitated.

You brushed me off.

What?

You sent me the brush-off email.

I never send emails, you know that. Must have been my PA. She's too efficient.

He *didn't* send it?
OK, now I can't cope. I'm going to cry, or laugh hysterically, or *something*. I had it all sorted in my mind. I knew where everything was and where everything stood. Now my head's a maelstrom again.
The phone beeps with a follow-up text from Sam:

You're not offended, are you?

I close my eyes. I have to explain. But what do I— How do I—
At last, without even opening my eyes, I text:

You don't understand.

What don't I understand?

I can't bear to type the words. Somehow I just can't do it. Instead, I stretch out my arm as far as it will go, take a photo of myself, then examine the result.

Yes. It's all there in the shot: my veil, my headdress, a glimpse of my wedding dress, the corner of my lily bouquet. There's absolutely no doubt as to what's going on.

I press Sam Mobile and then Send. There. It's gone through the ether. Now he knows. I'll probably never hear from him again after this. That's it. It was a strange little encounter between two people and this is the end. With a sigh, I sink down into a chair. The bells above have stopped pealing and there's a strange, still quietness in the room.

Until suddenly the beeps start. Frantic and continuous, like an emergency siren. I pick up my phone in shock, and they're stacking up in my in-box: text after text after text, all from Sam.

No.

No no no no no.

☹

Stop.

You can't.

Are you serious?

Poppy, why?

My breaths are short and ragged as I read his words. I wasn't intending to get into a conversation, but at last I can't stand it any more, I have to reply:

What do you expect, I just walk away? 200 people are sitting here waiting.

Immediately Sam's reply comes firing back:

You think he loves you?

I twist the ring of gold strands round and round my right-hand finger, trying desperately to find a path through all the contradictory thoughts thrusting their way into my head. Does Magnus love me? I mean . . . what *is* love? No one knows what love is, exactly. No one can define it. No one can prove it. But if someone chooses a ring especially for you in Bruges, that's got to be a good start, hasn't it?

Yes.

I think Sam must have been poised for my answer, his replies come shooting back so quickly, three in a row.

No.

You're wrong.

Stop. Stop. Stop. No. No.

I want to scream at him. It's not fair. He *can't* say all this now. He *can't* shake me up now.

Well what I am supposed to do???

I send it just as the door opens. It's the Reverend Fox, followed by Toby, Tom, Annalise and Ruby, all talking at once in an excited babble.
'Oh my God! The traffic! I thought we wouldn't make it . . .'

'Yes, but they couldn't start without you, could they? It's like planes.'

'They can, you know. They once took my luggage off the plane I was on, just because I was trying these jeans on and I didn't hear the announcement . . .'

'Is there a mirror? I've *got* to do my lipgloss again . . .'

'Poppy, we got you some biscuits—'

'She doesn't want biscuits! She's got to be slim for her big moment!' Annalise swoops down on me. 'What's happened to your veil? It's all bunched up. And your dress is crooked! Let me . . .'

'All right, missus?' Ruby gives me a hug as Annalise tugs at my train. 'Ready?'

'I . . .' I feel dazed. 'I guess so.'

'You look great.' Toby is crunching on a digestive. 'Much better. Hey, Felix wanted to say a quick hello. Is that OK?'

'Oh, of course.'

I feel powerless, standing here, with everyone milling around me. I can't even actually move, because Annalise is still adjusting my train. My phone beeps, and Reverend Fox gives me a frosty smile.

'Better turn that off, don't you think?'

'Can you imagine if it went off during the service?' Annalise giggles. 'Do you want me to hold on to it for you?'

She holds out her hand and I stare back at her, paralysed. There's a new text from Sam in my in-box. His reply. Part of me is so desperate to read it, I almost can't control my hands.

But another part is telling me to stop. Don't go there. How can I read it now, as I'm about to walk up the aisle? It'll mess me up. I'm here on my wedding day, surrounded by friends and family. *This* is my real life. Not some guy I'm connected to through the ether. It's time to say goodbye. It's time to cut this thread.

'Thanks, Annalise.' I turn the phone off and gaze at it for a moment as the light dies away. There's no one in there any more. It's just a dead, blank, metal box.

I hand it to Annalise and she thrusts it into her bra.

'You're holding your flowers too high.' She frowns at me. 'You look really tense.'

'I'm fine.' I avoid her gaze.

'Hey, guess what?' Ruby comes rustling up in her dress. 'I forgot to tell you, we're getting a celebrity patient! That businessman who's been all over the news. Sir Nicholas something?'

'You mean . . . Sir Nicholas Murray?' I say incredulously.

'That's the one.' She beams. 'His assistant phoned up and booked a session with me! Said I'd been recommended by someone whose opinion he regards very highly. Who on earth d'you think that was?'

'I've . . . I've no idea,' I manage.

I'm so touched. And a bit freaked. Never in a million years did I think that Sir Nicholas would take me up on my recommendation. How can I face him again? What if he mentions Sam? What if—

No. Stop it, Poppy. By the time I see Sir Nicholas again I'll be a married woman. The whole, bizarre little episode will be long forgotten. It'll be fine.

'I'll alert the organist that we're ready to go,' says Reverend Fox. 'Take your places for the procession, everyone.'

Annalise and Ruby are standing behind me. Tom and Toby are flanking me, each with an arm loosely crooked in mine. There's a knock at the door and Felix's owlish face peers round.

'Poppy, you look amazing.'

'Thanks! Come in!'

'Just thought I'd wish you luck.' He heads towards me, skirting my dress hem carefully. 'And say I'm so chuffed you're joining the family. We all are. My parents think you're brilliant.'

'Really?' I say, trying to hide my dubious tone. 'Both your parents?'

'Oh yes.' He nods fervently. 'They love you. They were so gutted when they heard it was all off.'

'*Off?*' echo four astonished voices, all at once.

'Was the wedding off?' says Tom.

'When was it off?' demands Annalise. 'You never told us, Poppy! Why didn't you tell us?'

Great. This is all I need, the third-degree from my entire wedding party.

'It was only temporary.' I try to downplay it. 'You know. One of those last-minute wedding-jitter things. Everyone has them.'

'Mum gave Magnus such a hard time.' Felix's eyes gleam behind his glasses. 'She said he was a fool and he'd never find anyone better than you.'

'Really?' I can't help feeling a glow.

'Oh, she was livid.' Felix looks highly entertained. 'She practically threw the ring at him.'

'She threw the emerald ring?' I say in astonishment. That ring is worth thousands. Surely even Wanda wouldn't start chucking it around the room.

'No, the gold twisty ring. That ring.' He nods at my hand. 'When she was getting it out of her dressing table for Magnus. She threw it at him and cut his forehead.' He chuckles. 'Not badly, of course.'

I stare at him, frozen. What did he just say? Wanda got the gold twisty ring out of her dressing table?

'I thought . . .' I try to sound relaxed. 'I thought Magnus bought it in Bruges?'

Felix looks blank. 'Oh no. It's Mum's. *Was* Mum's.'

'Right.' I lick my dry lips. 'So, Felix, what happened, exactly? Why did she give it to him? I wish I'd been there!' I try to sound light-hearted. 'Tell me the whole story.'

'Well.' Felix screws up his eyes, as though trying to recall. 'Mum told Magnus not to bother trying to give you that emerald ring again. And she got out the gold ring and said she couldn't wait to have you as a daughter-in-law. Then Dad said, "Why are you bothering, it's obvious Magnus doesn't have the sticking power for a marriage," and Magnus got in a fury with him and said yes he does, and Dad said, "Look at the Birmingham job," and they had this massive argument like they always do and then ... we got a takeaway.' He blinks. 'That was pretty much it.'

Behind me, Annalise is leaning forward to listen. 'So *that's* why you switched rings. I *knew* you weren't allergic to emeralds.'

This is Wanda's ring. Magnus didn't buy it especially for me at all. As I stare at my hand I feel a bit sick. Then something else occurs to me.

'*What* Birmingham job?'

'You know. The one he quit. Dad always gives Magnus a hard time for being a quitter. Sorry, I thought you knew.' Felix is eyeing me curiously as loud crashing organ chords from above make us all jump. 'Oh, we're starting. I'd better beetle off. See you in there!'

'Yes, OK.' Somehow I manage to nod. But I feel as though I'm on another planet. I need to digest all this.

'Ready?' Reverend Fox is at the door, beckoning us out. As we arrive at the back of the church, I can't help gasping. It's filled with spectacular flower arrangements, and rows of people in hats, and a crackling air of expectation. Right at the front I can just glimpse the back of Magnus's head.

Magnus. The thought makes my stomach turn over. I can't— I need time to think—

But I don't have any time. The organ piece is gathering momentum. The choir suddenly joins in with a triumphant swell. Reverend Fox has already disappeared up the aisle. The fairground ride has begun and I'm on it.

'All right?' Toby grins across at Tom. 'Don't trip her up, Bigfoot.'

And we're off. We're moving up the aisle, and people are smiling at me, and I'm aiming for a serene, happy gaze, but inside my thoughts are about as serene as the particles whizzing about in CERN.

It doesn't matter . . . it's only a ring . . . I'm overreacting . . . But he lied to me . . .

Oh wow, look at Wanda's hat . . .

God, this music is amazing, Lucinda was right to get the choir . . .

What job in Birmingham? Why did he never tell me about that?

Am I gliding? Shit. OK, that's better . . .

Come on, Poppy. Let's get some perspective. You have a great relationship with Magnus. Whether he bought you the ring himself or not is irrelevant. Some ancient job in Birmingham is irrelevant. And as for Sam—

No. Forget Sam. This is reality. This is my wedding. It's my wedding and I can't even focus on it properly. What's wrong with me?

I'm going to do it. I can do it. Yes. Yes. Bring it on . . .

Why the hell does Magnus look so sweaty?

As I arrive at the altar, all other thoughts are temporarily overcome by this last one. I can't help gaping at him in dismay. He looks terrible. If I look like I'm sick, then he looks like he's got malaria.

'Hi.' He gives me a weedy smile. 'You look lovely.'

'Are you OK?' I whisper as I hand my bouquet to Ruby.

'Why wouldn't I be OK?' he retorts defensively.

That doesn't seem quite the right answer, but I can't exactly challenge him on it.

The music has stopped and Reverend Fox is addressing the congregation with an ebullient beam. He looks as though he absolutely loves taking weddings.

'Dearly beloved. We are gathered here in the sight of God . . .'

As I hear the familiar words echoing around the church, I start to relax. OK. Here we go. *This* is what it's all about. *This* is what I've been looking forward to. The pledges. The vows. The ancient, magical words which have been repeated under this roof so many times, for generations and generations.

So maybe we've had some blips and jitters in the run-up to our wedding. What couple doesn't? But if we can just focus on our vows, if we can just make them special . . .

'Magnus.' Reverend Fox turns to Magnus, and there's a rustle of anticipation in the congregation. 'Wilt thou have this woman to thy wedded wife, to live together after God's ordinance in the holy estate of matrimony? Wilt thou love her, comfort her, honour and keep her, in sickness and in health; and, forsaking all others, keep thee only unto her, so long as ye both shall live?'

Magnus has a slightly glazed look in his eye, and he's breathing heavily. He looks as though he's psyching himself up for the 100-metres Olympic final.

'Magnus?' prompts Reverend Fox.

'OK,' he says, almost to himself. 'OK. Here goes. I can do this.' He takes an almighty, deep breath, and, in a loud, dramatic voice which rises to the ceiling, announces proudly, 'I do.'

I do?

I do?

Wasn't he *listening?*

'Magnus,' I whisper with a meaningful edge. 'It's not "I do".'

Magnus peers at me, clearly baffled. 'Of course it's "I do".'

I feel a surge of irritation. He wasn't listening to a single word. He just said 'I do' because it's what they say in American films. I should have *known* this would happen. I should have ignored Antony's snarky comments and made Magnus rehearse the vows.

'It's not "I do", it's "I will"!' I'm trying not to sound as upset as I feel. 'Didn't you listen to the question? "Wilt thou." *Wilt thou.'*

'*Oh.*' Magnus's brow clears in understanding. 'I get it. Sorry.

"I will", then. Although, it hardly matters, surely,' he adds with a shrug.

What?

'Shall we resume?' Reverend Fox is saying hurriedly. 'Poppy.' He beams at me. 'Wilt thou take this man to thy wedded husband . . .'

I'm sorry. I can't let that go.

'Sorry, Reverend Fox.' I lift a hand. 'One more thing. Sorry.' For good measure I swivel round to the congregation. 'I just need to clear up a tiny point, I won't be a moment . . .' I turn back to Magnus and say in a furious undertone, 'What do you mean, "it hardly matters"? Of *course* it matters! It's a question. You're supposed to *answer* it.'

'Sweets, I think that's taking it a *little* literally.' Magnus is looking distinctly uncomfortable. 'Can we crack on?'

'No, we cannot crack on! It's a literal question! *Wilt thou take me?* A question. What do *you* think it is?'

'Well.' Magnus shrugs again. 'You know. A symbol.'

It's as though he's lit my fuse-paper. How can he say that? He *knows* how important the vows are to me.

'Not everything in life is a bloody *symbol!*' I explode. 'It's a real, proper question and you didn't answer it properly! Don't you mean *anything* you're saying here?'

'For God's sake, Poppy—' Magnus lowers his voice. 'Is this really the time?'

What's he suggesting, that we say the vows and then discuss whether we meant them or not *afterwards*?

OK, so we should perhaps have discussed our vows before we were standing at the altar. I can see that now. If I could go back in time, I'd do it differently. But I can't. It's now or never. And in my defence, Magnus knew what the wedding vows were, didn't he? I mean, I haven't exactly sprung them on him, have I? They're not exactly a secret, are they?

'Yes it is!' My voice rises with agitation. 'This would be the time! Right now would be the time!' I swing round to face the congregation, who all gaze at me, agog. 'Hands up who thinks that at a wedding, the groom should mean his vows?'

There's absolute silence. Then, to my astonishment, Antony slowly raises his hand into the air, followed by Wanda, looking sheepish. Seeing them, Annalise and Ruby shoot their hands up. Within about thirty seconds, all the pews are full of waving hands. Tom and Toby each have *both* hands up and so have my aunt and uncle.

Reverend Fox looks absolutely flummoxed.

'I *do* mean them,' says Magnus, but he sounds so lame and unconvincing, even Reverend Fox winces.

'Really?' I turn to him. ' "Forsaking all others"? "In sickness and in health"? "Till death us do part"? You're absolutely sure about that, are you? Or did you just want to prove to everyone that you can go through with a wedding?'

And although I wasn't planning to say that, as soon as the words are out of my mouth, they feel true.

That's what this is. Everything falls into place. His belligerent speech this morning. His sweaty forehead. Even his proposal. No wonder he only waited a month. This was never about him and me, it was about proving a point. Maybe this is all about his father calling him a quitter. Or his zillion previous proposals. God knows. But the whole thing has been wrong from the start. It's been back-to-front. And I believed in it because I wanted to.

I can suddenly feel the pressing of tears behind my eyes. But I *refuse* to crumble.

'Magnus,' I say more gently. 'Listen. There's no point doing this. Don't marry me just to prove you're not a quitter. Because you *will* quit, sooner or later. Whatever your intentions are. It'll happen.'

'Rubbish,' he says fiercely.

'You will. You don't love me enough for the long haul.'

'Yes I do!'

'You *don't*, Magnus,' I say, almost wearily. 'I don't light up your life like I should. And you don't light up mine.' I pause. 'Not enough. Not enough for forever.'

'Really?' Magnus looks shocked. 'I don't?' I can see that I've pricked his vanity.

'No. I'm sorry.'

'You don't need to be sorry, Poppy,' he says, clearly in a huff. 'If that's really the way you feel . . .'

'But it's the way you feel too!' I exclaim. 'Be honest! Magnus, you and I, we're not destined to be together forever. We're not the main event. I think we're . . .' I screw up my face, trying to think of a way to put it. 'I think we're each other's footnotes.'

There's silence. Magnus looks as though he wants to find a riposte, but can't. I touch his hand, then turn to the vicar. 'Reverend Fox, I'm so sorry. We've wasted your time. I think we should probably call it a day.'

'I see,' says Reverend Fox. 'Goodness. I see.' He mops his head with his handkerchief, looking flustered. 'Are you sure . . . perhaps a five-minute chat in the vestry . . .'

'I don't think that'll fix it,' I say gently. 'I think we're done. Don't you, Magnus?'

'If you say so.' Magnus looks genuinely gutted and for a moment I wonder—

No. There's no doubt. I'm doing the right thing.

'Well . . . what shall we do now?' I say hesitantly. 'Shall we still have the reception?'

Magnus looks uncertain – then nods. 'Might as well. We've paid for it.'

I step down from the altar dais, then pause. OK, this is awkward. We didn't rehearse this. The congregation are all just watching, still agog, to see what happens next.

'So . . . Um . . . should I . . .' I turn to Magnus. 'I mean, we can't exactly walk down the aisle together.'

'You go first.' He shrugs. 'Then I'll go.'

Reverend Fox is signalling at the organist, who suddenly starts playing the Bridal March.

'No!' I squeak in horror. 'No music! Please!'

'So sorry!' Reverend Fox makes hasty 'Cut it' gestures. 'I was trying to signal "*Don't* play". Mrs Fortescue is a little deaf, I'm afraid. She may not have followed exactly what's been going on.'

This is such a shambles. I don't even know whether to hold my flowers or not. In the end, I grab them from Ruby, who gives me a sympathetic squeeze on the arm, while Annalise whispers, 'Are you *insane*?'

The music has finally petered out, so I start making my way back down the aisle in silence, avoiding everyone's eye and prickling all over with self-consciousness. Oh God, this is hideous. There should be an exit strategy for this eventuality. There should be an option in the Book of Common Prayer. *Procession For Ye Bride who Changèd Her Minde.*

No one's talking as I make my way along the paved aisle. Everyone's watching me, riveted. But I'm aware of phones being turned on, from the cacophony of little bleepy noises up and down the pews. Great. I expect there'll be a race to see who can post it first on Facebook.

Suddenly a woman at the end of a pew thrusts a hand out in front of me. She's got a big pink hat on and I have absolutely no idea who she is.

'Stop!'

'Me?' I come to a halt and look at her.

'Yes, you.' She looks a bit flustered. 'I'm sorry to interrupt, but I've got a message for you.'

'For *me*?' I say, puzzled. 'But I don't even know you.'

'That's what's so odd.' She flushes. 'Sorry, I should introduce myself. I'm Magnus's godmother, Margaret. I don't know many people here. But a text arrived in my phone during the service, from someone called Sam Roxton. At least . . . it's not for you, it's *about* you. It says, *If you happen to be at the wedding of Poppy Wyatt . . .*'

There's a loud gasp behind her. 'I've got that message too!' a girl exclaims. 'Exactly the same! *If you happen to be at the wedding of Poppy Wyatt . . .'*

'Me too! Same here!' Voices start chiming in around the church. 'I've just got it! *If you happen to be at the wedding of Poppy Wyatt . . .'*

I'm too bewildered to speak. What's going on? Has Sam been texting the wedding guests? More and more hands are flying up; more and more phones are bleeping; more and more people are exclaiming.

Has he texted *everyone at the wedding*?

'Have we *all* got the same text?' Margaret looks around the congregation in disbelief. 'All right, let's see. If you've got the message in your phone, read it out. I'll count us in. One, two, three . . . *If you happen . . .'*

As the rumble of voices starts, I feel faint. This can't be real. There's a crowd of two hundred people at this wedding, and most are joining in, reading aloud from their phones in unison. As the words echo around the church, it sounds like a mass prayer or a football chant or something.

'*. . . to be at the wedding of Poppy Wyatt, I'd like to ask a favour. Stop it. Stop her. Hold it off. Delay it. She's doing the wrong thing. At least get her to think about it . . .'*

I'm transfixed in the aisle, clutching my bouquet, my heart thudding. I can't believe he's done this. I can't believe it. Where did he get all the phone numbers from? Lucinda?

'*Let me tell you why. As a clever man once said: a treasure such as this should not be left in the hands of Philistines. And Poppy is a treasure, though she doesn't realize it . . .'*

I can't help glancing over at Antony, who is holding his phone and has raised his eyebrows very high.

'*There isn't time to talk or discuss or be reasonable. Which is why I'm taking this extreme measure. And I hope you will too. Anything you can do. Anything you can say. The wedding is wrong. Thank you.'*

As the reading comes to an end, everyone seems slightly shell-shocked.

'What the fuck—' Magnus is striding down from the altar. 'Who *was* that?'

I can't answer. Sam's words are going round and round in my head. I want to grab someone's phone and read them through again.

'I'm going to reply!' exclaims Margaret suddenly. '*Who's this?*' she says aloud as she taps at her phone. '*Are you her lover?*' She presses Send with a dramatic flourish, and there's a rapt silence in the church, till her phone suddenly bleeps. 'He's answered!' She pauses for effect, then reads out: '*Lover? I don't know. I don't know if she loves me. I don't know if I love her.*'

Deep down inside, I feel a crushing disappointment. Of course he doesn't love me. He just thinks I shouldn't marry Magnus. He's just putting right what he sees as a wrong. That's a totally different thing. It doesn't mean he has any feelings for me whatsoever. Let alone—

'*All I can say is, she's the one I think about.*' Margaret hesitates and her voice softens as she reads. '*All the time. She's the voice I want to hear. She's the face I hope to see.*'

My throat is suddenly full of lumps. I'm swallowing desperately, trying to keep my composure. He's the one I think about. All the time. He's the voice I want to hear. When my phone bleeps I hope it's him.

'Who *is* he?' Magnus sounds incredulous.

'Yes, who is he?' pipes up Annalise from beside the altar, and there's a ripple of laughter around the church.

'He's just ... a guy. I found his phone...' I trail off helplessly.

I can't even begin to describe who Sam is and what we've been to each other.

Margaret's phone bleeps again and the hubbub dies down to an expectant hush. 'It's from him,' she says.

'What does he say?' I can hardly trust my voice.

The church is so silent and still, I can almost hear my own heart beating.

'It says, *And I'll be standing outside the church. Warn her.*'
He's here.

I don't even realize I'm running until one of the ushers backs out of my way, looking alarmed. The heavy church door is closed, and it takes about five tugs before I manage to wrench it open. I burst out and stand on the steps, panting hard, looking up and down the pavement, searching for his face . . .

There he is. On the other side of the road. He's standing in the doorway of a Starbucks, in jeans and a dark-blue shirt. As he meets my gaze, his eyes crinkle, but he doesn't smile. He keeps looking at my hands. His eyes have a huge question burning in them.

Doesn't he know? Can't he *tell* the answer?

'Is that him?' breathes Annalise beside me. 'Dreamy. Can I have Magnus?'

'Annalise, give me my phone,' I say, without taking my eyes off Sam.

'Here you go.' A moment later the phone is in my hand, lit up and ready to go, and I'm sending him a text.

Hi.

He texts something back and a moment later it arrives:

Nice outfit.

Involuntarily, I glance down at my wedding dress.

This old thing.

There's a long silence – and then I see Sam typing a new message. His head is bowed and he doesn't look up, even when he's finished; even when the text arrives in my phone.

So are you married?

I carefully line up my phone and take a picture of my bare left finger.

Sam Mobile.

Send.

A crowd of wedding guests is jostling behind me to see, but I don't move my head an inch. My eyes are glued on Sam, so that I see the reaction on his face as the text arrives. I see his brow relax; I see his face expand into the most brilliant, joyous smile. And finally he looks up at me.

I could go to bed in that smile.

Now he's texting again.

Want a cup of coffee?

'Poppy.' A voice in my ear interrupts me and I turn to see Wanda, peering anxiously at me from under her hat, which looks like a massive, dead moth. 'Poppy, I'm sorry. I acted dishonourably and selfishly.'

'What do you mean?' I say, momentarily confused.

'The second ring. I told Magnus . . . at least, I suggested that he might . . .' Wanda breaks off, wincing.

'I know. You told Magnus to pretend he'd chosen the ring for me especially, didn't you?' I touch her arm. 'Wanda, I appreciate it. But you'd better have this one back, too.' I pull the twisty gold ring off my right hand and give it to her.

'I would have loved you to join our family,' she says wistfully. 'But that shouldn't have clouded my judgement. It was wrong of me.' Her gaze drifts across the road to Sam. 'He's the one, isn't he?'

I nod, and her face softens, like a crumpled rose petal being released.

'Go on, then. Go.'

And without waiting a beat longer I walk down the steps, across the road, dodging the cars, ignoring the hooting, tearing off my veil, until I'm a foot away from Sam. For a moment we just stand there, facing each other, breathing hard.

'So you've been sending a few texts,' I say at last.

'A couple.' Sam nods.

'Interesting.' I nod back. 'Did Lucinda help out?'

'She turned out to be pretty keen to derail the wedding.' Sam looks amused.

'But I don't understand. How did you even *find* her?'

'She has a pretty fancy website.' Sam smiles wryly. 'I called her mobile and she was only too eager to help. In fact, she sent the text for me. Didn't you know that you have some state-of-the-art automatic mechanism to contact all the guests?'

Lucinda's text-alert system. It finally came in useful.

I shift my bouquet to the other hand. I never realized how heavy flowers were.

'That's a pretty fancy outfit for Starbucks.' Sam is eyeing me up and down.

'I always wear a wedding dress for coffee dates. I think it adds a nice touch, don't you?'

I glance back at the church and can't help giggling. The entire congregation seems to have spilled out and is standing on the pavement like an audience.

'What are they waiting to see?' Sam follows my gaze, and I shrug.

'Who knows? You could always do a dance. Or tell a joke. Or . . . kiss the bride?'

'Not the bride.' He wraps his arms around me and gradually pulls me close. Our noses are practically touching. I can see right into his eyes. I can feel the warmth of his skin. 'You.'

'Me.'

'The girl who stole my phone.' His lips brush against the corner of my mouth. 'The thief.'

'It was in a *bin*.'

'Still stealing.'

'No it isn't—' I begin, but now his mouth is firmly on mine and I can't speak at all.

And suddenly life is good.

I know that things are still uncertain; I know that reality hasn't gone away. There'll be explanations and recriminations and messiness. But right now I'm entwined with a man I think I might love. And I haven't married the man I know I don't love. And from where I'm looking that's pretty good going, for now.

At last we draw away from each other, and across the road I can hear Annalise whooping in appreciation. Which is pretty tacky of her, but that's just Annalise.

'I brought you some reading matter, by the way,' Sam says. 'In case there was a dull moment.'

He reaches inside his jacket and produces a bundle of coffee-stained A4 papers. And as I see them, there's a thickening in my chest. He kept them. Even after we parted so badly. He kept our texts.

'Any good?' I manage a nonchalant tone.

'Not bad.' He flips through them, then lifts his head. 'Looking forward to the sequel.'

'Really?' And now the way he's looking at me is making me tingle all over. 'So, do you know what happens next?'

'Oh . . . I have a fair idea.' He trails his fingers down my bare back and I feel an instant bolt of lust. I am *totally* ready for my honeymoon night.[109] I don't need the champagne or the canapés or the three-course dinner or the first dance. Or even the last dance.

But on the other hand, there's the small matter of two hundred people standing across the street, watching me, as though waiting for instructions. Some of them have travelled for miles. I can't bail out on them.

'So . . . we've got this party,' I say tentatively to Sam. 'It's like, all my friends and family, all at once, in a really

---

109. OK. Perhaps not 'honeymoon night' exactly. They should have a special word meaning 'night spent with lover one has jilted fiancé for'.

intimidating bunch, plus all the friends and family of the guy I was supposed to marry today. And sugared almonds. You want to come?'

Sam raises his eyebrows. 'You think Magnus will shoot me?'

'Dunno.' I squint at Magnus across the road. He's standing there watching us, along with everyone else. But as far as I can tell, he doesn't look too homicidal.[110] 'I don't think so. Shall I send him a text and ask him?'

'If you like.' Sam shrugs, taking out his own phone.

Magnus. This guy I'm standing with is Sam. I know this isn't exactly usual – but can I bring him to our wedding reception? Poppy xxx

PS why don't you bring a guest too??

A moment later I get a response:

If you must. Mag

Which isn't exactly enthusiastic, but doesn't sound like he's planning to shoot anyone, either.[111]

I'm about to put my phone away when it bleeps again and I stare in surprise. It's a text from Sam. He must have just sent it, a few seconds ago. Without looking at him, I open it, to see:

<3

It's a heart. He sent me a love heart. Without even saying anything. Like a little secret.

---

110. In fact, he looks a lot better than he did when he was going to have to marry me.
111. Personally, I would bet a *lot* of money that Magnus is snogging Annalise by the end of the night.

My eyes feel hot but somehow I manage to stay calm as I type my reply:

Me too.

I want to add more . . . but no. More can come later.

I press Send then look up, with a bright smile, take Sam by the arm and draw up my train out of the dusty pavement.

'So. Come on, then. Let's hit my wedding.'

THE END[112]

112. Footnotes by Poppy Wyatt.

ACKNOWLEDGEMENTS

I would like to take this opportunity to thank my publishers around the world. I am so grateful for all the fantastic editions of my books, which you work on so lovingly.

A huge thank-you also to my readers for continuing to turn the pages, with a special wave to all of you who follow me on Facebook.

In particular I am eternally grateful to Araminta Whitley, Kim Witherspoon, David Forrer, Harry Man, Peta Nightingale, Nicki Kennedy and Sam Edenborough and their wonderful team at ILA. A special thank-you to Andrea Best – you know why! At Transworld I am lucky enough to be supported by a fabulous team and would like to thank especially my editor Linda Evans, Larry Finlay, Bill Scott-Kerr, Polly Osborn, Janine Giovanni, Sarah Roscoe, Gavin Hilzbrich, Suzanne Riley, Claire Ward, Judith Welsh and Jo Williamson. Thanks to Martin Higgins for everything. And a special mention to the copy-editing team, who put so much care into the fine-tuning of all my books – a huge thank-you to Kate Samano and Elisabeth Merriman.

Finally – as ever – thanks and love to my boys and the Board.

Sophie Kinsella is an international bestselling writer and former financial journalist. She is the author of ten number-one bestselling novels, including the fabulously popular Shopaholic series, the first of which is now the Hollywood movie *Confessions of a Shopaholic*. She is also the author of several bestselling novels under the name of Madeleine Wickham. She lives in London with her husband and family. Visit her website at www.sophiekinsella.co.uk